Praise for Carol Steward
and her novels

"Carol Steward masterfully combines danger
and intrigue with a charming love story."
—*Romantic Times BOOKreviews* on
Her Kind of Hero

"It's worth the journey. Ms. Steward's
writing is a pleasure to read."
—*Romantic Times BOOKreviews* on
Second Time Around

CAROL STEWARD

Her Kind of Hero

&

Second Time Around

Steeple
Hill®

Published by Steeple Hill Books™

STEEPLE HILL BOOKS

Steeple
Hill®

ISBN-13: 978-0-373-65274-7
ISBN-10:   0-373-65274-7

HER KIND OF HERO AND SECOND TIME AROUND

HER KIND OF HERO
Copyright © 1999 by Carol Steward

SECOND TIME AROUND
Copyright © 2000 by Carol Steward

www.SteepleHill.com

Printed in U.S.A.

CONTENTS

Books by Carol Steward

Love Inspired

There Comes a Season #27
Her Kind of Hero #56
Second Time Around #92
Courting Katarina #134
This Time Forever #165
Finding Amy #263
Finding Her Home #282
Journey to Forever #301

CAROL STEWARD

wrote daily to a pen pal for ten years, yet writing as a career didn't occur to her for another two decades. "My first key chain said, 'Bloom where you're planted.' I've tried to follow that advice ever since."

Carol, her husband and their three children have planted their roots in Greeley. Together, their family enjoys sports, camping and discovering Colorado's beauty. Carol has operated her own cake-decorating business and spent fifteen years providing full-time child care to more than one hundred children before moving to the other end of the education field. She is now an admissions adviser at a state university.

As always, Carol loves to hear from her readers. You can contact her at P.O. Box 200269, Evans, CO 80620. She would also love you to visit her Web page at www.carolsteward.com.

HER KIND OF HERO

For when we were with you, we told you beforehand that we were to suffer affliction; just as it has come to pass, and as you know. For this reason, when I could bear it no longer, I sent that I might know your faith, for fear that somehow the tempter had tempted you and that our labor would be in vain.

—*1 Thessalonians* 3:4-5

To my father, Tom Bohannan, for a lifetime of insight on law enforcement and showing me that there's a hero in each of us. Ken, Todd, Tim, Ed and the Greeley Police Department for their insights and for letting me experience firsthand the excitement and danger of police work.

My husband and kids for their never-ending encouragement. Anne for having faith in my ability to write this story. Helen, Sally, Ellen, LeAnn, Lynn, Margaret, Linda and Bette for motivating me to write through this challenging year. And to the Creator for inspiring me to share these stories.

Chapter One

❧

Calli Giovanni walked through the stained-glass doors praying that she would someday experience the peace of forgiveness.

Why can't I let it go?

"You can't get discouraged," her cousin Hanna said, following her through the doors. "Don't expect healing to happen all at once. It isn't easy. Like tonight's speaker said, it's one miserable step at a time. For tonight, go home. Stop patrolling."

"I can't, Hanna. I would think *you'd* understand. He was my kid brother. I want justice served. I can't let it go."

"I do understand, Calandre. More than you think." Hanna took Calli by the shoulders. "Who can't you forgive, Calli? The killer? Or yourself, for not seeing Mike slip out of the house?"

Calli turned and stared into her cousin's moist eyes. "Neither." Her own tears dried up years ago. All that was left was this numbness. She was an emotional zombie.

"Don't you see what this is doing to you?" Hanna asked.

"It's not worth it. You don't laugh. You don't cry. You barely exist." Hanna paused, then unlocked her car door. "Go home. It's time for you to stop."

Calli never finished her college degree. Her brother had been killed at the beginning of her last semester. She'd set new priorities. Priorities that cost her dearly. Her family, her fiancé, her happiness. All in hopes of finding answers. "That's easier said than done."

Hanna hugged Calli. "You can do it. Just don't give in. Sorry I have to rush off, but I'm expecting a call at nine-thirty. Take care." Her petite cousin slid into her sports car and waved.

"That's my problem, Han. I don't ever give up. I don't know how." Calli took off her down-filled coat and tossed it into the passenger's seat, her voice a whisper into the darkness. She watched Hanna drive away without a care in the world. "It's cost me everyone I loved, and I still can't let it go."

Her mother, father, older brother and even her sister were like distant relatives. They had put the past behind them and moved on. Recovered. Only she was stuck trying to erase the shadows lurking in her mind. Fighting the unknown in a city of dark corners and unlit alleys. Doing the only thing she could to avenge her brother's death.

Thinking of Mike, she closed the door and reached under her seat. Calli pulled out a zippered bag and stared at it, considering giving up on this thankless mission. She zipped the pouch open and emptied the contents into her lap. "Just one patrol before I head home. Maybe tonight's my lucky night." She tugged the long blond wig over her own hair and covered her lips with tropical punch-colored lipstick. Horn-rimmed glasses completed the disguise. *Good grief, I even look like Aunt Calandre.*

It was a quiet night in Palmer, Colorado. Calli spent over an hour cruising without anything to report. Feeling a sudden chill, she reached for the heat control, only to find it was already set on high and pumping hot air into the small compartment. *Calm down, Cal. There's not even any action.*

As she continued down the alleys and streets lined with dilapidated buildings, Calli prayed. "Though I walk through the valley of the shadow of death, I shall fear no evil, for thou art with me."

She perused the business district, then paused to consider what she was doing before turning toward the city's core. It was a neighborhood within a neighborhood. A place where nothing was sacred. Not property, not values and especially not human life.

The only thing flourishing here was the Eastsiders, a gang that preyed on the weak and helpless.

Maybe they would provide her with some clues. After all, that was the gang her brother had allegedly been joining when the "initiation" went too far.

Adrenaline pulsed through her veins as she turned into the parking lot of a dimly lit apartment complex. Her breathing became shallow and ragged. *Why do I keep doing this? Is it even worth it anymore?*

A shiver raced up her spine and Calli quickly glanced left, then right. The rays of the streetlight reflected off of the glistening ground. She dialed "911 send" on her cellular phone just as three figures bolted from the icy parking lot toward the apartments, dodging cars and jumping wobbly handrails. "Gotcha."

One threw a small crowbar at her, hitting the front fender.

"911 Emergency."

"Columbia Boulevard and 15th Street." Calli swallowed, trying to smooth her raspy voice as it scratched through the wires. "The Willows Apartments. There's broken glass everywhere."

One teenager slipped and fell to the ground. Calli skidded to a stop inches from him. He got up and looked at her, his dark eyes filled with fear. He glanced behind him, then stumbled ahead to where his cohorts had disappeared.

"Ma'am, are you there?" the 911 operator repeated.

Calli's heart pounded faster and she dragged in another breath. Shadows wrapped their arms around her. Streetlights flickered. Vines covered apartment windows like victorian lace curtains. Calli shivered. *Where'd they go?*

"Are you okay?"

"Fine. I'm fine. Three kids…" Calli pressed on the accelerator. She searched beyond the tinted glass for any movement as she drove slowly toward the exit to conclude the loop. She wanted desperately to leave before the officers arrived, armed with endless questions and expectations.

"They're wearing dark clothing, bulky coats." She paused, hoping to recall more. "One wore a starter jacket…and a bandanna. A blue bandanna." She turned the last corner before the exit. "They weren't very tall. Around sixteen, maybe younger."

The woman stopped her and repeated the information, then asked for more details.

Calli knew the more she could remember, the better the chance that justice would be served. "One had bleached blond hair, the other two had dark hair. I think one's hurt."

Sirens wailed in the distance, then abruptly stopped.

They'd be here any minute. *Time to go.* Calli thought of the gang's leader with a wretched sense of pleasure. Another bust. She may not be able to find the proof she needed to put the gang's leader away, but she could make Tiger's "work" more difficult.

She stepped on the gas pedal but it was too late. A white police car fishtailed as it rounded the curve. It slid on the ice and headed toward her.

Calli pumped the brakes. Time stopped, and the terror seemed to continue in slow motion. It was no use. Her tires couldn't grip.

She pressed the brakes again. Harder. Still nothing. Finally she slammed her foot to the floorboard and gripped the steering wheel, directing her skid away from the police cruiser.

Her four-wheel drive slammed into the curb and jerked to a stop. Seconds later, the officer pulled closer and rolled down his window. The set of his strong, square jaw personified authority. She couldn't look away from the deep-set eyes and rugged features that expressed sincere concern.

Trembling, Calli opened her window. The dark-haired officer leaned out of his car. "Are you okay?"

She nodded stiffly, and they drove on, into the parking lot. *Pull yourself together, Cal. Get going.* She shifted into first and stepped on the gas.

The truck didn't budge.

Depressing the clutch, Calli turned the key. "Come on, start." Without allowing the engine to settle into an even idle, she pulled away.

"That was too close for comfort. I've got to get out of here. Where's the phone?" She found it in the far corner of the floorboard and shut it off, then turned south on Columbia Boulevard. A few minutes later, flashing lights beckoned in her rearview mirror as backup turned into the apartment complex. "They're all yours, guys. I've done as much as I can."

Calli's heart raced in an unsteady rhythm as the motor purred down the street. Four miles later, she pulled into the parking lot of Teodoro's, the Quonset hut-turned restaurant she frequented. She clicked off the ignition and leaned her head against the seat. *Darn it, Calli. You're pushing too hard. You've got to stop.*

Tugging the bristly hair from her head, she stuffed the blond wig into the bag and let out a deep breath. She gazed into the rearview mirror, removed the glasses and studied herself disapprovingly. After wiping the gauche color from her lips, she applied ointment to help remove the remaining tint. The near-accident replayed in her mind as she yanked a brush through the matted mess of black curls. She had hung around too long, almost long enough to meet the cops in person. That was one complication she didn't need.

Stuffing the sundries and the makeup bag into her purse, she slammed the truck door, then walked to the restaurant entrance. Calli took a deep breath and tugged the glass-and-iron door open, anxious to meet friendly faces.

"May I help you?" the young woman asked.

Calli didn't even consult the menu. "Barbaccoa with black beans instead of pintos, and a large diet cola." She watched as rice and beans were piled onto the tortilla, then salsa and shredded beef. Last was the cheese and sour cream.

Teodoro's owner, "Teddy" Chavez, greeted her with a smile. "Your usual, eh, Calli? What are you doing out this late?"

She let his friendly wink soothe her nerves. A member of her neighborhood watch group, he knew very well what kept her out this late. Yet he always shared her silent celebration at making it through another night safely. She glanced at the staff, and went along with the conversation. "Couldn't wait for one of your burritos. Just thinking of them keeps me awake at night."

"That's no good. Ah, well, eat and enjoy." He turned to his employees and rattled off directions to them while Calli crossed the room and seated herself in the plywood chair. She rested her head in her hands and begged her heart to slow down.

Eating alone beneath the dangling halogen light bulb was much too comfortable. She sliced the giant burrito into two halves and set one aside for tomorrow's lunch. Her kid brother had always teased her about eating when she was upset. If he could only see her now. Listening to alternative music in a dingy restaurant, trying to forget the good-looking cop who'd nearly run her over.

Calli pulled the journal from her purse and turned to today's date.

January 22, 11:05 p.m.

She documented her evening's patrolling events, descriptions and response time of the local law enforcement on the blank pages.

Calli had started journaling in her early teens, as a way to deal with the loneliness of frequent moves, foreign languages and the other drawbacks of being an army brat. But in recent years the pages were filled with fewer emotions, and more details.

She thought through the events of the day, then wrote.

Has no one ever realized the guilt I feel? Surely they have. Over and again, Mom and Dad tell me it wasn't my fault—that Mike had snuck out before, that nothing anyone had tried had helped him. Why can't I move on?

It was not my fault. But maybe if someone had called the cops, maybe he'd be alive today.

She closed her eyes and whispered, "As in David's day, I see violence and strife in our streets, on city walls. Be my shelter and my strength, Father."

How can I stop now? Community involvement is making a difference. The neighborhood's crime rate has dropped. I have to keep trying.

The media tries to convince us that gangs are losing their appeal. They say gang members are frightened off by friends getting hurt and others sent to prisons. Yet, every week, I still see them out there, luring innocent kids into believing that they've found a place to belong. Tempting them with the promise of easy money. Trapping them into a life without hope.

Calli recalled the look in the youth's eyes as he stared at her. Fear, raw and exposed, spoke to her.

What was that kid looking back for? A way out, or someone they left behind?

Police sirens jolted her back to the present. The cruiser sped past the front of the restaurant. The officer she'd nearly collided with reappeared in her mind. His concerned gaze lingered there, like an unwelcome guest. Reflections of light glimmered over his handsome face. She shook her head. *He's just another cop. They all have that look.*

Thankful that she took the time to don her disguise, Calli wondered if they would place her as the caller. Did they get her license number? Hopefully she'd gotten away before they had the chance.

How can I give up now? There has to be a way to help kids like that.

The pen stopped.

Kids like Mike. She never believed that he wanted in to the gang. Never allowed herself to see him as needing something more in his life. Maybe she'd been wrong. About Mike, and the gangs, and thinking she could make a difference—to anybody.

She noticed the employees wiping Formica-topped tables, wrapping stainless-steel food bins and polishing the glass block room divider.

"Calli, we're closing." Teddy set a foil sheet next to her plastic basket. "For your leftovers."

She finished chewing and gulped her soda to wash the bite down her dry throat. After closing her journal, Calli wrapped the extra half. "Thanks, Teddy. Have a good night."

"You be careful out there."

"Always." She left the eatery, climbed into her truck and turned west, toward her apartment. It was after midnight, and morning would come early.

Fog rolled in from the river and a fine mist coated the streets with black ice. Even four-wheel drive wouldn't help in conditions like this. The light ahead turned green and Calli took her foot off the gas pedal. From the side street, a truck spun out of control.

She tried to determine a way to avoid it, but there was no escape. The truck rammed the passenger door, pushing her vehicle into another car parked along the street. Her head slammed into the driver's side window and shattered the glass.

Calli screamed, then covered her eyes with her hands, feeling a cold draft. She tried again to open her eyes, but they hurt too much. She pulled on the door handle, but the door didn't move.

"Help! *Help!* Someone help me." A few minutes later, sirens wailed. Voices commanded that she not try to move. Louder and louder the noise grew, then stopped. The fireman knocked away the remaining glass from the door. After the paramedic took Calli's vitals, he reassured Calli that they would have her out soon.

Calli awoke to pitch black. She tried to blink and found her eyes were covered. Reaching out, she felt a hard rail to her side. Her head hurt and her left arm ached. She vaguely remembered an accident and an ambulance.

Where am I?

The room was silent except for beeping noises in the distance. She licked her parched lips and grimaced. She heard breathing, then footsteps, followed by a warm deep voice.

"Calandre Giovanni? I'm Sergeant Northrup, Palmer Police Department."

The police? What are they doing here? Am I just imagining an accident? Or is this about the break-ins at the apartment complex? For all she knew, he may not even be a cop. "Where am I?"

"University Hospital. You were in an accident."

Calli gasped, then let out a moan as she tried to move.

She must have been seated, as her mind was fuzzy. "What's wrong with me?"

"Let me call the nurse for you." He stepped out of the room, and was gone for a few minutes.

His voice sounded familiar. What were the chances that he was the patrolman who'd nearly wiped her off the road? Next to zero, she assured herself. If the officers who'd responded to that call had caught the kids, they were probably still at the juvenile facility booking them at this very moment.

When the cop returned, Calli decided she'd rather ask questions than answer them. She needed time to clear her mind. "Where's the nurse?"

"It'll be a few minutes before anyone can come down. Emergency room's a busy place tonight. You okay?"

"Do I *look* okay?"

He stammered a minute, then apologized. "I meant, you're not going to be sick or anything, are you?"

"I'll live. Were you the officer at my accident?"

"No. That would be Jake Williams. He asked me to take your statement while I'm here. I came in with an unrelated ambulance call."

Hysteria threatened to return to her voice. She swallowed, trying to soothe the scratchiness. Absently she ran her dry tongue over her lips.

"Need a drink?" Without delay she felt the officer lean against the bed. "Here." She lifted her hand, ready for him to place a paper cup in her hand. Instead she felt a strong hand wrapped around a huge insulated-type mug. Pursing her lips to drink, she jumped when she felt the brush of his fingertip against her lower lip as he placed a straw in her mouth.

He chuckled. "Sorry, I forgot to tell you what to expect."

Embarrassed that all of her assumptions were wrong, making her feel even more helpless, Calli resented the warmth of the personal contact between them. She jerked her hand away. "Thanks. That's enough." The sooner she got rid of him, the better. The last thing she needed was a cop to keep her company. "So what do you need from me?"

"Just need to ask a few routine questions. No hurry. I'm here waiting to talk to another patient. My partner's still on the streets. Sheesh, they're a mess tonight. You'd think these drivers had never seen ice before."

Calli tried to sit up, and failed. She heard him bump into something, then felt a strong hand on her arm.

"Can I help?"

"I want the nurse. Where's the call button?"

His warm hand fumbled with hers and gently guided her fingers toward the side of her bed. His baritone voice was edged with control. "Here's the call button."

A calm confidence echoed his voice, and the scent of his aftershave sent a shiver of awareness through her.

Memories from her past tainted the image of this knight in shining armor. Calli realized that not only did she not have a clue as to what Officer Northrup looked like, but she had no idea if this man was really a cop. *I've been watching too much television. He couldn't be the one I saw earlier.*

"I'm sure it's frightening not to be able to see anything. You may not even believe I'm a police officer. Who could blame you, after the night you've had?"

The fact that he'd read her mind made her more suspicious. "Sorry, I'm not used to…" *trusting people.*

"You're cautious, just as you should be under the circumstances."

"Cautious." Now that *is an understatement.*

Calli struggled to pull herself out of the fuzziness and remember more about the accident.

Shuffling noises followed by a nearby clank dragged her back to the present image of a cop sitting next to her bed, as if he planned to stay a while.

I've managed to avoid the officials for three years, and now, over a simple car accident, I'm trapped. "So, what did you want to ask me?"

"Can you tell me what you remember?"

Chapter Two

Luke finished Miss Giovanni's statement just as his partner radioed from the car that he was ready to call it a night. With all the reports they had to fill out, Luke didn't argue, but silently confessed he wouldn't have minded spending a little more time with Calandre Giovanni.

Back at the station, Luke opened the locker room door; a strange mixture of aftershave and gun metal slapped him in the face. After the night he'd had, a room full of his fellow officers should have been a relief. It wasn't.

He shrugged the blue shirt off and straightened his uniform on the hanger, trading it for his street clothes. The young officer next to him was doing just the opposite. "What a night," Luke said.

"What's wrong, lucky Luke? Tired of leaping tall buildings in a single bound?" Vic Taylor drawled with distinct mockery.

Luke felt the muscles in his jaw tighten when he saw the smirk on the rookie's face. In no mood to confront the kid, Luke attempted to be civil. "Nah, piece of cake,

Taylor. One kid in a coma, a woman who narrowly escaped losing her eyesight, and a city full of drivers who act like they've never seen icy roads before. Not to mention the two punks in the slammer for breaking into a dozen cars and nearly beating the life out of a friend. All in a night's work.''

"You are so lucky. You always get the excitement.'' Taylor spat a four-letter word as he poked a finger in Luke's face. "All week I've been called off before I saw any action. You'd think my wife worked in dispatch or something.''

Luke laughed before he lost what little self-control he had left. "Don't be so eager, kid. The action's not all it's cracked up to be.''

The rookie adjusted his belt and puffed his chest out, as if ignoring Luke's advice.

"And by the way, it has nothing to do with luck.'' Luke tugged the gray T-shirt over his shoulders and rubbed the ache buried deep in his muscle. He noticed his partner, Tom, coming into the locker room.

When Luke turned around, the rookie was strutting into the briefing room.

Luke flung the leather jacket over his shoulder then slammed the metal locker door closed. "What's Taylor's problem? If he thinks two hours of paperwork and tagging thirty items into the evidence room is fun, he's got a lot to learn.''

His partner chuckled and slapped Luke's shoulder sympathetically. "Let it go, Luke.'' Tom continued. "I've learned the best way to deal with people like Taylor is to let their ignorant comments roll off your back.''

The reality of his best friend's comment sobered him. Luke glanced at Tom and shook his head. "I'm sorry,

Tom. After all these years, it just isn't right that a person's race still brings such discrimination."

"Nothing for you to apologize for."

An icy draft followed the command sergeant through the door from the parking lot, his shotgun slung from one shoulder and bag in the other hand. "Good work tonight," he said, nodding toward Luke and Tom. "One by one, we're putting those gangs out of business. Did the kid come out of the coma?"

Luke shook his head. "I'm going to check in on him throughout the day. If he doesn't, we really need that witness. The two suspects won't talk." Luke chugged the last of his cold coffee, watching as Tom moved his duty weapon from his belt to a waist-pack "holster."

After securing his handgun, Tom looked at Luke. "I still think we had a break tonight. I'll lay you odds that our anonymous caller is that blonde you nearly wiped out in the parking lot."

"Just what we need. A woman determined to eliminate Palmer's worst gang single-handedly. Why doesn't A.C. volunteer at one of the after-school programs or something safe?"

"Maybe she already has gang connections."

Luke didn't like that possibility at all.

"We should check out gang members' ex-girlfriends. Could be one trying to settle a personal vendetta."

"Against the whole gang?" Luke shook his head. "No way. But whatever the lady's reasoning, she's playing with fire." An image of the flustered blonde in the white truck flashed into his head. Couldn't be her. After three years, A.C. would be too used to the streets to get that upset over a little skid.

He rinsed his coffee mug and set it in the cupboard to

dry, then tossed his taped report to Tom. "Can't believe neither of us got a look at that license plate."

His partner placed both microcassettes in the manila envelope and filed them for transcription. "Nothing more we could've done. It was a bad angle. No light. Backup hadn't arrived. You know as well as I do, she was low priority."

"I should have told her to stay put so we could talk to her," Luke mumbled, continuing down the hall to the parking lot.

"Go home and chill. We're going to find A.C. It's just a matter of time." Tom disappeared from view, leaving only his footsteps echoing on the marble stairs.

"Don't hold your breath. She's as elusive as the East-siders' leader himself." Luke knew there were few on the force who believed that the same woman was re-sponsible for the majority of their tips. Thank goodness, his partner happened to share his theory.

Tilting his head from one side to the other, Luke hoped to shrug off the tension in his shoulders and the headache lurking behind his eyes. Tom was right, he needed to loosen up. Twelve years on the force was going to be the end of him if he didn't find some way to enjoy life again.

He recalled the woman's dark eyes and fair skin— recalled the quick recovery she'd made, slipping back into control in those brief seconds of their encounter. Tom's suspicion that she was their informant crossed his mind again. *No way. I'm just not that fortunate.*

"Hey, Northrup. Hear your lady tipped you off again! One of these days, you're going to have to introduce us. Bet she's hot." Laughter followed as the officers from the next shift made their way to the squad cars and loaded their gear.

Luke feigned a good-natured rebuttal, too tired to care

if they were being funny or serious. "Better watch it, boys. A.C. is good, and she just may be after your job."

The laughter stopped abruptly. Luke pulled his legs into the sports car and closed the door to the hoots and jeers that would follow his idle banter. Revving the engine, he backed out, then shifted into drive.

"Lord, help me find this lady, before it's too late."

Mrs. Maloney had already prepared Jon's breakfast and done the dishes when Luke arrived.

"Morning, Dad."

"Hey, sport. I'll take you this morning. Don't forget to return your spelling test today."

"I have it."

"Then let's get going. Traffic is a mess."

After he dropped his son off at school, Luke decided to stop for breakfast, then go by the hospital to check on the kid. And Calandre Giovanni.

Luke wasn't sure what it was about the woman that intrigued him. *Maybe it's that interesting name—Calandre.* He smiled. The name itself sounded strong. Determined. Spunky. And the woman? Well, the name fit. Perfectly.

He tried to justify seeing her again. *Am I crossing the line between personal and professional?* He didn't like the answer, so he looked at the situation from another angle. Deciding the least he could do was make sure she found someone to help her until the doctor allowed her to remove her bandages, Luke proceeded. Even one day without his eyesight would send him up the walls. *Nothing wrong with offering to help.*

Luke stopped at Teodoro's and greeted Teddy warmly.

"Good morning, Luke."

"Make me two breakfasts to go. Say, do you happen

to know a blonde who drives a white 4 Runner in your neighborhood watch group?'' Luke dug his wallet from his pocket.

"Blonde, 4 Runner," Teddy repeated, frowning. "No. Doesn't sound familiar. Something wrong?"

"We're looking for a witness. Thought she may have been the one. Thanks anyway, Teddy." Luke waited for his food, then paid and left.

Walking into Calli's hospital room, he felt helpless. Before him was a woman who was totally vulnerable. She lay on her side, her left arm propped on a pillow. Her short black hair was a mess, her thin lips pale and dry and her delicate features were mottled with bruises. *What in tarnation am I doing here?* Just as he considered turning and walking away, she moved.

"Mmm…Teddy's breakfast burritos." Her voice was soft.

"That's quite a nose." He wanted to elaborate, but figured he was pushing the boundaries by coming back at all. After all, he had met her in the line of duty. He'd consoled his conscience with the knowledge that he wasn't the primary officer on her case, and, since completing the statement, was now officially "off" the case.

"Sergeant Northrup…"

"Just Luke. I'm off duty." He opened the paper sack and unloaded two foil-wrapped packages.

"Oh," she said, her voice unable to conceal her puzzlement. She fumbled with the pillow, then the bed controls, obviously uncomfortable with his return. "Did you need me to answer more questions?"

He cleared her untouched breakfast tray from the bed table, glad she couldn't see the guilt-laden grin across his face. "No, I uh, wanted to check on the kid, and thought I'd stop in to see how you're feeling…. As long as I'm here. I have an extra burrito if you'd like one. I see you don't think much of the food here."

There was a long pause, then the corner of her mouth lifted. "I plead the Fifth. But I never turn down Teddy's burritos. Thanks. You're off duty, and you're here? Aren't you tired?"

"Takes me a few hours to wind down after a crazy shift like last night's." Luke unwrapped the burrito and placed it in her long fingers. She was enchanting—even in this state. Visiting her was not the best way to unwind, he reflected.

"How *is* your other patient?"

Here she lay uncertain of her own future, and she seemed more concerned about a total stranger's condition. Luke wished he could brush her worries away. "Still in a coma."

"I'm sorry."

She didn't ask for the details, for which he was eternally grateful. He didn't know how he could've politely told her he couldn't discuss an open case. Especially when one witness lay in a coma and the other had left without a trace.

It seemed like forever since there'd been anyone he'd been remotely interested in. Which made it even more difficult that Calandre Giovanni's case had to involve him. "I understand you get to go home today." *Ingenious, Northrup. You'd think this is the first woman you'd talked to.*

"I guess so. The doctor says there's no need to hang around here. The bandages make it look worse than it is. I think they're trying to slow me down." She ran her fingers over her head. Or what little hair was exposed anyway. She tentatively explored the gauze and slipped a finger under the edge and scratched her temple. "My things...from my truck. Are they here?"

"Just your clothes and purse. Whatever else you had, you can pick up at the salvage yard where your car was towed."

"Salvage yard?" She nibbled her lower lip.

"That's where vehicles are taken until the damage has been determined." He wondered if she had someone who could take her to get her belongings. "If you'd like, I could take you to clean it out."

Again, the silence was ominous. Her tone changed from the friendly exchange they'd established to one of total skepticism. "Thank you for offering, but I'll manage. My cousin is on her way with clean clothes."

"Okay. If you need anything, feel free to call me. Here's a card with your case number, the responding officer's name and my number if you have any questions." After visiting for a while longer, he placed his business card in her hand and left.

At home two days later, Calli found the switch to turn on the radio, and rocked in the antique chair. Music was the only thing she could enjoy without her sight. Running her fingers over the card in her hand, Calli wondered why Sergeant Luke Northrup had really returned. She inhaled, flustered as much by the fading aroma as she had been the man.

At first she thought he'd discovered a connection to the apartments when filling out the remainder of the report, but later she began to wonder if the personal interest was mutual. Yet she still couldn't allow herself to call, even to thank him for his kindness. He was a cop.

It didn't matter that he had a soothing voice that made her forget her past. Or manners that her grandmother would applaud. Or enough compassion to rewrite her personal definition of *law enforcement officer*. He was still a cop.

Until she met with the doctor to get the bandages removed, Calli could do little besides rest and wonder if Luke Northrup was really as wonderful as first impressions left her believing. Even if the nurse was exaggerating about Luke's appearance, it wouldn't matter. Looks weren't at the top of her list. But then again, cops weren't, either. In fact, they were no longer anywhere on her list. For more than one reason she reminded herself.

From the little she'd talked with Luke, her instincts said he wasn't a typical police officer. When he left her hospital room, Calli felt a longing to be someone she wasn't. An innocent bystander instead of a silent witness. Suddenly she wished she'd been born to a washer repairman instead of to an army officer. She longed to know Luke better, if only circumstances were different. If only *she* was different.

She'd tried to change. Even her grandmother had tried to help. Tried to teach her to crochet baby blankets and bake angel food cakes. Had tried to instill in her the more "delicate" aspects of women's traditional roles. Calli had almost succeeded in dousing the embers of her fiery temperament. Until that night three years ago.

The shrill ring of the telephone startled her from the unsettling walk down memory lane. She fumbled for the receiver and answered.

"I see from the newspaper that you're still patrolling."

The gruff tone caught her off guard, but it didn't take more than a second to recognize his voice. It had been months since she heard from him, yet she immediately felt herself cowering to his authority. With a blind search for her glass, she took a drink of water to smooth her vocal cords. "Yes."

"I worry about you, Calli." His voice softened.

Her hand moved to the bandages on her head. She couldn't even argue that point with him today. So how could she ever make them understand? Patrolling wasn't something she wanted to do. She had to. Someone *had* to care enough to stand up against the criminals who were tainting the city. Yet she said nothing.

"It's too late to help Mike. It's not too late to help yourself," he added.

Calli took a deep breath, then swallowed. "You taught me to be careful. I know how to protect myself."

"Your best protection is to stop. It's *not* your job," he insisted. "Let the police clean up the streets."

You taught me to care, to stand up for what's right. This may not be two countries fighting, but it's still war. How can you not understand? she wanted to scream at him, but the words caught in her throat.

"We've already lost a son."

"I have to go, Daddy. Give Mother my love." Calli hung up. She rested her bandaged head in the cradle of her hands. *Oh, Daddy, don't you see? Just because I'm a girl it doesn't mean I can't fight my own battles. I have to do something to protect the helpless.*

She knew the day would come when she would have no choice but to blow her cover, mission accomplished or not. Once she testified on any case, everything would change. She wouldn't be able to keep a job working with the public. She'd have to watch over her shoulder. And, she realized, it could even mean losing her own identity. Each night she asked herself the same question: Is it really worth it?

Chapter Three

Calli zipped the ski parka, adjusted her earmuffs and pulled on the bulky gloves. She checked her gear then felt her pocket to be sure she had remembered lip ointment, tissues and sunglasses.

Everything accounted for, she skied toward the footprints marking the loading zone for the tramway that would carry her away from the pressures of the city. Since the accident two weeks ago, she'd done little besides work the checkout lanes at the grocery store, then go home and struggle with the temptation to patrol again. With any luck at all, she'd be too tired tonight to care if the whole town crumbled at her doorstep.

She wanted this ski trip to revitalize her senses. Wanted it to make her forget the urge to protect the weak and helpless.

Experts said forgiveness was the key to moving on in life after a tragedy. Yet try as she may, Calli found it impossible to forgive—a hit-and-run driver, an unfaithful fiancé or an elusive murderer.

Calli took a deep breath of the crisp clean air and

closed her eyes. *Okay, Father, I'll quit patrolling. But there has to be some way I can help. Show me how. Take my life, my heart, and change it. Starting today, Lord, remind me how to relax and have fun.*

She watched tufts of clouds floating in from the west. "For I know of the plans that I have for you...plans to give you a hope and a future." Today she would be carefree. Happy. Relaxed. *Today I'm starting over.*

She noticed the broad shoulders ahead of her, and again found herself daydreaming about the cop with the resonating voice and tender touch. Though she'd never actually seen Luke Northrup, her mind had created its own image. His business card was still in her purse, with his home number scrawled on the back. She'd read it over and again, too stubborn to succumb to the temptation to actually call him. As kind as he had been, he was still a cop.

"Excuse me, sir."

He didn't respond.

As she waited, another chair passed. She looked at it, then to the man who was now struggling with the binding on his ski.

Calli watched as the next seat approached, then tapped the man's shoulder. "Excuse me. Are you going up?"

"Just a minute." he snapped. He stepped aside and Calli eased forward, her gaze climbing the ski slope.

Calli heard a clamor as the chair rounded the curve of the pulley. She hurried past the man to the loading zone for the lift. When the chair bumped the back of her legs, she instinctively sat down and knew immediately that something was wrong. She wasn't on the chair. She was on *somebody*. "What's going on?"

"Hang on!" a deep voice commanded. Calli grabbed hold of the vertical bar connecting the chair to the cable,

then looked down and realized three things. The chair
was already twenty feet above the frozen ground. To her
right, skis dangled from jean-clad legs, confirming her
suspicion that she was sitting on someone. And she didn't
dare let go.

"How—how did you get here?" she stammered. As
Calli yanked the safety bar down in front of them, she
felt his hand grab the back of her parka. "What are you
doing?"

"Trying to keep you from falling, ma'am." He shoved
her to one side, then kicked his long legs in a final effort
to sit upright.

The chair jolted from side to side. "Watch out! The
pole." She heard the snap as his skis hit the huge metal
post. The chair jerked to a stop, bumping Calli off the
seat again. She screamed.

"Don't worry. I have you." He hoisted her back into
the chair, then pulled her into the circle of his arms.

Calli whispered a prayer, unable to stop clinging to the
man who'd brought her to safety. He held her securely.
Tenderly. Sympathetically.

"It's okay now. You'll be fine, miss." The deep timbre of his voice was somewhat disconcerting and the
spicy scent of his cologne sent a shiver up her spine.

Slightly perturbed that he did nothing to dissuade her
from clinging to him, Calli concentrated on slowing her
breathing before she totally collapsed into his arms, further making a fool of herself.

"It's okay. Take a deep breath—let it out." She could
feel the rise and fall of his chest as he imitated his instructions.

Her breathing was ragged, and with each gasp the cold
air burned her throat. How long they clung to one another, she wasn't sure. Calli could feel his heart pounding

against her own, and, with determined control, she pushed herself away from the security of the man's embrace. Looking into his eyes, she felt as if a warm blanket had just been wrapped around her. His rough cheek brushed hers, and she fought the temptation to lean close again. Calli straightened her jacket and took another cleansing breath, the thin air only intensifying the dizziness.

"I...I didn't think you were going up...." she said, her words trailing off as she lost herself in his jade-green eyes. Her gaze strayed to the black stubble framing his smile, and it was suddenly a struggle to think.

A voice bellowed from the ground below. "Everyone okay up there?"

Her companion glanced down, then back to her. His voice held none of the irritation she'd first heard, but was strangely warm and comforting. "Are you okay?"

She swallowed with difficulty and finally a raspy sound emerged. "Fine. But you. Your ski. And..." She raised her body off the seat again, and reached under her. "Oh, no, I bent your ski pole."

He yelled to the ski patrol and confirmed they were both fine. The lift started with a jerk, and both grabbed for each other.

She watched the play of emotions on his rugged face. His eyes searched hers and they broke into laughter. His laugh was warm, deep and fully masculine.

"You couldn't have bent that pole if you'd jumped on it. There's hardly enough of you to—" He abruptly stopped midsentence.

It couldn't be. The laughter ended and she felt her cheeks heating up, despite the cold wind on her face.

Did he feel the same unexplainable bond as she did? It was crazy; they'd just met. Or had they? This wasn't like her at all. Every time he spoke, it sent a ripple of awareness through her.

"I'm very sorry, miss...." When she didn't answer, he continued. "I lost my balance and couldn't stop with these skis on." A smile immediately softened his rugged features and further melted her indignation. He lifted the faded baseball cap covering his unruly short black hair, swiped his brow, then replaced the cap. "I am sorry."

She nodded and looked the other way.

Calli couldn't help but wonder if her attraction to this stubborn, arrogant and attractive man was God's will. Heavens, she thought, He could have broken me into this new plan of His a little easier.

Her mind must be playing tricks on her, she decided. Not only did this man sound familiar, if she really used her imagination, he almost looked like the police officer who nearly ran into her that last night she patrolled. *Couldn't be.*

She wished she could think of something clever to say. Anything. She hesitantly admired his strong square jaw and thick brows which arched over the deep-set green eyes. *I am not ready for this, God.* She shivered, then felt a warm sensation relax her body.

Already she'd seen a gentle side of this man replace the severity of his earlier arrogance. He measured her with an unnerving silence.

He extended his hand, firmly grasping hers. "I'm Luke Northrup."

Her heart stopped beating. She'd just convinced herself that her mind was playing tricks on her. Convinced herself that the nurse exaggerated. She was stunned—Luke was as handsome as the hero conjured up by her crazy imagination. Searching her pockets, she found what she needed and slipped behind the screen of mirrored sunglasses. "Calli," she said simply. No need for more.

It didn't matter that she'd thought of him on a daily basis. Or that she'd promised God she'd give up patrolling, Teddy's burritos...anything, if she could just resist falling in love with another police officer. What did matter was she couldn't see him again. *This isn't fair, God. And I showed such restraint not calling him.*

Luke obviously didn't recognize her without her bandages and she quickly decided it would be safest to play dumb. "You must see stupid things like this all the time up here."

"Up here?" Luke's brows furrowed, with a glint of wonder in his eyes.

"On the slopes," she added, relieved that he'd not made the connection between her given name and her nickname.

He chuckled. "You think I'm a ski bum? I'm flattered."

Just like a cop—arrogant. Calli straightened her back and handed his bent pole to him. "I'll be glad to pay for the damage."

"Don't think a thing of it. If this binding had been working properly, none of this would have happened. They could be more careful about training employees, too. I'm not sure that guy even knew how to stop the lift."

"Are you security?" The rasp in her voice was getting worse. She had to calm down. The crisis was over. Everything was fine. He wasn't making the connection.

"No, but I'm sure the folks who run this place will trust my credentials."

An uncomfortable silence was avoided as she cleared

her throat and nodded. If Luke Northrup didn't want to admit to being a law officer, she wouldn't push.

They bounced along in silence. Minutes later, Calli looked up at the signs telling them to prepare to unload. Reminded of his accident, she assessed the situation. "So how are you going to get down off this mountain with a broken ski?"

"We'll just ride the lift back down. That ought to get their attention."

Calli yanked her sunglasses from her face and turned to him. "We?"

"I'll need you to file a statement…to verify what happened."

"I thought you said they would trust your credentials. It took me… Well, you can't imagine what I've gone through to arrange *this* ski trip!"

"Better safe than sorry. And we'd better have your arm checked. You gave it a pretty good yank. I don't think either of us will be safe on this slope today." He smiled, then added, "And, I think I at least owe you a cup of coffee for ruining your morning."

Her arm *was* sore, but she knew it wasn't broken. As she considered Luke's logic, the dismount ramp approached. He wasn't thinking of himself, but of her safety, as well as the other skiers. She, of all people, should understand his protective nature.

He waited for her answer. "Consider it a peace offering."

She looked at the glint in Luke's eyes and felt that crazy magnetism between them. *Just one cup of coffee couldn't hurt. He doesn't even remember me.* "If you insist. But I'll warn you, I'm not the forgiving type." *A cup of coffee. What could happen over a cup of coffee?*

Chapter Four

Luke unlocked the apartment door and hobbled inside, greeted by his son and an overwhelming garlic aroma. Jon must be toasting hoagie buns for his favorite after-school snack.

"Sorry I'm late. How was school?"

"Okay. We're out of garlic salt, but I added it to the grocery list." He walked around the corner, carrying a plate overflowing with bread. One glance at Luke and the thirteen-year-old stopped short. He brushed the dark bangs from his eyes. "Wow! What happened to you?"

"Nothing out of the ordinary. A little investigating. Some crisis intervention. Rescuing damsels in distress. Filling out paperwork." Luke collapsed in the brown recliner nearest the door and took off his boots. During the fifty-minute drive down the mountain, his sprained ankle had swelled and stiffened.

"I thought you were going to use the ski pass I gave you for Christmas today."

Luke released the footrest and pushed the chair back. "I did." After asking his son to bring him an ice bag and something for the pain, Luke told him about the excitement, minus the part where he'd struck out with the damsel. He could have sworn that beneath Calli's cautious exterior, she was interested.

When he awoke two hours later the television was blaring. Jon, seemingly oblivious to the racket, surfed the channels until he found a college basketball game. His son tossed a fringed pillow from the sofa at him. "How're ya doing?"

Luke stretched, yawning aloud as he folded the chair under him. "Ask me after I shower." He stood and limped across the room without the pain he'd had earlier. "Your grandma left a casserole in the fridge yesterday. Would you put it in the oven? I'll be out in a few minutes to finish making dinner."

Jon was slow to respond. "It's not that potpie thing, is it?"

"Yeah. Why?" Luke placed his hands on his hips and stopped. "You didn't throw it out, did you?"

"Not exactly." His son remained slouched on the sofa, peering at the TV from under the curtain of hair.

Luke waited for a further explanation. "Well?"

Jon raked his hand through his long bangs. "I ate it."

"You ate the whole thing?" Luke couldn't believe he bothered to ask such a stupid question. Of course he did. Jon was thirteen. He was supposed to eat them out of house and home.

"Well, I didn't know it was supper."

"Do me a favor. Don't tell me how great it was." Turning back to the kitchen, Luke rummaged through the freezer, hoping to find a replacement. There was none.

Kneeling in the middle of the kitchen, a pain shot up his leg and into his hip. From the cupboard, he pulled two empty peanut-butter jars and a few nearly empty boxes of crackers. His son was obviously going through a growing spurt. Jon only needed another six inches to reach Luke's height of six foot three, but the way the boy was eating, that would take less than a couple of months.

Luke settled for an overripe banana on the way to the shower. Between bites, he told Jon to clean up so they could grab dinner on the way to the grocery store.

After showering, Luke and Jon ate, then went to buy groceries. Luke bought double what he figured they needed, hoping there'd be a few crumbs left for his own meals after Jon finished eating.

Halfway through the store Luke found himself thinking of Calli. She'd mentioned that she'd almost completed her teaching degree, but was working at one of the downtown grocery store chains. He paid special attention to the employees as he browsed, certain that she also said she usually worked evenings. When he didn't see her, he made a note to start shopping in the evenings so he could run into her. *A few phone calls should turn up a "Calli" at one of them. It's not that common a name.*

As they were driving home, Jon was unusually quiet. They discussed another Nuggets loss and their tickets to the upcoming Avalanche game against the Red Wings. All the while, Jon barely uttered two words that wasn't an answer to a direct question. It was twice as tough to keep the conversation going, when all Luke could think about was the gorgeous woman he'd spent two hours trying to charm, only to be ignored when he asked if he could call her sometime. Before he had a chance to ask any more questions, Calli had slipped back into her cautious camouflage and politely excused herself. He drove home, replaying their conversation, trying to figure exactly what they'd been talking about when he'd blown it.

"Dad…did you hear me?"

"I was thinking of something else. Sorry. What did you say?"

"Nate wants me to stay with him Friday night. He's kind of bummed since his dad left. Can I go?"

"Friday, as in tomorrow?"

"Yeah. I know we were going to the hockey game, but… Well, it's important."

Nate lived upstairs, and the two had been friends since preschool. Only a few months earlier, Nate's dad had left his mother for another woman. The family was devastated. Especially Nate.

Luke thought of Friday's Avalanche game and how long they'd waited for these tickets. "Sure. Go ahead. Nate's more important right now."

"Really? Thanks, Dad. You're all right."

Hang on to that thought. It won't last long. Luke stuffed the disappointment away. He wasn't ready for his son to choose friends over him. Yet here it was. They unloaded the groceries, Jon finished his homework, then went to bed as Luke got ready for a night at the station. With his leg hurting like this, he knew he wouldn't be able to handle full duty.

Mrs. Maloney knocked quietly and came in.

"Hi, Marge. Jon has finished his homework and is already in bed. I should be home early tonight." He limped to the table and loaded his notes in his briefcase. Motioning to his foot, Luke offered an explanation. "Officially I'm off until I see a doctor, but I need to catch up on some paperwork. Shouldn't take more than a few hours."

"That's fine, Luke. I'll just watch the late shows."

"Feel free to go to bed. I can wake you when I get home."

He went to tell Jon good-night, but the room was dark and silent. Luke closed the door, remembering when Jon was a baby and his mother had just walked out on them. Jon had gone to child care when Luke worked the day shift, and had gone to Luke's parents at night. It became more difficult as Jon got older. Luke and Jon had argued about the neighbor coming to "baby-sit," but in the end, his son didn't give either of them any problems. It was a teenager's obligation to argue, but inside, Luke suspected his son was as relieved as he was that their favorite neighbor was here.

The command sergeant watched Luke try to walk without a limp. "Face it, Northrup, you're going to be at the front window for a month with that bum leg."

"Not a chance. A week, maybe two at the most. I'll do anything, Sarge, but not the front."

The front window was known as the department "Miracle Cure," known to heal any ailment twice as quickly when an officer was assigned there. Unlike dispatch's duties, working the front meant answering the phone, dealing with stupid questions, handling complaints due to "cold calls" that were filed at the bottom of the priority list.

The sergeant tossed a file on his desk. "For now, see if Angel and Dunn need help with their case."

Luke reviewed the file, looking for anything to tie a white 4 Runner to the case. They too needed their witness to come forward. Angel had asked Luke to listen to the tapes to confirm that it was the anonymous caller.

Luke pressed Play and again listened to the female caller on previous 911 tapes, including the calls from the night of the auto prowls two weeks ago.

He compared the voices one more time.

Tom shrugged. "You must know this by heart, Luke. Let it go. She'll call again soon."

Her voice was soft. "Is she whispering, or scared to death?" Luke asked Tom. Sirens wailed and Luke held up a hand, quieting his partner. There was a gasp, a rattle, then a clunk, like the receiver had fallen. The voice was quiet, but urgent. "Turn it up. She said something."

Tom rewound the recording and pushed Play and raised the volume. The transcription was full of static. "Come on. Start." He heard more static. Then, "Too close. Get out of here." Static and her voice saying, "Phone?" The line went dead.

After a quick drive back to the scene to reenact the call, Luke shook his head. "The lady in the 4 Runner was the anonymous caller. We could have had her." His frustration became more evident as they returned to the station. Tom left the room, seemingly aware that Luke needed time alone. The man knew him too well.

Luke rubbed his rough jaw. This anonymous caller case was getting to him. Of that, there was no doubt. After several minutes, he decided there wasn't much he could do besides turn it over to a higher power, one with more insight than his.

Tom passed by the desk for the fourth time in ten minutes.

"Would you stop pacing. My ankle hurts just watching you. What is it?"

"You okay?"

The bite of anger subsided. "I'll be fine. Just checking in with the Boss." Luke pointed up.

Tom nodded. "We're going to need it. Captain was just telling me Tiger came to the jail to visit Marlow yesterday. The guard says it looked like there was plenty of tension between them. Money must be getting tight."

Luke understood Tom's silent implication. It was time for the Eastsiders "to put in some work." They were bound to be getting edgy. Luke twirled his pencil, "walking" it from one finger to the next, then back again. "You said it yourself—there's nothing we can do besides wait for her to call."

Tom sat down and leaned back, folding his hands behind his head. "She's digging herself in deep, Luke. If we're looking for her, you can bet *they're* even closer to finding her."

Friday night Jon and Nate finished supper and went to Nate's bedroom. Nate's little brother ran into the room, screeching about not getting to watch his favorite show. The eight-year-old wouldn't be quiet.

"Mom! Tell James to leave us alone."

"I sent him to his room. He won't leave your sister alone, and I can't take any more of their fighting."

"And what're we supposed to do?" Nate argued with his mother as if she had the power to mend all of their problems. Jon felt sorry for her, but he couldn't tell Nate that. As far as his friend was concerned, he was the only one hurting. Nate felt like no one understood. Jon was trying.

"We're going to Jon's."

Jon didn't argue, though he knew he should have. His dad had gone ahead to the hockey game with Tom and they wouldn't be home for hours. He knew his dad didn't like him having friends over when he wasn't home. It wasn't that his dad didn't trust him, but he knew other kids sometimes didn't think before doing stupid things. For a dad, his was okay.

"C'mon, Jon. Let's get outta here."

Nate led the way down the stairs and out the front door of the building.

"Where are you going?"

"Out. I'm sick of this place."

"Let's just go to my apartment like you told your mom, Nate. What if she comes looking for you?"

"She never checks up on me—she's too tired to think of it. You coming or not?" Nate's language turned foul more often these days, and nothing anyone did was worthy of his attention. Jon didn't know what to do to help. But he had to try.

They headed down the street, meeting a couple of kids Jon recognized from school. From the way Nate greeted them, Jon realized this wasn't the first time his friend had escaped to the streets.

He looked around uncomfortably.

"Daddy on duty tonight, Northrup?"

He shook his head. That didn't matter. Everyone in the precinct knew him.

"Come on, Nate, let's split."

"In a minute."

Nate continued to talk with the group, which had doubled in size since they arrived. The gang headed down an alley. Jon lagged behind, unsure what was going on, but he knew he didn't want to be here.

They walked to a park, meeting up with a couple of older guys. After a few minutes, Jon got up the courage to tell Nate he was going home.

"You can't. Your dad'll ask questions, and if you go to my house, my mom'll get all uptight."

He pulled Nate away from the gang. "This is stupid, Nate. Let's go to my apartment. We can play video games, order a pizza, whatever."

"Time for business." The guy they called "Tiger" looked at them. "You in or out?"

Jon watched as everyone looked at him, expecting him to chicken out. Daring him. He'd heard what happened when they suspected a snitch. If he ditched out now, he'd be in deep trouble. And if his dad found out, it would be even worse.

Chapter Five

Calli picked up her paycheck and rushed past the checkout lanes. She tucked the paper and two videos into her backpack, waving to her boss on the way out.

Ten minutes behind schedule already, she parked the rental car and ran into the recreation center. Hanna met her in the lobby and they rushed to the women's locker room where Calli changed into her sweats and a T-shirt.

"It's a class of women." Calli said, watching Hanna brush her hair then freshen her makeup. "We're practicing self-defense, Hanna," she said with a laugh. "There's no need to primp."

Her fair-haired cousin was an easy target for muggers. Precise schedule, expensive car, drop-dead attractive. Over the years, Calli had tried telling Hanna to vary her routine, as well as other safety precautions. It wasn't until a woman had been attacked a block from Hanna's office that she'd been persuaded to pay attention to Calli's advice.

"I don't know, Bart's kinda cute."

"And kinda married." Calli laughed. "Not your type."

Hanna tossed the brush down. "I didn't see a wedding ring." Then as if there'd been no interest at all, she changed the subject. "Do we have to do anything 'real' tonight? Like flips or anything?"

"Probably a few moves. You'll do fine. Let's go."

Hanna pulled her hair into a ponytail at the top of her head and they rushed out the door. "Easy for you to say. You've been tossing men over your shoulder since you were a kid."

"I was merely defending myself. If you had brothers you'd know how to take care of yourself, too." Calli had carefully locked those memories away, and yet with that innocent reminder, they returned. Calli would never forget the first time she successfully flipped her older brother. Her dad took her for an ice-cream cone right before dinner, ignoring her mother's protests. To this day, Calli never figured out why her mom had been protesting; had it been the nature of the celebration, or the fact that the ice cream would ruin her dinner?

"Did you know that your dad tried to convince my mother to let him teach me self-defense once?" Hanna acted as if this was entertainment.

Calli stared ahead, afraid to open the door to the past any further than a tiny crack. Few people could overlook her father's tough militaristic exterior, and even fewer saw the loving emotional side that he reserved for his family. She slipped back through that door and slammed it closed. "Dad was a good instructor, but so is Bart. He knows what he's doing."

Hanna told her about her latest date, and the two started laughing. Calli didn't enjoy the dating game like her cousin did. For Hanna, meeting new people was fun, but Calli rarely went out, and only with men she knew well. Calli and Hanna joined the rest of the class on the mats and they began stretching.

Suddenly, hushed voices buzzed around her. She turned just as Luke Northrup introduced himself as their new instructor. Calli's smile disappeared.

"Bart broke his leg and asked me to take his place. I'm a certified instructor, and have taught personal safety with him before."

The other women seemed to have the same reaction to the handsome man as she had. Tonight he wore a black tank top and sweats, and as before, his hair looked as if he'd just used his fingers as a comb. His five o'clock shadow wasn't as pronounced as it had been at the ski resort, but he still had that air of authority which commanded instant attention.

Okay, God, what are you up to? I thought we agreed, no cops. Then she recalled Luke's gentler side. The care and concern he had shown at the hospital. The way he comforted her when she clung to him after the skiing accident. His tenderness was as startling as an ice cube on a hot summer day.

As they visited over coffee, she had relaxed and temporarily put the past behind her. Luke had never recognized her from their meeting at the hospital. But once again, he teased and tormented the emotions she'd long locked away. Then suddenly she caught herself entertaining the notion of seeing him once more. Before he could ask her for her phone number, she politely thanked him for the coffee and ran.

There wasn't room for a man in her life. Especially not this one. Not one who made her forget her past, her mission, her mistakes. Not even for a minute.

Luke's steady gaze bored into hers in silent expectation. Their eyes met—dueling, dancing, laughing. There was that maddening hint of arrogance again.

She found herself studying him as he turned his attention back to the class. Was she imagining it, or had his back straightened, his shoulders become broader and his determination grown stronger?

"We're going to start with a defensive move. I'm going to need a volunteer to help me demonstrate." Hands flew into the air, yet he looked right at Calli, as if waiting for her objection. "Miss...?" he teased.

Begrudgingly she stepped forward. "Calli."

Luke explained the move, then demonstrated the steps in slow motion. He wore the same spicy aftershave as that night in the hospital. She silently searched for a plausible explanation to the shiver that went up her arm as he held her wrist. His hold was firm, challenging her to break loose. Her move was quick and instinctive.

She expected him to call on another volunteer for the next demonstration, but he stepped behind her as she turned to leave and wrapped his arm around her neck, as a mugger would.

Calli braced herself on her left leg. She tugged at his arm, leaned forward, and "swept" at Luke's legs with her foot. The move was enough to knock him to the floor so she could escape.

The class watched wide-eyed as Luke lay sprawled across the mat, laughing. He rose to one elbow. "A perfect example of the benefits of the element of surprise. Great job...Calli."

Her heart raced. "Glad to help." She returned his smile, careful to hide her pleasure at seeing him again. Class resumed, and Calli fought the constant temptation to join in his gentle sparring. He'd explain a move, then the class would pair up to practice. As he made his way to her group, Hanna seemed to enjoy seeing Calli's discomfort escalate with each step Luke took.

"How's it going here?" His voice seemed deeper than before.

Hanna spoke first. "I don't quite understand." Calli watched Luke go through the steps again, this time, wrapping his arm around Hanna's neck. She couldn't explain the crazy longing she had to trade places with her cousin at that moment.

"You kind of elbow the attacker in the stomach as you reach up...." Calli's eyes met his, and she stopped. "Sorry. I didn't mean to interrupt."

"We're here to learn, from one another or from me, it really doesn't matter. Care to try it again? I'm ready this time."

"I'll give you a break."

Luke smiled, then turned to the class. "I'll be the first to say that one can never underestimate the opponent. That in itself could be a woman's best defense." Luke looked at his watch. "That's it for tonight. Have a good week."

Several women thanked Luke, then Calli for her "help." A wave of giggles followed, and he shook his head.

"Calli, I'd be willing to forgive you, if you'd agree to help with the class. We seem to make a good team."

Despite her laugh, Calli felt an unwelcome reaction to his innuendo. "Think the third time's a charm, huh?"

"Third time? Unless I'm mistaken, we've only met twice." He crossed his arms and put his back to the wall.

Great, Calli. How're you going to get out of this one?

When she didn't answer, he added, "Unless you consider tonight memorable enough to count as twice, which

I happen to agree. Can't remember being knocked off my feet by a more beautiful woman.''

Calli stepped aside, struggling to find an answer to his question before his flirting turned her brains to jelly. "No way," she said, realizing she was way behind in the conversation. *Forget it, Luke Northrup. No way am I going through this blessed torment every week! Enough is enough.*

"Hanna, does your friend always back down from a challenge?"

"Cousin," Hanna corrected.

His eyebrows arched and his mouth fell open. "Cousin?"

Calli watched as he eyed the two of them. Hanna and her long blond hair, blue eyes and robust figure, then Calli's classic Italian coloring and willowy body.

"Plead the Fifth, Hanna, or you'll be walking home." She turned to leave, feeling Luke's challenging stare.

Hanna leaned close and whispered. "What's going on here, Calli?"

She couldn't answer. Couldn't admit the truth—that she was falling for another police officer.

"Just think about it. It's one thing to have an instructor who can tell them what to do, but it's something else altogether to see one of their own succeed. These women could learn a lot from you. I'll call *you* this time."

"Don't bother. The answer's no…*Officer* Northrup."

Hanna looked at her, then to Luke and began laughing. "You're kidding. Not again."

Jon tried phoning Nate after dinner, but according to his five-year-old sister, Nate was supposedly at Jon's. Jon had become his best friend's alibi more than ever before. He wouldn't have minded at one time, but fact was, he rarely saw Nate at all anymore, and Jon didn't like his friend's new pals.

He finished his algebra and threw his reading book aside. "I'm going to take the trash outside, Mrs. Maloney."

She looked up from her knitting and seemed to know he had something on his mind. "Don't take long. You haven't finished the dishes, and I assume you still have reading to do."

"It's a stupid book," he muttered.

"That may be your opinion, but I don't think that will answer the questions on your test. Take a break, then get back to your homework, young man."

Jon grumbled, then walked out of the apartment. He checked the stairway, then headed outside.

Nate's recent hangout seemed to be the park. Without hesitation, Jon rounded the corner and sauntered to the end of the block. He saw Nate and his new friends near the picnic table, laughing. Jon paused, then backed behind a budding lilac bush and watched. The huddle tightened, then Nate backed away from the group and looked around.

A few more minutes passed, and the group broke up. Jon stepped into the alley and ran home. He rode the elevator to the third floor, waiting for his breathing to slow before going into the apartment. It was about ten minutes later that he heard the sirens, and wondered if they'd caught Nate this time.

The next morning, Jon went to school alone. Nate finally showed up third hour, unprepared for the reading test. After another of Nate's outbursts of profanity, the teacher ordered him to finish the class period in the office. Wearing a smirk, Nate turned to Jon as he left the classroom. It was all Jon could do to meet his friend's gaze.

In the lunchroom, Nate approached Jon. "So what's up, Jonny boy?"

"What's with you, Nate?" Jon kept eating.

His friend ignored the question. "Saw you at the park last night."

Their eyes met. "You're asking for trouble with them, Nate."

"They're my friends."

"Whatever."

Nate pushed his tray closer to Jon's. "You the one who called the cops on us last night?"

"I wouldn't do that to you. Besides, I'm not stupid enough to cross the Eastsiders."

"They're not so bad," Nate insisted. "Give 'em a break."

Jon looked at his empty tray. "Nate, don't tell your mom that you're at my house next time you ditch out." He stood and backed away from the table. "I'll see you around."

Chapter Six

❧

"How soon's that cellular tracking system supposed to be active? That may be our best chance to find the anonymous caller."

"A few weeks." Tom took a swig of pop. "Typical glitches in the system. Tested it the other night. The call was made right outside the station. Showed in the system near Golden Acres."

"A lot of good that does us." Luke turned on the alley lights, looking for anything out of the ordinary.

"Let's hope she can stay out of trouble until it's ready." Tom cleared his throat. "Say, you never finished telling me about Bart's class last night."

Luke proceeded to tell his friend about Calli. Tom laughed, making a few good-natured comments. "You haven't had that look in a long time, bro."

"Don't get any ideas." Luke shone the spotlight behind a trash can, then up a dilapidated fire escape.

"Doesn't look like I need to. Vanessa's been nagging me to plan that night out. Thought I got away from dating when I said 'I do.' Did you ask Calli?"

"Who said anything about a date?" Though Luke would like nothing more than to ask Calli to dinner, he wasn't fond of beating his head against brick walls.

"Last week I told you to find a date for dinner and a movie. You did ask her, didn't you?"

Thinking of Calli's reaction, he shook his head. "I need to spend some time with Jon. Sorry. Maybe next time."

"You didn't get her number, did you?" Tom tossed his head back and began laughing. "You are out of touch with women, Luke. No wonder you're still single."

"I have her number. For your information, she's going to help me teach Bart's class. Then I'm going to convince her to help with the classes at the high schools."

"She agreed to work with you, but she won't go out with you? Did you even get her name?"

His partner knew all of his downfalls. "What do you think I am, a rookie?"

"I don't have to think, I *know*. You're so out of touch with women, you'd have fallen for any lame alibi."

He thought of the way she'd avoided telling him her name, and hated to admit his friend could be right. Though he didn't blame Calli—or whatever her name was. He continued the thought aloud. "A single woman can't be too careful nowadays. There's a whole lot of kooks in the world. I'm not going to push her."

"A man of integrity. One of these days, I'll teach you everything you need to know to find the *right* woman."

Throughout their patrol, Luke thought about Calli. He was ready to call the registrar for the self-defense classes, when he remembered where else he had seen her. *Why didn't I see it before? Sassy, short dark hair. Tall and thin. Calli—Calandre. Calli Giovanni. That's it.*

Luke radioed dispatch to end their patrol as Tom

shifted the cruiser into park. He was still razzing Luke about letting Calli slip away. Hoping to get Tom off his back, Luke mentioned the blonde in the 4 Runner. Contrary to what he wanted Tom to believe, Luke had just made his own plans, with Calandre, a.k.a. Calli Giovanni. "You have plans for tomorrow?"

Taking the bait, Tom nixed his idea of researching the anonymous caller. "Get a life, Luke. You can't be married to the job. It'll kill you."

"Thanks for the vote of confidence, partner."

A shrill ring woke Luke before he'd even had a chance to fall into a deep sleep. He moved the phone from one ear to the other and flopped onto his back, listening to his ex-wife's whining. At one time he'd have sympathized with her, but not any longer. She'd changed her mind too many times. This time she thought she wanted to take Jon for the summer.

"If you want to see Jon, I don't have any problem with you coming to visit."

Along with a few remarks meant to upset him, she threatened to contact a lawyer. Now, in addition to the summer, she wanted to petition the courts to let Jon decide whom to live with.

"Nancy, have you forgotten that you signed away your maternal rights twelve years ago? I never had to let you see him at all. It's been at least six months since you've even called. You missed his birthday, Christmas…"

She hung up. Without even asking how her son was doing. Nothing had changed. Luke set the receiver in the cradle and let out a deep breath. *Kids do stupid things, Jon. I was a kid once, I know.*

An hour later the apartment door clicked closed. Luke heard his son open the fridge, take a glass from the cupboard and close the refrigerator. Luke could imagine Jon chugging down his usual quart of orange juice. Footsteps approached the bedroom and his door creaked open.

"I'm home, Dad. I'm going to shower and go back to bed for a while."

"You're home awfully early. Things go okay with Nate?"

Jon grumbled a response and disappeared.

The phone conversation left him wide-awake. Luke got out of bed and pulled his sweats on. Before his son went to sleep, he ran the vacuum, then straightened the rest of the apartment. His mind returned to Nancy's phone call. At least a million times in the last fourteen years Luke had regretted his carelessness that night. They'd been dating for several months, and with stars in their eyes, one thing had led to another. And before they'd stopped to think about repercussions, they'd become parents.

He walked to the door of Jon's room and leaned against the doorjamb, watching his son's peaceful slumber. Luke would always regret his irresponsibility that night, but he had never once regretted having a son or being a father. Not even when his seventeen-year-old wife had walked out of their short-lived marriage, dropping their baby off at Luke's parents' house while he was at school. He gave up dreams of the military in order to give Nancy time to grow, adjust and change her mind about leaving the two of them. Two days after Jon's first birthday, she returned, just long enough to hand Luke the papers giving up her son.

That had been a dark, difficult time in his life, but Luke had found that, as his faith had grown stronger, so had his ability to cope as a single parent.

He wouldn't back down now, either. He had to think of what Jon had been through. Consider his son's feelings. His mother's rejection hurt, though Jon would never admit it.

Luke remembered the day about a month before Jon's fifth birthday when he first realized his family was different. Sure, they knew other single-parent families, but those kids went back and forth between Mom's house and Dad's house. Jon didn't.

"I want a brother for my birthday."

Luke had never believed in lying, especially to a child. In fourteen years he'd faced some doozies, but he'd never lied.

Luke stared at the anger and confusion in the five-year-old's eyes. His own emotions were mirrored on his child's face. "I can't give you a brother. I can buy you a present at the store. Would you like a bicycle?"

"No. I told you what I want," Jon growled. "I want a brother."

"Come on, Jon, you've never seen a brother for sale at the store, have you?" Luke chuckled, groping for some levity. "Do you want a doll? Is that what you mean?"

"*No!* I want a baby, just like Nate's mom had a baby."

"I see." He paused to swallow the lump in his throat. "Babies need a mom and a dad." He wasn't ready to go into this discussion, but he felt the questions coming. "I'm not married, and it's best to be married to have a baby. Babies look like a lot of fun, but they're lots of work, too."

After Luke told Jon a simplified version of how babies are made, the two embraced. As if he finally understood, Jon's smile faded. "But *I* don't have a mom."

It hurt to tell his own son that he had a mother who didn't want to be one. "So we can't have another baby without someone to be a mom. Someone who wants to

be a mom as much as I want to be a dad and you want
to be a big brother."

Even now, Luke still noticed Jon's interest in babies.
Tom and Vanessa and their new twins were great fun for
Jon. Every few days, Jon stopped by after school to visit
the Davises. It was painfully obvious. His son still
wanted the one thing Luke couldn't give him: a family.

Calli watched the leader of the gang walk past as she
checked Mrs. Polanski's basket of groceries. Every Saturday afternoon, her neighbor came to check out in her
lane.

"How are your eyes doing, Calli?"

"They still tire easily, but other than that, just fine,
Mrs. Polanski. The doctor says there doesn't seem to be
any permanent damage."

"Is there any loss of vision?"

Calli smiled and shook her head in lieu of an answer.
She ran the boxes past the scanner, thinking about Luke
Northrup's request for her to help him teach the self-
defense classes. She did little but think about it since their
class. On one hand, she firmly believed in the cause. But
on the other, she had to be crazy to consider spending
even one evening a week with the very man she should
be avoiding.

She glanced nervously at the kids wearing gang colors,
and totaled her neighbor's order. "Twenty-five dollars,
fifty-three cents, Mrs. Polanski." While the elderly
woman dug through her tapestry bag for money to pay
her bill, Calli turned to the bagger and whispered, "Jake,
help Mrs. Polanski into her car, and be sure it's locked
before she leaves." He nodded. Feeling a bit easier, Calli
watched Jake and her neighbor walk out the door.

The manager tapped Calli on the shoulder. "It's time for your break."

"Thanks." She turned her light out, signed off her money drawer and strode to the back of the store for some fresh air. It had been a long day already. She stepped outside and headed for the abandoned loading docks. Taking a deep breath, Calli leaned to one side, the other, then forward, stretching her tired back.

She took a sip of soda, admiring the clear sky. The brisk wind tousled her hair and refreshed her senses. Finding a clean spot on the cold cement, Calli sat down. The breeze and drastic drop from the dock reminded her of the day she'd met Luke at the ski slope.

Don't get any ideas, Calli. That man is off-limits. Her watch beeped, alerting her that it was time to get back to work. She went down the steps and around the corner, surprised to find three kids spray painting graffiti on the wall of the store in broad daylight.

"Hey, guys. You need to clear out of here."

They laughed. "You going to make us?" the kid with the blue bandanna around his head taunted.

Calli took a deep breath and quickly dispelled the notion of doing just that. The odds were stacked on their side. Tiger glared at her. "Just a bit of advice. Take it or leave it. It's your choice." She hurried past them and turned the corner to the front of the store, relieved to see the flurry of activity.

Knowing they had followed her inside, she went straight back to her lane and entered her number into the register. For the next half hour, they lurked nearby, she supposed to make sure she didn't call the police. One picked up a candy bar and started eating it. She pretended not to notice, until he opened the second one. Calli was ready to confront him, when he stepped up to the register and handed her two one-dollar bills.

"Remember this, lady, you talk, you pay."

She snatched the bills from his hand and waited for him to take the change from the automatic dispenser at the end of the counter. "Your bill is paid, now leave."

Another customer stepped into her lane, and she decided to ignore the boys. *Why me, God? Why did I have to find them out there? I'm trying to convince myself that these kids aren't all bad, and this happens. I'm not convinced. If you don't want me to get involved, why do you keep bringing trouble to my door?*

"Good afternoon. Would you like plastic or paper?" Calli addressed the customer absently, pulling the cart forward until it rested against the stainless-steel counter.

"What a coincidence meeting you here, *Miss Giovanni,*" a smooth voice answered.

Calli looked up, stunned to see Luke. He looked over her shoulder, also surveying the boys she'd been watching. She looked nervously at him, then at the teens. "How did you find me?"

"What, you don't believe in coincidences?" Then he lowered his voice, still smiling. "Just keep checking, Calli. I'm watching them. Why are they bothering you?"

He reached under his leather jacket.

When she saw him release the snap of his holster, her shoulders tightened. Then her neck. She could feel her throat constrict. "Call me a skeptic, but no, I don't believe in coincidences," she said, squeezing each word out. In no time at all, she'd sound like a child with croup.

Calli turned toward the gang. Tiger was gone, and the remaining kids acted as if they'd never seen her. "Nothing. They're just loitering," Calli added.

Luke's rigid profile exemplified power and control.

"Loitering?" Smiling, he leaned over the counter and whispered, as if he was flirting. "You're lying through your teeth, Calli Giovanni. They have you terrified. Now what's up?"

She looked at him wide-eyed, stunned at the sparkle in his eyes, despite the seriousness of his words. "That is quite a performance, Sergeant. You should get an Oscar."

"All in a day's work. Now are you going to tell me why they are harassing you and none of the other clerks?"

She thought of the kid's threats and backed away. "I can handle it myself, but thank you anyway."

Luke paid for his groceries in silence and took them just outside the door. He asked an employee to watch his basket and stepped back inside and behind the pop display. Easing his way closer, he listened as the two remaining gang members grilled Calli about their conversation. After hearing implications that threats had already been made, Luke addressed the suspects, obviously surprising Calli as well as the kids by his return. "Afternoon, boys. I don't know what this is about, but it's obvious that you're not shopping. Why don't you get on your way?"

"What you talkin' about, Sarge?"

"Well, Pete, maybe you'd like to tell me what the lady here won't."

The two looked at Calli, then back to Luke. She recognized the steely look in Luke's eyes. A cop's eyes.

"Nothing. We didn't do nothing."

"Then I suggest you leave before I haul you all downtown to get answers."

The two left the store without any more "encouragement."

Unable to deny her relief that he'd returned, Calli struggled to maintain her composure. They had shaken her. There was no doubt about that.

Luke touched her shoulder. "You okay?"

She nodded, knowing her scratchy voice would again give her away.

"How long until you're off?"

She'd walked to work this morning, not concerned with walking home alone midafternoon. Now she couldn't deny the fear. Calli wanted company, even if it was Luke. "About an hour."

"I want to make sure you get home okay. Will you wait so I can get these groceries home and let my son know I'll be out for a while longer? He was still asleep when I called."

Calli assessed him openly, her doubts softened by the silver cross dangling from the chain around his neck, and the surprising news that Sergeant Luke Northrup was a father. "I'll wait. I don't want to walk home alone after this."

The hard-edged cop again faded, replaced with a caring, gentle man. "I'll hurry back."

Surprisingly enough, she wanted him to do just that.

Chapter Seven

Before she had time to consider leaving without Luke, he appeared in the employees' locker room. When he gazed at her, she fought to conquer the involuntary nervousness that overcame her.

"The manager told me where I could find you."

She smiled weakly. "Hi. I really don't need a police escort."

"Good, because this isn't official." He tilted his head to one side. "To be honest, it wasn't a coincidence that I came here."

She'd been unable to take her mind off Luke Northrup since he stepped into her checkout lane. This guilty feeling was due to the joy of his return. "Oh, really? Isn't it a little unethical to use police records for personal interests?"

Luke leaned against the wall and folded his arms across his chest. "It certainly would be. It is not, however, unethical to ask your cousin which store you work at." He stepped closer, a grin of amusement softening the stubborn set of his jaw.

Calli shook her head and pulled the miniature back-pack-style purse from her locker and tossed it over her shoulder. "I should have figured."

"She said to tell you she won't argue with you this time. Considering the grilling she gave me before giving me any information, I'll deduce that comment has to do with your usual choice of men?"

Calli slammed the locker door closed and collapsed against it. She felt her flesh color. "I'll…I'll get even…"

"Ah, Calli, don't forget, I'm a cop. I take all threats seriously, even toward obnoxious cousins." He smiled suggestively, then laughed.

She twisted her mouth, then smiled. "It's not considered a threat if I didn't finish the sentence."

Shaking his head, he said, "Considering the afternoon you've had, I'll forget I heard anything. Let's start over." He paused, then extended his hand. "Good afternoon, Miss Giovanni. May I see that you make it home safely?"

Calli crossed her arms over her chest. Luke reached past her and turned the combination on her lock, then followed her through the warehouse and down the stairs. They walked in silence through the produce section and past the customer-service counter. When they turned to go outside, she took his hand for support.

Figuring out why Calli had looked so familiar at the ski area wasn't any relief. After the car accident, he'd come to the conclusion that it was for the best that she hadn't called. All of that was immaterial now, he decided. He'd met her twice outside the line of duty. It couldn't be a coincidence. There was a reason the two of them kept running into each other.

Luke saw the strain in her face return as she remem-

bered the violent afternoon. He had told her the truth—
he planned to come back after she got off work, even
before everything had happened. But now it was even
more obvious that she needed someone. And he prayed
that he was the right person.

She remained silent, her lips pressed tightly closed, her
eyes dry.

He opened the passenger door and closed it behind her,
scanning the parking lot for any unwanted company.
There was none. He got in and started the engine.
"You'd better let it out. Cry. Scream. Yell. Something."

"I'm fine."

He gave her a sideways glance before laughing. "Considering your response to Hanna leading me here, I find
it hard to believe you have no reaction to what happened
this afternoon. Have you forgotten, I've seen you under
trying conditions before?"

"Well, this is different. I'm not falling off a chairlift."
Calli's gaze skipped along the street, as if she were looking for someone. Or maybe watching to see who had seen
her. "Did you see the other kid?"

"No, but I can guess who it was. This kid is trouble,
Calli."

"I can handle myself, Sergeant."

He was tired of sugar-coating the truth. "Let me put
it this way, Calli, if I had been trying to push you off
that ski lift, I wouldn't have failed."

"Would that be anything like the self-defense class?"

He wanted to kiss that smirk right off her face.

"Like I said, if I'd been trying…"

Calli's retort was sassy, quick and on target. "Face it,
Officer Northrup, I got you."

*In more ways than one, Calli. Trouble is, what in the
world am I going to do about it?* "Lucky break." He

grimaced as the words slipped from his mouth. "Now, about this afternoon…"

"I don't want to talk about it. Tell me about your son. How old is he?"

He'd seen people break down after experiencing less than she had been through today. Even those trained to deal with those situations.

"I've been a single dad for over thirteen years. Jon's a good kid." He saw the way her blink faltered, hiding her beautiful eyes. The fringe of her long lashes formed shadows on her cheeks. "What about you?"

"No family, just me." He didn't miss the wistful inflection in her voice.

"And what about Hanna's comment?"

Calli looked out the window, yet remained silent. He pulled into an old-fashioned drive-in restaurant and turned off the car. "Would you like something?"

She shook her head. "Thanks anyway."

He ordered, then waited for her to answer his question.

"Hanna and I have a long-standing disagreement about men."

"All men? Or just yours?"

She looked at him quickly, then turned away. "If it matters, mine. I seem to be attracted to men who are completely wrong for me."

He put their few conversations together and decided to test his only theory. "Because I'm a cop?"

"Yes."

"So if I was a banker, or a mechanic, you'd go out with me?" Not that that mattered much. He was a cop. Had no intentions of changing that for anyone. "Is that why you introduced yourself as Calli instead of Calandre on the ski lift?"

"My name *is* Calli. If your parents had named you

Calandre, wouldn't you go by another name? I didn't even think about it."

The food came, interrupting the conversation. He paid, and pulled his bacon double cheeseburger and fries off the metal tray hanging on the car window. As soon as the young waitress left, Calli went into some analogy of cops seeing things in black and white, trying to make him understand her reasons for not wanting to get involved with a police officer. Unfortunately he didn't.

"So, because I'm a cop, you wouldn't consider going out with me?"

She remained silent, shook her head, then nibbled on her lower lip. Calli looked like a fragile porcelain doll. Her ivory skin was smooth, her eyelashes feathered over those incredibly dark brown eyes and her full lips made a beautiful pout.

"Look at me, Calli. Please."

She hesitated, then turned to face him. "Luke, it's not the right time in my life. We're just too different, okay?"

"I don't buy that. Is there someone else?" He didn't want to know, but he had to ask. If there was, Hanna didn't approve, or she wouldn't have led him to Calli.

Calli's gaze met his, then she looked down. Wisps of hair fell around her face, and she pushed them away. There was a tangible bond between them, if only she'd let him tap into it. "Leave it alone, Luke. Please."

"Fine." He took an oversize bite of his hamburger, too mad at his own foolishness to say much else. He wasn't looking for anything serious anyway. So why was he acting like she'd just ripped his heart out?

He hadn't heard a word she just said, but she looked as low as he felt. It was as clear as daylight that she was lying. "If I was a gambling man, I'd say you're a loner, Calandre Giovanni."

She glared at him, then laughed nervously. She didn't answer. Didn't deny it, either.

"I don't know who's responsible for your unhappiness, but I do know someone who could help you deal with it."

Her eyes widened. Then she glanced quickly to the cross around his neck. Luke reached up to touch it.

He nodded. "God can handle anything."

"Sometimes I truly believe He's stopped listening."

"He's stopped listening? Sounds pretty serious. Why do you think that?"

As if she realized someone finally heard what she was feeling, she let out a quick gasp. "It's nothing," she insisted.

He lowered his head, saying a silent prayer for Calli. "It's not nothing when you think God doesn't care about you anymore. Whatever happened, it must have been pretty painful."

"Yeah, well, 'A purpose for everything' as my mother says. You deal with it and move on."

"That's what they say. Supposed to make us feel better, but it never worked for me." He held out his box of fries and offered her another chance to have a bite when he heard her stomach growl.

"Isn't there some regulation about officers fraternizing?"

"Yeah, we're right up there with priests," he grumbled, feeling guilty again. "But thankfully I'm not on your case."

She laughed aloud. "You have an answer for everything, don't you, Officer?"

She was pushing him. It was time to do a little pushing himself. "All but one. Have you decided to teach the class with me?"

"Why should I do that?"

"I understand you've kept after your cousin to take the class for years. You're just the kind of partner I need. One who really believes in the program. Need I say more, Miss Giovanni?"

"Oh, and I suppose the wise move would be to throw myself at your mercy before you learn *all* of my secrets, right?"

"Yup. And while we're at it, I'm taking a group of kids from our church in-line skating tomorrow. Why don't you come along? No strings. Just a chance to see that all kids aren't the same."

"I offered to fill in at work."

"After what just happened?"

"I was given the choice. I *offered* to work."

She is *stubborn.* "I'll pick you up after work, then. Make sure you get home okay."

"Luke."

He grinned. It was the tender way she'd said his name, and hiding his satisfaction was useless. "I don't want you to have to use that self-defense on anyone else. Okay?"

A smile peeked through her mask of uncertainty. "You're impossible."

"I guess that makes two of us. Give me your hours for the week." He pulled out his notepad and pen, ready to copy them down.

"Is that an order, Sergeant?"

He wanted to say yes. He didn't dare. "I wouldn't think of ordering you around."

Chapter Eight

The questions niggling Luke's conscience surfaced again as he drove away from Calli's apartment. He was puzzled by his sudden interest—not just the attraction to Calli, but the feeling that this wasn't about a date. He wanted...more. He didn't know how else to say it. He wanted...understanding...companionship...friendship.

Trying to talk to Tom was useless. Every time Luke mentioned Calli, Tom's answer was "Love at first sight." That *wasn't* it; she had been bandaged and bruised, her hair tangled and taped, and she was as feisty as a six-month-old puppy. Yet he definitely felt a bond with her from the first time he met her.

Am I crossing that fine line between personal and professional?

Luke rubbed the tension in his shoulder, as if he could swipe the difficult question away. "If I knew, I wouldn't keep asking."

What will the squad say about my seeing a woman involved with a case? "She's not a suspect. It's not a problem."

But you wouldn't have met her if it hadn't been for your job, his conscience probed. "Give me a break. That'd take away half the available population! Besides, we met skiing before I knew who she really was."

You gave her your card at the hospital with your phone number on it. She never called. What makes you think she's interested now? Luke revved the engine and turned the corner. "Who asked for your opinion?"

Since that morning in the hospital, he'd tried to understand this longing to ask a woman he'd barely met out to dinner. And each time he sees her, that unexplainable sense of purpose only grew stronger.

Reasoning through the circumstantial evidence wasn't enough to justify his yearning to know her better, and the battle waged on. After wasting his time on relationships that had gone nowhere, Luke didn't want to make the same mistakes again. Contrary to his partner's philosophy of love at first sight, Luke planned to approach women differently. Simple as having a relationship once seemed, he was beginning to have his doubts that God ever planned for him to be happily married.

He and Calli may have gotten started on the wrong foot, but it wasn't too late to set things straight. Friendship. That left plenty of room for growth and change.

There was a lot more to think about in a relationship now. He had a teenage son, a stressful career and no room for some woman who couldn't deal with either. At this point in his life any woman he'd consider a relationship with had to accept both.

He and Nancy had never really been in love, something he once thought could change. They'd made a baby together, and he was convinced that he'd done the right thing by marrying her. He did admire the fact that Nancy never tried to lie about her feelings. She didn't want to be married, didn't want children and didn't want to be tied down. It took years to accept that both he and Jon were better off without the additional stress of the rocky relationship.

The next relationship was the total opposite. Jessica was agreeable with everything he said and did. Beautiful—and spineless. Then Gretchen, who was strong yet boring. And Dana, who was fun, but possessive. He discovered there were as many combinations as there were flavors of ice cream.

Through Jon's childhood, Luke continued his search for the elusive match, until he'd recently come to the conclusion that *he* wasn't relationship material. And despite Tom's constant attempts to find Luke the right woman, he'd become content with being a father and then a cop.

Until Calli came along.

Calandre Giovanni. Spunky and...impetuous.

"Hmmph. Just what I need—a headstrong, impulsive, unpredictable woman in my life." *Is there really any other kind?*

This thing with Calli—who knew for sure? Beauty and excitement? Beauty and youth? Beauty and trouble? Whatever the combination, it would pass. Friendship... Now that was a new angle. So what was he doing complicating the equation with thoughts of being a husband?

Luke pulled into the underground garage and shoved the gearshift into park. *Father, I'm struggling here. I've worked so hard to understand why I'm not meant to be married, and just when I think I've got it figured out, you send Calli Giovanni into the picture. What's going on?*

Walking past the elevator, he sprinted up the seven flights of stairs hoping to exhaust some of the energy he was wasting creating reasons why he shouldn't see Calli. He paused at the top of the stairs.

You promise peace and understanding to those who ask. I don't even know what I'm asking for, Father, but something tells me, You have a reason for bringing this fireball into my life. So I guess I'll leave it to You to lead the way.

Luke unlocked the apartment door, shocked with the surprise greeting him.

"Nancy." He froze in the doorway. Jon's mother was sitting in his recliner. "You didn't tell me you were in town."

"I wanted to surprise both of you." She glanced at Jon, who was sitting on the sofa, looking less than thrilled.

Luke looked from one to the other. One was working hard to look confident, the other trying to look totally ambivalent, neither succeeding.

"I'd like to take you both to dinner tonight."

One look at his son told him to decline whatever the cost. "Sorry, Nan. We're busy. If you would have let me know you were coming, we could have made other arrangements."

She blinked, an uncertain expression flashing across her face. "It was a spur-of-the-moment decision."

"From California? Is everything okay? Nothing's happened to your folks, has it?"

"No, they're fine. They send greetings." Her voice turned sticky sweet.

"I'll bet." He watched as she tipped her nose in the air and flicked her hair over her shoulder. From the look on his son's face, the last hour hadn't been easy. "Jon, why don't you let Nancy and I have a few minutes to talk?"

Jon sent him a look of gratitude that would be etched in Luke's mind forever. Launching himself off the sofa, Jon headed for the front door. "I'll see if Nate's home." He turned to leave, then paused. "Oh. Bye…Nancy."

"Goodbye, son. I'll see you soon."

Jon eagerly dashed out the door, slamming it behind him.

The look of confidence on Nancy's face disappeared and Luke was feeling less than cordial. He placed his hands in his pockets, trying to ignore the floral scent of her expensive perfume. "So, tell me what's really going on, Nancy."

"I needed to see my son."

Luke propped himself on the edge of the desk, trying to appear more nonchalant than he felt. "And?"

Nancy shifted in the chair and crossed her legs. "I'm not some suspect you're interrogating, Luke."

He lifted his hands, simultaneously shrugging his shoulders. "Didn't realize I was out of line. You haven't contacted Jon in months, you hang up on me when you finally call, then I find you sitting in my living room that very afternoon. I can't turn off my instincts, Nan. Especially when Jon's involved." Luke moved to the antique chair facing Nancy.

"Don't call me Nan."

"Sorry. Thought you liked it." He waited, anticipating an argument.

"I'm getting married." She ran her hand down the leg of her jeans. An obnoxiously large diamond blinded him clear across the room.

Luke was mildly surprised. Shouldn't have been, but he was. Nancy lived a fast-paced life. If the diamond was real, she had finally hit easy street. If not, she had hit bottom and hadn't figured it out yet. Either way, he didn't care. He knew just enough about her current life to know that there was no more room in it for his son now than there had been in the past thirteen years. "I hope you'll finally be happy."

"I want Jon to spend the summer with us. See how it goes."

He stiffened, as though she had just punched him in the gut. "See how it goes?"

"You've had Jon for twelve years, Luke. It's my turn to have him now."

In thirteen years she'd taken her son no farther than across town to visit her parents. And even that had never been for more than an obligatory "showing." Her parents had made it clear that Luke wasn't good enough for Nancy. They had plans for her, and he didn't fit into that mold—neither did a child. Now she wanted to play mommy. "I didn't think you were into sharing. You gave him up. Call a lawyer, Nancy. I've been more than fair."

"I'm pregnant." Her voice cracked and she looked at her hands. "I want Jon and this baby to know one another. I want them to be a family."

Luke stood up and walked into the kitchen. He needed a glass of water before he choked on his own words.

All this time he'd been both father and mother. Struggled to raise his son alone. To make a family from just the two of them. And now, after walking out of their lives, she wanted to offer Jon the one thing Luke couldn't.

She followed him. "I'm sorry to break it to you this way, Luke."

"What did you tell Jon?"

"That I want a chance to know him."

"Does he want to go?"

"No," she said bitterly.

"Then I'd suggest you listen to him." Luke took a deep breath, struggling to remain calm. "No offense, Nancy, but Jon hasn't spent more than a couple hours with you every other year." He felt little more than pity for the spoiled woman he'd once married. "I'm no lawyer, but I think you'd have a stronger case if you'd shown a little more consistent interest. If you really want to be part of his life, take it one step at a time."

"Still giving orders, aren't you, Luke? You seem to think you can decide what's right for everyone. I think it's up to Jon to decide if he wants to see me. I think he will, too, if you'd let me have some time alone with him," she demanded just as Jon walked in the door.

Jon stared at his mother, disgust in his eyes. "I don't want to have anything to do with you!"

"Jonny," Nancy whispered, looking at Luke, her eyes pleading for help. "Please don't do this. I'm sorry."

"I'm never going with you. My family is here. You don't care about me."

"I'm your mother."

"You're nobody's mom, especially not mine. I don't want your stupid family. *Dad* and I are a family."

Luke sensed his son's pain. He embraced the young boy who was trying to stand up for him. "Settle down, Jon. Nothing is going to be forced upon you."

Tears brimmed in Jon's eyes. "I won't go!"

"We're not going to talk about that now." Luke lifted Jon's chin. "I'm going to walk Nancy to her car. Just try to calm down. We'll handle this together."

Luke took Nancy by the arm and led her to the door. She paused momentarily. "I'll see you soon, Jon."

In the elevator, Luke backed against the wall, arms crossed in front of him. "Anything else you want to say?"

"I can't believe you let him talk to me that way!"

"Under the circumstances, I think he has every right to voice his feelings."

"And where were you today? Is he always left alone like that?"

"Before you start, I think you'd better face the facts. Number one—before I'd even consider letting Jon go to *visit* you, he'd have to agree to it. Number two—you *have* no maternal rights where Jon is concerned. And number three—just to set your mind at ease, he's of legal age to be left alone for a few hours." Having unconsciously worked his way toward Nancy, Luke backed away. "I'm sorry—always have been—that you made the choice to give him up. But then, you never asked me, did you?"

"You'd really deny your son the chance to have a complete family?"

"How can you think that you can make a family by throwing a few people into a house together? A family is a huge investment, Nancy. And being a parent means one hundred percent investment. Is that really what you have in mind?"

When the elevator door opened, Nancy ran past Luke and through the lobby door. He followed her, and blocked the car door when she tried to open it. "I've *never* tried to stop you from seeing him. All I'm asking is that you take this slow. He needs a mother, more than two hours a year."

"You don't have to throw my mistakes in my face, Luke."

"You're the one who's threatening me with legal action. I'm merely stating the facts." Luke stepped back and opened the door. "Keep in touch."

Luke went back upstairs. Facing his son was agony. Defending his ex-wife was worse.

"I won't go with her. She's never cared about me."

"That's not true. She was only four years older than you are now when she had you, Jon. She had tough decisions to make."

"Lots of kids keep their babies."

"I don't know what to tell you, Jon. It may have been the best decision for her—for all of us. I can't say. You and I moved on and did the best we could."

"What did you *ever* like about her?"

Luke thought, then blew out a deep breath. This kid knew how to go for the jugular. "I guess all the usual things a teenage boy likes about a teenage girl. She was pretty and fun, and paid attention to me. What we did wasn't right, or even very smart. We made a poor choice, and faced the consequences."

"But you kept me, and she ran."

"Our priorities were different, but that doesn't make her a bad person."

"Do you still love her?"

Luke shook his head. "She gave me you, Jon. I don't love her, but I do care about her. I would never change the way things turned out. I wouldn't trade being a father for anything."

Jon remained silent. Luke knew it was a lot for a kid to think about. There was nothing he could have done that would have prepared him for this day.

Luke again thought about the time Jon asked for a baby brother for his birthday. Year after year, they had the same discussion, with the same end result. No. And now Nancy was giving Jon the opportunity to have what he'd asked for.

Chapter Nine

Calli closed the door to her apartment and groaned, upset with herself for giving Luke her phone number.

Not only was she upset at that, but also because she had agreed to help him teach the self-defense class. He was right—she did believe in the cause. Anyone who knew Calli knew she preached personal safety. It had nothing to do with the fact that Luke would be the instructor, she silently insisted. If Bart had asked, she'd have done it, as well. *But not with such anticipation.*

She dropped onto the checkered couch, hugging her well-loved rag doll with the incriminating smile. "Don't look at me that way, Bessie. He may *not* be the cop from the apartments. And even if he is, I didn't see anything that would help his case." Running a hand through her hair, Calli immediately stifled the smile that resulted from thinking of Luke Northrup. In three years, no one had broken through the cold shell of hostility she had wrapped around herself. Until Luke.

Could she ever completely let go of the anger that had become so comfortable? Would she ever feel the peace of forgiveness? Or the satisfaction of seeing justice served?

She reminded herself that Luke Northrup was a sergeant for the Palmer Police Department. For all she knew, Luke could be one of the many officers who loathed the mere idea of citizens joining the fight against crime. There could be nothing personal between them.

Calli fixed herself a sandwich and salad. Sitting at the table, she automatically pulled the journal from her purse. Calli paused, then tossed the book aside. She hunched over and rubbed the tension tightly strung between her eyebrows and her shoulders. *Why me? Why Mike? Why God?* Then in a faintness she didn't dare acknowledge— *Out of all the possible men in this city,* Why *a cop?*

The ache traveled from her stomach to her heart as the anger overwhelmed her fragile emotions. In desperation, she took a bite, choking it down with determination. *I cannot cry.* She guzzled milk, then took another bite, willing this guilt to quit eating at her from inside out.

Calli recalled the pain of her brother's untimely death. The torment of losing the man she'd loved to the system of justice. So determined was her fiancé to impress superiors with his ability to disassociate himself from a case that Brad had watched the family bury her brother—then closed the case, stating there was not enough evidence to go for a conviction. As the months had passed, her entire family moved on with their lives, leaving Calli alone, hiding in the shadows.

Love and betrayal. They went together like fire and ice. And she knew better than to play with fire.

Calli opened a bag of chocolate sandwich cookies and took a handful with a glass of milk. Dipping a cookie, she thought of Luke's suggestion that she "let it out."

She'd caught the concern in his eyes. He cared that she didn't react; he worried about her anger.

She didn't want to feel again. Not for Luke. Not for anyone. With a deep breath of resolve, Calli opened the journal and started writing about the afternoon's events. Reading back through the entry, she was startled by her own words and the feelings expressed.

Her fiancé had never been able to handle emotions. He constantly badgered her to forget the past. The more she tried, the more she failed. Even as a cop, Brad couldn't understand her need to do what little she could to protect the innocent. In his opinion, that was up to the police. She tried to change for him, but in the end, lost everything anyway. Lost the love and support of her fiancé and her family.

Where are you, God? All around me the enemy strikes, and each day I see a little less of You.

"They can't get away with this! Tiger can't elude justice forever." Memories of Mike came to mind, and tears blurred her vision. "Don't go turning to mush, Calli. Get back out there and patrol."

"Refrain from anger and turn from wrath." The verse brought peace, loosening the hold guilt had on her conscience.

She rinsed her dishes then splashed water on her tired face. Calli snuggled into the sofa and pulled out the tea towels she was embroidering for her grandmother's birthday.

The phone rang, and Calli was surprised to hear Luke's deep voice. "I wanted see if you gave me a working phone number."

"Don't trust me, Officer?" She realized that her smile was growing wider; her grip on the receiver tightened and a spark ignited in her chest.

"Let's just say I'm in the hard evidence line of business."

Her heart sank. "Everything in black and white."

"So to speak."

The reality of the situation was returning. She'd been this route before and wasn't ready to repeat it. Luke Northrup, like all the other significant men in her life, seemed to look at life logically; he was used to being in control, and would never understand her life in the shadows. Why did she let herself hope he would be any different?

"You there?"

She blinked, and realized she'd tuned him out. "Sorry. I was thinking of something else. What did you say?"

"I was saying that this isn't like me."

She giggled softly. "What? You're not usually arrogant and pushy?"

"Afraid that goes with the job. No, I don't…"

Calli found herself worrying her bottom lip between her teeth. She was sinking fast. If he asked her out one more time, she wouldn't be able to decline. Mission or no mission. "Go on, I'm listening."

"Great. *Now* I have your attention. I'm not doing something right here, am I? What I'm trying to say, Calli, is that I don't date much, and I'm not usually this…direct in my personal life. I want to apologize if I've come on like a bulldozer."

She laughed. Calli couldn't believe her ears. He was humble and honest. And she'd just laughed with Luke. Again. There was something warm and captivating about his humor.

"I don't usually go to such lengths to find someone, I mean personally…off duty." His voice echoed her unspoken longings.

"I'm glad you did," she whispered before thinking. *I shouldn't have admitted that. I can't help but hurt him.* "Luke, I…I was en…" She tried repeatedly to tell him about Brad, but the pain went too deep. How could she ever trust another cop? *No, I can't do this.* "Luke, I have to be honest with you…." *Slow down, Calli. He's obviously not like Brad. Think about this before you do something you'll regret.* "I'd like to be friends, but that's all I'm interested in right now."

On the other end of the line, she heard Luke exhale. "That's exactly what I wanted to say."

Calli and Luke met before class the next week to review the course objectives. Luke looked across the table, old fears and uncertainties dousing him in constant showers of reality. Nancy's visit served as a bitter reminder that he wasn't the marrying kind.

Teaching the first class with Calli was awkward, but uneventful. They both rushed off afterward, as if equally hesitant to give anyone the impression there was any sort of attraction between them.

Annoyed with himself for letting Nancy's return interfere with a possible relationship with Calli, Luke found himself reassessing every nuance of the time they'd just spent together.

Patrolling that night would have been impossible alone. Tom didn't say much, except that Luke "had it bad." Then Tom dropped the subject, knowing the silence would torture Luke all night. They had three routine speeding contacts and followed a lead on the case they were working on, but nothing panned out.

Luke found himself cruising Calli's neighborhood more often the next week. And as promised, he met her at the store each evening to make sure she made it home safely. In hindsight, he was kicking himself for insisting to do so. The agony of seeing her every day was like buying candy when you couldn't eat it.

Calli seemed annoyed with the arrangement, as well, and before class that Thursday finally told him about it.

"I'm perfectly capable of seeing myself home after work, Luke. You don't need to bother." Calli unzipped her bright pink-and-navy jacket and tossed it onto a chair.

It had already been a long day, and Luke was anxious to get through the class and away from the sweet temptation of Calandre Giovanni. "Just trying to do my job."

"Then do your job! I don't need a personal bodyguard."

He shook his head and chuckled. "Fine, Calli. Take care of yourself."

As if she was prepared for him to play the possessive fool, she stared at him for a brief moment before satisfaction lit her coal-black eyes.

"Happy now?" He yanked the sweatshirt over his head and tossed it into his bag, ready for class in his tank top and shorts.

Calli stepped back. With her eyelids lowered, she looked coy and more alluring than ever. "Thank you. It's just that I know what a bother it is, and there's really no reason for it." A softness lingered in her voice.

"Nope, no reason at all." Luke spread mats across the small gym floor, taking advantage of the few minutes to let out his irritation.

"Shouldn't I move these chairs?"

"They're fine."

"But when we break into groups, there won't be enough room. Will there?"

"We're not doing much role-playing tonight," Luke snapped.

"Well, you could have told me earlier."

"If you want to do something, get those canisters out of my bag. We're going to review some optional weapons tonight."

Calli hesitated, then looked in his bag, and held one up for his approval. "This?"

"Yeah, slide the one off my belt, too."

Hanna nudged Calli when she came into the classroom. "So, how's it going with the cop?" she whispered.

Calli turned to her cousin and saw the laughter in Hanna's eyes. "Where have you been? I've been trying to call you for two weeks. What in the world were you thinking when you told Luke how to get hold of me?"

"I was on a business trip." Hanna said innocently. "I was thinking he's just your type."

"Says *who?*" she growled.

"Ladies—let's save the combat for class. Calli…"

"Would you quit telling me what to do!" she snapped, accentuating the annoyance within herself.

Luke walked toward her, his mouth clenched tighter with every step. Calli felt her heart beating faster as she backed herself into the wall. "In case you forgot, *I'm* the instructor. When I tell you to do something, I don't need a debate! Now, would you *please* quit arguing with *everything* I tell you?"

Looking into his jade-green eyes, Calli fought her attraction to the dynamic vitality and control Luke exuded. Realizing she'd taken her frustration out on him, she bit her lip to stifle a defensive outcry while Luke pivoted and strode to the front of the room.

Hanna smiled as if to say "I told you so!" Calli straightened her back, vowing not to reveal his effect on her. She couldn't fall in love with another cop, and she had no intention of permitting herself to be snared in his trap. Girding herself with resolve, she rushed past her cousin and to Luke's side. Women filtered into the room, and Calli met his accusing eyes without flinching. "So, what is on tonight's agenda?"

"Just follow my lead," he said, leaving no room for discussion.

She stiffened at the challenge. "No problem. You're the boss."

Calli watched Luke "perform," using his sense of humor to make everyone more comfortable with the frightening topic that could make a difference between life or death. She admired his ability to laugh and poke fun at human nature while leaving no doubt of his intolerance for violence.

"Another mode of protection we highly recommend women carry is pepper Mace. You can find it at most sporting-goods stores."

Calli held up the canister that Luke had set on the desk.

"Pepper Mace is an oil-based spray which is as effective on dogs as it is on humans. That's why the postal carriers use pepper Mace instead of the older version of chemical Mace. It's also more intense."

Without looking, Luke added, "The canister Calli has is what we call an inert, which is used for training." He walked across the room. "You spray it in a zigzag pattern to form a 'wall' between you and the assailant. Go ahead."

"But Luke…"

He backed up, the humor disappearing from his voice. "Come on, Calli. Just spray it."

The class was laughing.

Calli looked up from the hairspray-type can, surprised to see Luke barreling toward her.

She pointed the nozzle and pressed the trigger, madly waving her arm.

Luke ran straight into the foggy "wall."

"Don't stop until… A-a-a-ugh." Luke coughed and dropped to the floor.

Calli ran toward him. "Luke…"

"Stay back. It's Mace."

She stepped away, eyes wide. Instantaneously the class stopped laughing.

Unable to open his eyes, Luke stood up and reached for Calli. "Help me to the rest room. I have to wash this off."

Grabbing his arm to lead him, she felt her eyes sting. "I'm so sorry, Luke."

"Water. Quick. This stuff is killing me," he complained.

Calli's eyes began to water from the residual spray. "Oh, I'm sorry. But you told me to…"

"I know what I said," he growled.

Rounding the corner, Calli paused in front of the two locker room doors.

Men's. I can't go in there.

Women's. He can't go in there.

"What're we waiting for?"

"Nothing." She pushed through the door, rushing him past the dressing room and to the showers. She turned on the water, and guided Luke into the spray of water.

"Soap." He rasped, gulping water and spitting it out.

"There isn't any. Hang on." Calli spun around. "Is there *any* soap in here?"

"Check the sink," a man in a business suit suggested. Luckily, he was the only other occupant in the locker room at the time.

At the sink, Calli pulled the lever to dispense the soap and ran back to the shower.

"It's liquid soap. Hold out your hands."

Luke lathered his face and arms. "What do you think you're doing in the men's locker room?"

"Where did you want me to take you? Into the women's?"

"It's not like *I* could see anything!"

Calli grinned, beginning to see the humor in the situation, now that he was out of intense pain. "Don't worry. There's no one else in here but a guy in a suit. Actually, his tie is so bad, I think my eyes hurt a little, too," she added in a hushed tone.

Luke laughed. He finished rinsing, opening his eyes under the flow before turning off the water. Then he sloshed to the bin for a towel.

Calli labored to keep a straight face as Luke marched out the door, sopping wet and straight into a crowd of wide-eyed women.

"Class dismissed." Luke squished down the hall to the gym.

No one moved.

"I think Luke would appreciate some privacy right now. I hope he has dry clothes in that bag of supplies." Calli watched him in silence.

Hanna was the first to laugh. "I can see it now. Grandma Giovanni is going to ask, 'How did you meet Luke, Calli?' 'Oh, I sprayed him with Mace.'"

A round of laughter shot from Calli's mouth before she regained her control.

Most of the women had already gathered their belongings from the room and were leaving. Hanna and Calli visited in the lobby until Luke joined them. "This bag was still in the room." He tossed Calli's jacket to her.

"It's mine," Hanna admitted. "Hope you get feeling better, Luke. I'll talk to you tomorrow, Calli."

Calli faced Luke. "Are you okay?"

"Other than my pride, you mean?"

"I've never seen a better demonstration of the effectiveness of Mace. Everyone was totally impressed." She bit her lip, trying to keep the corners from turning up.

"I'll bet."

"I don't know what you're worried about, Luke. I'm serious. They were speechless."

"After my spiel, it's a good thing someone could stay speechless."

She smiled sympathetically. "It was nothing to beat yourself up over, under the circumstances. One day you're going to laugh at this."

"You can tell which side of the demonstration you were on."

"Do you have time for a cup of coffee—as a peace offering?"

His eyes sparkled with the love of combat. "I wish I did, but I have to go back home to get dry clothes before work. How about Sunday afternoon?"

She could hardly say no after tonight. Neither of them had acknowledged the friendship had moved past the platonic level. Not aloud anyway.

Chapter Ten

Calli pulled the Indian blanket jacket over her turtleneck sweater. She'd spent the past two days practicing her apology for being so rude before the incident with the Mace.

Luke had left a message on her answering machine with the time and Tom's address. She'd played the message over and again just to listen to his voice. Still, Calli had to remind herself that this wasn't a romantic dinner. Unsure she was ready to take this step to a closer friendship, Calli had tried to back out, but finally consented when Luke admitted it was dinner with him and Jon at his partner's house. It couldn't even be considered a date.

Calli picked up her keys and the piece of paper with the Davises' address. Somehow, she thought, this should be less intimidating than a date. But it wasn't. She was not only meeting Luke's best friends, but his teenage son, as well. Not that anything had changed between them. There wasn't any point trying to kid herself. Calli had vowed that she would never fall in love with another arrogant, egotistical law enforcement officer.

Immediately recognizing Luke's cherry-red sports car, she parked behind it. Before she had a chance to look for the house, Luke stepped from the arched doorway. Calli watched him cross the street, his stride long and easygoing. The faded denim hugged his lean legs and the gray T-shirt made his shoulders look even broader than usual. His arresting smile and wink made her glad she'd come, despite her plans for later.

His friendship was as tempting as a healing dose of Colorado sunshine, yet dangerous as the scorching heat that accompanied it.

"There aren't any numbers on the house, so I've been watching for you."

Calli opened the hatchback of the rental car and removed a platter of layered dip and a bag of tortilla chips. "Hope I didn't keep you waiting."

"Why was I afraid you were going to stand me up?" he whispered, standing behind her.

Trying to ignore her hammering heart, Calli took a deep breath and let it out slowly. "Instinct. You're a cop. You've learned not to expect anything from anyone."

Luke chuckled. "You're only half-right, I am a cop. But I've learned to expect the worst, from everyone. And you, Calli Giovanni, have proven how wrong that is. I'm very glad you came." Luke held the door as Calli admonished herself for being so frank with him.

She had to be crazy to think she could go into a friendship, putting her own motives against those of one more man whose legal, moral and ethical obligations were to protect and serve. Tonight she'd explain to Luke that she couldn't see him again. There was no need complicating her life any more than it already was. She'd tell him everything, and it would be over. Surely the truth would convince him that they weren't meant to be together.

All she had to do was stay in control. *Easier said than done!*

Luke introduced her to his son, Jon, Tom's wife, Vanessa, and their twins. Calli was surprised to see how captivated Jon was with the babies.

The group played a round of table tennis and ate snacks, taking turns entertaining the newborns. She hadn't held a baby in years, and was enthralled with the warmth of such a tiny child. When the baby cried, Jon rescued her, and Joseph quieted instantly.

Calli could see immediately that Tom and Luke were much closer than just partners. They joked around and shared family tales. Jon was polite and comfortable with his father's repetition of his baby stories, and even joined in, ribbing Luke in return.

While the two men played a tie-breaking round, Vanessa, Jon and Calli talked about Jon's school. Then Jon excused himself to go to Youth Group with a friend.

Luke wrapped his arm around his son's shoulder and discreetly hugged the boy. "I'll pick you up at eight."

Jon nodded, grabbing his coat from the rack. "It was nice to meet you, Calli."

"You too, Jon."

He stopped to say a special goodbye to each baby, then ran out the door and down the street.

Calli looked admiringly at Luke. "Jon reminds me of my younger brother." As soon as Calli said the words, she froze.

"I hope that's good. I know how younger brothers can be."

A lump in Calli's throat prevented her from responding immediately. She blinked away the temptation to let her emotions take over. This wasn't the time. "You've done a fine job raising him, Luke."

He smiled, a soft smile that confirmed what that job had meant to him. Calli looked away, unable to meet his gaze. Baby Joseph wailed from the corner of the room. Vanessa was upstairs checking dinner, and Tom was changing Jordan's diaper.

Luke turned and rescued the fussy infant from the swing and walked back to Calli. She marveled at the sight of Luke's long fingers cradling the baby and declined his silent offer to let her hold Joseph. The man was a natural with babies. Luke was a father first, she noted, then a cop. *Just like Daddy.*

Calli cooed at Joseph as he whimpered in Luke's arms, uncomfortably aware that Luke's gaze was nowhere near the baby, but on her instead. The child quieted momentarily, then began to fuss again.

Tom returned, seeming flustered by his frantic twins. "So I'm not Superdad."

Luke made a lame attempt to sympathize. "One was tough. I can't imagine two at a time. But if anyone deserves this, it's you, bro." He chuckled mischievously and snuggled the baby next to his shoulder, undaunted by the noise.

Calli smiled. Jordan started screaming in Tom's arms. "Ah, Vanessa, I think your son needs something we can't give him."

Vanessa joined them in the basement and cradled the baby. "We'll be back in a while. Excuse us. Tom, would you mind helping me." She jerked her head to the side, motioning for Tom to follow.

Ducking under the low ceiling light, Tom backed away. "I'll go change Joseph. I'd tell you to make yourself at home, Luke, but you already do."

Luke shook his head, and tipped his head down, seemingly to hide his embarrassment. Calli felt his discomfort at being so obviously left alone.

"How long have you two been partners?"

"Too long." He motioned toward the Ping-Pong table, and suggested another game.

Getting ready to serve, Calli picked up the white ball and lifted her paddle.

"This time, cut the act."

"Act?" He'd figured it out. Somehow he'd placed her at the scene. It was over. She wanted to cry. Why? If she wanted to bring an end to this before it got more complicated, why did she suddenly feel an ache of loss?

"You are one dreadful actress, by the way, if you don't mind me saying so."

"What do you mean?"

"Pretending you don't know how to play this game. If my ego needed boosting, you'd be the last person I'd hire for the job, Miss Giovanni."

Calli felt as if a huge weight had been lifted from her shoulders. *He's not talking about the anonymous calls.* Wondering if she should feel guilty for the relief she felt, Calli turned toward the table, glancing over her shoulder to Luke. "There you go insulting me again. And I was about to apologize for being so rude in class the other night."

"It's not an insult at all. Thankfully my ego is more than capable of handling a fireball like you. In fact, it's growing *very* fond of the challenge."

He stepped closer, first setting his paddle aside, then hers. Their eyes searched each other's, until his gaze settled on her lips.

She couldn't move. Couldn't think. His nearness made her senses spin. Without a touch, he'd brought her back to life. "You're arrogant."

"Yup." The intimacy of his smile soothed her.

"And relentless."

"I suppose so."

"You're…"

"Calli, don't talk." His lips brushed against hers as he spoke. It was a silent challenge, and she was determined to meet it. After a series of slow, shivery kisses, Calli succumbed to his sweetness, giving up her own agenda. Her knees weakened as Luke coaxed her lips into unison with his.

When the kiss ended, Calli relaxed, snug in his embrace. For the moment, there were no shadows across her heart. Only a warm sunny glow. One that had faded long, long ago. Too long, she decided. This was what she needed. Someone to care about.

Not just anyone, she realized, but Luke. He was exactly the type of man she wanted. Witty and compassionate. Exactly the type of man she needed. Stubborn, yet funny. He knew who—and *what*—he was. He had his priorities figured out and didn't need anyone to affirm his convictions.

Luke Northrup was a man of integrity, and the last thing he needed was a woman with none.

With that realization, Calli backed away, letting her hands drop to her sides. She tried to speak, but couldn't form the words.

Luke smiled. "You were getting ready to throw another insult at me."

She laughed, too stunned by her own reaction to argue. Tears burned beneath her eyelids, and she blinked away this foreign urge to cry. "You're incorrigible."

"You're slipping, Calandre. Surely you can do better than that."

* * *

During dinner Luke and Tom began discussing a current case. They were careful to avoid using names, and if Calli hadn't been on the scene, she'd have never figured out what they were talking about. The hospitalized kid Luke had been waiting for the night they'd met *was* the boy who'd fallen in front of her four-wheel drive.

Luke took a bite of enchilada immediately followed by a swallow of milk. "We have to find out what A.C. saw."

Calli furrowed her brows. "Who's A.C.?"

"Stands for anonymous caller. She's been calling in for years. We can't seem to catch up with her."

They gave me a nickname, she thought.

Trying to look genuinely innocent, yet curious, she pressed for information. "And what do you think she saw?"

"Maybe she saw the Eastsiders beating up the poor kid. Maybe just the break-ins. That's what we need to find out."

Calli nodded in silence. She didn't dare ask anything more for fear of giving herself away. She listened as the two discussed other cases, wondering when and how she could tell Luke.

After dinner, Calli and Vanessa took the twins for a walk while Luke and Tom did dishes. Calli instinctively held the baby's bottom through the denim of the carrier.

"Luke looks happier than I've seen him in years, Calli."

Calli swallowed a lump of guilt. "He's easy to be with."

"He and Tom are quite a pair. Little did I know they were preparing me for twins. What one doesn't think of, the other does. I think that's why they are such a good team at work."

Calli laughed, more at the irony of this entire mess than Vanessa's comment. Here she was falling for the cop that happened to be looking for her. *Hide in plain sight.*

"I can see that in them." Calli longed to know more about the man who made her laugh, and cry and live again. "How do you deal with being a police officer's wife?"

Vanessa raised one eyebrow and looked Calli square in the eye. "It's like living for God. You live each day as if He would come back for you any time. With Tom, I don't leave things unsaid. I don't go to bed angry. We just don't know what tomorrow brings."

"Do you ever worry about him?"

"Every day. Some wives don't, but I think most of us worry more than we let on. Tom doesn't tell me everything, but I can tell when something is bothering him." They walked in silence, then finally Vanessa continued. "It's worth the risk. Loving Tom, I mean. I just can't imagine who I'd be without his love."

Calli rubbed her hand over the curly-haired infant cuddled against her.

What would it feel like to have another human being love her unconditionally? To have someone know everything about her and love her anyway? Right or wrong, to accept who she was and what she did? She wasn't sure she believed it possible.

Would Luke understand her silence? She thought of her brother and her long-lost mission, and losing Luke.

She once thought there would never be a man who could chip through this bulletproof vest she wore to protect her heart. But here he was. And just her luck, he was a cop.

Chapter Eleven

Calli and Hanna met at the park for lunch and a walk to enjoy the first day of spring. After listening to her cousin's complaints about recent dates, Calli told her about joining Luke for dinner at Tom's the previous Sunday. "The man is arrogant."

Hanna laughed. "Arrogant? Luke?"

"Of course Luke. You saw him before class last week, ordering me around, playing 'macho man,' in control…" Calli felt the warm Colorado sunshine on her face and looked at the tall skyscrapers surrounding the park.

"What I saw was a man with the patience of a saint. It's you who's painted that arrogant image of Brad on every uniformed officer you meet, Calandre. Luke is *nothing* like Brad. And as for class last week, *you* were every bit as responsible for that squabbling."

She couldn't argue that point. "Okay, enough. Luke and I already settled that."

Halfway around the path, Calli heard her name.

"Calli? Is that you?"

She spun around. "Hi, Vanessa. How are all of you?"

Calli knelt next to the stroller to say hello to the two fuzzy-haired boys. The twins appeared to be enjoying the beautiful day, intently watching the ducks and geese as they passed. Their mother's rosy glow made Calli wish for a family and that same happiness. "Looks like Jordan and Joseph are having fun. Vanessa, this is my cousin, Hanna Giovanni. Hanna, this is Vanessa Davis, Luke's partner's wife."

"Oh, yes, Luke has told us about you, Hanna. It's nice to meet you. We sure enjoyed having you over, Calli. I'd like to do it again. You and Luke interested?" The sparkle in her dark eyes made Calli wonder what Luke had told his friends.

"I'd like that. With all of our crazy schedules, it's tough to find time, isn't it?"

The three women chatted a bit, and laughed again when Vanessa mentioned the incident with the Mace. "They stopped by that next night for a cup of coffee and Luke actually blushed when Tom told me."

Hanna lifted her eyebrows. "Luke blushed? Ooh-eee. Love is in the air."

Calli laughed nervously, afraid to admit that she wanted more than anything for the words to be true.

Vanessa turned toward home, and Hanna and Calli continued around the lake. "I spent a lot of time thinking about what you said, Hanna. I wasn't after revenge when I started this mission. I simply wanted to find enough evidence to let justice be served."

"I know. It's a fine line to draw."

"And I think I crossed it. I lost sight of my goal. After Brad destroyed what little evidence there was against Tiger, I... Well, it doesn't really matter now. What does matter is I'm through patrolling."

Hanna let out a little squeal. "Really? Completely through?"

Trying to free herself from her cousin's suffocating hug, Calli laughed. "Don't get excited yet. That's not all."

Hanna's arms dropped and she held Calli at arm's length. "And?"

"I'm through patrolling, but I'm not through with my mission. I'm still looking for a way to prevent gang problems. I'm going to go back to school and finish my degree. I'm going to change my major to counseling."

Her cousin's face lit up. "That's my cousin!"

"It's not as easy as it sounds. I still find my resentment taking over at times. But I am trying to let it go." She told Hanna about the graffiti incident at the store and the anger the gang member's threats renewed.

"Remember Philippians 4:13 says, 'I can do all things through God who strengthens me.' Don't forget where your source of strength comes from, Calli. He won't let you down."

"How could I forget with you here to remind me?" *You and hopefully Luke. Maybe that's why we keep meeting. He's as stubborn as you, Hanna. Neither of you seems to give up on me.*

Later that evening, she shifted in her seat as the speaker's monotone drifted to mere background noise. The lecture hall had been filled with community leaders, law enforcement personnel and social services workers. Calli was among the few "interested citizens" who wanted to understand more about the gang culture and what could be done to help.

She looked around the room, wondering what others were doing to change the situation. Since she was no longer actively patrolling, Calli was particularly interested in information on programs that worked to prevent the problems gangs represented. Throughout the workshop several of the speakers referred to gangs as a "single-parent syndrome," claiming that there was a severe lack of role models for youths to reach out to when trouble strikes.

Calli had felt the repercussions of the single-parent household, and guessed that it had been even tougher for her brother. At least she had had her mother. But her mother had been totally exasperated by Mike's strong personality. And with her father away so much…it made sense now.

She didn't want to agree with one of the opinions expressed that members of gangs were also "victims" in their own rite. Yet, she realized, sometimes the truth was a double-edged sword.

Clapping startled her from her daze and concluded the program. When she realized the speaker had finished, the room was quickly emptying. Calli had no idea how long she'd been in her trance. Gathering her bags from beneath the chair, Calli saw Luke walking across the lecture hall, toward her. His badge glistened against the dark blue shirt—a glaring reminder of what stood between them. He looked even more handsome and confident in uniform.

All week long Luke Northrup had occupied her thoughts. She'd tried to come up with a way to stop her feelings for him from growing. She didn't want either of them to be hurt. They were going to be. More than she wanted to admit. He hadn't a clue who she really was.

Not only that, but Luke could very well have been one of the officers involved. One of the officers who'd dismissed her claims that Mike had not been interested in gangs. If Luke was one of them… No, she didn't want to know. After tonight, the foundation of her argument was on shaky ground, even in her own eyes.

Her parents had tried to convince her that there was no way she could have prevented what had happened. Yet to her, it was she who was responsible for Mike that night. She'd never forget the phone call from the hospital asking if her brother was home, and the horror that had followed when she'd discovered he'd snuck out of the house through his bedroom window.

For three years she'd tried to prove her brother's innocence. To find the gang member responsible for taking Mike's life. She'd struggled to move on. She had done what little she could to prevent the same thing happening to someone else's brother, or son or nephew. For three years she'd put her own life on the line. Spent her time, money, her very soul chasing the ever-elusive justice. What else could she do?

"Commit your way to the Lord." The words came to Calli from nowhere and a calm washed over her. *God? Is that you? Or the enemy trying to make me feel guilty about staying home?* Calli could no longer deny that everything that happened the night of her accident still frightened her.

Her decision didn't come without a struggle. She had promised Mike she would find his killer. A promise was a promise. Yet her mission had already cost her plenty. And if she didn't do something, her friendship with Luke would be the next casualty.

She avoided his gaze, knowing she couldn't avoid him.

"I didn't realize you were interested in gang intervention. What did you think of the program?"

"The officer's talk was…very informative." And a bit idealistic, she reflected. There are a lot of facts they conveniently left out. She couldn't look him in the eye. Not when all she could think of was telling him the truth, and then telling him goodbye, forever.

"You okay?" Luke asked, as if she looked ill. He folded the burgundy theater chairs, clearing a path for Calli.

Calli stood and backed away, trying to forget the peace she'd felt when wrapped in Luke's arms. There was no use wishing for something she couldn't have. "I'm fine." She stepped past Luke and headed for the stairs of the antiquated college building, hoping to steer clear of the chatty stragglers who were also making their exit.

"Let me walk you to your car. It's dark out there."

Calli deduced it wasn't really a question, but a statement. Arrogant or not, Luke had a protective nature. She couldn't believe he'd like the extent of her involvement in amateur crime fighting. To a cop, interest didn't directly translate to action. She knew that from past experience.

Pulling the radio from his belt, Luke informed Tom that he'd be escorting a citizen through the parking lot. A macho confirmation reverberated through the walkie-talkie.

"Unfortunately, Tom and I officially went back on duty when the class ended. Three officers called in with the flu tonight." Luke held the outside door as Calli fished her keys from her purse. Within a few yards of the building they were enveloped into the shadows.

Calli subconsciously wove a key between each finger. "Think you could join me for lunch tomorrow?"

The courage she'd felt a minute ago waned. "We agreed to keep this platonic, Northrup."

He crossed his arms over his chest. "You agreed, and

'platonic' doesn't exclude eating. We need to discuss this week's class.''

Calli pushed her shoulders back and glanced at him. Even in the dark, she could see something sparkling far back in his eyes. Confidence. Determination. Interest. She may be able to avoid the attraction between them temporarily, but she knew that Luke Northrup wouldn't give in easily. Nor did she want him to. This time though, she wouldn't get what she wanted, and neither would Luke.

She knew that she couldn't start a relationship this way. Without the truth, she would eventually have to choose—her mission, or Luke. Even with the truth, Calli was on shaky ground. As much as she wanted to think Luke was different than the other men she knew, she doubted it. He'd taken the same oath as her ex-fiancé. He, too, saw things in black and white.

Luke reached down and took her hand in his, wrapping his fingers around her fist. Calli tried to move the keys before they gouged his hand, but didn't have time.

''What's this?'' He took hold of her wrist and raised her hand to look. ''You don't trust me to protect you?''

Pulling her hand from his grasp was no easy feat. ''It's a habit. Doesn't mean anything.''

''It does to me. You're scared of something—or someone. Me?''

''Of course not! How did you come up with that?'' Annoyed by the contempt in his voice, Calli sidestepped when Luke reached for her arm. The radio on his belt squawked and Luke turned it down. At the same time his pace increased.

A patrol car zoomed up to them and stopped.

His partner lowered the electric window and leaned across the seat. ''Luke, we've got a hot one. Evening, Calli.''

"Hi, Tom."

A muscle flicked angrily at Luke's jaw. "I'll talk to you in the morning."

Calli recognized the look in his eyes. She didn't want to get on the wrong side of the law with Sergeant Northrup on the case. "Be careful out there."

Luke winked, and she smiled back.

She thought of the first time her and Luke's "paths" had crossed—the night she'd witnessed and reported the auto thefts. She recalled that it had been that night that the support group had talked about letting go of the past. After all this time, was she finally going to succeed?

After Luke's kiss, the mission was losing its appeal. She wanted love, and happiness and a family.

Chapter Twelve

When Luke and Tom and their patrol car were out of sight, Calli crawled into her sport utility vehicle, relieved that the repairs were finally complete and that she had thought to have it painted a different color. That gave her some comfort—anonymity from Luke and the gangs.

She closed her eyes and whispered. "What do I do, God? I really care for Luke. I know I can't keep going like this."

Anxiety crept through her. Calli lifted her cellular phone and dialed Hanna. "Are you busy?"

"Not too busy to listen." Calli heard the television in the background.

"I'm already out. Would you mind if I came over?" The traffic was heavy but it still wouldn't take long to make the trip to her cousin's new house in the suburbs.

"Come on over. I'll make some popcorn."

Calli headed west and turned the stereo up. Listeners were calling the radio station, requesting love songs to dedicate to lovers, ex-loved ones and special friends. She wondered if Luke listened to music, if he was the type to cuddle up and watch movies or if she would ever have a chance to learn all about what he liked and disliked.

Hanna's house was bright with landscaping lights edging the sidewalk. The crab apple tree stood stark against the deep azure sky, and bright yellow crocuses peeking through the dried leaves in the flower beds glowed in the moonlight.

Calli rang the doorbell and Hanna answered immediately. "So what's up?"

"My life is such a mess!"

Leaning out the door, Hanna said, "I thought you got your sport utility vehicle back, but this one's black! What happened?"

"It's hunter green. They offered the color change at a price I couldn't refuse." Shrugging, Calli continued. "I thought it would make everything with Luke easier, but it doesn't—that's half the problem."

"How's that?" Her cousin turned on the stereo and the two sat on the sofa with an enormous bowl of fluffy white popcorn between them.

"I told you about dinner with Luke at Vanessa and Tom's house Sunday." She continued to tell Hanna about learning that Luke was the cop that had nearly run her off the road. "So now, even though I haven't patrolled since that night, I know Luke needs to ask me questions." She brushed her hair off her face.

"I didn't see anything that will help Luke on the case, but he doesn't know that. Every time I look at the truck, I think of how I'm lying to everyone, myself included...."

Hanna shook her head, as if it was a lost cause. "I hate to state the obvious, but maybe the truth would be best. Either way, Luke probably won't be happy that you've waited this long to tell him."

"I don't want to lose him." Calli's voice cracked with the blatant admission.

"If you don't tell him, you're going to make yourself sick worrying about when he's going to learn the truth." Hanna took Calli's hand. "Besides, once you answer his questions, it'll be over."

"Do you really believe that?"

Hanna shrugged. "Well, that part will be over."

"And the relationship will be over." Her mind wandered to the night he questioned her in the hospital. She couldn't believe that he'd never asked nor noticed the make of her vehicle and convinced herself that it wasn't lying if he never asked for the information.

The two cousins talked for hours among the plush sofa pillows and soft music. Through a yawn, Hanna finally said, "Calli, I don't have the answer you want."

"No one does."

"You sure about that? When was the last time you bothered to ask?" Her cousin never was one to mince words.

It was after midnight when Calli went home, still thinking about the symposium, and the voice she heard, and Luke. She walked into the apartment, finding it difficult not to compare her tiny apartment to Hanna's new house. They were dusk and sunrise, a warrior and a princess, simplicity and elegance.

She thought of Hanna's disturbing question, unable to put it aside and fall asleep. She recalled the calming voice she'd heard at the end of the symposium. "What did it say? Something about returning…" Calli went to her bookshelf and pulled her dusty Bible from the shelf. Calli closed her eyes and hugged the book to her heart. "What are you trying to tell me, God?"

"Commit your way to the Lord."

Calli had attended church with her family as a child, and explained the voice with having memorized verses and now His words of comfort were subconsciously returning.

The words echoed in her mind. "In quietness and trust, shall be your strength."

What is that supposed to mean? Calli looked up the verse listed in the back of her Bible and read silently, "In returning and rest you shall be saved; in quietness and trust, shall be your strength."

Punching the numbers almost as she took the phone from the receiver, Calli trembled. "Come on, Hanna."

Her cousin's greeting was garbled, as if she was still asleep.

"Hanna, the strangest thing has happened. You have to help me. Wake up." Calli waited, then repeated the plea.

After a few minutes, Hanna woke, dismayed to learn it was four in the morning. "Couldn't this have waited?"

"No." Calli had no idea how to explain.

"Are you okay?" The question was followed by a breathy yawn.

"I'm not sure. Something weird is happening, Hanna. I don't know what to do." Calli told her cousin about the voices and how the Scriptures seemed to speak to the events in Calli's life.

"Wow."

"Wow what? What is God saying to me? Or is it me imagining things?" She gasped for another breath, then babbled on.

"Calli. You do have to be careful when looking at a single Scripture. Just a minute. Let me get my study Bible and we can look the verses up. I'm no theologian, but maybe I can help you find them."

Calli heard noises in the background and shivered as she wrote in her journal what the voices said. She turned to a clean page so she'd have room to write.

Hanna's voice was calm. "Okay, tell me again what happened. I was half-asleep before. We'll start with the verses you heard, then read the whole chapter to see if it still fits the circumstances." When Calli finished, Hanna claimed that she had goose bumps on her arms, as well. "This is stuff you read about."

Together, with the miles of cable connecting them, Hanna led Calli on her search. Hanna looked up key words, then gave Calli a few verses to look for, and she looked for the others.

While the two raced on to the next reference, Calli added, "It doesn't seem that long ago that I was reading this, Hanna. How could I have strayed so far away so quickly?"

"You've been through a lot, Cal. Between the stress and grief, it's understandable."

"Not everyone understands."

"I do."

"You try, but…"

"I do, Calli. There are things you have to let time heal. I couldn't change what you were going through, as much as I wanted to. I knew that God was always with you. He was just waiting for the right time to let you realize it, I guess." There was a long pause. "Or maybe He's been talking to you all along, and you couldn't hear Him. Oh, listen, here's the one! 'Commit your way to the Lord; trust in him and he will do this: He will make your righteousness shine like the dawn, the justice of your causes like the noonday sun.'" She paused, then gasped. "Here it is, Calli—the clincher. 'Be still before the Lord and wait patiently for him; do not fret when men succeed in their ways, when they carry out their wicked schemes. Refrain from anger and turn from wrath: do not fret—it only leads to evil.''

Tears welled in Calli's eyes, and she read the last verse on their scavenger hunt through the Bible. A chill shook her body as she spoke. '''And after you have suffered a little while, the God of all grace, who has called you to His eternal glory in Christ will himself restore, establish and strengthen you.'''

The silence of the night was a gentle breeze that warmed her soul. ''I think He's telling me it's time to stop patrolling. You think so?''

Hanna's voice was soft, as if she too had been greatly affected by their journey of discernment. ''Yes, I think so.''

Calli thanked Hanna and crawled into the soft warm bed, laying the Bible on the other side while she closed her eyes to pray. In exhaustion, His words helped her to relax. ''Come to me, all who labor and are heavy laden, and I will give you rest.'' Calli drifted off to sleep.

The phone rang before eight, and Calli pulled herself from the bed, as emotionally exhausted as she was physically.

''Did I wake you up?''

Calli dropped her head into the pillow, images of Luke still in his uniform from the night before. Her world had turned one hundred eighty degrees since he'd reached for her hand and had been insulted that she didn't trust him.

''Calli?''

''Yes, I was asleep.'' *And having the most wonderful dream.*

''Sorry. Do you want me to call back later?''

''No. I have something I want to say.'' For some

strange reason, she wanted to tell him about last night. She wasn't sure yet about coming forward as the anonymous caller. They had all the information she could give anyway. Telling Luke would mean rehashing three years in the dungeons. She wanted to put that part of her life behind her.

Calli's voice was deep and husky. His own was loaded with ridicule, ready for another battle with the spunky woman he was beginning to have very strong feelings for. "Good, because I'm ready for some answers."

"To what?"

"Questions. Do you want to go first, or shall I?"

There was a long pause, then in a velvety voice she said, "I had an incredible talk with God this morning."

She had no idea how her news affected him. He'd been praying for her to trust again, but had to admit he'd selfishly asked that God would let her learn to trust him. "Do you want to tell me about it?" Luke poured a glass of juice, waiting for her to continue. "What did you talk about?" he prompted.

"Putting my trust in God." The statement revealed no hesitancy.

God's eternal wisdom brought a smile to Luke's care-worn face. "That's great, Calli," he said in a soothing voice, prompting her to continue.

As she told him about her and Hanna looking up verses and the way they fit circumstances in her life, there was a calm he'd never detected in her voice before.

Breathlessly she added, "I have a long way to go."

Luke struggled to control his voice. "You aren't alone. Don't ever forget that. We all struggle to remember who is truly in charge."

A tired laugh tickled his ear through the wires. "That's comforting."

"It's true. I should let you go back to bed. I just have one question I have to ask before I can go to sleep."

"Shoot." He could almost see the sleepy smile in her eyes.

"Was the man who hurt you a cop?"

She spoke in a broken whisper. "Yes."

He didn't like being right, especially when the truth hurt. He wished he were with Calli, to hold her and reassure her that he would do anything to erase the painful memories from her heart. "Trust me, Calli. I won't hurt you."

"That isn't the issue, Luke. It goes much deeper, and I'm working on answers to those questions, too."

"Would you come to church with me tomorrow?"

"That's two questions, Northrup. I thought cops dealt in details. You're walking a fine line here." Calli giggled.

"Answer the question, smarty."

"What time?"

"Is that a yes?"

"That's three. You're losing it."

His mouth twitched with amusement, glad to have his sparring partner back. "I'll pick you up at nine o'clock sharp."

"I get the 'point.'" Her sleepy giggle was a deep and rampant river.

Luke laughed. "Get some sleep, Calandre."

"See you tomorrow."

After nearly dressing Jon himself, Luke decided that teenagers had no sense of urgency. He tossed Jon's pants and shirt onto his son's bed.

"Why are we leaving so early?" Jon groaned.

"I'm picking up a friend."

"Calli? It has to be her, or you wouldn't be so uptight." Imitating their favorite sitcom star, Jon's razzing reassured Luke that his son liked Calli.

"She's a mighty fine lady, Jon. And I'm already walking a fine line here. Don't blow it for me, okay?"

"Don't worry about a thing."

"Famous last words. Go comb your hair. And I think it's past time for a haircut." Ignoring Jon's protest, Luke went to his bedroom and got his Bible from the shelf.

Jon wet his hair down and met Luke at the door.

Calli was waiting out front of the apartment when Luke pulled up. She was wearing a beige skirt and two-tone wool blazer with matching shoes and purse. As soon as Luke parked, Jon jumped out of the two-door and climbed into the back seat. "You look really awesome, Calli."

Luke and Calli looked at each other, then into the back seat and smiled. "Thank you, Jon. I'm not overdressed, am I? It's been a while since I've been to church. Have things changed that much?"

"You look great, Calli. Your outfit is fine."

She smiled impishly, and Luke knew he was in trouble. "Just fine? Not really *awesome?*"

Luke turned away and shook his head. *No wonder I'm still single.* He glanced at Calli; her smile was sympathetic and warm. *Could Calli be the woman to change that, God? Keep my eyes open, Father. I can't let my own dreams blind me.*

The church parking lot was full, so Luke parked across the street. Calli's hand felt cold as ice when he helped her from the low-slung car. In her heels, she lacked but an inch of six feet. Luke was grateful when Jon ran ahead to join some friends, leaving them with a minute to visit.

"I hope you didn't mind the teasing. I was afraid Jon would be offended if I treated him in any other way than

I would any young man. He *is* quite a young man, you know."

"He's a teenager. He wouldn't know how to feel offended. I, on the other hand, do. After ten hours on the beat, I'll be doing good to keep my eyes open. And you want me to see my mouthy son as a young man."

"Don't worry, I know how to wake you up. A little Mace does the trick every time."

He groaned, squeezing her hand. "You have a very warped sense of humor."

Calli enjoyed teasing him. "Levity, Northrup, levity."

Luke's deep voice carried a tune with the same strength and vibrancy that he exemplified in the rest of his life. When another couple stepped into the pew next to Jon, Luke moved closer and she could feel him tapping his toe to the rhythm of the music.

She smiled, the combination of the words of the song and his powerful voice served as nourishment to her starved soul. In the years she had strayed, even the music had changed. She was drawn into the enthusiasm of the repetitious verses. Words of encouragement and praise lifted her heart.

The music ended, and they sat down. She glanced at Luke, surprised by the contentedness of his smile.

He leaned close, whispering into her ear. "Are you okay?"

Calli felt the radiance spread through her as if God was healing her inner hurts one by one. She nodded. Tears stung her eyes, and she was powerless to stop them. She pulled a tissue from her purse and dabbed at the cleansing droplets.

Luke discreetly took her hand and held it tenderly. When the pastor closed in prayer, she added her own thanks for His grace, and for the gift of Luke's friendship.

Chapter Thirteen

Calli plopped down onto the couch and twirled the cord around her finger. "I don't know, Hanna." She wanted to put the past behind her. All of it. Mike's death, her mission, the patrolling—everything. Since the church service Sunday morning, Calli felt a peace she hadn't experienced in a long time. She wanted to see where this relationship with Luke would lead.

"You've said it for yourself. Luke is different. What purpose would telling him serve? It's not an issue anymore. Don't make it one."

Maybe Hanna was right. Telling him wasn't necessary.

"Think of all the people you've helped, not the ones you're not. If it's that important, maybe you should…"

"I do *not* want to be a cop, Hanna. Believe me, there's no pleasure in patrolling. It scares me more than anything. Every night I was out there, and even more since my accident."

"Well it's about time you've come to your senses." As if everything was settled, Hanna started talking about plans for her spring vacation. "You need to learn to enjoy life. Be carefree once in a while. Do something absolutely crazy, just for the fun of it.''

"Yeah, right. That's why Luke's already nicknamed me 'Cautious Calli.'"

"That man has you figured out, girl. *Platonic,* my foot!''

"I promise you, there's nothing going on.''

"There's a whole lot going on, cousin. You're just blinded by love, is all.''

It was a warm spring Friday, and Luke's day off. His parents were taking Jon to the mountains after school for the week of spring break. He'd worked the rookie's shift yesterday so he could join the family for three days at the cabin later in the week.

He and Calli had seen one another three of the last five days. It had been a challenge, but then, everything about her was a challenge. She was full of spirit. Stubborn and elusive. And one of these days, she was going to give in to the pressure of his charm. And he hoped that day would be today.

Luke pulled up on his motorcycle just as she stepped onto the balcony of her third-floor apartment and sprayed the glass with cleaner. He leaned his forearms onto the handlebars and removed his helmet, then peered over his sunglasses. "Hey there, gorgeous!''

Calli pretended to look up, then to both sides. "I think the sun's in your eyes, mister.''

"I think it's your blinding beauty.''

Leaning against the rail, she looked at him, obviously amused at something. He was sure it was more than what he'd said. Because his comment wasn't that funny.

"What are you doing here? I didn't think we had any classes today.''

"We don't. I just missed your fiery personality." If he ever had doubts about his attraction to Calli, he couldn't remember one reason why. She had a natural rapport with teenagers. She didn't flinch when he talked about work. She had the uncanny ability to take him right past the stress of his job and back into life.

"You're in sad shape, Northrup. Miss your morning coffee and doughnut or something?"

"Or something. Come to think of it, I haven't had my coffee."

She smiled. "Come on up. I'll make you a pot."

"I'm okay, don't bother. But I will join you."

"Good. I'll buzz you in the main lobby. Come up to the third floor. I'm in apartment 3E."

A door opened and Calli peeked out, obviously looking for him. Her smile instantly made him glad that he'd come today. Out of habit, he'd stepped to the left of the doorway and she looked surprised to find him there. "Why are you hiding? Think I might have a guard dog back here?"

She was just as dangerous, standing there in faded denim jeans and a formfitting top.

"Luke?" She waved her hands in front of his face.

"Morning." He swallowed, uncomfortable with his sudden loss of concentration.

"Come in."

Luke walked past her, trying to ignore the overwhelming temptation to kiss her. He tried to remind himself of how good an idea this appeared to be an hour ago. Tried to remind himself of Calli's skeptical nature. Tried to tell himself it was going to take time to win her over.

"So what's going on?"

"Can't a friend stop by?"

"Of course you can. I'm just surprised." Calli stepped

into the living room, inviting him to follow. "Pleasantly surprised. I was trying to figure a way out of cleaning today."

Pleasantly surprised? You're serious? Was Calli hinting that she wanted to do something together? Or was his hopeful optimism leading him into a blind alley? Luke thought of sitting on the sofa, and eyed the variety of dolls inhabiting the room. He reached down to move a floppy rag doll that had seen better days.

"I collect dolls. Excuse Bessie." She tucked the baby into a full-size wooden cradle that had also been around a while.

"Dolls, huh? Was that yours?" He motioned to the baby bed and smiled.

She nodded, seeming oddly uncomfortable with the admission.

"It's beautiful. And I bet you looked adorable in it." Envisioning her as a child was easy—she'd have had big brown eyes, so dark they looked black, like they most often did now, and wild curls tumbling around her face, and one of those angelic smiles that wrapped her daddy around her little finger. Not much had changed. She was doing the same to him at this very moment with that subtle glow on her cheeks and tight-lipped grin.

She deserved to be carefree as the little girl who'd once held these dolls and sat in the security of her parent's lap. Could Luke offer her that? Could he show her how to be carefree again? Or was he a lost cause himself?

"Are you sure you don't want some coffee?"

"No thanks. I wondered if you'd like to head to the hills with me for the day. I need to buy my parents an anniversary present."

The expression in her brown eyes seemed to plead for

friendship, yet caution clouded the way. "To the mountains, shopping, on a motorcycle?"

"Unless you're afraid of bikes."

Trust Me. Calli licked her lips nervously and thought of pointing out the dangers involved. Some of which had nothing to do with the highway *or* traffic. *Okay, God. I'm trying. Really I am. But a motorcycle?* Despite her fears, she needed to learn to give up control. *Well, Hanna, is this crazy enough for you?* "Okay."

"Okay?" He furrowed his brows, then leaned forward, resting his elbows onto his knees and intertwined his fingers. "You're afraid, aren't you?"

She shook her head.

"It's okay. We can take the car."

"No," she argued, then remembered the night he'd asked her to trust him, and inside she knew she had failed. She breathed deep, and exhaled. "I want—need to take your cycle."

As if he realized the significance behind her statement, he simply nodded. "Fine. Let's go. We'll stop for brunch along the way. If you have hiking boots, they'd be best. I brought Jon's leather jacket for you to wear. It's warmer and cuts the wind."

Luke waited as she layered a blouse over the top. When they reached the street, he opened the saddlebag and took out the jacket and helped her put it on. She snapped it up while he detached the extra helmet from the backrest.

"I don't picture you as a cyclist." Calli noted the mischievous look in his eyes.

"Ditto with the dolls. We all have our secrets, don't we?"

He had no idea.

"Jon and I take off every summer. Take time to get back in touch—with each other, and God. Everything's so much clearer on a bike." Luke proceeded to fit his son's helmet to her head, then put his own on and spoke. She jumped when sound echoed into her ears.

"There are speakers in the helmet, so we can talk while we drive."

"Oh, how convenient," she said, wondering if the nearness of her voice would leave him as unsettled as his did her. Luke helped her onto the seat and showed her the footrests. He cautioned her not to tilt the cycle off the automatic kickstand. His long legs straddled the machine easily. Muscled thighs stretched against the thin denim. His brown leather jacket fit his broad shoulders as if it were a second skin.

He kick started the engine and slid back in the seat. "Hang on."

"To what?"

"Me. Wrap your arms around my waist." He twisted the handle and the engine roared. "Put your visor down."

Calli reached up and pulled the dark glass over her face. She tentatively placed her hands on his waist and heard him chuckle. He revved the engine again, and they surged forward. She screamed and clung to his entire torso. She felt a hard lump along his left rib, and realized that he was wearing his gun.

He laughed aloud, that soft laugh that had an uncanny way of soothing her nerves. Or at least it would have, had they been anywhere but on this glorified mode of "transportation." "That's better, but it would help if you let my lungs have room to breathe. I hope the gun doesn't bother you."

"Not at all. No more than my keys bothered you."

"Okay, so I overreacted. I'm not used to… Never mind."

"Women who can take care of themselves?"

"I didn't say that."

"May as well have."

"I know plenty of women who can take care of themselves. What I didn't say was that I'm not used to *dating* women who can."

"Thank you. I'll take that as a compliment."

She loosened her grip until he turned the first corner. He and the cycle dipped to the right, and Calli jerked left in hopes of keeping them upright. "Relax, Cal. Just follow me. When I lean you follow, stay with me."

"I'm no motorcycle babe."

He mumbled something, but when she insisted he repeat himself, Luke said, "I'm not about to let anything hurt you."

Once on the turnpike, headed out of town, the traffic thinned and Calli finally felt herself relax. His deep voice was reassuring. "You're getting the hang of it. What do you think?"

"I'm thinking God has an awfully strange sense of humor."

"Oh, yeah? You mean watching you squirm back there, learning to trust me?"

Calli hoped he couldn't hear her swallow the gasp. "*No*. That He thinks you and I have *anything* in common."

"You have a lot to learn, Calli. And in spite of your bullheadedness, He's going to see that you do."

Luke turned on a tape of men singing praise songs, some of which she'd heard months ago, some last Sunday in church. The road narrowed, winding among the rock cliffs and ponderosa pines, crossing back and forth over the gushing river below.

The words of the song reverberated in her mind over and again, with every twist of this path she followed. Her path was far from clean, far from free.

Luke pulled into a parking space and shut off the engine. They went inside the lodge and climbed the log steps. Calli studied the historical photographs and antique keys hanging from the log support beams. Once seated, they could overlook the moraine valley.

They'd visited very little on the drive up the mountain. Calli had listened intently to the music and let Luke's wide shoulders block the wind.

"How did you like the ride?"

She met his smile and the hand that was offered. "I don't remember feeling anything quite as wonderful. I guess I don't like taking risks."

With a slight squeeze of her hand, his smile broadened. "You don't say. What do you want to eat?"

"The muffins and fruit look good."

"No eggs and bacon?"

"The muffins are my splurge."

"You could splurge more often."

"You have a lot of room to talk." Hugging his body for the last hour, she could assure the pickiest of dietitians that there wasn't a wasted gram of fat on Luke Northrup. He was solid. Emotionally, physically and spiritually.

A very pretty young waitress took their order. Calli expected some kind of reaction from Luke when the girl complimented him on how *good* he looked in his leather jacket. But he ignored her flirting and politely thanked her, then placed his order.

"Did you like Pastor Don's sermon?"

"I thought about it all day. At first I thought it was

talking about street violence, but when he said it was written about a friend's betrayal, I was surprised."

They discussed the scripture, and how not much had changed in the two thousand years since King David's day. "Isn't it sad that after all these years, humans still make the same stupid mistakes?"

With all of her own mistakes, Calli found it difficult to criticize anyone else's, and she decided to change the subject. "With all of the violence you see every day, how can you stay so optimistic?"

"It's all part of His plan. There's nothing to fear."

"You mean you're not afraid to go to work each day?"

"To go to work, no. But there's a keen edge of fear that has to be there constantly. It keeps me alive. A cop ignores that, and he's dead. So yeah, I'm cautious of who could be waiting around the next corner, but afraid of my own end, no. What's waiting for us is absolutely awesome."

Calli remembered her father's reassuring voice before he'd leave on each tour of duty.... *If I don't come back one day, honey, I'll be waiting for you in heaven. We'll have eternity together.* She looked at Luke and forced a smile.

"You okay?"

"It's a lot to absorb, but I'm beginning to see how it all comes together." The sermon scripture had been from the fifty-fifth Psalm, and had spoken directly to Calli. She saw herself patrolling the city, saw Tiger and Mike. When the pastor explained the betrayal aspect, and the pain of the betrayed, Calli had choked back tears of remembrance. Of the love that had once betrayed her. "My dad was a commander in the military. He had a dog tag engraved with a verse on it. It was something like 'Be merciful, O God, for in thee my soul takes refuge.'" Calli paused and Luke finished the verse. "'In the shadow of thy wings I will take refuge, till the storms of destruction pass by.' That's a good one to remember, especially in law enforcement."

"You already knew it."

"I have a whole list in here." He pointed to his head. "Best armor we have against the enemy."

Chapter Fourteen

"Why don't you just go to the mall for a gift?" Calli asked as they went from one tiny, craft-filled gift shop to the next. They'd been browsing the touristy mountain town for half the day, and hadn't found "just the right gift" yet.

"Too much work. Here it isn't crowded, everyone's friendly. And it's fun. I'm having a great time, aren't you?"

Without thinking, she took hold of his arm and pulled him close. "I'm having a wonderful time. Thank you."

Luke tipped his head and kissed her cheek. "This is nice, Calli."

She backed away and pressed her hand against the spot on her cheek where the warmth of his kiss was making a beeline to her heart.

He stared at her, his gaze a mixture of anger and desire. "I get the message. Friends it is. You're probably right. Why ruin a good thing?" Luke turned away, pretending to look in the window.

"That's not what I meant at all, Luke," she whispered.

Unsure if he'd heard her, she repeated it again, louder this time.

"I heard you," he answered. "I just wanted to hear it again. To make sure you meant it." His eyes met hers and her heart raced.

"Do you work tonight?"

"Not until Monday." She was so stunned by the absurdness of the conversation, she didn't consider the wisdom of her honesty.

"What luck. Neither do I. You want to do something together?"

"That depends."

Luke grumbled in her ear. "You should know me better than that by now."

Calli felt the tension in his voice and laughed. "I was teasing, Northrup."

"Right. What I was leading into is that Mom and Dad are bringing Jon up here to their cabin for the week. I thought we could deliver their present and have dinner before we head back."

"You want me to meet your parents? Like this?"

"Like what?"

Calli motioned to her faded jeans and the conglomeration of shirts. "I look horrible. I don't want to make a bad impression. I mean, even as *just* a friend, I care what people think about me."

"Don't worry, Mom and Dad love 'biking babes.' And besides, you look awesome in everything you wear." His devastating smile turned to a mischievous chuckle, then he dragged her past the candy store and into another quaint shop.

Luke found his parents a set of ceramic coasters and a matching pine tree candle holder. They drove down the canyon, arriving at the cabin before Luke's parents and

Jon. Luke unlocked the door and started a fire. It was already dark when the three Northrups walked in the door, obviously surprised to find Luke and Calli waiting.

"What took you so long?" Luke joked, totally missing the panicked glances exchanged between his parents.

"Gramps had some business he needed to take care of. Hi, Calli."

"Hi, Jon. How's it going?"

"It's cool. *Vacation!*" He ran out the door to get another load of gear from the pickup.

"Mom, Dad, this is a friend of mine. Calli Giovanni. Calli, meet Joan and Ted Northrup."

Mrs. Northrup's smile crinkled the corners of her eyes. She was a petite woman with Luke's coloring. "Good evening, Calli. Jon was telling us about you. He's quite impressed."

Luke's father was stocky and slightly shorter than his son. He nodded quickly then said, "It's nice to meet you, Miss Giovanni. If you'll excuse us, I need to talk to Luke privately. Family matters."

Luke shrugged, raising his eyebrows.

Calli smiled, feeling like an intruder.

"I'm sorry about his gruffness, Calli. It isn't you. This problem has him on the defensive." Mrs. Northrup touched Calli's arm. "And as you probably know by now, a cop on the defensive isn't in any shape to socialize." Ted pulled his son into the next room. Calli heard the deep, hushed voices, mixed with an occasional harsh word.

"I understand, Mrs. Northrup. My father is a retired military man. They're a special breed, aren't they?"

His mother laughed. "Well, well, there may be an answer to my prayers yet."

Jon came in, dropped a load of bags, then dashed out

the door again. It was clear that he looked forward to spending time with his grandparents.

With a grim expression, Luke nodded to his father and walked toward her. "Calli, I'm afraid we'd better head back right away. Sorry. I'm going to talk to Jon for a few minutes, then we'll leave." He disappeared, leaving an awkward silence in the room. Even Mrs. Northrup's chatter stopped as she turned toward her husband. "He's going to tell Jon?" she asked incredulously.

"That's not our decision, Joan. He's Luke's son."

Calli smiled uncomfortably, anxious to know what was going on. When Luke and Jon came back into the cabin, Jon looked at his grandparents. "You don't have to worry, Grammy, I'm not going anywhere."

"I'll call you tomorrow and see what you've decided, Jon."

The teen's chin jutted forward, just like Luke's when he was mad. "I don't want to see her."

"Just think about what I said." Luke wrapped his arm around Jon's shoulder and kissed his forehead.

"I won't change my mind." Jon picked up a duffel bag and headed for the ladder to the loft.

"I'll be back tomorrow. We'll talk more about it then." Luke straightened his shoulders and hugged his parents. When Jon was out of sight, Luke gave his mother a stern look. "Don't push him, Mom. He has to make his own decision."

Luke helped Calli into Jon's jacket and helmet. Jon ran down the stairs.

"You still look awesome, Calli, even in *my* stuff."

She laughed and patted him on the shoulder. "Thanks for sharing, Jon. Have a fun week."

"We will. See you later."

Luke hustled her out the door and helped her onto the

bike. Calli waited uncomfortably for Luke to start the conversation. If he wanted her to know what the big emergency was, he'd tell her in his own time. They were out of the foothills before either said a word. "Jon's mother was in a serious automobile accident today. Nancy's father called while Dad was at the apartment picking up Jon's bag. I guess he demanded that Jon go to California with them tonight." Even through the mikes she could hear the turmoil in Luke's voice.

Not sure if Luke wanted to talk about it, she hesitated before delving further. "Jon doesn't want to see her?"

"Nancy was only seventeen when we were briefly married and had Jon. Her parents didn't like me much, and talked her into walking away from both Jon and I. One day, she dropped Jon at Mom and Dad's while I was at school, and never came back. A few months later she showed up with papers giving up her son. I've had full custody since."

She hugged Luke from behind, and he patted her hand, as if she was the one who needed consoling. "How old were you?" Calli was surprised at how easily he opened up to her, and longed for the same courage.

"Eighteen."

"And you've raised him alone?"

"We lived with Mom and Dad for a while, but as soon as I found a decent job, we found our own place. I wanted my space to raise Jon, and let my folks be grandparents. They'd already raised their family, though they still have a good time together."

"That's the way it should be, and it's clear that your parents and Jon have a great relationship."

"That's for sure. Of course, they spoil him rotten."

Calli chuckled. "Spoken like a true father. So if Jon's mother doesn't see him, why the big issue tonight?"

"Nancy made a surprise visit recently. She threatened to take us to court to get her custody rights back. Of course, that's been almost a month ago now, and we haven't heard a word since. Jon doesn't want anything to do with her."

"She doesn't understand how he feels?"

"Nancy's pregnant, getting married and wants Jon to join the cozy family. She always wanted what she couldn't have. I suggested she get to know her son first, let things grow from there."

His bitterness was subtle, much less obvious than her own opinion of Brad. Calli wondered if that was why Luke had never married again, because he was still in love with Jon's mother.

Luke turned off the interstate.

"Where are we going?"

"To talk to Nancy's father. I'm sorry you have to go with me, but he and Gayle leave in two hours. I don't want to miss them."

A few minutes later, Luke drove through the open iron gates.

He pulled to a stop in front of an elegant rambling ranch-style home. Luke turned the key of the cycle and climbed off, pausing to help Calli. He tucked the helmet under his arm and mumbled. "I'm probably wasting my time. Newt and I haven't spoken in years."

From the rigid set of his jaw, she sensed his determination to do the right thing for Jon and Nancy, even if it meant facing his former father-in-law. She admired Luke's willingness to work with Jon's mother at all.

Taking Calli's icy hand in his own, Luke led her up the steps. "We won't stay long."

There was no answer when he rang the doorbell. He

pushed the button again. Finally a middle-aged woman answered.

Luke explained who he was and asked for Nancy's parents.

"I'm sorry, sir, they were able to get an earlier flight. It doesn't look good for Miss Nancy."

"Do you know where I can reach them?"

She retrieved the phone number and handed it to Luke. "Mr. Newt told me to give this to you when you called."

"Thank you." Luke placed the paper in his shirt pocket and they left.

The silence was broken only by the rush of traffic. Though Calli knew what a special man Luke was already, this added to her admiration. He could let bitterness stand in the way, yet he didn't. He was ready to offer people who had caused him and his son years of pain and loneliness support when they were hurting.

A few minutes later, Luke turned off the freeway. She gazed at the familiar landmarks as they passed through her neighborhood. Why did the dilapidated buildings look brighter from the seat of a motorcycle?

Luke pulled up to the curb and swung his long leg over the cycle, then helped her off. "Come in for a while?" Calli asked.

"I should get home," he said with staid calmness.

Removing the leather jacket, she felt as if she were peeling off another layer of the shield around her heart. Wondering if Luke regretted opening up to her, she wanted to share her own pain with him. Wanted him to see that she, too, had a past that she'd rather not face. But tonight he was the one who needed to talk. "Go if you want. I just thought you could call the hospital from here. We could order a pizza and visit. An empty house isn't very comforting when you're miserable."

Luke listened to her steady voice of reason. Going home held no appeal, yet was it fair to dump this mess on Calli? *God, I need someone to listen and share this load. You know I want a wife to go home to and hold. I can't hash through everything with someone who isn't willing to stick around and help me pick up the pieces afterward. So if Calli isn't the one you have in mind, God, don't let me be tempted.*

"Luke?" Calli's hair tumbled from the restraint of the helmet. Her eyes looked like onyx and twinkled in the moonlight, reflecting her tears. "I know there isn't much I can do, but I can listen."

He waited to speak, emotion constraining his throat. "You sure you're up to it? It isn't pretty."

"We all have shadows to deal with. Maybe one day I'll share mine." The wind gently fluffed her hair and she pushed a lock behind one ear. Her smile was tender and compassionate.

Once in her apartment, Calli handed him the phone. "Go ahead."

He sighed heavily as he landed in the oak chair. He felt the color drain from his face as the conversation concluded. Luke hunched over, resting his elbows on his thighs. *Dear God, be with Nancy. And help me to say the right words to Jon.*

He looked up to find Calli leaning against the wall. She possessed strength and stamina at odds with the slenderness of her body. Her smooth cheeks glowed from the cold ride home. Her beauty was exquisite and fragile, and he wanted nothing more than to escape in her arms and hide from what he needed to do.

"How is she?"

"In stable condition. She lost the baby."

Calli could see the pain Luke felt and couldn't bear

the sight of him without breaking down herself. Biting her lower lip as a reminder to let him do the talking, she simply touched his shoulder.

"I shouldn't have been so stubborn. I wouldn't have been, had I known." His shoulders shook.

Calli knelt in front of Luke. "This afternoon you told me that we all make choices, good or bad, based on our life experiences. Based on your past with Nancy, you did what you thought was best. Now there are other factors."

"I don't know whether I should take Jon. She may not even know us. They can't even say she'll make it."

Calli nodded. She took Luke's hand in both her own and waited for him to speak again. After a long silence, he lifted his head.

"I'd rather err on the side of trying. This may be the last chance Jon has to talk to her. Someday he'll understand."

"I hope so."

They sat together for a few more minutes before she ordered a stuffed pepperoni pizza and salad. She set the table while Luke called the station, then Tom.

When he was through, she sat next to him and wrapped an arm around him. He buried his face in the crook of her neck and silently snuggled against her. He smelled like the fresh mountain air.

Calli's emotions whirled and skidded, coming to a sudden halt when Luke turned toward her. She felt his bearded chin prickling the sensitive skin beneath her jaw. Torn between jealousy that Luke was crying over Nancy, and happiness that he was with her, Calli prayed. *God, be with Luke and Jon, and Nancy. And help me to do the right thing, for all of them.*

One hand supported her back and the fingers of his

other hand played with her earlobe and the tangled curls she'd tucked behind her ear. "Calli?"

"Yeah?" she rasped.

"Did you hear a buzzer?" The doorbell rang again, and Calli jumped to her feet.

Calli pushed the intercom, releasing the door. "The pizza!"

He looked at her uncomfortably. "Saved by the bell."

When Luke and Jon returned from California three days later, Luke stopped by Calli's. She invited him in and they sat at the table with a glass of lemonade.

His voice was deceptively calm as he broke the news. "She's improving."

Luke sat across from Calli, drumming his fingers on the table. He told her about the awkward time spent with her family and Jon's apathy about the situation. "Jon's upset, and he won't talk about it. He's mad that I ruined his spring break. His attitude didn't help matters with her parents."

"You can't blame him, Luke. Hospitals are frightening places for kids. Throw in the factor that he's expected to be upset about someone who walked out on him, well, I just think her family should be more understanding."

"Jon doesn't understand what he's walking away from."

"How could he understand something he's never had? They're the ones who walked away. You didn't have to go, but you did."

He looked at her blankly. "This is frightening, but I'm starting to understand the way you think."

Calli slapped his shoulder playfully. "Gee, thanks a lot."

Luke grabbed her hand and held it firm, studying it. "That isn't the main reason I came today."

Calli felt her throat constricting.

"I don't know how to say this, Calli. You've made it clear that a cop doesn't fit into your plans. After what happened the other night, I'm not sure we're both ready to move on."

She considered arguing his point, wanting to remind him that less than a week ago they had been communicating quite well, before the pizza had arrived. Yet she sensed it was more than her fears in the way, that after seeing the effects Nancy's accident had on Jon, *Luke* wanted more space.

He picked up a quarter from the dish on her table and walked it from finger to finger. "I don't want to mess things up between us."

Puzzled, Calli stared at him.

"You asked to keep it platonic, and I blew it. I promise it won't happen again."

"Fine, Northrup."

"It's what you wanted. I should have listened."

She concentrated on the table. It wasn't what she wanted at all, but she knew it was best. They should have gone their separate ways long ago.

Luke stood and rested a hand on Calli's shoulder. "I'll see you Thursday, then."

She brushed the hand away. "You're right, Luke. It's best for us to keep it platonic."

Chapter Fifteen

~~

Calli sat on the step of Luke's apartment building. Waiting. She heard the news on the radio as she headed home from work. A rookie had been killed in the line of duty.

What am I doing here? Luke made it clear last week. He doesn't want to get involved right now.

She looked up to the stars and wondered what she could say to Luke when he did show up. How could she ever explain running to stay with Vanessa until she'd heard who the downed officer was. Or more importantly, who he wasn't.

It had been Vanessa that suggested she'd feel better after seeing Luke in person. The two women had talked about God, and about why Luke was backing away from Calli. Vanessa concluded that Calli was crazy to agree with Luke. The yearning to explain everything to Vanessa grew stronger as they visited, but Calli simply couldn't reveal why *she* should stay away.

Calli went home, even crawled into bed, then proceeded to soak the pillow as she struggled with her feelings for a man she could not have. She closed her eyes, remembering Vanessa's praise for the protection God had provided for Tom and Luke. Sleep still had not come.

Wondering if he'd get off early because of the shooting, she dressed and drove to Luke's. An hour and a half later, and she was still waiting for him to arrive. *We're just friends. I shouldn't be sitting here like some lovesick schoolgirl.* She looked again at her watch, then stood up to leave. Just then Luke pulled around the corner.

Well, it's too late to chicken out now.

Luke took his time getting out of the car. His rangy body unfolded from the low-slung vehicle and towered above it when he stood. He looked tormented.

When he spoke, his voice was raw. "Morning, Calli."

"Hi. I heard the news. I thought you might need a friend."

His disapproving look sent chills up her spine. *Then again, maybe I was wrong.*

Without a word, he sat on the cold cement next to her and stared into the predawn sky. In the dim light, his bearded chin and eyes were even darker, more intriguing. And the more she thought of what he'd experienced earlier, the more she wanted to know Luke Northrup. How did he cope? Surely in a city this size, he dealt with death and loss often. From his appearance, it bothered him. A lot.

Luke twisted his head, leaning it toward one shoulder, then the other. "What I need right now, you can't give me."

Calli slid up one step and rested her hands on his shoulders. Her thumbs began to make small circles, kneading his tight muscles. "And what's that?" She pressed harder, unsure that touching him was at all wise.

He remained silent. She could feel his pain, the emptiness of loss. With each rotation, Calli acknowledged that her feelings for Luke went far deeper than friendship. "I'm here, Luke." *Don't ask or expect more.*

"For how long, Calli? An hour? A day? A lifetime?"

Unaware that she'd stopped rubbing his shoulders, Luke took her hands and turned to face her.

"Why not?" he demanded as if they'd been through this a thousand times.

Puzzled, Calli searched his face, hoping for a way to avoid the ugly truth. She was here to make him feel better, and the truth wouldn't help. Not today. "You know why."

"Lots of men are cops." Luke muttered a curse. "Am I anything like the jerk that hurt you?"

Calli was totally taken aback by this interrogation.

"Then why are you here?" He studied her, then stood and unlocked the building door. "You shouldn't have come, Calli. Because Jon and I need someone who'll be around tomorrow."

"*You* can't promise *me* tomorrow, Officer Northrup!" She watched as the door closed behind him. Calli felt all of her dreams fading into the light. The more risks she took, the more she lost.

Luke climbed the stairs and unlocked the apartment door. Mrs. Maloney rose from the sofa. "I tried to run interference, but Jon already heard it on the radio. He took forever to fall asleep. How are you?"

"I feel a whole lot more vulnerable this morning."

"Fix yourself a cup of tea and spend the day with your loved ones. Every day is a precious gift. It'll do you good, both of you." She patted his arm as she walked past him.

Luke considered Mrs. Maloney's advice, immediately recalling the way he'd yelled at Calli. Regret waged a war within him. He didn't want her to be hurt. He couldn't promise he'd make it home at the end of his shift. He knew that.

Yet he couldn't let her go.

He followed Marge out the apartment door and rushed to the stairs. She turned for the elevator and looked at him, puzzled. "I forgot something downstairs. Go on home, Marge. I'll be right back."

"Good day to you, then."

He reached the street just as Calli was pulling away. He ran to catch up with her, and knocked on the window of her vehicle. Calli braked and rolled the window down.

Out of breath from the sprint down the stairs and chasing her down the street, Luke gasped, "I'm sorry, Calli." He offered her a sudden, arresting smile.

She smiled. "You're forgiven."

They stayed there in the middle of the street, saying nothing, but gazing into each other's eyes. It was a day to be with those he cared for—his son, and Calli. Life was too short.

"Would you join Jon and I for breakfast? I could use the company."

"Jon won't mind?"

"Are you kidding? He's crazy about you."

"If you were my dad, I wouldn't want to share you today."

The tip of his tongue touched his lower lip just before he grinned. "Since I'm *not* your dad, how *do* you feel?"

"It's part of being a cop—taking risks. I understand that." Her eyes grew moist and she quickly blinked the tear away.

"That's not what I was talking about, and you know it, Cal."

She swallowed, afraid to take another chance.

Trust me.

Nervously Calli bit her lip. "I was worried about you."

A car honked from behind them and Calli pulled ahead to the curb. Luke followed, thinking of the courage it took for this woman to come to him today. In the two weeks since he and Jon returned from California, he'd made no attempt to call her. And after the self-defense class ended, he doubted he'd see her again. Yet here she was.

She'd obviously not slept a wink, been waiting in the cool morning air, and from the puffiness of her eyes, she'd spent a good while crying, as well.

According to Tom, she'd kept Vanessa company while the two of them waited for the official announcement of the officer's name. A day like this was typically followed by the majority of cop's girlfriends breaking off relationships.

Luke crawled into the passenger's side and took hold of her cold fingers. "You didn't have to come. Why did you?"

"I may be a lot of things, Luke, but I'm *not* a fair-weather friend."

For better or worse, through good times and bad. Luke fought the hope building inside. He'd been hurt too many times by women who tried to convince themselves—and him—that they could handle the stress of his career. That, combined with full custody of his son, had marked the end of his few relationships.

Yet here was a woman who claimed to want nothing more than a friendship and was ready to stand beside him and his son after one of the worst months of his life. "I could use a friend today, and maybe if tomorrow works out, that'd be okay, too. We can take it one day at a time."

"It's a deal."

Calli flipped a U-turn and headed back to his apartment, and Luke covered his eyes. "I didn't see that."

"Good. It's been a long day. I'd hate to make you write up another ticket."

"Gee, thanks." He laughed, relieved that she was with him. "You like waffles?" Calli parked and they walked inside.

"Only homemade ones with my grandmother's secret syrup."

He pushed the button for the elevator. "Okay, I'll make the waffles, you make the syrup."

The elevator opened, and electricity seemed to arc between them as the doors closed them off from the rest of the world. Luke moved close. The mere touch of his hand holding hers sent a warming shiver through her.

The light conversation from a moment ago was suddenly jolted by Calli's intense feelings and the awareness that Luke was silently demanding such an admission from her.

Neither of them had tomorrow to promise, she repeated, desperately trying to convince herself that Luke's friendship would be enough. Calli knew the value of appreciating what she did have—each other—today. One day at a time.

Since the elevator was barely quicker than a snail, she assessed that the tingle in the pit of her stomach was the result of Luke's blatant appraisal of her.

"I know I agreed to keep this platonic, Calli, but I'm going to have to renege on that promise."

"Really?" *It's about time.*

"I can't help but wonder what it would take to fluster Calli Giovanni."

Calli laughed, silently daring him to try.

"Tell you what, if I succeed, you agree to fix dinner for me. If I don't, I make dinner."

She put her hands on her hips in defiance. "Wait a minute. Either way, you…"

"Win. And what's wrong with that?" He stepped closer, his intense gaze ripping her willpower to shreds.

Calli's eyes widened as Luke pulled her against him and whispered, "I'm falling for you, Calli."

She gasped. Her eyes drifted closed as his hand rested against the small of her back. He kissed her, deeper than ever, the instant warmth sending another shiver up Calli's back.

"Luke…" she rasped.

"What?" he murmured into the tender skin below her chin.

"You win."

He laughed, and she felt his chest relax. "You're slacking off, Miss Giovanni. I at least expected some resistance."

"I'm too tired to argue with you today. Anyway. You flustered me." The elevator stopped, and Calli backed away, afraid of making another mistake. "You coming, Northrup? You did promise me breakfast."

"Wait just a minute."

Calli stopped and looked into his green eyes. There was a need there that she wasn't sure she could deny— a commitment. A hope for tomorrow.

Could she give it to him?

His gaze held her tenderly.

How could she not?

"This isn't much of a life to offer you. Sitting at home

worrying about whether I'll make it home from work each day. And you waiting with Vanessa last night tells me you want more than friendship, too.''

"I asked her not to tell you.''

"She didn't.'' His expression stilled and grew serious. "Tom told me.''

"What happened to black and white? That's a definite gray area, Officer Northrup.''

Luke's expression was one of pleading. "Look at it this way. With me you'll always know where you stand. If you want to leave, do it now.''

Calli knew what he was saying. If she turned and walked away, it was forever. She tried to push her confused emotions into some sense of order. "Then I guess we'd better do some serious talking.''

Luke pressed the Close Door button, then sent the elevator toward the parking garage. "So talk. We have plenty of time.''

After weeks of testing, her willpower was dissipating in front of her. "I've already tried to walk away, Luke. I've even asked God not to let me care. But tonight terrified me. I've never worried about anyone like this.''

"What is it, Calli? Is it my job that worries you?''

She shook her head. "No, I know you're careful and well trained.'' She took a deep breath, then let it out. "I was engaged to a *very* domineering man.''

"Mmm-hmm.'' he nodded, his arms crossed in front of him.

"I don't want to make that mistake again.''

"Good.''

She looked at him, startled. "What do you mean, good?''

"I mean good. No one should live with someone else

pushing them around, telling them what to do. And I, for one, don't plan to let you marry the wrong man.''

"And you don't think that's domineering? Or conceited? Or…''

"I call it love. I'm not saying that I'm perfect, Calli. Yet I'd like to think I have just enough confidence to keep me alive. Too much, a cop begins to think he's invincible. Too little, he just isn't able to do the job. And in case that balance gets out of whack, I think you're perfectly capable of setting me straight.'' Luke leaned against the carpeted wall inside the tiny cubicle.

"You don't know me, Luke.''

"Is there something you think I *won't* like?''

"Yes.'' She breathed deep, silently asking God for strength to tell him everything. The words wouldn't come. *Not today. He has enough to handle right now.*

"I'm in no rush, Calli. If it's that upsetting to you, wait until you feel more comfortable.''

The door opened, and an older gentleman carried his groceries into the elevator. The silence stretched thinner with each floor that passed. When they reached the third floor, Luke led Calli into his apartment.

"When you're ready. Not until then.'' He kissed her cheek, then walked away.

Luke left Calli in the living room while he went to tell Jon that he was home. She overheard the relief in the two masculine voices, a cold reminder of the tragedy that Luke had been through earlier. Today wasn't the time to tell him. She wasn't ready, and Luke and Jon needed today to heal.

Calli studied the pictures on his walls. Wooden frames held photographs of himself and Jon, hiking and canoeing. There were some pictures of waterfalls and mountains, and one snapshot of his parents' cabin, with Luke and Jon and several other people standing in front of it.

Wrapping her arms around herself to fend off the sudden chill, Calli was startled when Luke leaned over her shoulder and pointed to each person, "introducing" her to each sister, brother, in-law and "out-law" as he affectionately referred to the nonfamily members. His rough cheek grazed hers, and she smelled the faint remains of his cologne mixed with that fully masculine scent of a long stressful night. Strangely, just knowing he'd come home unhurt made the pungent aroma soothing.

"It sounds like you have a very close family."

Luke led her to the kitchen. "Yup. You don't have time for meaningless squabbles in this line of work. Dad is a retired street cop. Mom was a teacher. We learned young not to take family for granted."

Pulling the waffle mix from the cupboard, he paused, then turned to Calli. "What do you need for the syrup?"

"Sugar and water."

"White sugar?"

Calli nodded. "Oh, and vanilla." She saw the disbelief in his eyes. "You just caramelize the sugar, add the water, let it boil, then add the vanilla extract and serve it. It's wonderful."

"Mmm... Sounds interesting. So what do your folks do?"

"Dad's retired from the military. Mom raised us kids." She waited for the "military brat" comments to start.

"Where are they now?"

Calli wanted to change the subject. She did not have the energy to go into detail about what had driven them apart. "In Glenwood Springs."

"Ah. Do I hear, 'Close enough, yet far enough away' in your tone?"

"Exactly."

Breakfast was a welcome break, working side by side. Jon set the table and made conversation. After breakfast, Calli yawned, then Luke did, and the circles under Jon's eyes confirmed that none of them had slept. "I don't think any amount of coffee is going to take this fatigue away, guys. I'm going home so you can get some rest."

Luke took her hand, and Calli found it hard to avoid his gaze. She felt Jon's eyes on them. Father and son needed time together, time alone to share their relief, their fear. They didn't need a stranger around.

Jon crossed in front of them and hugged his dad. "I'm really glad you're okay, Dad, but I'm going back to bed. I'm glad you came today, too, Calli."

Calli looked into Luke's eyes and felt the heat rush to her cheeks. Every time his gaze met hers, her heart beat a little quicker.

"I'm not going to be far behind. Go ahead, Jon Jon."

"See you guys later." Jon closed his bedroom door behind him. Luke took Calli's hands in his.

"I want you here today, Calli."

Chapter Sixteen

Calli heard footsteps and rolled over, rubbing the sleep from her eyes. Mrs. Maloney had left her belongings on the bed, and Luke insisted she take a nap on his. The furnishings were totally masculine. Totally Luke. The comforter was navy with white snowflakes and twinkling stars and elk running through pine trees. On the walls were old wooden snowshoes and more collages of photos. A poster of the Longs Peak in the springtime faced the bed.

It was nearly noon. Calli sat up in the bed and pulled her legs to her chest. She peered down the hall to the living room where Luke slept. He was still sprawled in the recliner like a guard dog protecting his domain. Jon tiptoed past the doorway on the way to the bathroom.

I should leave while Luke's asleep. He doesn't have a clue what odds are against us. She continued to think while putting her tennis shoes on and folding the blanket that she'd used to cover herself. She wasn't patrolling any longer, but that didn't take away from the facts. Luke was looking for a witness who he suspected was the anonymous caller, and unfortunately, it happened to be her.

"Afternoon, Calli."

She turned, surprised to see Jon come into the room. "Hi, Jon. How did you sleep?"

He shrugged, looking more his age than she'd seen him before.

"That probably makes three of us who didn't get much rest." *And probably all for different reasons.* She couldn't help but wonder how Luke had managed as a single father for all these years—and how both father and son would adjust to having a woman in the house.

The boy was nearly as tall as she was, yet he was already developing his father's broad shoulders. His hair wasn't as dark as Luke's, but his facial expressions were obviously copies of his dad.

And looking at the teen, she wondered how he felt about the danger of his father's job. Without really thinking, her thoughts were spoken aloud. "When I was growing up, my dad was in the military. I sometimes wished someone else's dad would save the world. I wanted *my* dad to stay home and teach me to play softball."

"Yeah, it stinks sometimes, but most of the time it's okay." He smiled tentatively, raising his already bushy eyebrows. "It could be worse. At least my dad isn't gone for long stretches of time like your dad must have been."

Calli smiled. Jon was a cop's son for certain. He didn't talk about the possibility that the day could come when Luke may not come home at all.

As a young child, she never realized the danger of her father's career or the pressure it must have put on her mother to create such normalcy for herself and her family. There was always plenty of love and security. Home was wherever they were, and each day spent together was what her mother called "a precious gift from God." Calli smiled. Today she understood what her mother's saying really meant. Her mother's claims that her faith had carried her through finally made sense. Calli wondered who that "buffer" was in Jon's life.

Was it Luke's parents who played the role of mother, protecting Jon from the harsh reality of law enforcement? Days like today couldn't make it easy on an officer's child, when everyone looked at you with unspoken fear—and heaven help the person who spoke the words aloud.

You can't promise me tomorrow, Luke.... All we have is today. One precious day at a time. She clung to the hope that she could live with that. She couldn't deny that her own fear had taken over as she'd watched Luke turn and walk away. She knew in that moment that life with Luke was an all-or-nothing proposition. And walking away was no longer an option.

"My ears are burning." Luke's voice relayed between Calli and Jon as the two exchanged glances.

"Afternoon, Dad. I'm going to shower." Luke pivoted to let Jon squeeze through the doorway.

"What's your hurry? You two planning some sort of conspiracy?"

"Nothing. Just talking."

Luke looked suspiciously at Calli. "Trying to figure out how to convince me to spring for dinner after all?"

Calli felt her insides warm and her fear dissolve. "That goes without saying. After all, you won the bet."

He smiled. "Excuse me, but I did win the bet, which means you fix dinner. So if that wasn't it, what *were* you two talking about?"

"What's wrong? Afraid I might be finding out some of *your* secrets for a change?"

"No way. Jon's been well trained."

The blanket was bunched in her hands as she paused midway through folding it. She quirked her eyebrows, gently teasing him. "Had a lot of practice at new girlfriends, has he?"

"Depends on who you talk to. According to Tom—not enough. According to me—too many."

Calli finished folding the blanket and set it at the foot of the bed and took two tentative steps toward Luke. "What does Jon think?"

"He doesn't get attached. Self-preservation."

"I don't know if that's good or bad. Did he get attached to someone?" Calli saw his expression soften as he watched her with a keenly observant eye. The magnetism of his gaze drew her closer.

He paused, tipping his head as he shrugged. "He was pretty young, seems to have come through it okay. Maybe you'd like to take care of that, once and for all."

This time, when Luke invited her into his heart, she took that perilous leap of faith. She lifted her trembling hands to take his. Luke pulled her close and wrapped his arms around Calli.

The water turned on, and Jon started singing obnoxiously loud.

Tucked comfortably in Luke's embrace, Calli felt Luke's smile against her cheek and the rumble of his laughter as he drew her closer. Their lips met and his kiss sang through her veins.

Later that day, Luke slammed his fist on the captain's desk.

"Settle down, Luke." Captain MacIntosh handed Luke a printed report. "It started with some spray paint incident. Rizzo was arrested last night, claims you had some connection to his arrest. I don't take kindly to threats toward my officers. I want you off the streets for a few days.''

''You've got to be kidding me. You're not going to let that scum run the precinct.''

''Come on, Northrup, you know me better than that. A couple of days of low-profile duty won't drive you to insanity, much as you'd like to argue that point.'' Captain MacIntosh informed Luke of related cases, and handed him another list. ''We need to inform the store manager and find out which employees may be involved. Think you can handle that?''

Calli was at the top of the list. He'd handle it.

''You putting a man at the store?''

Mac ignored the question. ''It's just for a few days, Luke. I don't want the streets to become a war zone.''

''Come on, Mac!'' He felt the blood surge to his brain.

His commanders' voice grew louder, while he continued to ignore Luke's protests. ''You might want to suggest that the store offer a few weeks' vacation to the involved employees.'' With a threat of suggestion, the commander added, ''A permanent transfer might not be a bad idea, either.'' The captain stood; a calm sense of authority overcame Luke. He may as well resign himself to the order.

Luke stalked out of the commander's office, mumbling.

''Northrup, be careful out there. Remember, you're on the list, too!''

An hour later, Luke was discussing the situation with the manager of the store.

Luke made note of the conversation on his daily log. His next stop was Calli's. In the lobby he studied the locks then rang the intercom.

''Hello.''

"It's Luke." In the lobby, fake ferns hung above the table with a chair on each side. Mailboxes graced one wall and the mirrored walls in the background gave the lobby that seventies feel.

There was a long hesitation before she responded. "Come on up."

"I planned on it," he mumbled. Luke prayed that, for once, Calli Giovanni wouldn't argue with him. "God, help me to get through to her."

She was waiting with the door open when he exited the elevator. When she saw the uniform, Calli's huge eyes doubled in size.

Calli watched Luke approach, his commanding presence evident with each step. Luke created a powerful image. From the navy blue of his uniform, to the belt full of gear and his own dark coloring.

She looked at the uniform again, then into his green eyes, hoping to find comfort from the Luke she had come to love. "Hi. What's up?" She'd been both cautious and lucky since getting her vehicle back from the repair shop. Cautious not to express her pleasure with the *new* color, and lucky to catch herself before inviting Luke to assess the beautiful results. After all these months she'd finally relaxed. There was no way he could have figured out that she was A.C.

"This is official." He followed her into the room, closed the door behind him and motioned to her to have a chair.

"I could tell." Her heart pounded against her chest. "I don't take bad news sitting down. Just spit it out."

The radio squelched and Luke adjusted the volume without a hesitation in his conversation. "Taylor's death wasn't an accident."

She watched the painful play of emotions possess him.

"I'm sorry." Calli fought the selfish sense of relief washed through her. Relief that it hadn't been Luke.

"The rear of the store is full of graffiti. We made one arrest and the kid is making threats. Is this why they were harrassing you the other day?"

Calli nodded. "But they have no reason to blame me. I didn't tell anyone."

Merely hearing the gang's name bristled her anger. Taking a deep breath, she hoped he missed her reaction.

"Don't pretend you don't understand, Calli. You're in danger."

Calli walked to the sliding door, looking at the lights of the troubled city. "I'm a realist, Northrup. I've accepted the risks."

"Good. Because reality isn't always pretty."

She leaned her forehead against the cold glass. When would this end? She'd finally found a man with integrity, and every time she turned around, they were being pulled apart. She was trying, really trying to listen to His plans, His instructions, and still felt under attack.

"I love this—a realist and a pessimist. We don't stand a chance."

"We just have to be cautious." Luke's voice was calm and reassuring.

"I know, but I still worry about you."

He stepped behind her and whispered in her ear, "My number-one priority each day is to make it home to Jon. Now I have you, too. Don't worry. I'm always careful. Remember that arrogance we cops have will bring me home at night."

Calli turned and wrapped her arms around him. "Promise me tomorrow, Luke."

He lifted her chin and placed a gentle kiss on her lips.

"I promise. Stay home tonight. Don't make me worry about *you*."

A chill went up her spine as Calli looked him in the eye. *Sometimes, I feel like you know all my secrets, Lucas Northrup.* "I didn't have any plans tonight."

"Good. And it goes without saying, don't let just anyone in."

"Is that an order?" Calli smiled.

Luke didn't. "It most certainly is. May I call you when I get home in the morning?"

She realized she didn't mind the order at all. And definitely didn't mind the love that was behind the order. Calli was afraid to admit how much she respected this man, and afraid not to. "You'd better."

He hugged her closer, and she felt the bulky bulletproof vest that was a vital part of him, just as vital, she realized, as his attitude and determination. She watched him walk out the door with tears in her eyes. "Please, God, if you're going to make me fall in love with a cop, give him enough arrogance to keep him alive."

Chapter Seventeen

After his shift ended, Luke went to Calli's apartment again. Warning Calli wasn't enough, he had to make sure she was safe. He approached the lobby of her apartment building and jiggled the locked inner door. After slipping his driver's license into the gap, it opened right up. "Just as I figured."

He rode the elevator to the third floor, then knocked on her door. There was no answer.

A woman with a tiny baby and toddler walked past, the woman eyeing him warily.

After the elevator doors closed behind the trio, he knocked again, louder this time. Fear began to churn in his stomach. *I should have done this last night.* Finally she answered, eyes sleepy and hair disheveled.

"Luke. What are you doing here? How did you get in the lobby doors?"

"Close your door and lock it. I want to check it out."

Calli yawned and brushed the hair from her face. "What?" He held up his license and waited as she followed his instructions. "It won't work. I've already tried," she said as she closed the door.

A minute later, Luke stepped into her apartment without any problems.

Calli stood there, blank, amazed and very shaken. "So what's your point? I can't keep you out of my life, or what?" Her tone turned very chilly for a woman who had just the night before asked him to give her a promise.

"Sit down, Cal. We need to talk."

She hesitated, then threw back her head and placed her hands on her hips. "If you think you can barge into my apartment and start ordering me around, think again. No one has the right to scare me like this."

Luke crossed his arms in front of him and nodded. "You're right. No one has that right."

"What are you talking about?"

"Somebody left a message painted on the store's parking lot."

Calli slowly sat on the sofa. Her body stiffened.

Luke squatted in front of her, resting his rump on his heels. "They've made more threats."

Fear showed in her eyes, though she tried to cover it. "Since last night? What kind of threats? What does that have to do with me?"

"You may have forgotten that scene I interrupted at the store, but I haven't. I want you to pack a few things and disappear for a while."

She sighed. "That was nothing."

He reached up and held her face between his strong hands. "Did you hear what I said? Your life is in danger."

Every nerve in her body fought her attraction to Luke. She twisted out of his hold and stood motionless. "I heard you. Did they threaten *me?*"

"Not by name, but we do have to take precautions."

"I'll be fine, Luke. I know how to take care of myself."

Calli proceeded to rattle off a list of precautions she'd already taken, including the key episode they'd argued over just a few days ago. "I'll be fine right here."

In place of a response, Luke gave her a look of disbelief, which she totally ignored. She then turned her back to him. He had to give her credit—she was holding up just fine. He watched the way she moved. Confident, determined, obstinate. Yet her strength did nothing to lessen her femininity.

"Besides," she added, "even if I do need to take precautions I'm not going to involve you and Jon. I've gotten myself into this...."

He pulled a ratty blue bandanna out of his pocket and tossed it to Calli. "I found this next to your car about four o'clock this morning. Is it yours?"

"They've tagged me? How could they? I'm careful, Luke."

"All it takes is one person sitting in the parking lot watching."

From the look of panic in her eyes, she was beginning to understand.

"Now, will you go pack a few things, please? We'll check your apartment occasionally to see if they press the issue."

Her face turned ashen. "But Luke..."

He lifted her chin and kissed her gently. "Ask questions while you're packing, Calli. You're the cautious one. For once, be cautious when it's necessary."

"Where are you taking me?" He could see ideas racing through her mind at lightning speed.

He shook his head, totally exasperated with Calli's

stubbornness. "You can stay with Jon and me. I don't want to endanger your family, or Hanna, or anyone else. I want to keep an eye on you myself."

"Oh, Luke. No."

Luke took hold of her hand. In one fluid motion, he stood, pulling her up with him. "Oh, yes, Calli. I have enough to worry about without you arguing with me. Let's boogie. We don't have all day. Be sure to take any valuables you have."

"I just have a few pieces of my grandmother's jewelry, I'll take it with me."

She packed a suitcase while Luke made sure the windows were locked. He looked around the cozy apartment with curiosity, trying to picture her dolls and cutesy things in his apartment. He chuckled. Jon would think his father had totally lost his mind. He picked up the rag doll she'd called Bessie, and tucked it in the crook of his arm. "From the looks of you, Bessie, you must have a lot of stories to tell about Calli."

Just as he said it, Calli walked up behind him and snatched the doll. "And she's not telling *you* any of them."

"Then I guess I'll have to find another way to get answers about you, huh?"

She tossed the doll into the cradle, and headed for the door. Luke again tucked the doll under his arm and followed Calli. She headed toward her car.

"Where are you going?"

"I'll follow you over. I need my own transportation."

He looked at her, ready to argue, then reconsidered. "Let me have it checked out first. They'll bring it over later."

He stepped up next to her, took the suitcase from her hand and firmly escorted her to his car. "Get in."

Calli couldn't miss the concern in his voice. He closed the door behind her.

He put her luggage into the trunk and slammed it closed. They drove in silence. As the sun rose, smog blanketed the city in an eerie glow.

"The store manager called after you left last night." Though Luke didn't comment, she knew from the smug look on his face that her assumption was correct. "You must have been very convincing. He tried to put me on mandatory leave until further notice."

"Tried?"

"I agreed to a change of schedule and a week's vacation."

He glanced at her from the corner of his eye. "I must not have been all that convincing then, because I pushed for a transfer."

She was flattered that he was truly worried about her. "He suggested it, but I'm planning to go back to school this fall. No need bothering everyone with a transfer if I'll be quitting anyway. It's time I get that last semester out of the way."

"You quit one semester before graduating?"

Calli swallowed the lump in her throat, praying for the courage to open up to him. "My brother died unexpectedly, and I just couldn't pull myself together in time to study for finals."

He let up on the accelerator. "I'm sorry."

"Me, too."

"That would do it, for sure."

She straightened her shoulders, refusing to let the past continue to pull her down. "I can do all things through Him who strengthens me." *I can do this.* "And now it's time to get on with my life." Calli reached for his hand.

"For the first time in three years, I have something to look forward to. So what do you have in mind?"

"Uh," Luke stammered. "Uh, in mind."

"The threats," she said, grinning. Knowing she had flustered him for a change gave her immeasurable satisfaction. "You do have a plan, don't you?"

He nodded, seeming to pull himself back to the business at hand. "When I told the captain about Tiger and his boys harassing you at the store, and me stepping in at the wrong time, he suggested I take a few days off, as well."

Calli was speechless. *Good thing he doesn't know about A.C., or he'd really be worried.*

Pulling up to the red light, Luke handed her a set of keys. "This is for the outer doors. This is to our apartment." He shot her a wary glance. "Ours, as in Jon's and mine, I mean."

Calli lifted her eyebrows. *I don't think I'd better tease him about that one. We're already walking a very fine line. And I'd better find a better solution to my safety— soon.*

"You have to lift the doorknob slightly to turn it."

"Extra security, I suppose."

"No, a royal pain. No one's getting past these locks unless they're authorized." He drove down a long cement ramp and pressed a lever. "Another pain, but under the circumstances, the precaution is necessary."

The garage entry was cold and dingy compared to the rest of the building, yet she had to admit, the place even felt more secure. It was just another reminder of the danger he, too, lived with each day.

They again took the elevator, and Calli remembered the kiss he'd given her right in this elevator. She wondered if he remembered it, too. He opened the apartment door and Calli felt an instantaneous discomfort, carrying a suitcase into a single man's apartment.

"Good morning, Marge. I'd like you to meet Calli Giovanni. There have been some gang-related threats, so she's going to stay with us for a while."

"Hello, Calli. It's nice to meet you, though I wish it had been under better circumstances."

Everything in black and white, down to the detail. He took her suitcase and set it along the wall. "Could we get another set of keys? I gave her my spare set."

"Of course. If you need anything, Calli, our apartment is the first door to the right of the lobby."

"Thank you, but I don't plan to be here very long. Since I'm on vacation now, I'll be glad to stay with Jon."

"If you'd like, Marge, take a few days off, then. I'll get in touch with you when this is over."

"That's fine. Call if you need me," Marge said. After an update on Jon, Mrs. Maloney left.

Luke's low voice was a little awkward as he showed Calli to the extra bedroom. "I'll clear out a couple of drawers for you. We'll have to wash the sheets. Marge sleeps in here when I work swing or graveyards."

"Why are you doing this, Luke? I could find some-where else. I could…"

"Do you really have to ask?"

She fought the dynamic presence he exuded. She wasn't ready to hear his feelings. Wasn't ready to face her own. His professional instincts seemed to cross that invisible line and read her thoughts.

"I'd like to talk to your parents, let them know you're here, and why."

"No." A sensation of nausea and desolation swept over her. "I don't want to worry them."

"That's why I want to explain the situation. If they

call and you're never home, well I don't want them to think anything is going on here. I don't want you to think so, either, Calli. I want you safe, that's it.''

There are no shades of gray, are there, Luke? Calli turned away, hoping the emotions he stirred would eventually settle to a dull ache. ''I'll explain it to them when I'm ready.''

His expression turned grim as he watched her move her suitcase to the bed. ''Feel free to make yourself comfortable here. Do what you want with the room. I know you'll want some space to yourself.''

''Thank you, but I don't plan to be here that long.''

The disappointment she saw in his eyes spoke volumes, and she was surprised to find her own instincts working on him.

''Yeah. I suppose you're right. I'm going to finish moving this stuff into my room. If you need anything, let me know.''

He walked into the next room, and Calli wondered how she was going to survive this. They had the entire day together. Several days together from the sound of things. At least there was only a few more days of school. Then Jon would be here to act as a buffer, or at least a distraction.

She noticed that Luke had carefully set Bessie on the pillow, and she hugged the doll to her chest. ''Luke?''

''Yeah?'' He came into the room for another load of clothes, then went back to his own while she followed.

Hearing his deep voice so near was comforting, she couldn't deny that. But she couldn't hide forever. Not from her feelings nor her past. And she couldn't inflict them upon Luke and his son. Jon needed his father, now more than ever. She didn't want to distract Luke and certainly didn't want Jon to feel she was here to keep tabs on him.

She rounded the corner to his room and watched Luke arrange his shirts in the oak dresser drawer. "How will Jon feel about all of this? He still seems upset about Nancy. I don't want to add to that. This should be time for you two to be together."

With his back to her, Luke placed his hands in his pockets. "I hope he'll do fine. Besides, I want the two of you to get to know each other."

"Are you going to tell him about the threats?" She narrowed her eyes in speculation.

"I don't lie to him—about anything." He turned to face her. "I won't lie to you, either, Calli. I'm worried. The Eastsiders are ticked off at something, or someone."

"How do you look these kids in the eyes, knowing what they're capable of?"

"They're lost kids who want rules. And they want someone to care enough to enforce them."

"I've noticed, they *love* rules."

"I never said they wouldn't push their limits, just to see if you have the backbone to stand up to them. Once you do, the majority of them will respect that. The rest, well, they get attention however they can." Luke packed the last of his clothes into the drawer and placed an arm around her shoulder, leading her to the living room.

"But they make victims of innocent people. I don't understand how can you overlook that." Frustration and confusion had given her a headache and she rubbed her temples to ease the pain.

He sat on the sofa and pulled her close. "Who said anything about overlooking anything? It's the same as when God disciplines us. We know His laws. Because we're human, we're going to sin, and there are going to be consequences. It would be nice if we learned the first time, but most of us don't.'' His gentle gaze was full of understanding. "We all make mistakes, but we still have to pay the consequences.''

She felt both disturbed and comforted by his tone. Once again, she found herself wondering if he suspected she was A.C. "I know that. I just don't know how to make them right again.''

He kissed her, and all of her loneliness and confusion welded into one swell of yearning. "When you're ready, remember, I'm here.''

Tears welled in her eyes, and Calli buried her head in the hollow of his neck, absorbing his strength. She had seen too much, witnessed too many painful scenes and lost everyone that had ever meant anything to her.

Yet sharing them with Luke could cost her more than her peace. She could lose the only hope she had.

The deep timbre of Luke's voice vibrated in her ear. "Father, be with Calli today, help her to fight the invisible battles that wage a very real war within her. King David claims the Lord is close to the brokenhearted and saves those who are crushed in spirit.'' He paused, running his fingers through her hair. "We know that the battle must be fought, but must rest assured that the victory is already ours. Amen. I love you, Calli.''

"I love you, Luke.''

Chapter Eighteen

Luke's phone rang and Calli stared at it as if she'd never seen one before. Luke was taking Jon to school. She looked around to see if he had an answering machine, feeling somehow obligated to answer if not. She jumped when the lock rattled on the door behind her.

Luke barrelled through the door and grabbed the receiver. Calli returned to the kitchen and wiped the counters, feeling strangely unlike a guest.

The low tone of Luke's voice made Calli hesitant to pass through the living room to go into hers. It was obviously a private conversation. Trapped, she dried the dishes, found where most of them belonged, then knelt in front of the opened refrigerator to take inventory.

"You hiding?"

She looked up at him leaning over the door, suddenly feeling terribly awkward being alone with him. "I didn't want to interrupt your phone call, so I thought I'd…I could…I was…"

He smiled up, the refrigerator door separating them.

"It was just something to keep me busy. I wouldn't presume to guess what you and Jon like to eat."

"If it's edible, we like it." Luke pushed the door closed, easing her out of the way. He poured himself a cup of coffee. "Would you like some?"

She shook her head. "You just got off work. Won't that keep you awake?"

"Better now than tonight. Since I won't be working for nearly a week, I'd best change my schedule now. If I nap now I'll be up all night. Since we have the day together, why don't we do some shopping? As you can see, the fridge is empty."

The thought of going to her grocery store brought a chill to her today, yet she couldn't admit to Luke that she was afraid of returning. Not after the brave front she'd put up earlier.

"Maybe we could check out the stores on the south side. We can grab a bite to eat and make it home before Jon is out of school. That call was Jon's mother, I could use some advice, from a unbiased party."

"And you think that's me?" She smiled. "You'd better think again."

"From a female perspective, then."

"That, I can handle."

They headed south out of the city. Luke clipped his pager to his belt and set the volume. "Nancy's coming to stay with her parents for the last few weeks of her recuperation. She wants to spend time with Jon."

Calli studied Luke as he stated the facts then waited for her response. Reading his emotions was impossible, his police training was so ingrained into his character. "And you want me to tell you…what?"

He looked at her slyly. "Very clever. What did you say your major was? Psychology?"

"Almost. Education." She looked out the window to the mountains in the west, then back to Luke. "Why don't you start with the benefits."

He grimaced. "Ouch. You go for the jugular."

"Get the pain over with early."

Luke shared his reluctance to believe Nancy could really stick around, and his relief that she finally wanted to know their son. After a short list of "hopeful" benefits, Luke and Calli discussed the drawbacks, which boiled down to one thing—Luke was afraid Jon would end up hurt if his mother changed her mind again.

"How do you convince a child to give his mother another chance?"

Calli remained quiet. She wasn't the person to ask about second chances. She thought of her own parents and the many times they had asked her forgiveness. The worst part was, she now realized that it wasn't them that should have been asking. It was her that needed to ask their forgiveness.

"Calli?"

"If it helps any, you've already convinced one child— me." Her voice broke as she struggled with the admission. "After my brother's death, my parents grieved and moved on with their lives. Because I couldn't, they had to make a painful choice. And I'm ashamed to admit, I still haven't asked them to forgive me for holding it against them."

He took her hand and apologized. "I just keep saying the wrong thing, don't I?"

"No, not at all. I'd say God brought us together for a lot of reasons. Thank you."

"You're welcome. Let's pray Jon experiences the same change of heart that you have. It would sure make this dad's job a lot easier." He smiled confidently.

"Nancy's getting into town late next week. I asked her to let me talk to him this weekend. Jon and I have plans to go to my parent's cabin. You will come with us, won't you?"

Luke turned into a shopping center and parked the car while Calli struggled with his invitation. "I've already intruded on you and Jon. I can go to Hanna's for the weekend."

"Jon's not the only one whose feelings matter here, Calli. While I won't say that I've always let him have his say when it comes to my relationships, well, this time our instincts match pretty well."

"And I pass the test?"

Luke leaned across the console between their seats. "With flying colors. I'm crazy about you, and so is Jon."

Calli laughed. "I guess we'd better keep the weekend in mind when we're shopping, then, hadn't we?"

The next few days went quickly. Jon finished the school year while Luke spent the time off catching up with odd jobs he'd let slip past. They had Tom and Vanessa over for dinner one evening. Calli let Hanna know where she was staying in case her parents did happen to call. And she and Luke checked her apartment daily. So far, there was no sign of trouble.

Luke was asked to return to work early because of the holiday weekend. After his shift was over Monday morning, they planned to head for the hills.

"Dad, where are my new jeans?" Jon's voice cracked, and Calli grinned, remembering her brothers' voices changing.

Calli zipped her own suitcase closed. "Were those the one's in the laundry, Jon?"

There was an uncomfortable silence followed by a sarcastic response. His behavior had progressively worsened in the past week.

She took a deep breath, trying not to let his attitude feed her guilty conscience. "Check the top of your dresser. Unless I put them in the wrong pile, they should be there."

There was a long silence followed by Jon's sarcastic response. "Thanks, Calli. I'm not used to having the laundry folded."

Luke stepped around the corner from his room. "You don't have to let her know all of our bad habits, Jon." He winked to Calli and smiled slowly. "I could get very used to this," he said quietly.

"I'll warn you, I'm only this efficient when I'm on vacation."

"That's a relief. These two bachelors might go into shock." He smiled, then called out over his shoulder, purposefully trying to lighten the mood, "My bag is ready. I'll be home around eight in the morning and we'll load up and leave."

"Don't you want to get some sleep first?" Calli stepped into his open arms, becoming increasingly comfortable with their closeness.

"You'd better not be late or Calli and I'll leave without you," Jon warned.

Luke laughed. "Does that answer your question?"

Calli gazed into his eyes and shrugged. "Be careful out there, Luke."

"I'm always careful. You and Jon take it easy. Don't let his attitude bother you. He's just anxious to get away." He kissed her cheek, whispering into her ear. "I love you."

She smiled. "I could get very used to *that*. I love you,

too." Calli felt a tug on her heart as he walked out the door. *Take care of him, Father.*

Later that evening Jon answered the phone, then stomped into Calli's bedroom where she was reading. "Did Dad tell you that Nancy's coming to visit?"

Calli swallowed hard, determined to avoid the question. "What did your mother say?"

"She told me she wants to see me. When I told her we were leaving tomorrow, she was in a hurry to get off the phone. Why didn't Dad tell me?"

Nancy must have not realized Luke's weekend wasn't the traditional Saturday and Sunday. "He must have wanted to tell you about it at the cabin."

Jon stared at her, his confusion obviously simmering. He dropped onto the sofa and pouted. "Why does she have to come here now?"

There was an awkward silence between them. "I went for almost a year without talking to my parents once." She set the photo frame back on the shelf and sat in Luke's recliner. "That first visit was really tough. It still isn't easy to talk to them. It's going to take time."

"I don't need her," he snapped.

Calli recognized Jon's anger all too well. "We can't ever have enough people who care about us, even if we don't *need* them."

"She doesn't care about me."

"She obviously does, or she wouldn't be coming." This conversation was supposed to be between Luke and his son, not her. "Why don't you talk to your dad about it in the morning?"

"I can't talk to him about *her.* He has enough to worry about without my mom showing up. Do you really think he knows already?"

He called her "my mom." He's making progress,

whether he'll admit it or not. Calli nodded. "Maybe your mother has realized that she made a mistake, and wants to…"

"She can't take me from Dad."

Calli shook her head, trying to calm his unspoken fears. "I'm sure she knows that. After her accident, she may have figured out that time is too short.…" Calli felt her own regrets of letting time slip away without telling her parents of her love and regret. "Give it a try, Jon. Your dad wants you to have the chance to know Nancy. To have some relationship with her, whatever that turns out to be. It's really okay."

"She's not cool like you."

Her heart swelled. "You don't know her well enough to say that. She's probably as scared as you are about getting together."

"Then why does she keep calling? Why doesn't she just leave Dad and I alone? We've done fine without her." Jon took an envelope from the end table and started tearing it into bits.

More and more, Jon reminded her of her brother Mike. She hadn't wanted to get into this conversation with him, but now she felt good that he'd confided in her. As she searched for the right response to his anger, she hoped she'd helped him sort things out. She knew talking to him about Nancy had helped her.

"Listen, Jon, have you ever had a friend hurt you, and you just keep thinking that if you keep trying harder, one day he'll like you again and won't hurt you anymore?"

Jon's eyes grew huge as he nodded.

"It isn't easy to keep trying to make amends when someone keeps saying and doing things that hurt. But when they come back again and again, I'd guess your friendship means an awful lot in order for that person to face the constant rejection.''

Calli wanted the impossible: to take Jon into her arms and soothe his pain, erase his confusion and tell him everything would be okay.

Chapter Nineteen

No sooner had they finished unloading Calli's SUV than Jon was ready to vacation. "Let's go fishing, Dad. I already got the canoe out."

Jon had ignored Calli all morning. *What in the world is wrong with you, Jon?*

"Later, Jon. I've got to get a little shut-eye. The three of us can go this afternoon." Luke picked up the cooler and took it down the short flight of stairs and began unloading the food into the refrigerator.

Calli was right—he and Jon needed time to let down. Next week he was going to have his evaluation for his promotion, and he and Jon hadn't even talked about Nancy's wish to be part of his life again. Like Calli, Luke had noticed his son's moodiness in recent weeks.

Mumbling, Jon disappeared through the front door, and Luke immediately stepped outside. "Don't leave the property, Jon." He dug three lounge chairs from the shed and opened them on the deck. He took a deep breath of fresh mountain air. "Have a seat, Cal."

"I thought I'd unpack. You go ahead and rest. Where do you want me to put my things?"

He led her up to the second level. "Jon and I'll share the bedroom, if you don't mind. It has a bigger bed. You can have the loft." Luke lifted her bag over the rail and motioned for her to climb up. She expected him to follow, but he stayed below. The room was hot and stuffy.

There were only five rungs on the ladder, and the ceiling in her room was, at its highest point, barely five foot high, causing her to hunch over when she stood. "I doubt you even fit up here, do you?"

"I haven't tried recently. Obviously, no one spends much more time than sleeping up there. You may not want to open the window now. When the afternoon sun hits, it'll be unbearable up here."

"Do you and Jon come to the cabin very often?"

"Every month or so we squeeze in a couple of days. When Mom and Dad bought it, they picked one that was close so all of us could use it as much as possible. Between the five families, it's rarely empty. We're going to add on in the back this summer. All of us kids are paying for the renovation. We'd like everyone to be able to come at the same time."

The concept of an entire family working on one project overwhelmed her. Her own family was scattered now, and barely kept in touch. Of her siblings, she was the nearest in proximity to her parents, and the furthest emotionally.

Calli gazed at Luke, who had folded his hands together, and leaned his arms on the loft floor. Pretty soon, his chin was rested on his hands and his eyelids closed. She knelt down next to him and whispered, "Luke, go to bed."

He jolted up and shook his head. "I'm going to nap

on the deck, enjoy this fresh air. Why don't you join me?''

"What about Jon?''

"He'll be okay. He knows there will be consequences if he doesn't stay close. It isn't your job to keep track of him. You could put your swimsuit on and sunbathe while I nap if you'd like.''

Calli laughed. "I didn't bring my swimsuit. You didn't tell me there was a pool.''

He grinned mischievously despite his droopy eyelids. "I didn't? Sorry. It's near the entrance to the development. There's a swimming pool, weight room and a clubhouse that we rent when the whole family comes at the same time. We had Christmas here once. If that wasn't crazy!''

She giggled at his sleepy babbling.

He was fighting to keep his eyes open, let alone stay in an upright position. Luke lifted his pointer finger and motioned for her to come closer.

When she did, he patted the carpeted floor for her to sit on the floor of the loft. Luke took hold of her hands and pulled her off. A moment later, she was wrapped in his long arms. She smelled the mingled scents of soap and his spicy aftershave. He locked his hands behind her and leaned back to look her in the eyes.

His gaze searched her face, as if reading into her thoughts.

"Just one more thing, this is supposed to be a relaxing weekend. Time to forget all the trouble at home. That's the one rule to this cabin. It's a retreat. There's *no* discussion of problems or work here.''

Calli swallowed. "Nothing?''

"I want us to have fun. And that's an order.''

"Yes, sir." *I guess that means no sharing secrets, either.*

He placed one hand on the middle of her back and pulled her toward him. "Have I told you that you're an answer to my prayer, Calli Giovanni?"

"You asked for me?" She lifted her hand to his cheek and admired his green eyes. She saw loneliness and love waiting for the right person to share his pain. Despite her fears she smiled. "Could've fooled me. You didn't even know which name to ask for."

"Calandre or Calli, somehow God knew just who I was missing in my life."

Luke looked at Calli and saw doubt behind her mask of caution. During a recent Bible study, he'd come across a verse in Proverbs. "A good wife who can find? She is far more precious than jewels. The heart of her husband trusts in her, and he will have no lack in gain."

Had he found the woman God had planned just for him? There had been others that he had once believed to be God's choice, but in the end, had been merely a distraction. Calli could certainly be distracting, but more than anything, she was a friend.

Calli lifted her chin and kissed him lightly. "Get some sleep, Luke. Jon's going to be bounding in here ready to go, and you won't have even closed your eyes."

He listened to her soft voice and wanted to ignore the advice, but in the end, he gave in to her words of reason. If he held her much longer, he wouldn't want to let her go. Luke took a deep breath and blew it out. *Why did you have to make her so tempting, God?*

"You know just how to keep me in line. I'll see you later."

"Sweet dreams."

His dreams were far from sweet, and Luke woke

crankier than if he'd not slept at all. Luke jumped from the chair and tripped over Calli who was in the chair beside him. His foot caught on her chair and he dumped her next to him.

Luke stared into her dark eyes, panting as if he'd just run for his life. "You must have been having quite a nightmare."

"You're okay?" Luke furrowed his brows.

"Fine, thanks. But I'm not so sure about you." She smiled. "What happened?"

Still sprawled against the railing of the deck, he raised himself on one elbow. "I think I just met your ex-fiancé."

Her face paled and the smile disappeared. She untangled herself from him and the chair and stalked into the cabin, turning briefly. "You don't want to go there, Luke. That subject breaks 'cabin rules.'"

Luke collapsed on the warm wood deck and took a deep breath of the thin mountain air. He closed his eyes. Whatever this man did, he'd left quite a scar to heal. *You sure I'm the right man for this job, God?*

He heard a rustling in the trees and peered through the slats on the railing. Tiptoeing through the woods, Jon was soaked from head to toe and shivering in his boots.

Without a word, Luke went to the back door and waited until Jon slid the door open. "Don't even think of coming in here in that condition."

Jon jumped. "But I'm cold."

"Not half as cold as you're going to be. Weren't you told to stay here?" The voice was that of a cop—stern with no vestige of sympathy.

"You said on the property."

"Have our property lines moved, Jon? It's always

meant *our* property, not the development's, and don't pretend that's what you thought."

Jon was quiet and stood with his arms around himself. "Can I come in *now?*"

"You know Mom doesn't let any of us step foot in here when we're dripping wet. Strip down," he said impatiently.

"But *Dad.*"

Luke followed Jon's gaze, surprised to catch a look of reprimand in Calli's dark eyes. "I'll go for a walk." After she'd pushed her way past them and hurried out the door, Luke ran his hand through his hair in frustration.

"I'll be right back with a towel. Guess you won't be going on the lake today, will you?"

"But Dad…" Jon said, removing his wet clothes.

Luke felt like a teakettle ready to boil over. "But Dad nothing, Jon. Every choice you make has consequences. You didn't follow the rules, did you?"

Jon lowered his chin to his chest in a full-grown pout. "No. But you were asleep."

"And so you went into the canoe alone? That's two rules broken, Jon. You could have been at the bottom of the lake, and I'd have been nowhere to be found." When he returned with the towel, Luke lowered his voice. "Jon, rules are rules, whether anyone is around to catch you or not. Vacation hasn't even started yet. It could be a very long summer at this rate."

Jon started to argue and Luke interrupted him. "Go shower and get warmed up." He waved his hand in a gesture of dismissal. "I'm going to catch up with Calli before she walks all the way home." His son's lanky legs shook all the way to the next room.

Luke ran up the mountain, in the same direction Calli started out. He saw her in the distance, sprinted ahead of her and turned around. "Okay, Calli, let's set things straight here. Jon was wrong, and it's my duty to discipline him." His eyes clung to hers, trying to analyze her reaction.

"Everything is black and white with you, isn't it, Luke? You didn't even listen to him. How do you know that he was going out in the canoe?" Calli walked past him without hesitation.

Arms crossed over his chest, Luke stepped in front of her. Not fond of giving the neighbors anything to gossip about, he lowered his voice. "How many thirteen-year-old boys have you raised? The canoe is gone and Jon came home soaked. He didn't fall into a mud puddle."

She deliberately invaded his space, to the point that he wanted to step back. Calli poked her finger on his sternum, and he was shocked to admit that it actually hurt. "All I'm saying is that you know he's excited for school to get out. He stretched the boundaries a little. Maybe you should listen to him. This was supposed to be a weekend for you two, Luke, and I'm in the way. He wants your attention."

He started to respond, but Calli continued.

"I had brothers, for your information, and let's just say that I gave the term 'tomboy' an all new meaning. You could have let him go. I was here, too." She reeled on, as if short-circuited, as if proving to both of them that she was immune to him. Every curve of her body screamed defiance.

Listening to her, he realized God knew exactly what he was doing, bringing Calli into his and Jon's lives. All around them the ground was turning green and wildflowers were beginning to bloom. Luke bent down and picked one. "I'm not used to sharing that responsibility. When we're with others, he knows he still answers to me. I may have been a little harsh, but thank you for not saying so in front of him. I'm sorry." He handed the yellow blossom to Calli. "I'll talk with Jon. Let's get him and go catch dinner."

She looked stunned. "Why don't you two bring dinner home? I'll make a salad and rice. Maybe you and I can go out on the lake tomorrow."

"Jon and I both need you, Calli. It doesn't bother him that you're here." He slid his arm around her waist and started walking back to the cabin.

"He's been sharing his home with this strange woman for three days, and then she horns in on his weekend with his dad. I just think he'd like time alone with you. He's not used to sharing you, either. Or is he?" Calli stopped suddenly and turned toward him, waiting for an answer.

Luke shook his head and drew Calli close. "No he's not, but he'd better get used to it. Real quick."

Two hours later, Luke and Jon came up the road with a stringer full of trout and smiles across their handsome faces. Calli nervously bit her lip. The argument with Luke that afternoon had renewed old fears and uncertainties. There was no way around it, Luke was *all* cop.

She hurried to the loft, leaving the kitchen so they could clean and prepare the fish. They had agreed to eat around six, so she had an hour to rest. The door opened and Jon called her name.

"I'm upstairs."

"You ought to see these fish! One is sixteen inches long. And it has *pink* meat. Those are the best. Dad caught one and I caught the other three of them."

"Congratulations, Jon, but I'm not good with blood. I'll enjoy eating it though."

"Okay."

Calli turned away from the railing, cherishing the comfort of their laughing voices. The sun was hot on her back and she closed her eyes. It had been years since she had felt such peace. Even at her apartment, guilt ate the comfort away. She'd come to expect herself to take care of everyone. For three years the weight on her shoulders had stripped her of her own life. With Luke around, she felt safe and loved, and at home.

Yet there was Jon. At this critical age was there any hope of the two of them forging a relationship? His mother finally wanted to know her son, and more than ever, he needed one. She knew the pressure on Luke had to be terrible.

Calli felt the tears sting her eyes. *Father, I don't know if I can be a mother to Jon. And I don't know that he can take another person leaving his life if I don't have what it takes to commit myself to them. And I couldn't bear to lose them, either.* She wiped her eyes on the pillowcase.

"In quietness and trust shall be your strength."

She sniffed. *I'm trying, God, really I am.*

"Are you okay, Calli?" Luke's hand rested on her arm.

She jumped. "I didn't hear you come upstairs."

"S.W.A.T training."

Surprised by his retort, Calli turned and looked into his green eyes, her tears turning to laughter. She wiped them away and rolled over to face Luke. He was on his knees next to the bed, a gentle smile on his unshaven face, the face she'd fallen in love with. After removing the baseball cap, his unruly hair stuck up all over. That, too, she'd come to find boyishly endearing about him.

"Why the tears?" Under his steady scrutiny, she found it impossible to sort out her thoughts.

She bit her lip and looked away. "I think it would be best if I go back home, Luke. I'll install a better lock. I'll move. I don't know what I'll do for sure, but I can't stay with you."

He leaned closer and lowered his voice. "Because of Jon?"

She nodded. "He's not ready."

"He's thirteen, Calli. He isn't an easy sale, so to speak." Luke's whisper was so low, she had to read his lips to verify what he was saying. "Don't worry about being a mother. If that's too much right now, just be his friend. He does like you."

She looked away, thinking of Mike, and the sister she hadn't been. Why would this be any different? "I don't want to let either of you down."

"He has nothing to compare a mother to. You can't let him down." Luke smiled.

That was exactly what she was worried about. Jon needed a mother, someone he could count on, someone to be there when his dad wasn't available. She didn't want to interfere with Jon's chance to start a new relationship with his mother.

She was getting attached to Jon. And there were times when she saw hesitation in Jon's expression. Like he wanted to be friends, then, realizing the risk involved, he would back away. They were spending more time together, yet she and Luke had never discussed her role with Jon. She wasn't his guardian, she wasn't his stepmother, and lately, she was beginning to wonder if she was his friend.

"I'm afraid to get close and have things not work out for us. I don't know what's bothering Jon—if it's his mom's accident, or his friends...or us. I'm afraid staying with you, even temporarily, isn't wise."

Luke's brows lifted. "Now, are you referring to Jon, or me?"

"All of us—" she turned away "—could use some space. There's a lot to consider, Luke."

His expression grew serious. "I suppose you're right. We'll talk about it later, okay? Dinner's ready." He took her hand in his and pulled her close. "Get ready for the best catch of the Rockies."

"I thought I already caught the best," she said jokingly.

Luke wore a smug grin. "Lady, that's what I've been trying to tell you for weeks now."

During dinner it was obvious that Luke and Jon hadn't talked about Nancy's impending visit. Jon looked at Calli defiantly. "Nancy called again last night. She's coming next week and wants to see us. Do I have to go with her?"

Luke choked on the French bread. How could Nancy have said anything after agreeing to let him talk to Jon this weekend? Luke looked at Calli, surprised to find her purposefully ignoring both of them.

While he and Calli had talked about Nancy and Jon, they hadn't discussed his determination to help Jon through every step of his mother's return. It was important that he encourage and support Jon throughout this adjustment. Though there was nothing left between him and Nancy, that didn't mean Calli, or Jon for that matter would understand or agree with his desire to make this work. After a long silence, both sets of eyes were fixed on his. "Yes, Jon." He could see the emotion rising in his son, and rushed on to defuse the anger before it got out of hand. "Your mother and I have hashed through a lot of things. I think it's important for both of you to give this a chance."

"You've got to be kidding. You told me…"

"I'm not going to force you. I thought we'd start by having her over for dinner, just to let you two have a chance to talk. I'll be there with you, as long as you want me to stay."

"But why do I have to do this? She's the one who dumped me."

Luke set down his fork and swallowed. "She regrets what she did. Right now, she doesn't even feel she deserves to have survived the accident. It's been a really rough few months for Nancy. She was pregnant and lost the baby. She's trying to pull herself back together."

Jon remained quiet.

Calli wiped tears from her eyes.

"I'm not asking you to do more than you're capable of. None of us are free from error. She's asked our forgiveness. Though it doesn't make up for all we went through, just knowing she wants to know her own son eases some of my pain. This could be a good thing, Jon. For all of us.

"Calli…" He glanced at his son, then into her eyes. "I didn't mean to discuss this with you right here, but now that it's over, I'm glad you heard. You may as well know how I feel. If things work out the way I hope, for all of us, this is a major issue that won't ever go away."

She looked at Jon, then back at Luke. Her gaze was gentle and understanding. "I don't feel our relationship has to change at all because of Nancy. There's room for all of us to learn how to show God's forgiveness. Like I said last night, Jon, your dad wants you to be happy. I'm sure finding out that your mom really cares about you will fill the spot inside that's always wondered."

"It does, kind of…." Jon shrugged.

"And Jon, no matter what happens, no one can take

that comfort away from you. You are loved, very much.'' She looked at Luke and the tears flowed.

She met his smile and accepted the hand he offered. He'd have never had the courage to address such an emotional subject with Jon tonight, yet Calli had barrelled right in and taken on that maternal role of making both of them face their feelings. ''Jon, all I've ever wanted is what's best for you. I think it's important for you to know your mother.''

Jon looked at Luke. ''If it's really okay with you, Dad, I'll give it a try. As long as you two will be there at first. I don't know what to say to her.''

Luke looked at Calli as she nodded. ''It's more than okay, Jon. I've prayed your mother would want to be a part of your life since the day she walked out. And don't worry, I doubt that she knows what to say to a son, either, so you're not alone. We'll work through it.''

After watching a movie, Jon went to bed, leaving Luke and Calli alone. Suddenly Luke felt as awkward as a sixteen-year-old on his first date. The earlier conversation had exposed so many emotions, he didn't quite know how to thank her for supporting him.

Seemingly unaware of the battle going on inside him, Calli gathered the popcorn bowl and glasses and headed for the kitchen. Luke took a deep breath and leaned his head back on the sofa. *Okay, Tom, I'll admit, I have it bad. Now what? I've already dropped enough bombs on her tonight.* When Calli returned, she'd changed from her shorts and T-shirt into jeans and a Colorado State University sweatshirt. Just looking at her warm clothing made him realize how cool the evening had turned.

''You want to watch another movie?'' She ran her hand through her glossy dark hair.

How could she stand there and pretend she didn't notice that he was being tormented? Trying to remind himself of the cool air outside, he cleared his throat. "Which one?"

She read the title, and he knew he was in trouble. He wasn't in any mood to watch a romantic movie with her tonight. "I'm not watching some 'chick flick,'" he grumbled.

"It's a comedy."

"It's about weddings. That's a romance. Besides that, true tomboys don't watch chick flicks, either."

"Oh, no?" She raised her eyebrows again, and a look of determination sparkled in her eyes. "Define tomboy."

He was sinking fast. "Well…" His gaze roamed from her head to her painted toenails. "Tomboys aren't beautiful. They aren't feminine."

She motioned to her shirt, then her jeans, and looked at him like he'd lost his mind. He had, and it wasn't coming back any too quickly.

"What is feminine about jeans and a baggy old sweatshirt?"

"I plead the fifth." He forced himself to look away and take a deep breath. He stood up and backed away, hoping to capture some of that cool air on the deck. "Tomorrow, I'll challenge you to the 'tomboy test.'"

Calli laughed. "The tomboy test?" She stepped closer, following him through the screen door and to the railing.

"I'll prove that you've outgrown your tomboy days." Luke pulled her into his embrace and kissed her thoroughly. "So you'd better rest up, Calandre Giovanni."

"Just what exactly is included in your little 'test'?"

"That's for me to know and you to find out."

Chapter Twenty

Calli smelled the coffee early the next morning, and peeked over the loft banister just as Luke carried his mug to the deck and quietly closed the door behind him. Enjoying the wonderful view, Calli watched as he took a long sip, then leaned his elbows on the railing and bowed his head. The muscles in his neck relaxed, and the weight seemed to left from his shoulders.

She turned away, smiling. *God, I can't begin to understand your awesome ways. But I thank you for bringing Luke into my life, for allowing me to grow and find hope again. What a precious gift you have given us. Amen.*

Though she wouldn't admit it, she had lain awake half the night wondering what in the world Luke was going to come up with for his crazy test. She'd already proven she could hold her own in class, for her size, anyway. Surely he wasn't going to put his brute strength against hers.

Calli pulled on her cutoffs and a T-shirt. After she ate a doughnut and drank some orange juice, she went outside to find Luke, and ended up hiking all over the mountain. An hour later, she still hadn't seen any sign of him and headed back. Unexpectedly winded, Calli stopped to rest against a huge boulder. Behind her she heard a rustling in the bushes.

"Luke?" *Trying to scare me, huh?* She waited a few minutes, then turned around to find a black bear sniffing her through the leaves.

Calli screamed. Too frightened to look behind her to see if the bear was following, she ran down the path. She rounded the curve and knocked Luke, Jon and herself to the ground.

Luke grabbed her, trying to calm her down as she kicked and stumbled in her feeble attempt to get back to her feet. "What's wrong?"

Jon jumped to his feet and ran on up the path. "It's just Eunice," he reported.

"Eunice?" Calli gasped. "It's a *bear!*" Calli felt the rumble of Luke's laughter as she pressed against his chest to stand up and brush herself off. She felt the sting of a scrape on her shin. She grimaced and tried to wipe the sand from the wound. "And don't you *dare* try to tell me that it's not!"

Jon returned. "You scared her off."

"Gee, too bad."

Though he tried, Luke failed to wipe the smirk off his face. "Eunice has lived here for as long as we've had the cabin. She rummages through the trash cans every morning, but never hurts anything."

He wrapped his arm around her and led her back to the cabin to clean up her leg. Calli sat on the counter by the kitchen sink, trying to get the courage to touch the washcloth to the cut.

"You want me to do that?" Luke stepped closer, reaching for the towel.

Calli pulled her hand away. "I can do it," she insisted. Thinking all night long about the endless possibilities Luke could conjure up for his ridiculous test, Calli was determined to prove she could handle a little scrape. After all, she had to do something to redeem herself—as she'd already failed miserably with her confrontation with the bear.

"You're turning white, Calli. Let me do it for you."

Refusing again, she took a deep breath and turned her attention away from the injury. Finally she lathered the soap and dabbed it onto the wound, then stuck her leg under the running tap water.

Then his warm hand held her leg still while he dabbed the raw skin with antiseptic. Calli bit down on her lower lip to muffle a groan.

"There, it's done," he said.

He carried her to the deck and set her on the lounge chair, then went back into the cabin. He returned a few minutes later with ointment, gauze and tape and applied the dressing.

"You're a good patient. Very brave," he teased her.

"Thanks. Do I get a lollipop, Doc?"

"How about a kiss?"

Their gazes met right before his lips touched hers.

She felt her cheeks regaining their color. "So far, I'm miserably failing the 'tomboy' test, aren't I?"

Jon ran up the steps to the deck. "The *what?*"

Luke lifted one eyebrow and laughed. "Calli says she's a tomboy."

"Oh." Jon turned into the cabin muttering something about being "The Hulk."

"At least he had the tact not to laugh."

Luke smiled without an ounce of regret. "One day, you'll laugh at this, too."

Calli fixed dinner for Hanna and told her all about the wonderful weekend she'd spent with Jon and Luke. About the romantic sunsets when Jon snapped pictures of her and Luke laughing in the canoe, all-day hikes and Luke's tomboy test.

"Sounds like it's getting serious. Have you told him yet about being the anonymous caller?" Hanna took another bite of crab salad and cracker.

"Do you always have to bring up the downside of everything, Hanna?" She set her fork on the edge of her ivy dish and took a sip of water.

Hanna lifted her eyebrows. "Reality check, cousin. You *are* the woman he's looking for—personally…and professionally. What do you think he's going to say when he finds out Calandre, a.k.a. Calli Giovanni, is A.C.?"

"I don't think about it anymore," she said, listening to the rumbling thunder outside. "He's not going to find out, at least not from me. I'm not patrolling—end of story." Calli opened the door to let the cool breeze inside. "I've spent months trying to put patrolling and Mike's death behind me. You were the one who talked me out of telling Luke before. Now you've changed your mind?"

"Humph. I never said that, exactly. I did say honesty was the best policy. I give up on you, girl."

After supper, she and Hanna sat down to watch the romantic comedy that Luke had refused to watch with her.

She smiled, thinking of Luke teasing her about true "tomboys" not watching "chick flicks." He claimed she must have outgrown the "tomboy" stage, and she'd spent the rest of the weekend failing to prove him wrong. Her heart swelled when she realized Luke really heard her lecture about listening to Jon. He had made a point to take time away from her to spend with his son. It was reassuring to know that Luke respected her opinion, even if he did grumble about it at first.

In the evenings, Luke and Calli had escaped to the deck to visit after Jon went to bed. They all came home happy. She and Jon had the chance to talk, hike and grow closer. She found herself wanting more then ever to reach out to kids like Jon, to make a difference.

And she and Luke came home closer than ever before.

Life was looking up. Jon was in a better mood. Calli was less stressed about letting Jon down and less pressured by their relationship. Things seemed to be going great.

After they got home from the mountains that morning, Luke and Jon immediately installed a new door and dead bolt for Calli's apartment while she was at work. The dream he had at the cabins drove him to convince the building owner to make improvements to the security system in the lobby as well.

Before Luke clocked in, he and Tom worked out together. They jogged a few laps around the indoor track then went to the weight room.

"How was the weekend?" Tom asked, as he began to lift.

"Really nice. Started out tense, but ended up great." Luke told Tom about the weekend as they moved on to the shooting range.

He thought of Vic Taylor and the threats that continued to pour into the precinct. Fifteen shots later, Luke dropped the magazine to the ground, reloaded and fired again, running around the barricades, then dropped to the prone position. Then Luke stepped to the background while Tom went through the course.

"Are you joining the racketball league this season?" Tom asked.

Luke shook his head and looked down. "I've got enough at home to keep me busy."

"I know what you mean," Tom said, then added, "Still in knots over Calli, huh?"

"There's something bothering her."

"Her?"

"Yeah, yeah, it's getting to me, too. I asked her about her ex-fiancé at the cabin, and she threw 'house rules' at me. Then I got mad at Jon, and she gave *me* grief for not listening to *him*."

Tom patted him on the back and laughed. "You'd better marry that lady so you can concentrate, bro." Tom finished and rested on the bench.

"I'm thinking about it." He watched the "I knew it" look spread across Tom's face. "Thinking seriously about it."

Luke wrapped a towel around his neck and headed upstairs to change. Tom followed close behind.

"I know she's a Christian, struggling with trust a bit, but she seems to be rooted on His word. She was upset about her taking time away from Jon and I. No matter what I said, I couldn't convince her that she's not going to let Jon down. What does concern me is that it doesn't sound like she gets along with her parents. When she came to stay with us, she refused to tell them."

Tom wiped his brow and turned into the locker room. "You blame her? Didn't you say her dad was military? She probably saved your hide, Northrup."

"Come on, Tom. It isn't like she 'moved in' with me.

I made those boundaries very clear. I just worry about who she would turn to if she needed someone. Hanna's fine, but it bothers me that she can't turn to her parents. What will she be like with Jon? And if her parents were strict, why'd she give me grief for disciplining Jon?''

Tom took a long drink at the water fountain, then slapped Luke's back. "Probably because you *didn't* listen to the kid. Sounds like maternal instincts kicking in."

"Yeah, yeah. Just wait until Jordan and Joseph are thirteen. We'll see how much guff you take off them." Luke laughed, knowing his friend's intentions were noble. Luke showered and dressed for work, ready to head to the lounge to eat his dinner before going on duty.

An ebony hand touched his shoulder. "Luke, give it to God. Hand your relationship with Calli to God."

"I have, again and again." He leaned against a locker, waiting for Tom to finish dressing. "Sometimes I wonder if this frustration isn't Him handing it back."

"So you moved her back home today?" Tom tied his boots and buckled his belt.

"New door and dead bolt are installed and painted to match the others. Jon and I did what we could on the windows and sliding door, though she's on the third floor. I have to admit, I'd still feel better with her at my place."

"I don't think this has anything to do with the East-siders. You'd better do some serious planning before you move her in this time."

Luke shot his partner a look of warning. "There was nothing going on. Nothing."

"I know that. And I for one think Calli's just what you need, along with a house, and a dog, and a few more kids." He laughed. "She needs more room than in your place."

Luke thought of the day he'd climbed up to the loft

and seen her sobbing. The fear that jolted him was something he'd never forget. He was almost relieved to hear
Calli admit she wanted more space from him. The other
part of him realized how much he liked her company.

It also made him realize he wanted her with him more,
and that installing a sturdier door and lock on her apartment was a long-term solution to a short-term problem.
He wanted her back, soon. Tom was right. He'd better
start some serious planning.

The thunderstorm arrived with a boom. Luke and Tom
ran outside to look at the sky.

"From the look of these clouds, we're in for a big
one," Tom said. "That is one cool breeze."

"In the briefing room now! We need to get out there,"
the drill commander bellowed. By the time they stocked
their bags and ran to the squad cars, the rain had turned
to hail. The wind whipped the pebbles back into the
clouds and spit them out again as stones.

They switched on the radio and listened to the weather
warnings, and Tom kept his eyes open for tornadoes. All
over the metro area, electricity was out and limbs were
ripped from the trees. Streets were flooding. It was going
to be another busy night.

Jon was at the amusement park with friends from the
Youth Group when the storm hit. The electricity flickered, sending the two miles of riverfront fun into a ter-
rifying hysteria. Rides stopped and started. Hail pounded
everyone and everything. Screams of terror took on an
all new meaning. Jon gave up trying to follow his scat-
tering group. They were to meet at the entrance at midnight, but that was three hours away, and the gates were
flooded with people trying to escape to the shelter of
their cars.

After unsuccessfully searching for his group, Jon found a phone. He called Information and asked for Calli Giovanni's phone number, relieved that she answered on the first ring. "Calli, I'm at Riverbend Amusement Park. Everything is a mess here, and I can't find my group. Could you come get me?"

"I'm not sure how long it will take, with the street flooding and downed limbs, but I'll get there as soon as I can. Is there a shelter near the entrance?"

"I'll be okay."

"Stay inside, Jon. There's another storm cell coming our way. See you soon."

He waited, keeping an eye out for his friends. Ten minutes later, they made a dash for their cars. Jon told them he had a ride on the way, and to leave without him. Luckily, none of their group was trapped on the rides. Rescuers were still struggling to free those people stuck on the rides from the threat of lightning and pummeling by golf-ball-size hail.

Calli pulled up and honked the horn. Jon ran, dodging the pounding stones, and jumped into her four-wheel-drive.

"What's going on here? Didn't they see the storm coming?"

"I guess not. I was playing a video game when it hit. Sorry about your car."

She shrugged. "Don't worry about it. I don't have a parking garage, so it was out in the weather anyway. Have you called your dad to tell him you're okay?"

He shook his head. "I'll call when I get home. I'm supposed to stop and get Mrs. Maloney when I get there."

Calli moved her purse out of his way. "There's a cellular phone under the seat. Hand it to me and I'll call him.''

''Can I do it?''

She laughed. ''Sure. Plug it into the cigarette lighter, then push the power button.''

''Will it work in this storm.''

''Should. I just used it to call help for the driver of a flooded compact car. Which reminds me, since we have to go out of our way to avoid the low underpasses anyway, I'm going to return these movies at the store. Do you mind coming with me?''

''No problem.'' The phone rang, and Jon asked to send a message to his father that he was with Calli, and they were both okay.

He told Calli about all the rides and hurt people while she drove to the market. The worst of the storm was over by the time they drove into the parking lot.

''You want to come in with me? We could get you something to eat. Then I'll take you home.''

''Sure.'' Food was always welcome.

They walked into the store and dropped the videos into the slot, then headed for the frozen pizza since the deli was closed. They checked out and got into the hail-battered vehicle.

As they drove down Columbia Boulevard, Jon noticed some of the storefronts broken. ''Did you see that?''

She looked in her rearview mirror and nodded.

''Go around the block.''

''I should get you home. Your dad's probably trying to reach you.''

''Then we should call on your phone.'' Just then Jon saw Nate and about ten other Eastsiders bashing in the storefront of an electronics store and begin loading stereos and televisions into cars. He turned as they drove by. "We have to do something."

He looked at her and wondered why she was hesitating.

A block away, Calli turned suddenly and lifted her foot from the gas. She didn't look happy. "Hand me the phone."

Chapter Twenty-One

Three days later, Calli stopped after work and bought groceries to fix dinner for Luke and Jon. Calli saw Jon enter the store, trailing behind several gang members. She looked again at her watch. School wasn't out for another hour. Careful not to draw his attention, Calli watched the group from the corner of her eye. Jon was obviously out of place with the group of hoods. He nudged a Hispanic boy and pulled him aside.

The two appeared to be disagreeing, then Jon backed away.

Calli paid for her groceries, and stalled, trying to find a way to approach him. He walked toward the door. "Hi, Jon."

He turned around, eyes wide. "Oh...um...hi."

She looked at the cart, and back to Jon. "I don't suppose you could do me a favor?"

"A favor?"

"If it wouldn't interrupt you and your friends, I could use some help getting all of these up the stairs to my apartment."

The Hispanic boy nudged Jon. "You don't have an elevator?"

"Broken. But it's okay, I'll manage."

His eyes pled with her to insist. Calli didn't know what was going on, but she didn't like the way Jon looked. "I'll see you for dinner?"

"Yeah. See you later."

The minute she got home, Calli ran to her closet and dug through the box where she'd packed away the wig and glasses she wore while patrolling. Clutching the pouch to her face, she stopped herself, reminded of her vow to commit her way to God.

"Let not your hearts be troubled: believe in God, believe also in me."

But Jon's in trouble. Calli hesitated, struggling with the temptation to handle the situation herself. *I know, God. Trust.* She closed the apartment door and tossed her pouch of makeup and the wig back into the box. *Okay, I can do this.* She walked back to the kitchen and unloaded one sack, then ran down the stairs to get another armful of groceries, determined to make herself leave it in God's hands.

When she reached the top of the stairs with the last load, she collapsed in the chair. Calli pulled out her information from the gang symposium. Flipping through the pages, she puzzled over Jon's choice of company. Reviewing the warning signs of gang involvement, Calli ruled out some signs completely, but couldn't deny there was enough reason to be concerned.

After Calli left, Jon argued with Nate again. "This isn't my scene, Nate. Yours, either. Come on, let's get home." He had to hurry home, before Calli could call his dad.

Nate pushed Jon away. "And what are we going to do, Jon, go home and baby-sit a house full of brats?"

Jon didn't know how to argue with that. He didn't know what it was like to have a brother or sister. He rarely had anyone but Nate over after school. "We can shoot some hoops or play hockey while your sister and brother play at the playground."

"It's Friday. I just want to kick back with the gang." Nate tied a blue bandanna around his shaved head and pulled it snug.

"You don't need them, and you don't need this trouble."

"If you want to wimp out, Jon, go on home to Daddy. These guys are the only friends I have who really care about me."

Nate strutted away.

"And what am I?" Torn between staying to fight for his best friend or doing what was best for himself, Jon backed out the door and ran home, tears blurring the way. He stopped in their apartment building lobby and pretended to get a drink from the water fountain, hoping to rinse the redness from his eyes.

He didn't want to tell his dad, because he would go straight to Nate's mom, and then Nate would be even madder. He wanted his best friend to trust him, to like him again. But most of all, he wanted Nate to be safe.

While he was walking toward the elevators, Jon heard his dad talking to the manager about renting a second parking place in the security garage. They already had one spot for the motorcycle and its trailer. Why was his dad wanting to pay more to put his old car in the garage now, after it was already dinged up from the hail storm? Jon went to the apartment and waited.

A few minutes later, the phone rang. Expecting Calli,

Jon snatched the phone before his dad had a chance. It was Mrs. Maloney calling to tell them she couldn't come tonight because she had the flu. Three more times the phone rang, and not once was it Calli. He began to think she might be different from his father's other girlfriends.

They were going to her house for dinner, and Jon couldn't figure out a way to convince his dad to stay home. And even if he had, what was the use? Calli was going to tell on him sooner or later. May as well get it over with. Jon started thinking about his excuse.

His dad really liked Calli. As far as he was concerned, she was all right. Calli seemed to care about him, too. The past girlfriends were always telling on him right away. But Calli was different.

They had been at her house now for two hours, and she hadn't mentioned seeing him at the store. Was she trying to make him squirm? Did she even know that Nate and the others were part of the Eastside gang? *Maybe she doesn't know who they are.* From out on the balcony, Jon could overhear Calli and his dad talking.

"Mrs. Maloney has the flu, so could you do me a favor and stay with him tonight? I know that's asking a lot…."

She looked at Jon, then his dad. "I'd be glad to, but would either of you mind if we stay here instead? That way you could go home and get some sleep before I need to go to work. I could drop Jon off at home on my way to the market in the morning."

"Is that okay with you, Jon?"

"I guess."

The three of them watched a movie together, then Luke went to work. After he was gone, Calli walked over and sat down at the other end of the sofa. There was an uncomfortable silence.

She changed the channels, then finally turned the television off. "I may be out of line here, Jon, but I would like to know what was going on this afternoon."

He shrugged. "I needed to talk to Nate."

She didn't smile or say anything for so long that he began to wonder if she'd heard him. "Does your dad know you cut classes?"

"No. Aren't you going to tell him?"

"Aren't I?" she repeated. "I guess that depends on you." She crossed her legs and swiveled toward him. "I don't want to see you get hurt. That's my first priority. If I think you're in danger, I'll talk to Luke about it."

Jon realized she knew exactly who he was with, and that coming up with some story probably wouldn't work with Calli any more than it would with his dad.

"So, why were you out of school early?"

"I told you, I needed to talk to my friend," he said, hoping she'd back off.

"How do you plan to keep your father from finding out that you missed part of the day? Did you forge Luke's name on an excuse?"

She wasn't any pushover. He nodded.

"How did you get hooked up with the Eastsiders, Jon?"

He leaned forward in his seat and opened his hands in front of him. "I'm not a member of the gang." He made the mistake of looking at her.

Her voice remained calm. "Then what are you?"

He didn't have to answer to her. She wasn't his mom—yet. "Why do you care?"

She looked sad. "Because the gangs are trouble, and I don't want to see you get hurt."

"What makes you think they'd hurt me? I told you, I'm not a member." He looked at all the dolls she had lying around, figuring someone with that many dolls would never understand guy stuff. *I hope she doesn't bring these to our house when they get married.*

"Because you were arguing with that boy. Was that Nate?"

"Yeah, so? We've been friends forever. He's not going to hurt me." He glanced at her and rolled his eyes.

She nodded. "Then why did you look concerned?"

"You sound like Dad."

Her eyebrows lifted. "I do?"

"He's always asking a hundred and one questions. If I'd known you were going to question me all night, I wouldn't have agreed to stay here. Dad could've taken me to Grammy and Gramps."

She smiled. "I am honored that you chose to stay here, but I won't ignore my concern about the kids you're hanging out with. You know they're trouble, and I hope you decide to keep your distance. I'm willing to listen, if you decide you do want to talk."

Calli told him he could watch television while she did some stuff, so he turned to the basketball game. She went to the kitchen and washed the plates and forks from the apple pie she'd made for dessert, then went down the hall to the bedroom area. Pretty soon she came back in, wearing pajamas and a housecoat. Calli reached into a basket and started stitching some towels. They talked about sports, and he was surprised that she liked to ski and play volleyball.

"Wait a minute."

Calli set the sewing in her lap and looked at him. "What?"

"You're the girl Dad met skiing, aren't you?"

She tried not to laugh. "Well, I don't know. How many times has your dad gone skiing this year?"

"Once. I gave him a ski pass for Christmas."

"Then I guess I'm guilty."

"You're the one who was hanging off the chair?"

"Guilty."

He started laughing. "Did you know Dad's afraid of heights? You're lucky to be alive." She seemed happy to be talking about his dad, as happy as his dad was when they talked about Calli.

"Your dad makes a difference in people's lives every day. I'd like to know that I made a difference in someone's life."

"Have you been married before?"

Calli shook her head. "Thankfully it broke up before that. Why?"

He shrugged. He'd be in big trouble if he told her about the ring he and his dad picked out for her just before they came over. "Just curious."

"It's nearly midnight. We'd better get some sleep. I work at eleven in the morning, so we'll need to get you home around ten. I left some extra towels in the bathroom, and if you'll move, we can put the sheets on the sofa. It pulls out to a bed." She put her needlework away and walked down the hall.

When she returned, she had an armful of pillows and blankets.

"Calli."

"Yes, Jon."

He looked at the floor. "Thanks."

Chapter Twenty-Two

Luke called the next morning when he got home from patrolling and updated her about the gang activity. Calli felt a pull to join the battle, but snuggled in her bed instead, remembering the commitment she was making—to God, to Luke and to Jon.

As Luke talked, she remembered her conversation with Jon the night before. She and Luke really needed to find a time when they could discuss parenting, and what role, if any, she should take with Jon. As Luke had admitted, he wasn't used to sharing that responsibility. For whatever reason, maybe he wanted things to stay as they were. Parenting a teenager was like walking a fine line anyway, without starting on the defensive. Yet she desperately needed reassurance that she was doing the right thing.

"You busy tomorrow night?"

Calli rolled over and curled into a ball, a smile on her face. "That depends, Officer."

"I'm only suggesting dinner. I thought I'd see if my folks could have Jon stay with them. That way we wouldn't have to worry about time. I think we're going to have a lot to talk about."

"You think so, do you?" She felt her face turn pink. "What're you up to, Northrup? I thought we were going to take some time to think about all of this."

"I guess you'd better be thinking then, because I'm ready to talk." His voice was low and husky.

She sighed. "Where are we going? How about that new café on the corner?"

"I'm talking about *dining,* Calli. As in a dress and tie."

Calli tried to moisten her rasping voice. "Luke, I think we'd better *talk* first."

"Isn't that what I just said?"

Her breathing was shallow and fast. She wasn't ready for his proposal. "Luke," she pleaded. "You didn't..."

He hesitated, and uncertainty crept into his voice. "I guess you'll just have to wait and find out."

She could tell he was tired, and she needed to fix breakfast for Jon and get ready for work. All night long, she'd wondered if Luke had learned she was the anonymous caller. If she told Luke about her patrolling now, he'd be awake and furious all day, and in no shape for work tonight. Fatigue could put his life in danger. By the time she got off work this evening, it would be time for him to report for duty.

Luke interrupted her thoughts. "Can you go to church with us in the morning?"

"Sorry, I work the early shift again tomorrow." By the time she got off, there would be no time to talk before dinner tomorrow night. She would just have to talk first.

Calli heard Jon get up and go into the bathroom. He turned on the shower and started singing. "Does Jon always sing in the shower, or is it just around me?"

"Always, but it's louder when you're around."

"I'd better get moving. What time tomorrow night?"

"Mom's fixing dinner for the family at two, so I suppose about seven. If you happen to get off early, everyone would love to meet you."

"Thanks, but I don't want to barge into your family dinner in the middle, especially the first time I'm invited. I'll talk to you at seven."

Calli hung up the phone, then let out a groan of frustration. *I have thirty-six hours to figure out how I am going to tell him.*

At the breakfast table, Calli couldn't relieve the pressure she felt sitting across from her prospective stepson. Luke said tension with the Eastsiders was stretching thin. What she did now would set the boundaries of their entire relationship.

"Jon—" Calli sighed "—I really think it would be wise for you to visit with your dad about Nate today."

The teenager shook his head. "No way. Nate would... be really mad."

She stared at him. "I know that, Jon. I also know what the Eastsiders are capable of doing. And so do you. You need to talk to someone who can help."

"I'm talking to you."

Jon looked at her with total confidence. He actually meant it. Calli swallowed. She was it. "Jon, I don't know Nate. Luke does. Nate might listen to your dad." *Welcome to parenting, Cal.*

"They already think I snitch on them. I can't, Calli."

"You know who's involved and what they're doing. You know way too much. Not to mention that your dad's a cop. Did you ever think they could be using you?"

He stared at his food. "I only went with them once. And yesterday at the store, Nate told me it was just going to be us. That's why I was mad at him. I thought we could be like we used to be, that maybe we could talk.''

Calli smiled wanly, feeling sympathy for the boy. ''I know it hurts to see him make poor decisions, Jon, but you could end up in trouble just trying to help him. Your dad works with gangs. He understands them, why they do what they do. He'll know how to help you and Nate without repercussions.''

He didn't answer.

''It's admirable to want to help someone you care about. But the problem is bigger than you are.'' Calli realized she could very well have given herself this lecture any time during the past three years, and she would have listened just about as well as Jon.

''I can handle it. I'm not going to stop until Nate's out!''

Calli saw reflections of her own stubbornness in Jon. ''Why won't you tell your dad?''

''He has enough to think about.''

Jon's compassion was inspiring. She could hardly believe he was only thirteen. Calli decided that there was no way around it—she had to be the one to try to reach Nate. ''Okay, Jon, tell me what you know about gangs.''

He thought. ''They cause trouble.''

After a long silence and deciding he didn't know more, or didn't want to elaborate, Calli responded.

''That's it in a nutshell.'' She tried to see this through Jon's eyes and saw Mike. She saw herself, in charge. Could she change the outcome this time? She had to; there was no choice. ''Do you know why kids get into gangs?''

''I used to think it was because they were bad kids, but Nate wasn't, until he started hanging out with these guys.''

"When did Nate get involved with them? Was there something stressful going on in his life?"

"I don't know."

These Northrup men were impossible. "Jon, I want to help. In order to do that, we have to know what might have made Nate turn to them. Kids that get pulled into gangs can be rich or poor, come from loving families and broken families, but the one thing that's most common is that they are hurting inside over something and they don't have anyone to turn to. The gang welcomes them, makes them feel loved. And then…"

"He's not bad!"

"I believe you. I do." *Neither was Mike.* Calli took a deep breath, groping for the words to help Jon, and Nate. *God, help me.* Calli struggled with memories, and unshed tears. She couldn't cry now, Jon needed someone to look up to as much as Nate did.

"And he has me to talk to, so that can't be it."

She knew how Jon felt. She, too, would have done anything for Mike. For three years she wondered why he had never tried to tell her what was wrong, or worse, that he had, and she didn't hear him. *Psychology 101—listen.* She waited, silently struggling with wanting to talk to Luke, to someone who could ease this pressure and guilt.

"I know what he's feeling, because my mom walked out on me when I was a baby!"

"Did that happen to Nate recently?"

"His dad left. Now he's supposed to be taking care of his little sister and brother after school while his mom works. Dad and I keep inviting Nate to do stuff, but he refuses."

"What does Nate's mom say?"

"He doesn't listen to her."

Calli felt the situation pulling her into a direction she wasn't prepared to handle.

"What about 'putting in work'? Do they drag you and Nate along?"

"I went once, because I was afraid to back away. They didn't do much, spray painted a few fences and walls. Now I don't stick around that long."

"Good. You have to leave Nate to make his own choices, Jon. If you want to talk to him here, or at home, that's different. But outside of that, steer clear. I don't know how to reach Nate. We aren't professionals. There's a local ministry we could talk to."

"You'd go with me?"

"Sure. I don't want to see anyone hurt. Maybe they can give us some ideas to help Nate."

"Us? You don't know him. Why do you care?"

"Because I don't like people hurting other people. It isn't right. If we hurry, we can go this morning." Calli made a quick phone call to the mission, then rushed through her shower and called the store to tell them she might be late.

They walked into the converted warehouse. The church looked less than spiritual. Posters of teens lined the walls. There were televisions and vending machines.

They walked past a room of young women, pregnant or holding tiny babies, apparently learning parenting skills. The kitchen was filled with teenagers studying stoves and poring over recipe books.

Hanna had told her about Pastor Ortiz, a dignified-looking man with dark hair and a friendly face. He greeted them warmly, and led them to his office, talking as they walked.

"You know as well as I do that every day we fight

battles. For some it's everyday survival. Some are invisible battles that we fight with invisible weapons.''

''Invisible weapons?''

''God's word. This battle you are fighting is very real, Jon. Indeed, it must be fought, but know that you already have the victory.'' Pastor Ortiz pulled out two chairs and sat down behind his desk.

Calli looked at the muscular man. ''I admire your efforts, but how do you work with these kids? Do you ever really 'reach' them?''

''It means digging pretty deep inside. Deeper some days than others. And I make them search, too. They need to find the desire to change before I can help them. All these kids are making that choice.''

Looking through the glass walls, Calli saw the kids' enthusiasm in the activities and knew there was still hope.

''What happens when they make the wrong choice?''

''The same that happens when the rest of us make the wrong choice—they pay the consequences. Maybe it would help you to understand if I told you that I see members of gangs as victims.''

Calli shook her head, fighting the temptation to understand. ''No, I don't think that helps.'' These were the kids that she'd spent years supposedly ''helping.'' But she hadn't helped them. Stopped them, maybe, but the mission was meeting these kids' needs. *This* was making a difference.

''Look at it this way. These kids are looking for love. For friends. They may be from broken homes, victims of physical or emotional abuse or neglect.''

Calli wanted to see the minister's point. Wanted to understand the flip side. ''I know the statistics.''

''Don't get me wrong, Miss Giovanni, I'm not approving of the negative behavior. That's why I opened these doors, to get kids off the streets and into a place where someone cares for them. Where they can try to overcome their problems.''

She wanted to believe him. Envied his generosity. Fighting the battle her way not only held no rewards, but was making no headway in the rash of gang involvement. She knew that, but it was all she could do to focus on the innocent victims. ''That's admirable.''

''And sometimes we succeed. So what can I help you with?''

''My friend's dad left, and his mom is so busy trying to work and make sure the little kids are okay, she doesn't know what Nate's really doing.''

Calli looked at the pastor, then at Jon. ''She knows he's not home. What does she think he's doing?''

''She thinks he's at my house.''

Calli touched his arm. ''Have you been covering for him?''

He looked away. ''Not since I found out how often he's with the gang, but his mom doesn't even bother to check. She believes him.''

The pastor took Jon's hand. ''You can't take responsibility, Jon. You're going to end up in the middle of a huge problem. We need to let his mother know what's going on.''

Jon shook his head. ''Nate won't listen to her. It's too late.''

''It's never too late,'' Calli said, praying that it would be true. For Jon, and Nate. For her and Luke. ''Jon, Nate knows you'll stay with him anyway. It's his parent's attention he needs. And if they don't know, they can't change.''

''I'm not going to be the snitch. I've seen what they do to snitches.'' The fear in his eyes was very real.

The pastor interrupted the duel between Calli and Jon. "I'll be glad to make a call on his mother. No one will have to know it was you that sent me."

Jon looked to her and then to the pastor and nodded. Jon wrote down the address and he and Calli went to Luke's.

When they arrived, Calli went up with Jon, just in case Luke would be awake and asking why they were late. There was a note on the table.

> Mrs. Maloney's still sick. Calli, can you pick Jon up after work today? If not, Jon, call Grammy and Gramps ASAP.
> Love you both.

"I'll see you after work. Go on in and make sure your dad's asleep." Calli waited for Jon to confirm that Luke was sleeping, then turned to leave. "And, Jon, please talk to your dad. He'll understand."

Luke leaned back in his chair, making notes on his pocket notepad while waiting for the commander to join them for the briefing. Tom repeated an address he overheard was related to one of their cases. "You think A.C. was the caller?"

Tom shrugged. "We'll check the address, make sure everything's quiet. Remind me to see if they got a trace on that cell number before we leave."

Luke closed his eyes and said a prayer.

"Hey, Fife," one of the officers bellowed, imitating Andy Griffith. Everyone looked at the sergeant entering the room. "You drop something, 'Barney'?" Bill's partner held up a shell. "Found this on the ground next to the car last night. Was that the clanging sound I heard when you cocked your shotgun last night?'' Muted laughter spread across the room. Bill turned red all the way to his necktie.

Soon everyone was poking fun.

Patricia asked if they'd had any follow-up reports on the alleged ''pool cue holdup.'' Across the room, the new recruit mumbled, ''Gimme a break. In the dark, it looked like a sawed-off shotgun.''

Luke chuckled, amazed that something so simple could relieve such insurmountable levels of stress.

The white-haired captain strolled into the room shaking his head. ''Children, children.''

Luke wiped the grin off his face, ready for the ugly side of his job to begin. Until they were home safe again, laughter wouldn't be nearly so easy to come by.

Mac continued. ''I hear love is in the air.''

Luke grinned. ''Northrup.''

He dropped the chair to all four legs. ''Yeah, Captain.''

''You have some earth-shattering news for us?''

He looked at Tom, who had a ''not me'' grin on his face.

''You'll be the second to know.''

''Keep us up-to-date on the progress of that case.'' Laughter filled the room.

Luke nodded. ''This place is worse than Aunt Nellie's gossip chain,'' he mumbled.

''*Now,* we can get on to business.'' Mac turned the page. ''There was more vandalism at the market on Columbia. Some windows busted, too.''

Luke looked up. Mac was staring right at him. ''That's right, Northrup. I should take you and Davis off the streets for a few more days.''

Calli was working this afternoon. ''Anyone hurt?''

"No injuries reported. We're not sure if it's related to the threats or not."

Luke lowered his voice. "With all due respect, Captain…"

"As I was saying, we're already shorthanded out there. So let's be careful. I don't want another officer down."

The room hushed in respect for Vic Taylor.

Tom put his hand on Luke's shoulder. "I'm sure she would have called if she needed you."

That was the real question. Did she need him? He listened in silence as the latest cases were discussed, and pushed his way through the door after roll call was over. "Let's get out there."

He made short order of inspecting the squad car and loading his gear, then got behind the wheel.

Tom closed the trunk and buckled himself in. "Guess I don't need to ask where you're headed, do I?"

Chapter Twenty-Three

Calli rushed to Luke and Jon's after work, lugging three bags of groceries and a bucket of fried chicken down the hall. She rang the buzzer and waited for Jon to open the lobby door. There was no answer. Stuffing her key ring into her pants pocket, she dug out the keys that Jon gave her that morning and searched to match the right key to the right lock. *I hope he just fell asleep, that he didn't go out with Nate.*

The elevator's slow climb gave her a chance to take a deep breath. It was a busy day complicated with the drive-by shooting at the store, a shortage of checkers and knowing she and Jon would be spending another evening together. So much seemed to ride on these first few days with him.

If she and Luke did decide to get married, her commitment would be doubled; she'd be a wife *and* a mother. Kids had always been a part of her dreams, but starting out with a teenager was far more than she expected.

More important to her at this point was earning Jon's respect. Everything with teens seemed to hinge on that.

According to her friends, kids that age rarely admitted to liking their parents' decisions, but if they listened, a parent could feel somewhat confident that they had the child's respect. She really needed to know how Luke would handle *this*.

She picked up her bags and balanced the load so she could get both locks opened.

"Jon!" She stepped into the apartment. "Jon, are you here?"

The silence grabbed her. She dropped the bags on the table. Calli ran from room to room calling his name.

He wasn't there. Remembering the police department's nonemergency number from her days patrolling, Calli dialed the precinct. "Luke Northrup. It's urgent."

"If it's an emergency, call 911."

She took a deep breath, trying to hold her patience. "No, I need to talk to Luke." She turned, frantically searching for a message from either Jon or Luke.

"Let me check his status."

Rushing through the apartment for any signs of where Jon could have gone, Calli waited for the answer on the other end. *Maybe Nancy had arrived sooner than expected…? No, she wouldn't have left with Jon without telling someone.*

"I'm sorry, miss, Officer Northrup isn't available at this time."

Without responding, she dropped the receiver onto the base and sprinted up the stairs to Nate's apartment. His mother answered her knock immediately, and seemed unconcerned that Nate hadn't told her where he and Jon were going.

Before Nate's mother could even close the door, she was gone. Calli paused at the elevator, then decided the stairs would be quicker.

"He is a shield for all those who take refuge in Him."

Please God, be with Jon and Nate. It can't happen again. I know I promised, but I have to go. I have to find them. Please. She prayed all the way to the parking garage. In the SUV, Calli dug the cellular phone from under the seat and plugged it into the car's lighter.

She tried to call Luke again, but the phone went dead. Jamming the plug into the socket, she tried again. It rang, then disconnected. She tossed the phone into the seat and pounded the steering wheel in frustration. Calli had no choice but to continue into the shadows of the city without the security of a connection to the police. Or a way to call the apartment to see if Jon had returned.

Fear consumed her, worse than ever before. She had spent three years wishing she could turn back the clock, change the outcome for Mike. All that time she'd been preparing for battle. She had a chance to make a difference.

"What would you do if you were here, Luke?" *This is no time for natural consequences. The stakes are too high already.*

She tried to remember the verse Luke and her father kept in their hearts. "'Be merciful, O God, for in thee my soul takes refuge; In the shadow of thy wings I will take refuge, till the storms of destruction pass.'" *Forgive me if I don't have it down perfect, Father.*

Calli started the truck and backed out, then stopped. She put the brake on, then jumped out and called Jon's name, hoping she was wrong. Hoping he'd just brought the trash downstairs, gone to the store...anything, except followed Nate tonight. She had to find them before either of them got hurt.

Luke's only been gone an hour. Unless someone had given them a ride, they had to be close. Getting back in the vehicle and zigzagging her way to the south, Calli checked the convenience store.

Then the sleazy café two blocks away.

Her heart raced, making the slow pursuit that much more difficult. She didn't have time to take it slow. Couldn't bear to consider the chances of missing him.

"Not Jon, too. Please God, not Jon. I can't let him down."

"He who began a good work in you will see it through to completion."

This time, there could be no peace from God's reassurance until she knew Jon was home safe. Anger welled within Calli, and she felt the pang of guilt for wishing harm to come to Tiger and the others who continued to make victims of the innocent. *They may be victims in their own way, but that doesn't give them permission to hurt others.*

"Trust me."

A group of kids congregated on the corner. After a careful search, she drove on. She checked the time. Another hour had passed. Calli quickly checked her apartment, then drove past the nearest gang hangouts. When nothing turned up, she went back to Luke's, through the puzzle of matching the right key to the right lock and finally into the apartment to see if Jon had returned yet.

There was no sign of him. She scratched a note on an envelope and not knowing where they kept the tape, set it on the table. Calli dialed the station again.

"Officer Northrup is still busy. May I take a message?"

"Yes, tell him to call Calli at 555-7995. It's an *emergency*."

Running down the stairs, she wove the keys between

her fingers. She pushed through the lobby door and turned straight into Jon, and the rest of the gang.

"This her, Jonny?" Tiger asked, yanking on Jon's arm.

Calli tried to hide her shock at seeing Jon already looking like he'd been used as a punching bag. Counting Jon, there were five of them. She presumed the other battered kid was Nate.

"No! I don't know her." Nate was silent.

Calli's gaze darted between the teens, her other hand clutching the canister of Mace.

"This is the same lady we met behind the store, isn't it, Pete? She was with you the night of the storm, too. Right, Jonny?"

"What do you want?" Calli moved her thumb to the trigger.

"We're after a snitch. And when we find her, she's dead."

She looked at Tiger. His hair was slicked back into a ponytail at the nape of his neck. Another kid wore torn jeans and a white undershirt with the sleeves rolled up.

Her heart raced, and her throat constricted. "Looks like you've already made your point. Let them go. This is between us."

"No." Jon started to protest, but Tiger pushed him to the ground.

A tough-looking gangster with a shaved head grabbed Jon by the collar, then dropped him again. "Shut up, kid."

Calli sprang forward. "He has nothing to do with this. I'm the one you're looking for."

Tiger nodded, and one of his punks shoved Calli away, but she quickly regained her balance. *A woman's best defense may be the element of surprise.* "You won't get away with this!'' Her voice was already raspy, yet Luke's advice spurred her on. Calli lunged at Tiger, using her entire body to slam him into the brick wall and jabbed the keys into his side.

"Get her off me!" he yelled.

Somebody picked her up from behind. Screaming for help, she broke her captor's hold with a kick to the knee and he dropped her to the ground.

"Stop!" Jon turned to his friend. "Nate, do something.''

Calli tried to stand, but it hurt to breathe and her legs would barely support her. She pointed the canister at Tiger and sprayed him and another kid with Mace. They both hit the ground, knocking her against something hard as they landed....

She heard voices. "Calli, wake up."

Calli realized she had passed out. Her head hurt. She opened her eyes.

"Jon? Where is he?" She rolled to her side and tried to blink away the blurry picture. "Jon?"

"Jon's right here. Lay still. Calli. George called the police.''

She looked up to the silver-haired woman staring at her. "Mrs. Maloney. Is he okay?"

Luke heard the call to a gang fight over the radio and recognized his address. He hit the light switch, flipped a U-turn and stepped on the gas.

"We were just there! How did we miss them?"

Tom picked up the mike. "Officers 1097 and 1120, E.T.A. four minutes.''

"Make that two.''

"Slow it down, Luke. It may not be them.''

Luke ignored him. It was Jon and Calli they were talking about. No way was he going to slow down. "If it is Jon and Calli, Father, take care of them."

"Amen," Tom added.

Swerving through and around traffic, Luke made it in just over two minutes. Calli's vehicle was parked right in front of the doors, as if she'd arrived in a hurry, as well.

He slammed on the brakes, and both men were out before the car stopped bouncing.

Mrs. Maloney waved her arms.

The ambulance sirens warbled to a halt. Backup officers followed.

Dodging oncoming traffic, Luke ran across the street.

Nate and Mrs. Maloney told Tom what had happened while Luke examined his son. The paramedics pushed Tom aside. Another pair of medics were treating Calli.

Luke felt the tears sting his eyes as he stood looking at Jon.

His partner touched his shoulder. "I'm sorry, Luke."

"Jon." His son was immobilized. Splints surrounded one arm, and an IV was already taped to the inside of Jon's other elbow.

Luke took a deep breath. "Jon, it's Dad. I'm here." With only a glance, he questioned the paramedic.

"Hi, Luke. This is *your* son?"

Luke nodded.

"He woke up for a few minutes. Looks like he has a broken arm, but my guess is it looks a lot worse than it is. Cuts and bruises will heal."

"I love you, Jon. We'll pull through this together." The paramedics lifted the cart into the ambulance. "I'll be right back. I want to check on Calli."

"She's about ready to go with us," the medic added.

"Good." Beads of perspiration blended with tears and dripped from his lip.

He went to the second group of paramedics. Calli's face was already swollen and bruised. "Oh, Calli. No."

"Is Jon okay?" Tears streamed down her face and she gasped for air. "I tried, Luke. There were too many of them."

Nodding, he patted her arm, and her eyes closed. He squeezed his own eyes shut and gulped air, trying to block out reality. "Thank you for trying. I love you."

The EMTs lifted the gurney and nudged Luke. "We're ready."

Luke followed them into the ambulance and offered to help. The paramedic handed him saline solution and gauze, and Luke gently washed his son's face. He spoke with barely checked anger. "Who did this, Calli?"

She answered in a suffocated whisper. "Eastsiders. And this time, Tiger isn't going free."

Chapter Twenty-Four

Luke walked into Calli's hospital room, his usually tan skin now pale, dark shadows under his eyes, his unshaven jaw tight with stress. "Jon's going to be okay. The surgery on his arm went well. It wasn't as bad as they originally thought."

"Good. The nurses kept me updated during the surgery, but I haven't heard anything since." She noted that he didn't make any effort to come closer. Try as she may, she couldn't stop the pain.

"Haven't you called Hanna?"

Calli shrugged. "She left a while ago. I didn't want her to be up all night." *And I hoped you'd be here with me.*

All along she'd been lying to herself, convincing herself that it was going to be different this time. Jon was going to make it. Her parents would finally understand. And this time, the cop would stand beside her.

She tried not to notice that Luke hadn't looked at her. Yet when he walked to the window, she couldn't ignore it. She felt that everything they had become was gone.

"Go ahead, Luke. Tell me I should have minded my own business." She refused to be intimidated. Yes, she regretted that Jon was hurt, but she knew from experience the outcome could have been so much worse. "You won't be the first."

Luke seemed to be studying the sunrise. The firm outline of his shoulders strained against his uniform and served as a painful reminder of the pressure Luke was feeling. "Why didn't you tell me?" A nerve along his jaw flinched.

Calli paused to wonder what he was asking, then decided it didn't matter anymore. It was long past time for her to tell him everything. "I tried. There wasn't time."

He turned and sat on the marbled windowsill. "How long have you known Jon was involved with the gang, Calli? One hour, two, twenty-four?" He turned his head, his gaze meeting hers. The anger in his voice turned to a tomblike silence. "And you didn't have time to tell me?"

She'd gone through everything regarding Jon a hundred times in the last few hours, and decided she couldn't have done anything differently. Except that she should have told Luke weeks ago about being the anonymous caller. She did regret that. She expected to hear Luke tell her, "It's time to face the consequences." But he just stood there in deafening silence.

Now there would be no more chances.

No more tomorrows.

"I tried to help. Jon wasn't joining, but he wouldn't give up on trying to get Nate out." She couldn't tell Luke that his son asked her *not* to tell him.

"So you put yourself right in the middle." His words were unforgiving. "Why didn't you let me handle it?" Luke's raw voice lowered, his pain excruciatingly evident with each word he spoke. "I'm his father, not to mention a cop."

"Everything happened too fast, Luke. I tried to convince him to talk to you, but Jon was afraid of the gang. I took him to the Mission to talk to Pastor Ortiz."

Luke picked up the straw from her tray and twirled it from finger to finger, pacing the room.

"I tried to call tonight, but you were on patrol. The dispatcher obviously didn't believe me when I told them it was an emergency. There wasn't time to explain."

"And look where that got you," Luke snapped.

"You can't hurt me, Officer Northrup. Three years of hearing Brad's insults reverberating in my mind have taken care of that. I knew the risks of what I was doing. I accepted them long ago."

"We're back to the jerk, huh?"

Calli swallowed the fear, denying that Luke would react like her ex-fiancé, blaming her, playing the perfect role of macho man. With quiet determination, she took a deep breath and recited her statement again. This time for Luke.

"When Jon wasn't home, I just knew he'd gone after Nate." Her mouth grew dry, her voice weakened as she now realized, she should have done more. "I had to find them, before they got hurt. As it was, I barely got there in time. With all the stress you've been under lately...I'm sorry, Luke, but I'd do it the same way in a minute."

"Who do you think you are, a psychologist?"

"It didn't take a degree to see Jon was upset. I only tried to—"

Luke pounded a fist into the foot of the mattress. "Save him? And what about Tiger? You trying to save that worthless punk, too?"

Bile rose in her throat. "Hardly."

"Oh, you *do* realize your limits, huh, tough girl?"

There was no use trying to hide her anger. "I'm not the only reason Jon was hurt. But if it wasn't for me, he could have died tonight."

He didn't argue. Luke just stood there in his filthy uniform, perspiration dotting his forehead.

Calli pulled herself to her feet and stepped closer. Luke took a step back. She followed, her blatant stare challenging him. "There *are* no limits when it comes to Tiger or any of the Eastsiders. And this time, finally, I have enough to put Tiger away. I'm the woman you've been looking for."

For a brief moment, there was an almost hopeful glint in his eyes.

She stepped past the IV pole and picked up her journal from the bedside table and held it in the air. "Three years, Luke. I've waited three years for this day."

"What are you talking about?" The lines on his forehead grew deeper. His eyes narrowed.

"Mike Giovanni. My kid brother." She swallowed the tears, and turned away from his angry stare. The words had a bite of their own. "I've spent three years trying to prove that my brother wasn't a gang member, and didn't want to be. That he was the victim. Maybe *now* someone will listen."

"Y-you," he stammered, staring at her with a look of utter disbelief, "are claiming to be the anonymous caller?"

She nodded. "Hanna brought me my journal. I finished my last entry this morning. Enter the book into your evidence, Officer Northrup. Every call is there, every step I've taken in the name of justice."

He stepped closer and closer, backing her against the

wall, the words grinding from his mouth. "It's bad enough that you used me! But you used Jon?"

Calli pushed him away. "You're the one who fell into that chairlift, Luke. I didn't even know you were a cop! And when I found out, I ran. Again and again. How many times did I tell you this wouldn't work? Did either of us have any control over falling in love?" She stared him in the eye. "I didn't tell you because I had nothing that would help."

"How do you know that?"

"Fine, Luke. Interrogate me. Ask me why there are no entries after you came to see me in the hospital, Luke."

Silence.

"I gave up my mission. For you. For Jon. For us."

Luke stepped closer, stopping just out of reach.

He shook his head. "All this time, you've been after Tiger? Why didn't you let the authorities handle it?"

"The authorities had their chance. Does the name Brad Burns tell you anything?"

Calli saw the connection being made. Luke's shoulders sagged. "That crooked cop was your fiancé?"

Calli looked away, unable to face the anger in his eyes.

"Brad determined that Mike wanted in, and the case was closed. Said there wasn't enough evidence. For three years, I've vowed not only to find my brother's killer, but to protect other innocent victims like him. Like Jon. I can't prove it, thanks to Brad discarding evidence, but I'm convinced that Tiger is responsible for my brother's death."

Luke lifted her chin and stared at her, his deep-set eyes filled with disbelief. "Why, Calli? Why didn't you tell me?"

"You showed me how to hope again…how to forgive and move on." She bit her lower lip and swallowed the lump of regret in her throat before continuing. "I was afraid I'd lose you."

Luke turned around and took several deep breaths.

"Tiger was with Jon tonight. But Jon didn't want in. I saw it in his eyes. Jon was the victim as much as I was. And if it kills me, I'll prove it. You can't stop me. I won't let Jon down, too. I've come to terms with the risks. That's something you should understand."

"I've had years of training. A few self-defense classes and seminars hardly prepare you for what's on these streets."

"Don't, Luke. I've made a difference and you've said so. Only, you didn't know it was me. But of course that alone changes everything, doesn't it?"

"It sure does. Everything."

"Check your records, Luke. I stopped patrolling the night of my accident—the night we met." Derision and sympathy mingled in his glare. He didn't seem in the mood to test her. Probably for the best, she decided. It had been a long night, and she was out of strength to fight anyone.

What she wanted, she couldn't have. Support. Luke and Jon. A family.

Tears fought for release—finally. After years of none, all she wanted tonight was to cry, to let it all out in Luke's embrace. To be held and comforted. Yet she had to remain strong for a while longer. She couldn't break down now.

Disappointment consumed her. She'd thought Luke was different. That he'd support her efforts. That he'd understand her need to protect her brother's reputation, her family name, as well as other innocent victims.

Calli walked to the window and heard Luke leave the room and the door close slowly behind him.

Chapter Twenty-Five

〜

"Luke, you've been up all night. Go home. We'll stay here with Jon. You have to get some rest." Luke gazed at his parents. His father's eyes looked tired. He had called them right after signing the waiver for his son's surgery.

"I can't go until Jon wakes up. I have to see that he's okay." Hunched over in the chair, Luke rested his head in his hands, noting the bloodstains on his uniform. Calli's blood.

"You're going to fall out of the chair, Luke. Don't they have someplace you can lie down? We'll call you when Jon wakes up." His mother rubbed his back, and he thought of the night he heard about Vic Taylor and Calli had been the one to ease his tension.

He hadn't been able to tell his parents the role that she played in all of this. Tonight he didn't have the energy.

He fought to understand Calli's reasoning. And soon the entire precinct would know, would think that he knew all along. *How could she have kept it a secret for five months?*

His father cleared his throat. "Is Calli doing okay?"

Luke nodded, too choked up to speak. He didn't know how to feel: betrayed, grateful or angry. Today he'd been planning to propose. They were going to have talked, and he'd hoped she would agree to be his wife. Now he couldn't help but wonder if she would have ever told him.

The nurse walked in, carrying the journal Calli had offered. "Miss Giovanni asked me to give this to you." She shrugged her shoulders and handed it to Luke.

"What's that?" Joan Northrup's brown hair still looked elegant, even after spending the night in the hospital waiting room.

He set it aside and ran his hand through his hair. "I'll look at it later."

"Luke? What's going on?" His father's voice held the same depth and authority that Luke had learned to rely on and respect.

He looked into his father's steely eyes. If anyone would understand Luke's struggle, it was him. "Mom, could Dad and I talk alone for a while?"

"I'd like to hear this, too."

Knowing there were no secrets between his parents, he almost felt asking her to leave was useless. "It's work related. And I don't think I'm ready to hear the emotional side of it quite yet, but I'm sure after Dad fills you in, you'll get your say."

"Just so I do. I think I'll go check on Calli. What room is she in?" His mother raised her eyebrows, waiting for him to protest. Luke didn't have the energy.

"Room 382." Once his mother was gone, Luke inhaled deep. He was sick of this antiseptic stench. He leaned back in the chair and folded his arms across his chest. "She didn't just happen upon the fight, Dad. Calli is the anonymous caller."

There was a moment of silence. "Your Calli has been cleaning up our streets? She's the superwoman we read about in the papers? Why didn't you tell me?" His father was acting like she was a national hero.

"I just found out tonight. They were waiting for her, Dad. They used Jon." Luke explained everything. He voiced his pain, and his doubts, and the love that felt like it had just been stabbed to death. Without trust, was there anything to build on? He longed for a relationship like his parents, where there were no such things as secrets.

"I'm not excusing what she did, but after being betrayed by Burns, it's no less than a miracle she's on the law's side at all."

"I know that. And I am grateful that she saved Jon's life. I'm just not so sure…"

"Marriage is forever, Luke. Good, bad and ugly times all go together. And I can guarantee you, a cop's marriage will suffer more than the average share of hard times. You'd better be more than sure this time."

Luke nodded.

"There will come a time, Luke, when you'll be ready to work through this. A marriage can't survive without forgiveness."

"It can't survive without trust and honesty, either," he said bitterly.

"Trust is built when we can face one another with forgiveness in our hearts. It's easier to be honest when you've built a foundation on trust and forgiveness. None of us could forgive if He had not first forgiven us."

"But you and Mom don't keep secrets. I don't know if I can deal with that. How can I be sure there aren't others?"

His father chuckled. "That has to be worked through together. When I worked undercover, there were plenty of secrets. It wore on our marriage. But our love was stronger than our differences."

Luke said nothing. His father offered again to let him go home, but he refused.

His parents went home to get some rest so they could stay later when Luke would consent to take a break.

Jon stirred but didn't wake. There was barely an inch of his face that wasn't battered and bruised. Mesmerized by the rhythm of the IV, Luke watched the liquid drip to the tubing and into his son's arm.

You've seen me through thirteen years of parenting, Lord. I could use another dose of reassurance right now. I know You're here, that You were with Calli and Jon last night. Help all of us to work through this.

While Jon slept, Luke read from the journal.

Two hours later, Luke put it down. Reading it had left him emotionally exhausted and mad enough to spit nails. There were several times Calli had taken on situations that were much too risky for a civilian.

In one entry, she'd written that when the police didn't arrive in time, she chased a thief away, preventing him from driving off in an expensive sports car.

Reading accounts of her state of emotions that first year after her brother's death, Luke had to admit he was touched at the tenacity she possessed. Included were details of her spiritual battle and her determination to protect the innocent. He closed his eyes, wiping the moisture from them.

"How's it going, partner?"

Luke jumped. "Do you really have to ask?" He filled Tom in on the surgery, his recovery and Calli's announcement.

Tom looked at Luke, yet remained quiet.

Luke looked Tom in the eye, reading the turmoil reflected in his eyes. "You know?"

"She told me when I took her statement last night. She asked me to let her tell you. I had to tell Mac, but no one else knows. For her protection, I'm not sure anyone else should know." Tom looked him in the eyes. "How are you doing with this?"

Luke started pacing. "Not good." He looked at his partner and motioned to the table. "Have you read any of the journal?"

His partner shook his head. "She wasn't finished. I told her I'd pick it up today."

"It's right there. Take it. It's frightening to see the risks she took. We were this close to catching her—" Luke held up his hand, measuring an inch with his thumb and finger "—dozens of times."

"You've read all of it?"

Luke nodded, struggling to keep the anger from his voice. "I can't believe it. The blonde I ran off the road, the voice I memorized, her determination. It was all right in front of me the whole time! Talk about love being blind. She played me for the perfect fool. But what really makes me mad is that she used Jon."

"You don't really believe that, do you? Come on, Luke."

Luke sat and crossed his ankle over the opposite knee. "Stay on the case, Tom. I want it handled right. I don't want Tiger to walk this time."

"It's by the book, so you'd best stay as far away as you can. Calli's pressing charges."

He nodded. "I never doubted that."

There was a groan from the bed. Luke looked at Jon,

who was fighting to wake up. "Jon. How are you doing? Tom, go get a nurse."

Jon mumbled, then ran his tongue along his lip. "Drink." As Luke helped him get a sip of water, he remembered the first time he and Calli met. Thought of the way her helplessness had lured him back to her again and again in the last five months. *Helpless? What a joke!*

Jon squirmed, then mumbled, "Dad, this isn't Calli's fault. How is she?"

Luke hated to admit that he hadn't been to see her in hours. "Not much better off than you. No broken bones, otherwise, you could be twins."

Jon twitched as the nurse checked his pulse and eyes, then jotted notes on his chart.

"You're doing fine," she told him.

Ignoring the nurse, Jon concentrated on his dad and Tom. "And Nate? Is he okay?"

Tom nodded dubiously. "He's at the juvenile center. A little beaten up, but nothing like you two. He's the one that ran into the apartment building to call for help. We arrested Tiger and two others in the park. All three are in jail."

Luke looked to Tom. "You sure they're the ones?"

"As sure as we can be until the blood tests are in. Calli marked them up pretty well. Can you believe she carries that triple-action Mace that dyes the suspect? I'd hate to surprise that lady in a dark alley." Luke heard the respect in his partner's voice.

"I'm sorry, Dad. This is my fault. I should have listened to Calli. I'm so sorry."

He kissed his son and straightened the sheets. "I am, too, Jon. I should have paid more attention."

"Luke, do you mind if I take Jon's statement now, while it's fresh on his mind?"

With a nod of permission, Tom pulled his recorder from his pocket and set it on the table, then pulled a form from his clipboard.

After Luke heard his son's version, the struggle was even worse. He knew he shouldn't be so angry, that he should be grateful, that he should thank Calli again for risking her own life for his son. He couldn't.

His partner told Jon to get better. He then put his supplies away and turned to leave. Luke followed him into the hall and handed him the journal. Just thinking of what she'd been through in the last three years, his eyes misted over. "Here's everything you ever wanted to know about the Eastsiders."

Without hesitation, Tom gave Luke a quick embrace. "Let us take care of this, Luke. You have other places to put your energy right now."

As the morning progressed, his fellow officers stopped by to give their support and assure Luke and Jon that nothing would slip through the judicial cracks on this case. Everyone was behind him.

Jon was asleep again, and this time when his parents offered to stay so he could go home and sleep, Luke accepted.

Unable to face the front doors where the attack had taken place, Luke entered through the parking garage and dragged himself into the apartment. First thing he found was the note she'd left on the table. The groceries she'd dumped on the kitchen floor greeted him, as well as a bucket of fried chicken for her and Jon's dinner.

He ignored all of it and went straight to the shower hoping the steaming water would pound the tension from his muscles and wash away the tears. Afterward, he called Nancy to update her on Jon's condition.

Despite the seemingly overwhelming support for Calli's courage, Luke could only concentrate on her betrayal and the five months that she hadn't told him the truth. Her comments came back to haunt him over and again as he tried to sleep. *"I'm attracted to men who are completely wrong for me... Keep it platonic... We have nothing in common."*

He recalled his prayers to find A.C. "Well, I've got to hand it to You, God, You led me right to her. Now what am I supposed to do?"

He slept, then woke, feeling rested, but still bothered by the pressing need to deal with this new list of problems. He wanted to be with Calli, to pretend this had never happened. The pain was too fresh. How could he trust her again?

Luke knew he should talk to Nate's mother, then decided he couldn't face her yet. Right now he was too angry. Because of Nate, Jon and Calli were in the hospital and lucky to be alive. He couldn't place all of the blame on her or Nate, he realized. If he had been paying more attention to *his* son, he may have noticed what Calli obviously saw happening. Then again, if Calli had told him what was happening, he may have been able to avoid the entire situation.

Luke went into the kitchen and put the groceries away, then took the chicken to the trash dump down the hall. He walked in the kitchen and again saw Calli's name on the scrap of paper. He thought back, trying to remember the exact time he and Tom left the station to look for her. Looking at the time she put on her note, he realized they must have just missed each other.

She had tried to call right away. Had wasted no time in looking for Jon. Put her own safety last. Which was exactly what he would have done. With startling clarity,

Luke recalled the nightmare he had at the cabin a few days earlier, and closed his eyes. "It's over."

Luke pulled a black T-shirt over his head and thought of Calli. *"You see everything in black and white, I see life in shades of gray…"* How could he turn his back on her now, after all she'd been through?

After straightening the apartment, he stopped at Teddy's restaurant for a burrito and went to spend the evening with Jon.

Luke walked into his son's room, glad to see him sitting up.

An honest attempt at a smile appeared on his son's face. "Hi, Dad. Calli came to see me this afternoon. She was on her way home. She said she's staying with Hanna for a few days."

Luke bit his lip to stifle his disappointment at missing her. "Was her cousin with her?"

"No, I think it was her parents. Her dad's even bigger than Gramps. Grammy says you didn't go see Calli today." From his son's animated conversation, Luke guessed Jon was feeling much better.

As his son again repeated every minute detail, trying to work through the trauma, Luke was unable to put Calli's courage out of his mind. Jon had fought for his friend and Calli had fought for them both.

Though Jon was still peaked and dozed off and on, he was talking constantly when he was awake. Much more like Jon's true nature than the quiet, troubled teen who had been lurking in their home recently.

"Dad? Why didn't you go see Calli?"

"I went to see her first thing after your surgery."

"But not later. Calli says you're pretty mad at her, that she should have told you something sooner."

"She tell you what that was?"

"No."

He switched the television to a baseball game, then turned the TV off and leaned his head against the back of the chair. "Yeah, she should have told me sooner. And she should have told me about you and the gang. Calli is the anonymous caller we've been trying to find."

"I said I'm sorry. And I know Calli is, too. I apologized to her this afternoon."

He held his son's hand. "I hope you've learned from this mistake."

Jon nodded.

Luke longed to hold Calli, to reassure her as he did the first night he learned about the threats. Her words still pulled at his heart. *"Promise me tomorrow, Luke,"* she'd said. *"I just don't know, Calli."*

Luke shook the memory away and looked at his son.

"We all make mistakes, Dad. You say that all the time. You're still going to give her the ring, aren't you?"

Chapter Twenty-Six

Calli's parents had arrived just in time to take her home from the hospital. Driving through the familiar neighborhood, she realized she couldn't return to her place. The memories of her painful journey would always haunt her there.

The time had come to start over. No more working at the grocery store. No more patrolling. Her mission was over. Successful or not, she had done all she could.

Hanna insisted Calli stay with her until she decided what she was going to do. Her parents immediately moved her few belongings into the empty basement of her cousin's new house.

What now, God? There's a whole world of possibilities, but You know my heart's desire. You obviously brought me through last night when I couldn't have stood alone. I'll trust You to show me Your plan.

Calli found Hanna's Bible the next afternoon while Hanna and her parents were cleaning her apartment. She hesitated, then picked it up. *I really blew it this time, God.*

As Calli studied His word, she realized that He had tried to prepare her for this. Warned her all along of the trials that would test her faith. Right now, she felt she had failed. Succumbed to temptation. *What other choice did I have? I couldn't turn my back on Jon.*

Calli fell asleep on the sofa, and woke to her parents' laughing. *What is there to laugh about?* Pulling an extra pillow over her head, she admitted that she wasn't even sure she wanted them here. They'd been very polite, but the closeness was gone. She didn't feel she had or she ever could live up to their expectations.

"We have some dinner ready, sweetheart. Do you feel like joining us?" Calli's mother was the same after all these years—quiet and strong. Her mother's emotions were never exposed. *The perfect military wife. Strong and silent.*

Rolling over was still a struggle, and pain throbbed in her lower back. Every part of her body ached. Her face was purple. She didn't want *anyone* to see her like this.

"No, thanks, Mom."

"I'll bring it in here then. We can eat together."

"Is everything out of the apartment?"

"Everything." There was a pause, and her mother returned. "I thought this might help."

Calli opened her eye and felt a tear form. Then another, until she couldn't see. It didn't matter now. It was long past time to have a good cleansing cry.

"Bessie," Calli said, straightening the handmade overalls her mother had sewn twenty years ago for her "tomboy" doll. Her mother placed the doll beside Calli and kissed her cheek before she left the room.

She remembered Luke talking to her lifetime friend, then tucking Bessie in his arm, caring enough to make

Calli comfortable. "I'm so sorry, Luke." The tears over-flowed like a creek in the spring.

The next day her father helped Calli up and insisted she get some sunshine. After helping her into the chaise longue, he took hold of her hand. "I haven't told you how proud I am that you stood up for Jon, Calli."

Despite his words, she felt empty. "Anyone would have done that."

"You'd be very disappointed to know how many people turn their heads and walk away. For three years I've been telling you to do just that. I'm sorry, Calli. I just wish you'd have gone to the academy and joined the force. It's not too late, you know."

"I *don't* want to be a cop, Daddy. I felt guilty. I was mad. By the end of those three years, I wanted vengeance. Patrolling was my cowardly way to get even with the criminals, gangs, the Brads of the world. They hurt others, I wanted them to pay. Whether or not it did any good, who knows? I don't even know if justice was served. Standing up for Jon is the only thing I've done worth remembering in three years."

"That's not so, Calli." He reached to the table and picked up his well-worn Bible. "God uses each of us in so many ways. You faced your fears each time you went out there. What may have been a gentle reminder to one person may have saved another person's life. Like that boy who was hurt at the apartments. Because you got there when you did, he's okay today."

Calli didn't look at it that way any longer. Seeing the price Jon had paid, she realized her reasons were no longer justifiable. She closed her eyes to the bright sunshine and warmth, regretting her stubbornness, and that it had brought pain to Luke, and also his son.

"And there were countless others. Your motives may

have started as vengeance, or justice—it doesn't really matter. In your heart, you were doing it to protect others. There's nothing to be ashamed of.''

''You really think so?''

''I do.'' He leaned over and gave Calli a hug.

My daddy is proud of me. Thank you for renewing our relationship, God.

Seemingly oblivious to her momentary escape, her father read, '''And after you have suffered a little while, the God of all grace, who has called you to His eternal glory in Christ will Himself restore, establish, and strengthen you.' Calandre, a warrior's battle is never won, and trust me, the way isn't easy. We're tested each day. And I'm very thankful you're okay.''

''If you call this okay.'' She grinned, longingly remembering the night Luke walked into her hospital room and asked if she was okay. ''You and Luke would have gotten along great. You're so much alike.''

''Don't give up on him yet, honey. Ask your mother. Our type can be pretty bull-headed. Sometimes takes a two-by-four to open our eyes.''

''And once in a while, it takes the whole tree trunk,'' Catherine Giovanni said as she carried three glasses of lemonade into the yard. ''But once he gets the idea, it's there to stay.''

''I'm not like you, Mom. I'm not patient, and quiet and…silent.''

''Well, sweetie, this is one time you'd better practice a bit of all of them. Because if Luke is like your father, it could take him a while to realize what he's lost.''

Calli unpacked a few of her necessities, wary of completely ''moving in'' until she'd found another job. She and Hanna were getting along fine, her bruises were going away and she was doing everything she could around the house to take her mind off Luke.

She'd hurt him, and there was nothing that could erase that pain. For him, or herself. The emptiness spread like the stifling smog along the Rockies, leaving her in a bleak existence. Tom had called earlier in the day to ask her a few more questions, and reported that Jon was getting better every day. Apparently, Luke felt the same way as she did about leaving the city and had started to look for a house in the suburbs where he and Jon could start over.

Before Luke went to the hospital to take Jon home, he stopped at the station. The commander confirmed that Luke could have whatever time he needed to take care of Jon. He suggested Luke consider a desk position when he completed his requirements for lieutenant, which would be as soon as Luke felt up to the evaluation.

"I probably blew all hopes of a promotion last night. I heard my address, and knew. I should have taken my badge off."

"You did just what any of us would have under similar circumstances. I'm just glad you stayed with Jon instead of going out there looking for the suspects." The commander raised his glasses to his forehead and rubbed his eyes.

"I'm sure you're right, Mac."

"Don't worry, Luke, no one's going to question your integrity on this." With a fatherly look of warning, Mac added, "Just don't give in to the temptation to stick your nose into this case. You want to know anything, you ask me. As for A.C.—Calli—we both know she didn't do anything illegal. And thanks to her, we may have broken up the Eastsiders. No leaders, no gang. We have our work cut out for us to keep it from gaining power again."

"What are the charges?"

"I think the list would be shorter to say what can't we charge them with. For starters, since Calli's come forward, we can also hit them with intimidating a witness."

"She's quite the hero, isn't she?" Luke said cynically.

Mac patted Luke's back. "I know it hurts." He stepped closer and rested his hand on Luke's shoulder. "Father God, provide Luke with the discernment to know the plans You have for his future with Calli. Give him the strength to help his family to recover from this tragedy. Help him to be an understanding father and have the integrity to be a forgiving husband. Amen." He lifted his head and winked to Luke.

"You think we have what it takes do you?"

"Any woman who'd go though that for my kid, I'd be a fool to walk away from, Northrup. Think about it."

After Jon was home and asleep in bed, Luke thumbed through the pictures that Jon had taken of him and Calli in the canoe. He understood her pain, her fears, her drive to find her brother's killer.

If he took himself out of the picture, he could even understand why she'd been afraid to tell him. Everyone else she'd known and loved had left when they could no longer deal with her obsession to find the person responsible.

And now he knew firsthand the anger that had driven her. It was the same emotion that consumed him after Jon and Calli's beatings. Right after it happened, his professional oath could have easily been set aside. The cop in him had wanted nothing more than to take this matter into his own hands. To solve this case himself. He'd wanted justice, without the judge, jury or anyone else. Just himself and Tiger, face-to-face.

He couldn't begin to understand the depth of his anger and pain those first few hours. He was extremely grateful that the greater fear was Jon's health, that God held him at his son's side where he was forced to deal with his emotions face-to-face.

Those two days in the hospital he'd prayed more than he thought was possible. Prayers of thanks. Prayers for Jon, and Calli, and the wisdom to make the right decisions.

Nancy arrived and came directly from the airport to see Jon. After a successful dinner, Nancy asked Jon if he would like to spend a few days with her family. Jon's answer was an immediate "Yes!"

The anger had forced him to come to terms with his own mortality. Coming home to an empty apartment made him face what his life would be without Jon. Without Calli.

He realized that he could turn his back on his love, like Nancy had Jon, but everything he believed said to forgive. "Seventy times seven times. Forever."

Jon agreed to look for a new school to attend the coming fall. They decided to find a house away from the hub of the city. After Jon's recovery would be complete, Luke's convictions would take him back to the precinct. He was a cop.

Luke was faced with the woman he loved, and how to win her back. How to ask her forgiveness. How to offer his own. The world was no longer black and white, but a million shades of gray.

The phone rang. He answered.

"Dad?"

"Yeah, Jon. How are you doing?"

"Okay. Nan…Mom and I had a talk about what happened. And I don't know…'' The silence reverberated through the wires.

''You don't know what, Jon? Whatever it is, we'll work through it.'' He and Jon were working hard to establish trust in each other again. Luke knew the next few months were going to be challenging, with moving and making new friends.

''I don't think I ever told you how great I think Calli is. I mean…''

Luke smiled. He knew Jon and Calli were right together from the start. And for a while, he began to worry that Jon was his main reason for wanting her so much. Thankfully, that fear quickly subsided as they'd become better friends. ''Are you trying to tell me how stupid I am to let her go?''

''She fought for me, Dad.''

''I know, Jon. And for the record, I agree with you. If she'll give me another chance, I plan to ask for her forgiveness.''

''Is that all?''

Luke chuckled. ''Is that from your mouth, or your grandmother's?''

''Gee, Dad, you think I'm blind? I'm sorry I messed things up for you guys.'' Luke stared at the photo of them canoeing. He'd had a copy framed for each of them.

''Don't even think that, Jon. You said it yourself. You and Calli have settled things between you.''

''Thanks, Dad. And thanks for letting me come here.''

''You have a good time. Just remember, lots of rest. Okay?'' His son had a lot of adjusting to do this summer. They all did.

''Dad, I'm fine,'' Jon moaned. ''Anyway, are you going to go see Calli? Maybe ask her to dinner at the apartment so you can talk. You should fix her your barbecued ribs and coleslaw.''

''Ribs?''

''Sure, you know, kinda symbolic, like God taking one of Adam's ribs to create Eve.''

''Enough, Jon. I'll handle the details.''

His son laughed. ''G'night, Dad.''

''Night, Jon. I love you.'' Luke hung up the phone, torn between missing his smart-mouthed son and laughing at the accuracy of his analogy.

Yeah, he'd blown it with Calli. He hadn't talked to her since that night in the hospital, but offering himself to her on a platter seemed a bit much. Then again…

Chapter Twenty-Seven

"**D**ress casual," Luke had said. "Just in case dinner gets messy." *Forever the pessimist, Luke*. Calli's heart hadn't slowed down since she got the phone call.

She checked her watch again, having to hold her hand still, it was shaking so much. Never had she been so nervous to go out to dinner with anyone.

"Settle down, Calli. I'm not going to yell at him," her father said, sounding stern instead of comforting.

"Easy for you to say." Never had she had so much riding on one night, she realized. Never had she felt for anyone the way she did Luke. Never had ten days gone so slowly.

The doorbell rang, and Calli swallowed hard. Luke had never picked her up for a date before. Come to think of it, they'd never had an "official" date before. She wasn't sure this would qualify, either, since she refused to go to a restaurant or movie. Her bruises were uglier than they had been that first day, minus the swelling. Green and yellow and brown weren't her favorite colors, especially now. Though the makeup helped in one way, in others it made her look even worse.

She opened the door and struggled to get words from her mouth. Trouble was, it wasn't emotion choking her up. Luke stood in the doorway looking taller and more rugged than ever. His beard was a day or two old, just like the day they'd met at the ski slope. His black jeans and buffalo plaid shirt were boldly telling her she was about to be courted as never before.

"Hi," she gasped. She remembered the first time he'd worn the shirt. She'd teased him about the black and white checks being his true nature. He'd argued that there was no gray in his line of work. She'd said there were gray shadows all around them. He'd missed the point.

"That's it? I was hoping for this wildly romantic reunion, and you whisper, 'Hi.'"

She managed a small, tentative smile. "You flustered me." Luke laughed, just as she hoped he would. Calli stepped back to let him in.

"I know the feeling." His smile broadened and Calli felt herself relax.

She turned to her father and made introductions. While the two men visited, Calli called her mother to come meet him. After a few minutes of conversation, her father excused them. "I'm sure you two have plenty to talk about. We can visit later."

Calli gave him a quick hug. "Thank you, Daddy, for everything." She hugged her mother and turned to Luke. "I'm ready."

Luke turned to her parents. "Thank you for being here for Calli this week. I won't keep her out too late tonight."

"Luke, there are no hard feelings about this. You had your son to care for, and we were here for Calli. I'd have been more upset if you'd have rushed right back without taking the time to think everything through.''

"Thank you, sir. I'll take good care of her.''

"Have a nice evening.''

Luke helped Calli into the car and closed the door for her. He climbed in and leaned over to kiss her.

"I'm truly sorry for everything, Luke.''

His finger lifted her mouth to his lips. "You're forgiven,'' he whispered before kissing her again.

Calli asked about Jon. After answering, Luke told her they were going to his apartment for dinner and maybe a movie. "I don't know that I can go back there, Luke.''

"We'll go in through the garage, but I think you need to face your fears. I just thought we could talk easier here. If you get tired, you can go lie down.'' He reached over and took her hand in his. "I'll be right here for you.''

They walked into the elevator and Luke wrapped his arms tenderly around her waist. "Does this hurt your back?''

"No.'' Calli closed her eyes then dropped her head against his chest and ran her fingers along the squares of his shirt, not feeling anything except his warm embrace.

He placed a gentle kiss on her forehead and released his hold and she backed away. "I found those gray areas.'' One by one, he pointed to the gray checks on his shirt, then stepped closer.

Tears filled her eyes.

"You were right, Cal, they were there all along. I never noticed. There are probably some more that I haven't found yet. Maybe you could point them out.''

"I'm not chasing shadows anymore.''

"Even if you were, that's okay by me. We can use all the help we can get out there.''

She shook her head. "I'm breaking out of that trap. I'll leave the bad guys up to the pros."

"We all have to face our fears."

"Don't worry, Northrup. I'm still facing my fears. Right now." She wanted Luke to take her in his arms again. Even with the pain, she longed for the security of his embrace.

"I'm sorry I didn't come back to see you, Calli. There's no other way to say it besides I was a coward. You were so independent and brave to go out there alone, night after night, fighting back. I didn't want to understand, but I do now. I see your shadows, and I want to share them. I don't want you chasing them alone."

Luke wanted to heal the hurts that kept Calli from him, though he knew he didn't have that power. But he sure wasn't going to walk away. That was just what she expected him to do, because everyone else in her life had given up on her.

They went into his apartment and sat down. Luke brought out some chips and dip and sodas. "Are you comfortable?"

She nodded unconvincingly.

"Calli?"

She nibbled her lip, avoiding his gaze. Luke knelt next to her and lifted her chin. She closed her eyes. A single tear escaped, yet she refused to give in and let herself cry.

"Let it go. Let your tears wash away the pain. Don't let the guilt crush you any longer."

She gasped for breath. "I can't." She shook her head. "I have to be strong."

"God gave you tears, and He gave you me. Trust me, Calli." He brushed the wisp of hair from her eyes. "You don't have to take care of everyone and everything all by yourself. Let me share your pain.'' His hand gingerly touched her face and wiped the tear from her eye.

"I should have told you…"

"You were right where God needed you, all along." Luke smiled. "I love you, Calli. I need you. Jon needs you." He looked deep into her eyes, his gaze soothing her soul. "Don't you see?"

Tears flowed freely, and Luke sat next to her, then wrapped her in his arms. "I don't know what I'd do without you, Luke." He felt her body relax and tears drip on his shoulder. "I was so afraid you wouldn't call."

"I did, though. You'd do just fine, honey, but I don't want you to have to face anything alone again."

"No, I wouldn't. I'd quit praying, Luke. I didn't think He was listening anymore. Nothing was going right." She inhaled quickly, then babbled on and on. He couldn't understand her words anymore.

Luke closed his eyes, sending a silent prayer upward before speaking. "Being submissive is the *real* challenge."

Calli pushed herself away.

Luke had a grin on his face. "Don't go getting all riled up here, Calli."

"Then I think you'd better start explaining yourself, Lucas Northrup. That sounds a bit domineering."

"We need to give control to Him. We're told not to worry, to give our troubles to Him. That goes against our instinct. Submission is trusting."

"I've tried. Really, I have."

Luke found his fingers in her hair. "I'm not criticizing you. I'm the same way. It wasn't until I came to terms with being a single father and quit trying to make a relationship where there was none that He gave me you.

And I'll admit, it's going to take some time to learn to submit myself and my responsibility for Jon to anyone else.''

She gazed at him with admiration. "Then you get two women to deal with at the same time. I take it Jon and his mother are getting along since he's staying with her family."

Luke filled her in on their meeting and Jon's eagerness to visit with Nancy's family.

"Dinner should be ready in about an hour. Why don't you lie down for a few minutes, while I get everything ready?"

She furrowed her brows at him. "Wait a minute, Northrup. One minute you're telling me to be submissive, then you start telling me what to do. Get back here. You aren't going to tease me like that, then go fix dinner."

He knelt on one leg in front of her and placed his arms on the supporting knee. "I also promised your parents that I'd take care of you, and I have every intention on spending the rest of my life doing it. Starting right now. I don't want your back to get sore and tired."

"Really? The rest of our lives?" The sparkle returned to her eyes. "It's that easy for you to forgive me, after all I did wrong?"

"Well, you still have a problem with dating a cop?"

"No."

"Still think we should keep it platonic?"

She was silent.

"Just give me your honest feelings, Cal," Luke continued.

"No," she said in the whisper he'd come to recognize as A.C.'s raspy voice.

"Please don't be afraid, Calli. I was mad and hurt. I won't deny that. But my love for you is stronger than anything the enemy can throw in our way. You are a gift from God for Jon and me." Luke pulled something from his shirt pocket and held it firmly in his hand. He looked into her eyes. They were filled with a curious and deep longing. He moved forward and kissed her, in hopes of answering her unspoken request.

"Each time I tried to refuel the anger, God had erased more and more of it, until it sunk in how many times He's forgiven me." Luke let his gaze roam, lovingly taking in the way Calli had dressed to cover her injuries. He realized she must be suffering on a hot summer day like today.

"I promise there will be no more secrets, Luke." She stared into his eyes and blushed at his loving appraisal. "What?"

"Calli, I love you. Will you be my wife?" He opened his hand, revealing a diamond surrounded by rubies. "'A good wife who can find? She is far more precious than jewels. The heart of her husband trusts in her, and he will have no lack in gain.' I'm in no position to argue with the wisdom of God."

She lowered her thick black lashes, another tear escaping from the corner of her eye. "Oh, Luke, I want nothing more than to be your wife and the mother of your children. This ring is so…awesome."

He took her hand in his and placed the ring on her finger. "Now will you lie down and rest for a few minutes? Jon planned this wonderful dinner for us, and he won't let us forget it if I chicken out."

"Chicken out?"

An hour later, Luke led Calli to the table and turned the lights out, leaving the room in candlelight shadows. Luke pulled the chair out for Calli and helped her into the cushioned seat. "I think a promise of tomorrow should start with a symbolic gesture.'' He turned to the kitchen counter and set a plate in front of Calli with a single barbecued rib on it. ''I'd give anything for you, Calli.''

The corner of her lips turned up as she held the rib in the air. ''This looks like something Jon would come up with.'' She pulled the meat from the bone and smiled. ''I didn't think your ribs were this meaty.''

''I guess you'll just have to set a wedding date so you can find out.'' Luke's chuckle was deep and tormenting.

Calli leaned over and whispered in his ear.

''Tomorrow?'' Luke said, managing no more than a hoarse whisper.

''My parents are here, your parents already have plans to take Jon to the cabin for a few days. I'm not working yet, and you have a few more days off. That way we can look for a house together. Promise me tomorrow, Luke.''

''You can have all my tomorrows, Calli. I promise.''

Epilogue

Jon braked to a stop by the emergency room entrance. Calli had called Luke at the precinct from her cellular phone and he was already waiting at the hospital. After two years of marriage, the sight of him in uniform still did make her heart beat faster. His smile was welcome reassurance. "If I'd known you were having contractions when I left for work, I wouldn't have gone."

Calli slid out of the SUV and waddled to the wheelchair. "I wasn't. My water broke a block from Jon's school. Contractions are already coming five minutes apart. Glad I wasn't the one driving through this traffic." She took a deep breath. "It's not supposed to happen this fast with a first baby."

He turned the chair around and started to close the truck door. "Jon, go ahead and move it to a parking place. I don't want to leave Calli. Be careful. We'll be on the third floor, labor rooms." His voice was amazingly calm.

"Wait, don't forget the labor bag. It's in the tr..." Calli gasped, arched her back and took a cleansing breath, clutching the arms of the chair so tightly that her knuckles turned white.

"Jon'll bring it in. I admitted you already. They're ready for us." Luke closed the door and pushed the chair up the ramp, then took the elevator to the third floor. Before they reached the labor room, Calli's breathing had become more shallow and rapid. "Slow down, honey."

"I'd love to, but I don't think the baby is crazy about the idea."

They both laughed. "I hear impatience is inherited." The irony of the statement hit him as they rushed down the hall.

The nurse helped Calli move to the bed and into a gown. "Your doctor has been called, Mrs. Northrup. How are you doing?" After all the formalities and making sure Calli was as comfortable as could be expected, she reminded them to do their breathing.

Luke held her hand. "Come on, honey, breathe slow. In, out." Luke dabbed a cool washcloth on Calli's face, and gave her a kiss, hoping to distract her for a minute. "Want some ice chips?"

Calli squeezed his hand. When the contraction was over, she relaxed and stared into her husband's green eyes, feeling less anxious already.

"Did either of you call the Youth Outreach Center to tell Pastor Ortiz that you wouldn't be able to keep your appointments today?"

She nodded. "Shelly started covering my counseling schedule a week ago. I was just taking drop-ins."

Jon peeked his head into the room. "Can I come in?"

Calli smiled, motioning for him to join them.

"Hand me the T-shirt from the bag, son. I need to change."

The almost sixteen-year-old tossed the shirt to his dad. "Here you go."

Calli had a serious look on her face.

Almost ready to change, Luke paused and leaned close. "What's wrong, honey?"

"I can't decide if I want to kiss you for giving me a baby, or kick you out of the room…forever." Luke laughed, not feeling a bit threatened.

"Isn't transition wonderful?" Suddenly she grabbed his hand and squeezed as an intense contraction began.

Luke struggled one-handed with the last button, and the remainder of the navy shirt dangled between them. "Honey, you've got to let go of my hand for *just* a minute so I can take this thing off." When she didn't let go, he tugged the bulky shirt back to his own wrist until the contraction ended, then tossed it into an empty chair and quickly pulled the other shirt on.

"What brought this on so suddenly?"

Jon stepped forward. "She let me drive to school."

Luke nudged his son with an elbow. "Well, that explains everything. Give me a break, Cal. I'd think you'd have better sense than to take a fifteen-year-old driving two days past your due date."

Calli's smile was cut short by the intensity of the contraction. She squeezed his hand tighter. He grimaced. She let go, then immediately grabbed his shirt and pulled him closer. "Ou-uee."

"This is happening so fast I'm not even going to need that goody bag full of candy bars, am I?" She was beyond distraction. "Breathe, Calli." Luke bumped into the bed and held her face between his hands. "In, two, three. Out, two, three."

Jon continued the story, unaware that the baby's birth

was imminent. "All of a sudden, Calli was laughing, and said something about her water breaking. I didn't…"

"Jon, go get the doctor. Come on sweetie, breathe with me. Pant, Calli. Hee, hee, hee, haw." His heart swelled with love as he watched her pained expressions.

"C…a…aaan't," she gasped, then held her breath.

"*No*, Calli don't push yet. You've got to wait a minute, honey. Just a few more minutes, sweetie. Jon… The doctor."

The teenager's eyes grew wide. "Y-you mean?"

"Pant, Callie. Jon, go get the doctor, *now!*"

"I'm out of here."

"Luke…" She gasped when the contraction ended. "Is it supposed to happen this fast?"

"You're doing great, Calli. Have I mentioned how much I love you?" He touched her round belly and smiled, then wiped her forehead again. "Looks like Jon's going to get that baby he's been asking for, and just in time for his birthday."

Tears filled her eyes, and she made no attempt to stop them.

"You okay, honey?"

"Do I *look* okay? I'm having a baby."

"You look beautiful." He kissed her forehead, half expecting her to push him away.

The doctor rushed into the room with the nurse following. "Have a little one in a hurry to get here, huh?"

Luke nodded. "She wasn't even having contractions three hours ago when I left for work."

The nurse scurried to get everything ready. "Your son changed his mind about watching. He's going to wait in the hall."

Luke nodded, peering past the woman to see what the

doctor was doing, and chuckled. "He lasted longer than I thought he would."

Everything started happening all at once, and soon Calli delivered a beautiful baby girl.

Two hours later, Calli closed her eyes, knowing little Cara Michelle was in her daddy's expert hands. "Luke, don't forget to call Mom and Dad." He spooned some ice chips into Calli's mouth and leaned over to kiss her.

"Already done. Grandma and Grandpa Giovanni are en route as we speak. And by now, all the aunts and uncles should have heard the news, too."

Calli was exhausted, but couldn't stand to fall asleep and miss all this excitement. "She's beautiful, isn't she?"

"Cara's as beautiful as her mother. Get some sleep, honey. Your daughter's going to need to eat before too long."

Luke sat on the edge of the hospital bed, the tiny infant wrapped securely in her daddy's strong hands with Grammy Northrup standing nearby watching.

"Who would have thought when you walked into Calli's hospital room that night that you'd wind up back here married and having a baby?" his mother reminisced, admiring her granddaughter.

Luke lifted his eyebrows. "I did." Luke leaned across the bed and pressed his lips to Calli's. She quivered at the sweet tenderness of his kiss. "You looked so helpless, I wanted to protect you even then. Little did I know…"

Calli blushed. "Yeah, yeah, enough already. Could you hand me my ice, Lieutenant Northrup?"

Luke chuckled as they both seemed to remember their awkward first meeting. "Here, let me help," he teased.

Luke's father wrapped an arm around each—his son and grandson. "What do you think, Jon?"

"She's okay, for a girl." The teenager beamed proudly, despite his nonchalant attitude. "It's a great birthday present. About time Dad remembered. Now, who's going to take me to get my driver's license tomorrow?"

Luke and Calli looked at each other and laughed. "Maybe your mother would like that honor."

"Mom and Jack are coming for my birthday? Cool." He slapped Luke a high-five, then froze. "Hey, wait. When's their baby due?"

"Not *that* soon," Calli interrupted, thrilled with Jon's adjustment to having not only one mother, but two.

Cara opened her eyes and looked at Luke. "Hi there, my little sweetheart," he cooed, gently rocking his tiny daughter.

Jon washed his hands in the sink and rushed to have a turn holding his little sister. "Come on, Dad, it's my turn." Luke carefully placed the infant in Jon's arms. His smile grew wider. "Good thing you weren't an October baby, or Dad would probably call you pumpkin!"

Calli smiled at her family. She hadn't a clue what she'd done for excitement before these two came into her life. And something told her, this was just the beginning.

* * * * *

Dear Reader,

My father was a law enforcement officer for twenty-five years, so I have always held in high esteem those men and women who every day face risks that many of us take for granted. I felt this was a perfect story to combine the tough and tender sides of a police officer hero who lives his Christian faith in spite of the overwhelming challenges of his career. Throw in a teenager and a heroine who has yet to overcome a painful past, and we see what it takes to turn ordinary people into our everyday heroes.

As Christians, we often hear individuals ask, "Why does God allow bad things to happen to good people?" That's not only hard to answer, but hard to comprehend. Moving on after something bad happens is often a sheer act of faith. It takes courage and trust in His almighty power. When we look back on difficult times and challenges, we frequently wonder how we ever made it through. It is during these time that we learn to cling to His truths and promises.

This past year, I've come to understand the promises made in Thessalonians. A few weeks after I lost a brother-in-law to leukemia, my father had a heart attack, and a few months later, my mother had a stroke.

God never promised an easy road, for believers or nonbelievers alike. We're all His children. For those who trust in Him, comfort comes in knowing that though we must struggle here on earth, the celebration of our victory is already being prepared.

I hope you enjoy Luke and Calli's challenging walk to forgiveness and love.

Feel free to write to me c/o Steeple Hill, 233 Broadway, Ste. 1001, New York, NY 10279.

Carol Steward

SECOND TIME AROUND

Two are better than one, because they have a good reward for their toil. For if they fall, one will lift up his fellow; but woe to him who is alone when he falls and has not anther to lift him up....
A threefold cord is not quickly broken.
—*Ecclesiastes* 4:9-10, 12

For my mother, Phillis Bohannan,
for teaching me never to give up. Thanks, Mom.

Acknowledgments:

To Robin and Michelle for your inspiration
even before God introduced us.

Many thanks to Marty, Deb and Bette for your
expertise and continued support.

Chapter One

F<small>ROM</small> the parlor, building contractor Kevin MacIntyre heard the church bells outside announcing the celebration. He ran a finger inside his shirt collar, suddenly feeling as stuffed as insulation between two-by-four studs. Why the suit bothered him today, he hadn't a clue. He wasn't the type to shy away from formal occasions. In fact, he typically enjoyed them. He guessed it was because his best friend was making the long-awaited trip to the altar, and Kevin had yet to find Miss Perfect. *With all the hours I'm putting in at work, I don't have time for anyone else, anyway. What do I care?*

Kevin picked up a miniature plastic football and tossed it to the groom. The music began softly, then grew louder and faster. Kevin opened the door to the chapel and peeked out to see if it was time for them to take their places. The usher escorted the beautiful guest down the aisle on his arm. Dr. Emily Berthoff was as gorgeous as ever.

Emily raised her eyes and met Kevin's. Her demure smile seemed to hold a touch of sadness, and the air whooshed from his lungs, leaving him with a burning need for oxygen.

He studied her intently, remembering… Suddenly, her hunter-green dress faded to white, a veil covered her face, and her smile was full of love.… Kevin furiously blinked the dream away. No longer concerned with starting any wedding, he pushed the door closed. "Why didn't you tell me Emily was coming?"

The groom looked unconvincingly baffled. "Did I forget to mention that?" Bryan threw the football back across the room, the ball hitting Kevin in the stomach before dropping to the floor.

"Yeah, I'd say you forgot to mention that!" Kevin mocked.

Bryan followed his chortling toddler across the room to get the toy, and the two embraced in a growling hug. "Just be glad Barb is feeling better. Laura was going to ask Emily to stand in as the maid of honor."

Kevin straightened his suit, then combed the unruly waves of hair back into place with his fingers. "Laura's trying to get even with me, isn't she? Your future wife has a warped sense of humor."

Bryan chuckled.

Jacob handed Kevin the football. He picked the toddler up and tossed Bryan the ball. "Go tackle your dad," Kevin whispered into Jacob's ear as he set the boy down. Then Kevin watched with envy as his best friend and son played together, casually waiting for Pastor Mike to come for them. *I'm going to miss having Jacob around.*

"She's a romantic. Thinks you and Emily should give it another try." Bryan checked his watch, stuffed the toys into a baby-size backpack, then pulled his suit jacket on. "You've got to admit, Emily is still available—not to mention as beautiful as always."

"Even if I did admit it, it doesn't mean anything." Kevin had chased away memories of Emily Berthoff long ago. Moved on with his life. Pursued his dreams and was on the verge of making them come true. And she was no longer a part of the plan.

"Maybe Laura's right, Kevin. A lot has changed in seven years."

He scowled at his friend. "Eight. It was the year the Buffs beat Nebraska. Yeah, a lot has changed. I've just made a bid that will put my entire business at stake, not to mention the risk I've let you take on this investment. I want to pay you back as soon as possible. I don't need some woman turning my life around to fit her agenda."

Bryan smoothed his son's tiny vest, while obviously trying to wipe the smirk from his own lips. "I wouldn't exactly call your ex-fiancée *some woman*. That in itself tells me how you feel about her."

"Wait just a minute here! Don't go assuming anything. Seeing her here surprised me. That's all." Kevin checked his pocket for Laura's wedding ring, wishing Bryan would let the issue die, just as his and Emily's relationship had died. "It's been too long to care what the doctor does. She made her choices."

Until he had unexpectedly run into Emily in Laura's hospital room two months ago, he'd successfully erased the enchanting woman from existence. Since then, unmanageable thoughts plagued his mind with reruns of the years they had been together: dreams of a family, of traveling across the country together, of waking up to one another—

Bryan's somber voice interrupted him again. "Put the show aside, Kevin. I know it hurts. You're not going to like this, but I'm going to say it anyway...."

Kevin wanted to walk out of the room in the worst

way. He didn't need Mr. Happy here to throw his own words back in his face. Problem was, on the other side of that door was a chapel full of smiling loved ones ready to celebrate "happily ever after." There was no escaping. No matter how desperately he wanted to leave, he couldn't do that to his best friend. Not today.

"It's time you put the past behind you and looked at your future. And Emily's as good a place as any to start."

Kevin started to say something, and was politely told to wait his turn. The echo of his own words reverberated in his ears. He couldn't believe it had been little more than a year since he'd used that same line on Bryan. "Just because it worked for you, don't count on it changing my life."

"Come on, Jacob, hold still." Bryan stood his son on the sofa and straightened the toddler's tiny bow tie. Returning his attention to Kevin, he added, "You never stopped caring for her. If it hadn't been for your dad, you probably would have gone after her then."

Kevin tugged on the knot of his own necktie, certain it was getting tighter by the minute. "Drop the subject, Bryan."

Bryan stepped in front of him and looked him in the eye as he readjusted the silk strip around Kevin's neck. "That's why you haven't stayed with any other woman. You only have feelings for the one who walked away. Swallow your pride, Kevin. Talk to her. You owe it to both of you to settle it, once and for all."

"Forget it." There was nothing more to say. He didn't want to see, let alone talk to Emily Berthoff, M.D., again. Not because it might rekindle the fire, but because his fire had never gone out.

The tall oak door opened and a middle-aged pastor

with a receding hairline nodded. "Morning, Kevin. You ready, Bryan?"

"Thought you'd never get here." Still staring Kevin in the eye, Bryan waggled his eyebrows. "Best day of my life."

Kevin walked behind Pastor Mike and the groom into the small chapel filled with candles and flowers and smiling faces. He watched the bride's father present Laura to Bryan. Their gazes were fixed on each other and love radiated between them.

"We are gathered here to celebrate the union of Laura Bates and Bryan Beaumont...."

Even in his sulking mood, he couldn't help but feel the happiness choke out the bitterness. He laughed at Laura's youngest son, who was fidgeting with his suit. Kevin lowered his eyebrows and shook his head slightly until the boy stopped. Bryan was going to have his hands full. In just over a year he'd gone from no children to four; from married, to widowed, to honeymooner. *You have my best wishes, friend.*

The soloist sang about love that never ended, and Kevin felt the noose around his neck slip another notch tighter.

He found Emily instinctively, yet stubbornly turned away. With beautiful red hair and a bright smile, she had always stood out in a crowd. Always would. His mind drifted to bitter memories of that day, a month before their wedding, when Emily had announced she'd unexpectedly been accepted into a prestigious medical school—across the country. The day when the very foundation of his dreams had crumbled like bad concrete.

Though they had known there was a remote possibility she'd be accepted at Johns Hopkins, they'd made their plans based upon her attending medical school in-state.

Time was supposed to heal all wounds, so the saying went. It hadn't worked in eight years, and he doubted it ever would. In that respect, Bryan was right; there would be no one for him, because the only woman he'd ever loved had walked away.

Bryan nudged his hand, and Kevin realized he had missed his cue. He reached into his pocket and pulled out Laura's wedding ring. He glanced at the bride, who had the smug look of a woman who already had a scheme in mind.

"Relax, your time will come," Bryan whispered as Kevin handed him the ring.

"Not a chance." He was supposed to be the one calming the groom. Not the other way around.

In what seemed like minutes, Laura and Bryan were pronounced husband and wife, and the two were joined by four rambunctious children for a walk down the aisle. Kevin waited for the music to change, then followed, trying to ignore the striking woman in the third pew.

Two hours later, the celebration was winding down. Kevin must have talked to every person in the reception hall, except the pretty doctor. Somehow they had managed to miss one another. He supposed he had the pastor to thank for keeping Emily company. Glancing quickly around the room, he consoled himself with the realization that she had left first, without making any effort to talk to him.

He backed through the arched doorway and spun around, ready to make a quick escape up the stairs, out the door, and away from this lousy trip into his unpleasant past.

"They're perfect for each other, aren't they?"

Kevin stumbled up the step as he turned toward the all-too-familiar voice. The slick sole of his shoes on the metal edge sent him sprawling across the stairs. Clenching his jaw to swallow the cry, a deep rumble vibrated against his vocal cords.

"Kevin! Are you okay?"

He groaned. "Why in blazes are you hiding in here?"

"I was paged and needed a quieter place to phone the hospital." Emily extended her hand to help him up. "I didn't mean to startle you."

He brushed her hand aside, stunned by the sincerity of her remark. After all this time, he wasn't going to let Emily get to him. "I'll be fine, thanks for the concern, Doc."

Children squealed and raced past them across the room in a raucous game of kissing tag. A look of admiration softened Emily's green eyes. She tipped her head toward the chaos. "Who would have pictured Bryan as a father of four? Laura is so much better for him than Andrea, isn't she?"

Tearing his gaze from Emily, Kevin looked at the bride and groom. "Like night and day. It took a while, but I finally got through to them."

She flipped her cellular phone closed and put it into a compact purse, her tone turning cold. "How generous of you. Must have been the jealousy routine. You were always so good at that one."

He studied her as she concentrated on the newlyweds. Emily's full lips turned into a smile that crinkled the corners of her eyes as she watched the giddy couple behind the tiered cake. Kevin closed his eyes, wishing after all these years he could forget how wonderful it was to hold her in his arms and kiss the soft fullness of her lips. *Don't be a fool. Emily is off-limits.*

Wishing she didn't still have the power to make his heart skip a beat, Kevin tugged the knot of his tie loose.

"So that was it. Your mother convinced you that all men were like your father, huh? And all this time, I thought it was medical school that lured you away."

The smile disappeared and her eyebrows arched up. "And apparently you still think I should have given up the opportunity of a lifetime to follow *your* dreams. I'm relieved to know I made the right decision." Emily turned to leave.

Following her through the doorway, he grabbed her hand. "We can both be happy you realized your career was more important than a family *before* it was too late."

"How dare you," she countered in a broken voice.

Kevin stepped in front of her, deliberately blocking her view of the festivities.

"Sorry if I hit a nerve."

"You're not a bit sorry."

"Oh, there you're wrong, Doc. There are a lot of things I'm sorry about." He could never forget the tailspin her announcement had sent him into. It had short-circuited his very existence. "But I guess you're not interested in hearing all of that, are you?"

Emily's green eyes widened like those of a cat ready to pounce, yet she remained silent.

He let go of her silky-soft hand, and she stepped back as if giving up without a battle. He should have remembered, their arguments always made her nervous, the tragic remains of a broken home. She lowered her head, and he could no longer see her face through her veil of red curls.

She glanced at him, then away.

Was that a tear? He yanked his tie from around his neck, unfastened the top button, and dragged in a quick breath, inhaling the sweet smell of her perfume. The last thing he had expected was that she would cry.

She cleared her throat and looked at the tie dangling in his hand. "You know, Kevin, I didn't notice you trying to contact me, either. The final decision was yours," she said with renewed determination.

Kevin backed away. The old Emily wouldn't have made a scene. Especially not in a public place. "There *was* no choice," he said quietly.

"No choice?" she repeated. "Funny, isn't it? You're here in Springville *now*. Yet the family's business that couldn't manage without you then, isn't."

He wondered if he should tell her why, then decided against it. It was best to leave things as they were. She was the one who had walked away. Let her think what she wanted. Their future was long gone.

Raw pain glimmered in her misty eyes.

He felt the rapid beating in his chest and wondered if he could have been wrong, then immediately pushed the thought away. He had his business to consider now.

"Fate is a funny thing for sure." He studied her puzzled look and laughed softly. Forcing the question away, he added, "Who would ever have guessed we'd wind up here together?"

"'Together' is a bit presumptuous, isn't it? We've managed to avoid each other up until now—that shouldn't be too difficult to continue. After all, we have no reason to see each other." She walked into the main reception hall, stopped by the crowd gathering around the bride and groom.

He wanted to tell her he was bidding for the project on her clinic, but couldn't risk placing her in an awkward situation. And because the bids were closed, he didn't want to jeopardize his chances, either. *This is business. Strictly business.*

Crowding in behind her, he whispered in her ear.

"Face it, Emily, we will see each other. I assure you."
He chuckled, then quickly chastised himself for entertaining the thought of walking into her office on a daily
basis to prove his point. *You're playing with fire, Kevin,*
said a voice inside him.

She spun around.

Gazing into her eyes was a mistake. He forced away
the sudden image of kissing her and putting that wedding
ring on her finger—for good this time.

He turned to see what the commotion was behind him,
just in time to see the bouquet bounce like a volleyball
from one female to the next...and into his own hands.
Cheers and laughs filled the room.

"Sorry, ladies, I'm out of the running." He shrugged
his shoulders and smiled, then tossed the bouquet back
into the air.

Emily had sidestepped her way past him and was escaping into the crowd. But the bridal bouquet arched toward her. Obviously surprised, Emily reached out and
caught it.

She spun around and shot Kevin a cold, hard stare.
Then she threw the flowers back at him, turned and ran.

Chapter Two

Emily frantically chopped the onion, tears rolling down her face. "Who does he think he is?"

"Sounds just the same as *I* remember him." Her younger sister looked at the cutting board. "Are we going to eat that onion, or drink it?"

Emily glanced at the pile of pulverized white mush. "When did you get so picky?"

"Well, normally I wouldn't argue, but we're making salad, not stew." Katarina scraped the mess into the garbage disposal, rinsed the wooden slab, then walked across the kitchen, drying the cutting board with a towel. "So Kevin still looks great, huh?"

"I didn't say anything about the way he had looked— did I?" Emily was certain she hadn't told her sister he looked so devastatingly handsome that she had even failed to notice what color of dress the matron of honor was wearing. She didn't tell Katarina Kevin's hair was blonder than before, his skin more bronzed and his laugh even huskier. She hadn't, and she wouldn't. She didn't dare.

Katarina disappeared into the other room, but her raised voice more than made up for the distance. "You may have the M.D. behind your name, sis, but *I'm* the heart specialist." Her sister's honey-blond head momentarily peeked around the corner. "And trust me, that onion was not strong enough to warrant that river of tears."

When Katarina reappeared from the living room, soft music floated in behind her swaying body. "Maybe ocean waves will help you relax. You really do need to lighten up, sis."

Her sister was right. She was too serious. Emily pulled another onion from the hanging basket and chopped a couple of slices, then set the cutting board in front of her cheery sister. "*There* is your onion."

"Why are you mad at me?" Katarina shrugged her shoulders, hands palms up in front of her. "I didn't tell you to break your engagement with Kevin to become a doctor for my sake. In fact, if you'd asked, I'd have said you were crazy to let Kevin go. My hearing was already damaged—nothing anyone could have done, including you. The job of Savior has already been filled—in case you need another reminder."

"That's not even funny, Katarina."

"Lighten up, sis. I was joking!"

Emily's focus instantly moved to the hearing aid tucked into her sister's right ear. "Oh, Kat. I'm sorry. I don't blame you." Emily set the knife on the ceramic-tile counter and rinsed her hands, then hugged her younger sister. "No, sweetie. It wasn't just because of you. It was for families like ours who grew up without the money to get proper medical care. If you'd only had the medicine for your ear infections, you'd be fine now."

Katarina's eyes clouded, and Emily saw sudden visions of their impoverished childhood. She leaned back and tucked a stray hair behind her ear, remembering arguments she and Kevin had had regarding family finances. "I'm sorry," she whispered. "Guess I haven't let go of my past after all, have I? I hand it to God, then I yank it back. Bet He thinks it's a yo-yo by now."

Kat reached out her hand and held Emily's, her ornery smile erasing the look of hurt from her blue eyes. "I think there's one part of your past you'd better examine very carefully before letting him slip away a second time."

Emily turned her sister's head and spoke into her ear. "Is your hearing aid on?" she teased.

Katarina nodded.

"Good, because I don't want you to miss what I'm going to say. I don't care about Kevin MacIntyre." Emily tugged the unruly curls to the top of her head and fastened a barrette, then continued. "I don't wish him any harm, but...I don't need him. I am perfectly happy on my own."

"Right. I don't believe a word of it, but the time will come when you'll realize what he still means to you."

Emily watched her sister dance to the back door and pull the Victorian lace curtains closed, seemingly mocking Emily's problems. Katarina was the only sane person she knew who could switch moods as easily as turning pages on a calendar.

"I am curious," Kat continued. "How do you plan to avoid him when both of you are friends with Laura and Bryan?"

"They'll understand." Emily placed the ivy-trimmed dishes on the antique table and added two glasses of iced tea. She thought of Kevin's promise that they would see each other again, and the seething anger started anew. "Oooh, he's so sure of himself."

Katarina didn't say anything, just smiled. The disk changed, and it wasn't long before she began humming with the music. Pretty soon, Emily heard an echo of the wedding processional behind her.

"Knock it off, Katarina."

"Mama always said your temper was because of that fiery red hair. Came from the Irish side of the family, I suppose."

Emily shook her head and rolled her eyes, remembering their childish arguments as if they were yesterday.

They continued preparing dinner in silence. Even though Katarina irritated her like only a little sister could, Emily was anxious for Kat's move to town so they could get together more often. They were the closest of the three siblings in age and in spirit.

If it hadn't been for her sister's youthful encouragement, Emily never would have made it through the broken engagement or medical school. Kat's zany sense of humor was a totally endearing quality that Emily had learned to appreciate, and had come to depend upon.

"Emily?" Her sister touched her arm.

She turned, shaking the daze away. "What?"

Kat had moved the food to the table, and now motioned for Emily to sit. In unison they bowed their heads, while Emily blessed the nourishment before them.

There was an unsettling quiet as they ate.

"Do you think Dad ever loved Mom?" After all these years, Katarina's voice echoed Emily's gnawing childhood fear.

Emily stared at her food. Would the mention of her broken engagement ever stop reminding all of them of their father? "I try not to analyze them, Kat. We both know how unforgiving Mom can be. Maybe Dad couldn't take it anymore. Maybe... Who knows?" Emily shrugged, then took a bite of chicken. She wished her sister would change the subject.

"Don't you ever wonder why he never came back to see us?"

Slurping the juice dripping from the bite of pear, Emily mumbled, "Of course I do. I doubt I'll ever get over it."

"What?" Katarina turned her head slightly, tears brimming in her bright blue eyes. Out of frustration, she combed her fingers through one side of her sporty hairstyle, as if the hair were preventing her hearing aid from working.

"I mean, there are parts of my past I can't seem to forget." The hearing aid in Katarina's ear was tiny and no longer bothered her, but it always would Emily. It was a constant reminder of why she'd gone into medicine. No matter how much she tried, Emily would never forget the pain she'd nursed her little sister through. She'd do everything possible to help prevent another child's suffering. "How do you deal with it? You're always so disgustingly cheerful."

The brightness of her sister's porcelain skin paled and the smile dimmed. "There are still days when I'm so mad I could spit nails. Trust me."

Emily took her sister's hand and squeezed it. "I'm sure there are, Kat." Caring for Katarina and their youngest sister, Lisa, while her mother had worked two jobs had made Emily realize the importance of an education. Which was why she and Kevin had agreed to wait until she finished her bachelor's degree to get married. Then came that letter—

Her mind pulled the plug on the memory. "Hey, we're supposed to be having a good time tonight. Who brought up this maudlin subject, anyway?"

Katarina grinned. "You're right. Let's change the sub-

ject. So, tell me more about the wedding. The part without Kevin, if you'd prefer.''

In between bites of chicken *cordon bleu* and salad,
Emily told her everything, *excluding* the charming way
Kevin had played with the kids during the reception. Remembering it made her heart swell. There he was in his
tailored suit, romping around on the floor with Laura's
sons so the bride and groom could enjoy the reception....

His thoughtfulness and boyish sense of humor were
what had first caught her attention so many years ago.
She had been sitting solemnly by herself under the golden
leaves of the grand old maple tree at the college-
sponsored concert, when Kevin spied her staring at him.
Even from a distance, she'd seen the way he made everyone around him feel. He had a contagious laugh and a
quick wit. As she blushed, he introduced himself. A few
minutes later they were sharing the shade, deep in conversation and laughter.

For three years he'd courted her, throughout it all putting up with her mother's ridicule. But Emily had stayed,
falling ever more deeply in love with the man her mother
had predicted would love her and leave her, just as Emily's philandering father had done.

''I'm going to Lincoln next week for a show. Do you
want me to take anything to Mom?'' If her sister noticed
Emily's distraction, she didn't mention it.

Emily welcomed the interruption.

''Mom... Oh, yeah, would you take her birthday present?''

''What did you get her? I haven't found anything yet.''

''It's an airline ticket. Thought I'd take her to the
mountains. Care to join us? I've borrowed Laura and
Bryan's cabin for a week.''

''Sounds fun. I'll check my schedule. With the move,

I may have to make a last-minute decision depending on how everything is going.''

"I thought I'd see if Lisa can join us, too. We'll make it a family reunion.''

After catching up on the latest on Lisa and her beau, they discussed Kat's growing business and her worries of keeping up with the demand for her designer dolls.

Clearing the dishes while Katarina called her on-again-off-again boyfriend, Emily let her thoughts return to their mother's influence on the three daughters' relationships. Katarina couldn't take that final plunge into matrimony. Lisa didn't date any man long enough to fall in love.

And Emily—the broken engagement to Kevin had been enough to send the frightened child in her running as far as possible from love and commitment.

Eight years later, she was still running.

Two weeks had passed since her sister's visit, and since she'd seen Kevin. Emily walked into the church's preschool to tell the children about being a doctor. She and the teacher visited for a few minutes before a little boy from Emily's Sunday school class grabbed her hand. "Dr. Emily, come see what a tall tower I can build.'' She followed Ricky, welcoming the chance to visit with the little boy away from the examination room.

For the next half hour, Emily watched as Ricky played with the children. After Circle Time, they prepared for the guests to talk about their careers. A cake decorator was first, and gave each child an ornately decorated cookie to keep each busy while she turned a mound of cake into a stand-up penguin.

Emily was next. She looked at the cake and the children eagerly eating cookies. *Great, how do I top this?*

After telling the children about how much she enjoyed

being a doctor, she pulled the stethoscope out of her pocket.

"Dr. Emily, can I listen to your heart?" Ricky blurted out, his raised hand flapping back and forth.

"Sure. You can each have a turn. Come up one at a time." The familiar boy with streaked brown hair jumped to his feet and nearly leaped over the kids sitting in front of him. Emily recognized most of the children, either from Sunday school or the medical clinic. Before she knew it, all the children were crowded around.

"Shh," Emily prompted. "We must be very quiet."

Ricky listened for a minute, then expertly moved the stethoscope. She wanted to cry at the extent of his knowledge of the workings of the instrument, which came from more hands-on experience than any child his age should have.

"I don't hear anything, Dr Emily." He frowned. "I think you have a broken heart."

A deep chuckle rumbled behind them. "An insightful young man."

Emily's heart raced at the sound of Kevin's voice.

The little boy's brown eyes grew larger. "Wow! There it is. It's beating as fast as Thumper's paw. 'Member, in *Bambi*?"

"Are you twitterpated, Dr. Emily?" a precocious little girl asked.

"Twitterpated?"

"You know, in *love*." The little girl sighed. "Like Bambi and Faline."

Emily felt the blood rush to her cheeks. "No, I'm not. We'd better let someone else have a turn now, Ricky." She gave him a hug and watched as he ran across the room...to Kevin.

Kevin knelt down and spent several minutes in conversation with the child. From the corner of her eye, Emily watched, angry at herself for paying Kevin any attention.

The other preschoolers filed past, and Emily helped them listen to each other's hearts beating. Ricky moved back to the circle of children after giving Kevin a high-five. Then Kevin visited with a parent, while Emily finished talking with the children and gave them the disposable masks and hats.

Then she turned the stage over to Kevin. He leaned close as Emily walked past. "Any time your heart needs a jump start, let me know."

"You'd be the last person I'd call," she mumbled, wishing she could dispel her reaction to him. Emily silently joined the parent volunteer in the back of the room. She and the other woman listened as Kevin told about the construction business, demonstrating with a toy log set.

The children were mesmerized by the rugged-looking man with the contagious smile and rumbling laugh. Other than the uncustomarily clean blue jeans, he looked every bit the brawny construction worker. A red-plaid flannel shirt over a blue T-shirt and a bright yellow hard hat completed the irresistible image. His strong hands moved the tiny logs with the same delicacy one would use to move fine china.

All the little boys proclaimed they, too, wanted to be builders after his enthusiastic description of tearing walls apart and building others. The energy in the room began to escalate.

"Why did you become a builder?" The teacher prompted the conversation back to the subject, her calming voice reminding the children to listen.

"My father was a builder, and it was something I always enjoyed. It's hard work, but I like bringing families together in a new home,'' he said.

It was obvious that he loved talking to the youngsters. The children drilled him with questions, and he took time to answer each one. He still had his way with kids.

Emily wondered why he hadn't married. Coming from a family with six children, he had wanted to have at least four of his own. He had chivalrously promised Emily that he'd support them all, yet that wasn't enough for Emily. She wanted a career of her own, one through which she could provide for her family, if necessary. She wasn't about to watch history repeat itself.

Emily stared critically at Kevin. Why was he here? How had he, of all people, come to be asked to speak to the preschool?

Kevin smiled lazily, then winked at her before saying goodbye to the preschoolers. She realized the desperate attempts she was making to taint her image of the only man who could touch her heart with a mere glance.

The children would be leaving soon, and this was Kevin's only chance to talk to Emily alone. As he exited the preschool room, he nodded for her to join him outside. He could see her reluctance.

"Why are you here?" she demanded as soon as the door closed behind them.

He folded his arms across his chest and smiled. "I heard there was a damsel inside with a broken heart. Thought I'd come to the rescue."

"Very funny."

He smiled. He had decided after the confusion at the wedding that he needed to find out if she was still interested—if that had been the reason for her tears. He challenged himself to make her laugh. Or at least smile. She had a beautiful smile. "Actually, I was just waiting for the rescue breathing."

Her eyes were clear as green ice. "I'm serious."

"It's obvious that hasn't changed."

Emily put her hands on her hips and waited. She had changed from the college co-ed he'd fallen in love with, he thought. Her shyness had matured to a quiet confidence, her insecurities had been replaced by a calm determination, and her wide-eyed look of fear reflected a love that hadn't died.

"Okay, the truth," he continued, hoping that reflection was wrong. "I'm working on developing a new image." He started to tell her about the bid, but she took an abrupt step toward him and flashed him a look of annoyance.

"I really would have thought you'd grow up a little in eight years." She turned and walked back inside.

"Just as I thought, you can't handle the truth," he mumbled, once she had turned the corner and disappeared from sight.

Kevin recalled Laura begging him to come talk to the preschoolers. He glanced through the narrow slat of a window into the preschool and watched as a little boy clung to the teacher, doing whatever he could to get her attention. There was no question in Kevin's mind that Laura was trying to set him and Emily up again.

"Better luck next time, lady."

Chapter Three

The conference room was filled with the aroma of gourmet coffee and glazed doughnuts. Sunlight filtered in through the broken slats of the blinds. The chief of staff addressed the doctors and board members, summarizing the top three clinic renovation proposals. At the mention of a small independent builder, Emily let out a quick gasp.

Her colleague Bob Walker leaned close. "What's wrong, Em?" he whispered. "You look like you've seen a ghost."

Ignoring him, Emily examined the different bid summaries with a sudden urgency. Why hadn't she considered this possibility earlier? Muffled voices buzzed around her. Her heart rate increased. *He wouldn't dare.*

Dr. Bob Walker pushed a note in front of her, a barely legible invitation to join him for dinner scrawled across the prescription pad. Sending him a reprimand from the corner of her eye, she scrunched the note into a tiny ball and tossed it into the trash can.

She thumbed back through the folders and, with a sud-

den chill of comprehension, looked again at the unbe-
lievably low bid. Kevin was vying for this job. That's
why he had been so confident he'd be seeing her again.

"Emily? What are your feelings about the bids?"

"Yes, Emily, what are you thinking?" Bob added, a
mischievous glint in his eye.

Still dismayed, she cleared her throat and brushed a
stray hair off her forehead. With a quick appraisal of the
spreadsheets before her, it was hard to argue the obvious.
"Since the project committee is behind on fund-raising,
I'll admit it does make this incredibly low bid very ap-
pealing."

The other committee members nodded. Dr. Roberts
agreed, adding, "With the incentives City Council is offering, I think it's critical that we make the commitment
now. Sonshine Medical Clinic is finally gaining the support we need."

Emily closed the folder, suddenly aware of what the
outcome of this vote could mean to her own peace of
mind. No matter what happened between her and Kevin,
she reminded herself, this was business. *If* the contractor
was Kevin...she'd learn to deal with it when the time
came. If not, her paranoia could cost both the clinic and
the company bidding a very important project. She had
to keep her personal turmoil out of the way.

"There isn't really any question, is there?" Dr. Walker
added.

Not regarding which sealed bid to accept, maybe, but
Emily had plenty of questions, doubts and uncertainties.

The company was offering incredible upgrades that the
clinic couldn't otherwise afford. How could Kevin afford
to be so generous? Surely his fledgling company didn't
have this kind of money to donate. And from the way
he'd reacted to seeing her at Laura and Bryan's wedding,

he wasn't trying to win her over again. *Surely I'm just imagining this. Kevin doesn't want to be near me any more than I want him around. He wouldn't do this.*

There was no question but that she wanted the clinic to flourish. She wanted to help their patients. And despite her and Kevin's history, she wished him every success, both personally and professionally. She just didn't like the idea of their goals being mutually dependent.

Turning her mind back to the meeting, she concentrated on the discussion. Others expressed gratitude at the upgrades, and Emily added suspiciously, "Can we trust his word on that?" The faces around the table looked puzzled by her sudden lack of enthusiasm. "It's just— I'm merely concerned that we be sure the company will follow through once it has the job in hand. Well, it does seem determined to win this bid, doesn't it? Question is, how many promises would the company make in order to get the job?"

Everyone began talking at once, and Bob leaned close. "You know something about this company, Em? I've never seen you so feisty. To be honest, I like it."

"What's wrong, Bob? Did the new receptionist break your date?" She edged away.

He smiled. "Come on, have dinner with me. No one need find out."

Emily looked around the table, then turned her head so that only Bob could hear. "I think you're making a big mistake, Bob. Your third strike with me was two receptionists and six months ago. One more, and you'll strike yourself out of the clinic, as well."

The doctor sobered, and leaned back in his chair, nonchalantly pretending he hadn't heard anything she'd said. That was fine with her. Just so he understood.

Emily let her mind wander back to Kevin as the board's discussion progressed without her.

Thirty minutes later the chief of staff spun his pen on the chipped tabletop. "I think it's obvious that number two believes in our mission. Unless there's any disagreement, I'll share our feelings with the board and let them make the announcement." All present turned and looked at Emily, anticipating another argument.

What if it's not Kevin? Can I take that chance? She shook her head.

As the others made their way through the conference room door, she opened the folder again, looking more carefully for some inkling of proof. Could Kevin believe in the clinic's mission? She saw no evidence, but decided he deserved a chance. She thought back to their conversation at the wedding. *Trust me, Emily. We will see each other again.* Kevin had gloated. But why did he want *this* job?

Unfortunately, her emotional struggle would have to be sacrificed for the good of the patients. She would learn to ignore Kevin, and his charming antics.

Silently edging her way past the board members, Emily considered Kevin's possible motives. Whatever his reasons, one thing was for sure: when Kevin MacIntyre went after something, there was no stopping him....

She recalled the weeks he had spent trying to convince her to go on that first date with him. Flowers, phone calls, surprising her between classes. Yes, Kevin MacIntyre could write the book on charm.

Emily wondered how she'd face him each day, then rallied. *It's over now. We've both moved on.* If *he gets the job, well, if I can work with Bob, I can surely handle Kevin. I have to. The clinic's future depends on this renovation.*

Emily returned to her office. If the staff needed her, they wouldn't hesitate to call. She needed a minute to breathe. Time to collect herself and banish Kevin Mac-Intyre from her thoughts—if only temporarily.

Emily closed her office door behind her and leaned against it. *Dear God, help me. I don't think I can handle this alone—*

The phone rang, and she knew her moment of reprieve was over. She took two calls, then began seeing patients.

Twelve hours later, Emily pulled into her garage. She walked into the house, dropped her purse and collapsed on the sofa. Ignoring the blinking light on the answering machine, she set her pager on the end table and closed her eyes. She flipped her shoes onto the floor and propped her ankles on the arm of the couch.

It was days like this when she asked herself what she was thinking when she gave up the man she loved for that miraculous acceptance into medical school. And the answer was always the same. She had been thinking of her mother's struggle to provide for her and her sisters when their father walked out. She had been thinking of Katarina's hearing loss. Of the people she wanted to help. The last person she'd been thinking of was Kevin—the one person she should have considered more.

Her stomach growled, proclaiming that the salad she ate for lunch was long gone. She was famished. Dragging her fatigued body off the couch, Emily rummaged through the cupboard until she found a can of beef stew. The wind howled outside as a winter storm moved in from the west; snow was already sticking to the streets. *Thank goodness I'm not on call tonight,* she thought. Emily dumped the stew into the pan, turned on the burner, then simply stared at it, waiting for it to boil.

Kevin's words had haunted her for the past two weeks.

We can both be happy that you realized your career was more important than a family before it was too late. They stung because after years of wondering, she finally knew why Kevin hadn't come after her. He felt she'd abandoned their dreams for a job. That truth was especially difficult after days like today. Days that started before seven and didn't end when the office closed. Days that melded, one into the other. Days when crises happened nonstop.

Help me to remember that it's not for my own glory, Father, but for Yours.

Emily couldn't accept credit for the many decisions that had led her through the last few years. For without Him, she couldn't have survived it at all. Medical school, internship, finding a clinic whose mission fit so perfectly with her own. It was nothing short of a miracle, finding her way back to Springville, Colorado. Or so she'd thought.

Until she saw Kevin MacIntyre standing in her patient's hospital room.

Until her past caught up with the present and threatened to crush her future.

Until Kevin made her realize she *couldn't* "have it all."

There were countless days when she wished for all the things that he'd accused her of rejecting for her career. Times when she longed for the serenity of a man's loving embrace. Nights when she dreamed of her own children. And still she battled daily with the green monster, envying women who had mastered that delicate balance between career and family. There were even moments when she cursed the day he had walked away. And days when she wondered if Kevin had ever felt the same.

Her eyes burned with tears she refused to shed.

It appeared she now had the answer. He'd moved on with his life. And on, and on, obviously not letting their broken promises slow his social life any. It appeared her mother was right. Kevin was like her father: a fifties type of man, who wanted his woman to raise the children and have dinner ready at six o'clock. Kevin MacIntyre was definitely *not* the man to offer support throughout her demanding career.

Snow swirled around the parking lot and drifted along the curb. Kevin closed the door of his short-bed pickup, ready to work out with Bryan at the gym before heading home. Cranky and ready to burn off some frustration, Kevin stepped through the glass doors and headed for the lockers.

"Hi, Kevin."

He turned, temporarily distracted by the silky voice.

"Evening, Kristen. Looks like life is treating you well."

"Could be better. You've been avoiding me." The brunette leaned her elbows on the handles of the stationary bicycle and flashed him an accusing smile. Perfectly shaped eyebrows arched high above blue eyes.

He returned the smile, inwardly calculating just when he'd last seen her, or anyone not related to the business. "No, it's not that," he stalled, suddenly tongue-tied and in a hurry to make an exit. "Work is keeping me busy. Maybe we can do something soon."

He ducked into the men's locker room, surprised when Bryan stepped in just behind him.

"Gone into hiding, have you?" his friend joked.

Kevin shrugged, wondering himself why he'd brushed the woman off. He and Kristen had dated a few times after she had decorated one of his model homes. Things had been going fine. Neither wanted a commitment. Both enjoyed the same things. So why did he find himself avoiding her as if she were trying to tie him down?

"How are Laura and the kids?" Kevin asked, hoping to change the subject.

It worked.

Bryan talked enthusiastically about his new family, and a few minutes later they headed for the weight room. Kevin was anxious to get back in shape before the longer days of the spring building season began. He'd put in more hours at his drafting table than actually working with the crew over the past winter, and it was beginning to show around his midsection.

"You okay?" Bryan eyed him accusingly some time later as he added another cast-iron disk to each end of Kevin's weight bar. "I've never seen you avoiding—"

"Fine, just bored with it all, I guess." Kevin lifted the barbell, only to be interrupted by another female acquaintance. After she left, Kevin sat up and wiped his hands on the towel draped around his neck.

Bryan elbowed him. "What were you saying about your life being boring?" His friend raised an eyebrow and chuckled.

"You're a newlywed. You shouldn't be noticing other women," Kevin grumbled.

Bryan snapped the towel in midair. "Don't worry, I'm perfectly happy where I'm at. Unlike you—"

"Let's get out of here. We aren't going to get anything accomplished in this place. Why don't we go get a bite to eat?"

"Thanks, anyway, I've already eaten."

"Oh." On the way to the locker room, Kevin suddenly realized that although he was busier than ever, his personal life had come to a screeching halt in the wake of his company's booming success. Now that he thought about it, he hadn't been on a date in months. What was wrong with him? No wonder he was irritable. *All work and no play...is bound to get on a man's nerves.*

Nothing was the same anymore. Dating had lost its appeal, second only to going home to an empty house and an answering machine full of jobs to pursue. Which was just what he had wanted—a successful business. He should be ecstatic. There were plans to evaluate, bids to make, orders to call in; business was right on track.

But something was still missing.

Bryan pulled his bag from the locker with a look of total satisfaction. To his credit, though, he didn't say a word. And there were plenty of choice comments he could have made. Kevin knew, because he'd used them all on Bryan little more than a year ago.

His friend got a drink from the fountain, then cleared his throat. "I still have that weight set I bought Laura at the house. Why don't we work out there?"

"I don't know if I'm in any mood to deal with disgustingly happy newlyweds and four energetic kids at this hour," Kevin muttered under his breath.

Bryan looked at his watch and laughed. "Another fifteen minutes and they'll all be in bed, anyway. Come on over. I need someone to push me before Laura's good cooking puts twenty pounds on me."

"You poor thing." Kevin considered going home, but quickly dispelled the unappealing idea. Unlike his friend, he had no one, nothing to greet him at home. No commitments. No leash. *Keep talking, Kevin. Maybe you'll convince yourself.*

"Come on. It'll be fine."

"Sure, why not." What was he bellyaching about? He had a business that was claiming more of his time each day. More than he'd ever dreamed possible. "I'll meet you back at Laura's—I mean, your house." He winced at the mistake. He still found it difficult to understand why his best friend had agreed to stay in the house his new wife had shared with her late husband.

"Don't let it bother you. I do it, too. It'll always be Laura's, no matter how many changes we make. She promises to start looking for our own house as soon as things settle down."

"With four kids, you don't plan on that being anytime soon, do you?" Kevin wrapped an arm around his friend's back and laughed. "Ah, wedded bliss."

Bryan elbowed him in the stomach. "I'll take the chaos of a house full of kids over a quiet one any day. You sure you don't have time to build a house for us this spring?"

"If I'd known you were going to be back in town and in the market, believe me, I wouldn't have filled all my slots. You wouldn't believe how many calls I've had this week alone. But if the bid for the clinic falls through, you'll be the first person I call."

"Not a chance. There's no way the committee can afford to turn you down. I'm glad to hear you're keeping busy." Bryan stopped beside his new four-wheel-drive and tossed his bag inside. "Let's get going. We can catch up while we work out. Laura will be glad to see you."

A few minutes later, Kevin stomped the snow from his shoes and followed Bryan into the turn-of-the-century home, half expecting an ambush.

The sound of happy children and the smell of fresh-baked cookies met him at the front door and tugged on his heart. Laura's youngest son, Chad, ran to Bryan and jumped into his arms. "Hi, Dad! Did you come home to tuck us in?"

"I sure did—wouldn't miss it for the world." Chad beamed at his stepfather's attention. "Have you brushed your teeth?"

The youngster scrunched his nose, then turned toward Kevin and said hello.

Bryan set his stepson down and patted him on the behind. "Get it done, and I'll be right up."

"T.J.! Kevin and Dad are here!"

"Chad, don't yell, please." Laura passed through the kitchen just as they did, and gave her husband a kiss. "You're home so soon? We've only been married a few weeks. You can't be that out of shape yet," she teased.

Bryan tilted his head toward Kevin and laughed. "Too many distractions there."

"And you came to this zoo instead?" Then, as realization hit her, she grinned mischievously. "Oh. You mean...*distractions*. Well, you may as well use that contraption you two brought me last year. It's going to rust if someone doesn't use it. I told you I didn't have time."

"I'm not giving up on you yet." T.J. ran into the room and gave Kevin a high-five, and Bryan let his embrace loosen. "Is Jacob asleep already?"

Laura playfully pushed him away. "'Already'? You haven't been chasing him since six this morning. I'm wiped out."

"Mom," their daughter beckoned.

"Just a few minutes, T.J. Kevin, please don't get him riled up, it's bedtime."

Kevin gave his friend's wife a salute. "Yes sir, lady."

Bryan kissed Laura again before she headed to the children's bedrooms, then turned to Kevin. "I'll help Laura tuck the kids in, and be right down."

Kevin and T.J. visited about school and sports for a few minutes before Kevin sent the young man up to bed.

He could see why Bryan liked this chaos. He paused. *Don't go there, Kevin,* said an inner voice.

He and Bryan lifted weights for an hour, taking time to catch up on each other's lives and discuss business before he left. Bryan insisted he wanted to remain a silent partner because he knew nothing about the construction business, but Kevin appreciated his friend's willingness to brainstorm business tactics, anyhow. Just talking helped clear things in his own mind. And there was certainly enough to muddle his thoughts these days.

One of which was the Sonshine Medical Clinic bid. With Bryan's business sense, and Kevin's construction knowledge, they had come up with what they hoped was a winning proposal—one that would help the company remain secure for generations to come.

Laura sent a plate of peanut butter cookies home with him, another reminder of what was missing in his life. Homemade cookies…and someone to share them with. *A lot of good building a company is going to do—you don't even have anyone to pass it down to when you're gone.* He immediately thought of his father, and pushed the bittersweet memories away.

Kevin pulled the truck into the garage and climbed the steps to his empty house. Here it was, nearly ten o'clock, and he'd done everything possible to avoid coming home.

While dinner was heating in the microwave, Kevin showered and threw on a pair of ragged old sweats. Clearing that morning's breakfast dishes from the table, he poured a tall glass of milk and turned the big-screen television on to catch the end of the late news and eat his ''dinner.''

After the sports segment ended, Kevin switched off the TV, immediately deafened by the silence. He turned it on again and tossed the remote control onto the sofa, then retreated into his office. He clicked on the radio, hoping the noise would drown out the emptiness so he could concentrate on work.

He had already waited a week past the deadline to hear from the clinic regarding the renovations. If they wanted to break ground in a month, a decision had to be made soon. He couldn't afford to put off other projects much longer.

Having spent a year looking for the right project to launch a commercial branch, he couldn't believe it when he learned the best prospect would mean facing Emily on a daily basis. This decision came with a bucketful of mixed emotions. He'd almost backed away because of her; yet Bryan had convinced him to go through with it, even agreed to remain a silent partner to show his support and assure Kevin that he'd have the money necessary. They both knew Kevin couldn't manage the financial end without Bryan's investment. There was a lot riding on this bid. It was one thing to jeopardize his own financial security, but Bryan's and his employees' was another issue altogether.

The renovation of Sonshine Medical Clinic was a high-profile project with a strong emotional tie to the community. Even if Kevin lost money, if all went well, it would bring in more work than his growing company could manage. He wasn't going to get anywhere in this business by playing it safe. His dad's experience had proven that. In order to prove to himself and his family that he could have kept the family business going after his father's death, he had to do this, and succeed. Nothing was going to stand in his way. MacIntyre Construction would make it to the top, and stay there.

He looked at the note Bryan had given him and read the verse from the Book of Proverbs: "Commit to the

Lord whatever you do, and your plans will succeed."
Kevin shook his head, trying to maintain his optimism.
If it's meant to be, it'll work out. *Think positively.*

Kevin perched himself on the edge of the chair, the
clinic's blueprints spread across his drafting table. He
took a deep breath and let it out, struggling to get his
mind back on business. He looked at his changes. "Okay.
We'll have to open this wall to do the extra wiring." He
jotted notes to contact subcontractors as he went along.
His eyes roamed down the sketch to the office with "Dr.
Emily" in the corner. His mind drifted back to the day
he went to visit Laura in the hospital and ran head-on
into his past...

"If you'll excuse us, sir." Emily had said. No hello.
Just that phony smile plastered across her face. Her dis-
position was as bristly as steel wool. Trying to ignore
Emily, he had joked with Laura, leaving the poor patient
in tears because it hurt to laugh after her abdominal surgery. Emily had mistaken Laura's tears for her feelings
having been hurt, and the doctor had actually *scolded*
him. So much for bedside manner.

Even angry, she'd attracted him. Affected him. Made
him look at the years without her and see how empty life
was. He faced the truth—he'd been living a superficial
and indulgent existence. After nearly eight years apart,
merely seeing Emily had changed his life—again.

Kevin slapped the ruler onto the paper and drew in the
new wall. *It's strictly business, Emily. Strictly business.*
He tried to erase the image of the unforgettable redhead
from his mind. He didn't need to be reminded of the pain.
Hers, or his. Eight years was a long time.

He had changed. The past was over. And love was out
of the question—something to be avoided at all costs.

*But handing my troubles to God just isn't as easy as
it sounds.*

Chapter Four

The phone rang, and Kevin let the answering machine do its job, glad the volume was turned down. He was in no mood to talk to anyone. The machine clicked off, and he returned to work. A couple of hours later he decided to call it a night. On the way through the kitchen, he pushed Play on the recorder, and was puzzled by the final message.

Kevin rewound the tape and played the last message again.

"How could you?" the woman's voice said.

"Emily?" He sat down at his desk and dialed the only listing in her name, but was intercepted by the clinic's answering service. She wasn't the doctor on call. He tried to explain the situation, only the receptionist wouldn't give out a home number.

He thought of calling Laura and Bryan to get her number, then realized it was far too late to call anyone. Besides, Laura would *never* give up her task as matchmaker if she knew he was trying to reach Emily.

That night Kevin slept fitfully, pondering what exactly

she had meant by her message. *How could I what?* Could she have found out he was bidding on the job? No, that couldn't be the case. They couldn't reveal names on a silent bid. Unless they'd already hired another contractor. No, he couldn't even consider that.

If he didn't get the bid, he'd be furious she found out he had even been interested in the project. Knowing the way women think, she'd jump to the conclusion that he'd done it to be near her. Not a chance. It was business, pure and simple.

By dawn, he was just plain mad. He wondered why she thought she should have any say in his life at all. It was still too early to reach Emily at the office, and he had plenty to do before the clinic opened, anyway. After breakfast, he loaded his briefcase, tossed it into the cab of his truck and headed to the job site.

Kevin inspected the equipment, gave directions to get the workers going, then went into his pickup and pulled out his cellular phone. He called his office manager, relieved that she had a message for him to call the clinic director. Kevin called right away, encouraged when the director wanted to set up a meeting as soon as possible.

When Kevin asked to speak to Dr. Berthoff, though, he had no better luck getting hold of her than he had had the previous night. He considered leaving his mobile number, but decided against it. *Sounds like it won't be long before I'll have plenty of opportunity to talk to her.*

After getting the crew started on the two houses they were finishing, Kevin left for the clinic. Trying not to be overly confident, he gathered his courage and walked inside. He was escorted through the lobby, down dingy halls, and into the director's office.

"Kevin, I'm glad you called." The balding gentleman pumped Kevin's arm enthusiastically and motioned for him to sit down in the vinyl-upholstered armchair. Kevin could see why they were renovating. *Run-down* didn't begin to describe the place.

An hour later he walked out of the meeting with a new contract that would drastically change his life, one way or another. If all went as planned, he'd be doubling his staff size within the year. If not, he'd be jumping into the market looking for a new employer himself.

He turned left and headed to the lobby.

"Kevin?"

He'd know that voice anywhere.

Pivoting, he realized he must have taken a wrong turn and ended up near the examination rooms. Emily and another doctor stood shoulder to shoulder, having been reading a chart. He looked at the man, then to Emily, then back again.

"Excuse me, Bob. Unless you need this immediately, could we finish discussing it later?"

Kevin watched as the doctor assessed him. "Sure, why not over lunch?"

Emily's gaze met Kevin's as she gave the preppy doctor a curt response. "You know why not."

As if her punch needed help, Kevin mumbled sympathetically to Bob, "I wouldn't let it keep you up nights."

Emily paused momentarily to scold him with her eyes, then motioned for Kevin to follow her. There was a tilt to the corners of her lips, but he could say with certainty that it wasn't a welcoming look. "How are you, Kevin?"

"From the sounds of your message, maybe I'd better let you tell me. That was your *charming* voice on my answering machine, wasn't it?"

She walked into a cubicle with her name on the door,

and he paused to examine the nameplate: Emily Berthoff, M.D.

Her answer was interrupted by the phone.

Taking the opportunity to collect information, he tapped on the wall, pretending to examine the structure. Her office was filled with books, books and more books. Same old Emily. Only difference was the titles. He could still picture her with her nose in those college textbooks. Heaven knows, he'd done his best to take her mind off her studies.... It hadn't worked then, and if he was smart, he wouldn't bother trying now.

The wallpaper here was outdated, even by his standards. There wasn't a plant, flower or photograph in sight. Nothing to indicate a family or a life beyond her career—

She ended the phone call and looked at him expectantly.

"I don't think I've had the chance to congratulate you, Doctor."

"Congratulate me?"

"On your degree." Kevin touched the rounded desk corner sticking out from under the stacks of books, files and journals.

"Oh." Her green eyes opened wide with surprise. "I never know whether to take you seriously or not."

Blast it, lady, don't look at me like that. I'm trying to be nice. How could one sentence throw him all the way back to the day she'd walked out of his life?

Emily walked back to the door and closed it. "The last time we discussed my career choice, you were less than encouraging."

And now she was back, he thought. Every workday for the next six months. He had to keep peace between them.

"Whether or not I liked your decision is no longer an issue. I said 'congratulations,' and I meant it. It took a lot of work, and you deserve credit for it."

Obviously confused, she said merely, "Thank you." Emily put her hands in the pockets of her yellow blazer and took a deep breath. "Why, Kevin?"

Same Emily. Right to the point. "Why? I thought the message said, 'How could you?'" He smiled. "Don't I get some sort of congratulations for accomplishing *my* goals?"

"The way I remember it, your plan was to run your father's business. In fact, as I recall, that's why you stayed—and I left. Alone."

"Things changed. I have my own company now, which just happens to have landed a terrific deal." The elation inside was fading fast. He hadn't expected a red-carpet celebration, but even a halfhearted welcome would have been appreciated.

"So I figured out. Which was the meaning of my message last night. How *could* you bid on our project?" She stepped around the desk and looked him in the eye, as if trying to intimidate him. "Why this job? Why not some other building project?" she asked with more than a hint of disapproval.

"It was purely a business decision," he said, meeting her challenging gaze. *Two can play this game, Doc.*

"A business decision?" Her voice caught.

"That's right, strictly business. Relax. It had nothing to do with you." He stuffed his hands in his pockets and jingled the change against his truck keys. He wasn't about to tell her how many times he had almost turned away *because* of her.

She ran her fingers through her hair, lifting it away from her face, and he felt his heart skip a beat. *Don't do this, buddy. She's off-limits. Business and pleasure don't mix. Remember that, whatever you do!*

"Surely there's another opportunity that would bring in a better profit than ours. As long as this is 'strictly business,' that is," she said tartly. Reaching for the desk, she closed a thick book and placed it on the jam-packed shelves. "How could you do this?"

Kevin crossed his arms and took a deep breath. "I could do it for the same reason you went across the country to your prestigious medical school. It was the best option available at the time."

She stared, a cold look that could build walls in an instant. Her phone rang, and she answered, still holding his gaze. "I'll be right there," she said into the receiver. Her eyes left his and she stepped around the desk. "I have an emergency."

He nodded, then opened the door and waited for her to go ahead. "Let's make a deal, Doc. I won't practice medicine, and you don't tell me how to run my business. Okay?"

Without responding, Emily rushed out of her office, and Kevin followed. Down the corridor, he saw a petite woman struggle to keep a stocky teenager, who'd obviously met up with someone's fist, on his feet. From the lobby, he heard the receptionist trying to get the woman to wait for a wheelchair.

"Here, let me get him." Kevin wrapped his arm behind the boy's back and followed Emily's directions. Once the patient was secure on an examination table, Emily put on gloves and began to clean his cuts. Kevin backed through the door, right into the doctor Emily had brushed off earlier. Through the opening, Kevin heard Emily tell the nurse to bring in novocaine and a suture kit, then turn to soothe the upset mother.

"Looks like Dr. Emily has it under control. Guess I'll go grab some lunch by myself," said the other doctor as he removed his stark-white lab coat and headed out the back door.

Kevin looked back at Emily, then walked down the long hall to the lobby. "If nothing else, this should be an interesting few months," Kevin muttered as he headed to his truck.

The remainder of the morning was a chaotic combination of reviewing applicants' resumes and ordering supplies. Always in the back of his mind was Emily, and the anger he'd seen in her expression when she saw him in the hallway.

But there was no room for second thoughts. He'd just landed the deal that could make or break his business. Emily had already met her goals, despite what they had cost her personally. He had let her go then, determined he wouldn't stand in her way.

Now, he'd be certain she didn't stand in his.

After getting his day back under control, Kevin called Bryan to tell him the news.

His friend bolstered his enthusiasm. "Told you they'd jump on your offer."

Kevin swallowed a lump of pent-up apprehension and felt a wave of relief, content that he'd done the right thing. "Yeah. They're having some publicity shindig Friday night to get the deal moving. As a partner in the business, you're obligated to attend, and bring your lovely wife."

"Sounds great." Bryan paused. "Hey, friend, don't forget, you're expected to bring a date, too."

A date. *Sure, why not. After all, this is a reason to celebrate.*

* * *

Emily zipped the crushed-velvet evening dress, then stepped into her black pumps just as the doorbell rang. "I can't believe I have to go to this reception for Kevin." She grumbled all the way to the front door. She tried to steel herself for a miserable night. Adding insult to injury, her car had had a flat tire when she'd left the office, and the first person to the rescue happened to be Bob Walker—Dr. Casanova.

She opened the door and met him on the porch. "Hi, Bob. I appreciate the lift."

"If I'd known a flat tire was all it would take to change your mind…" He smiled suggestively and lifted her hand to kiss it.

Emily pushed him away, amazed that a man with such a brilliant mind could be such a loser. "I don't want to go through this all evening. I won't. If I had *any* choice in the matter, I wouldn't even be going tonight."

"I wish you'd change your mind, Emily. All I ask for is a few minutes to explain."

"There's nothing to explain. I'm well aware of the facts of life. I think that was covered in basic pre-med, wasn't it? Maybe you missed that year."

"It was nothing," he began, following her to his car.

Emily opened her own door, ignoring his attempts to act like a gentleman. "One receptionist may have been nothing, the second one—"

"We never went out."

She dropped herself into a seat that barely cleared the ground. "Because she was married." Emily looked at him. "You just don't understand, do you, Bob? That is bordering on harassment."

"No harm in a little flirting." He shrugged, ignoring her warning.

She shook her head and closed her door to Bob's lame

explanation. He'd blown any chances of a relationship with her, or any woman in their office. And now Emily was getting a headache, complete with a sudden case of the jitters. The last thing she needed was Bob next to her whining all evening.

Everyone in the clinic would be there to kick off the renovation. It was critical that she and Kevin be on their best behavior. Neither could take a chance of endangering their positions by revealing their past relationship.

Kevin's employees would be there, as would his silent partner and best friend, Bryan Beaumont. At least she would have Laura to visit with.

When they arrived, Emily walked into the restaurant as quickly as she could to avoid being paired up with Dr. Casanova. She was immediately greeted by Laura.

"Emily, I thought you'd never get here," Laura exclaimed. "Is this your new boyfriend?"

Emily turned around to see who Laura was referring to, praying it wasn't Bob. *I can't believe I ever even considered dating him,* she thought. "No, he's not. In fact, if Bob is any indicator of men these days, I'm through looking. Men just can't be trusted." She glanced at Laura, realizing she'd stuck her foot in her mouth already. "Oh, I know Bryan's different."

Laura smiled. "Yes, he is. But he isn't the only trustworthy man alive, you know."

There was a dreadfully long silence before Emily explained the situation with her car, ignoring Laura's comment altogether. She didn't need to expose her jaded opinions of men to a woman who'd found another wonderful husband after the death of her first husband. *Just because all the men in my life walk out when I need them most doesn't mean a thing, I'm sure. Who needs them, anyway?* "Would you and Bryan be able to give me a lift home?"

"I'm sure Bryan wouldn't mind. Let's go find him. Kevin was introducing him to some of your partners. I went to the ladies' room and haven't caught back up with him."

"Laura, I'd rather not…"

Laura touched Emily's arm sympathetically. "Kevin brought a date, so there's no reason to feel awkward. She's actually pretty nice."

A date? Why was she surprised? There was no reason Kevin shouldn't bring someone. In fact, she should be thrilled. What better way to avoid him?

They made their way through the crowd and to the hors d'oeuvres, finally finding Bryan at a table near the front of the room. Laura invited Emily to sit with her, which Emily was glad to do, until she realized Kevin and his date were seated at the same table. She glanced around, quickly realizing that most everyone had quit mingling—she had a choice between Bob's table, or Kevin's.

Friends had informed her that Kevin had started dating soon after their breakup. That knowledge was unsettling, especially now that she was sitting across from him and his gorgeous girlfriend. Laura was right: Kristen seemed amazingly likable. If nothing else, Emily would love watching Kevin squirm.

Emily sat down, and was soon listening as Kristen explained her work as an interior decorator, though her attention drifted to Kevin and Bryan joking together. Emily remembered with fondness their friendly banter. Ignoring the emotion building inside, she distracted herself from admiring how handsome Kevin looked in a suit and tie.

The khaki blazer and baby-blue shirt accentuated the color of his eyes and complimented his curly golden hair.

She turned toward the raucous sound of laughter and the clinking of silverware against china across the room. Toasts were made to a successful project. Platters of shrimp scampi emerged from the kitchen. She and Kevin exchanged a glance. *Déjà vu.* Unexpectedly, the years between disappeared, and Emily found it impossible not to return Kevin's disarming smile.

Emily heard a pager beeping, and to her relief noticed Bob leaving the party.

Laura quickly jumped up and headed toward the ladies' room. Bryan quietly asked Emily to check on her, explaining that his wife had been battling the flu for a couple of weeks. Emily wanted to laugh, surprised at the naiveté of this father of four. Taking into consideration that his wife had left their marriage before telling him she was expecting, she simply patted his shoulder and followed Laura.

She went into the ladies' room, and wasn't surprised to find the newlywed blotting her face with a cold paper towel.

Laura looked up, a wan hint of embarrassment coloring her cheeks. "Are you here as a friend, or a doctor?" Laura took a mouthful of water, swished it through her mouth and spit it out.

"I'm not sure which you need more right now." Smiling, Emily stepped closer to the trim woman and felt her forehead. "No fever. Your husband seems to think you need a doctor. He hasn't a clue what's wrong, does he?"

Laura shook her head. She leaned her elbows on the edge of the sink. "He's had so much to adjust to. And contrary to what you think, we weren't trying yet. He wanted to wait a few more months," she mumbled through the soggy paper towel.

Emily let out a long sigh, struggling between her instincts as a doctor to agree with Bryan and the brief jealous longing of a woman. "Have you taken a test?"

"Who needs one? This is my fourth, Emily. The flu doesn't last two weeks. Besides, the office doesn't usually want to see a patient until they're ten weeks, right? I wanted to wait another week or two to tell Bryan. I don't want to worry him." Laura took a deep breath and exhaled.

"With your recent history, it wouldn't hurt to come in earlier, Laura—make sure everything's settled in the right place." Emily suggested Laura sit down in the soft chair in the corner for a few minutes before going back to the party.

Laura stood up straight and smoothed the front of her column dress, then brushed her hair back into order. She took a compact from her purse and applied some color to her pale cheeks. "That shrimp sounded so good, but when I smelled it..."

Emily could sympathize with a missed dinner.

"I wish I could see the look on Bryan's face when you tell him," she said to lighten the mood.

Laura's face paled again as she looked toward the creaking door behind Emily. "Looks like you may get your wish," she whispered.

Bryan peeked into the ladies' room and looked around uncomfortably. "Are you okay, honey?"

The concern in his eyes was obvious.

Laura closed the gap between them and hugged her husband, whispering in his ear. His face creased into a heartwarming smile. Bryan's hands were on her waist, and he pulled her closer.

Emily felt like an intruder watching the tender exchange of their kiss. Yet, much as she tried, she couldn't look away.

Bryan gave his wife one more hug, then held her at arm's distance and looked into her eyes. "Maybe I'd better take you home."

Emily interrupted. "I think that's an excellent idea. I hear jelly beans do wonders for morning sickness, which, by the way, can occur any time of day."

Laura glanced at Bryan, a guilty look on her face. "I should be fine now. This is Kevin's big night. You should be here for him."

Easing his way out of the ladies' room, Bryan shook his head. "You can't even stand the smell of the food, Laura. You know how protective Kevin is. He'd insist."

"You can't tell him the news now. I don't want to overshadow his night."

Bryan thought a moment, then turned to Emily. "Could you explain for us, Em?"

"I'll tell him that Laura wasn't feeling well, and I insisted you take her home. He wouldn't dare argue."

Laura broke into a wide smile, and exchanged a knowing glance with her husband.

"Don't get any ideas. Just doing my job." The two turned to leave, and Emily added, "Bryan, I want to see her on Monday, just to be on the safe side."

"Consider it done."

The two left, and Emily felt tears sting her eyes. *This is ridiculous. You deal with pregnant women every day, Emily. Why should Laura be any different?*

Emily sat down and took a deep breath, willing herself to relax. Other women came and went, and each time Emily claimed she had something in her eye. Finally, she dried the tears, then splashed cool water on her face. She allowed her eyes a few minutes to clear before returning to the table to get her purse and leave.

But the elegant decorations—calla lilies and spires of fresh greenery—had been cleared from the tables, and the guests were already gone. She must have lost track of time.

Kevin and his date were making their way toward her. Kristen released Kevin's arm when he turned toward Emily. "How is Laura?"

"She wasn't feeling well, so I insisted Bryan take her home." Emily looked toward the table for her purse. As if reading her mind, Kevin produced it. His hand looked incredibly tender holding the tiny evening bag, and Emily felt emotion choke her throat. "Thank you."

His gaze lingered, and Emily's heart raced despite the knowledge that Kevin's girlfriend had reclaimed her place beside him. "It seems your ride left already. Let us give you a lift home."

"No. Thank you, anyway." She glanced around, observing that the room was now filled with wait staff whisking dishes and linens into the back room. "I'll call a cab."

"It's bad PR to leave a member of the clinic board waiting for an unreliable cab service." He broke away from Kristen again, and pulled Emily aside. "Not to mention, I want to know what's really going on, and why you're upset."

She glared at him. "Now's not the time. You have a date." The last thing she needed tonight was to share her private misery with Kevin.

"I think that's up to me to decide." His eyes drilled intimately through her. "Let me get Kristen's coat."

"What?" She stared at him in amazement. "When did you become so cultured?" The words slipped from her mouth. So far, they had both been careful not to reveal their past relationship, and she hoped Kristen missed the inference.

"You might be surprised," he quipped, a teasing glint in his eyes.

When he returned, Kevin helped Kristen with her fake fur coat, then escorted them both to his truck. The awkwardness didn't end when they all piled into the cab, with Kristen crowded into the middle.

Emily gave Kevin her address and asked if he needed directions. When he turned in the opposite direction, Emily glanced at Kristen. The woman's resentment was apparent. "Kevin, I need to get home," Emily insisted.

"I need to call it an early night myself. I'm sure Kristen understands, don't you?" Kevin's voice carried a tone that Emily knew all too well. The discussion was over. And from the look on his date's face, so was their relationship.

Kevin pulled to a stop in front of the woman's town house. Trapped between them, Kristen looked at Emily, as if it were obvious that she refused to exit the truck from Kevin's door as she had entered.

"I—I'm sorry, Kristen," Emily stammered as she got out to let Kristen exit. Kevin walked around the truck to escort his date to the door.

"I don't know what's going on between you two, but tell Kevin not to bother calling back until it's over for good this time."

Emily stared at the woman, who turned and began walking so fast on her spiked heels that her legs wobbled. Kevin trailed behind, and didn't seem surprised, moments later, to have the door slammed in his face.

Emily hurried to climb back into the truck before Kevin returned to help her. She hiked the hem of her dress an inch to step up onto the chrome running board, but her foot slipped. From the corner of her eye, she saw Kevin rush forward, too late to catch her before she hit the ground.

Chapter Five

"**E**mily!" Kevin dropped to his knees beside her. "Are you okay?"

She groaned softly, rubbing the back of her head. "I can't believe I did that."

"Well, it's a first for me, too. Never had a lady hurry just to avoid letting me help her get in. Guess that'll teach me to take two women home at the same time, huh?"

Emily lay awkwardly on the cold ground trying to explain how she'd fallen, but finally her irritation won. "Oh, forget it," she said, trying to get up gracefully. "Would you mind helping? Please."

He placed a hand on her shoulder to hold her still and leaned closer to examine her head. "You sure we should move you?"

"Who's the doctor here?" She squirmed, struggling to get to her feet. "I'm fine."

Kevin pulled her away from the truck door, trying to ignore the way her auburn hair tumbled from the curved silver clip and shimmered in the moonlight. "Hang on." Kevin put one hand under her knees, the other behind her back, and lifted her off the ground. The touch of her hands on his neck brought back dangerous memories he would just as soon have kept locked away. He didn't move. He couldn't. His gaze dropped to her lips. All he could think of was the unthinkable.

"Kevin. Don't even…" she scolded, at the same time sending him a calculating gaze that half dared him to try.

He smiled, thinking about accepting the challenge, and his foolishness for even tempting fate. "Don't worry, Doc, I wouldn't dream of it." It didn't help when he saw the heart-shaped opening in the back of her otherwise conservative crushed-velvet dress.

She loosened her embrace, sudden panic in her eyes. "I think you should put me into the truck before your irate girlfriend finds us like this and gets the wrong impression—again."

He paused, then not-so-gently dropped her onto the seat and slammed the door closed. What was he thinking? He knew better than to play with fire.

They drove in silence for the first five minutes. "I've told you already, she's not a girlfriend. I mean, she was, but… She's not."

Her eyes glimmered with amusement. "You can say that again." Emily tugged the hem of her dress closer to her knees and began fishing around on the floor. "She certainly acted like she *thought* she was your girl, didn't she?"

I don't owe you any explanation. You can't even be civil! "What are you doing?" he asked instead to change the subject.

Emily continued to dig around on the floor. "Trying to find my evening bag and shoe."

"Your what? When did you lose those?" He pulled

the truck to the curb and shifted into Park. Once the dome light was on, he joined the search.

"Sorry, but I wasn't thinking of my feet when you tossed me into the truck and slammed the door in my face."

Kevin muttered under his breath when he realized he had no choice but to turn around and go back to Kristen's. When they arrived, they saw both items laying in the driveway. Glancing at the glowing windows to see if Kristen was looking, Kevin jumped from the cab, retrieved the dainty black bag and high heel, then returned to Emily.

"What would Kristen think if she found these? She already believes there's something between us," Emily said with concern.

Kevin slipped the shoe onto her foot and set the purse in her lap, giving in to the temptation to flirt. He quirked his eyebrows and smiled. "I'd say she's a mind reader." Emily yanked her foot away from his hand and turned away.

"Let's get you home, before anything else goes wrong." He should have known better than to tease her— even after all these years. *The sooner I get you home the better.*

Emily clutched her door when he spun the truck around, making it lumber over the bumpy curb. "We'd have been fine if you had taken me home first. Everyone would have been happy. I wouldn't have a concussion, Kristen wouldn't be furious with you, and you...well, you wouldn't be stuck here yelling at me over something I had no control over."

"A concussion?"

She cleared her throat. "Okay, so I exaggerated."

Kevin let out a deep breath, silently assessing her fall.

"First of all, if there's a chance you have a concussion, we should take you to the hospital and have you checked out." He drummed his fingers on the steering wheel, impatient for Emily to say something.

"I don't need to go to the hospital."

He wasn't about to leave her alone until he was sure she was okay. He'd had enough experience with injuries in college football to know the risks. It was too dark to tell much in the truck. It would have to wait until they got to her house.

"Second, I'm not concerned with how furious Kristen is. The only reason I called her is that Bryan insisted I should have a date." This was his fault. He should have called Emily a cab. Not that he cared one iota that this definitely ended any chances with Kristen.

He had known seeing Emily tonight would be rough, but he hadn't expected it to be this bad. It was a constant battle to remind himself that there was no longer any use trying to make the stubborn doctor swoon. It was obvious that she was convinced the breakup was his fault. Thinking back, he guessed it probably was as much his fault as it was hers, but would she see it that way? He doubted it.

In the long run, the family business was gone along with the original proprietor. His family hadn't been the same since.

She reminded him to turn south on Main Street. A few blocks later, he pulled into her driveway and ran around the truck to help her out. She stepped down, brushing him away. "I'm fine. I can see myself in."

"I'll leave just as soon as I'm sure you're okay, and not a minute earlier. Besides, you haven't told me about Laura yet."

Emily winced as she put her weight on her foot. She

couldn't let Kevin see her limping or she'd never get him to leave. And the last thing she could handle tonight was Kevin MacIntyre playing nurse.

"I couldn't help but notice that you showed up with Dr. Walker. Are you and he...you know."

"If it's any of your business, no, we're not!" Tempting as it was to make Kevin wonder, the thought of willingly allowing *anyone* to mistake her and Bob for a couple was out of the question. "I had a flat tire when I came out of the office tonight, and he gave me a ride." She took a step, tentatively lifting the good foot. Her leg crumpled, and Kevin caught her. "It'll be fine. I probably just twisted it a little."

"Yeah, yeah, it'll be good as new in a few days." He offered an arm to lean on and helped her to the front door. She had no choice but to accept. "Where are your keys?"

She opened the tiny bag, but realized she'd forgotten to move the keys from her carry-all in her rush to avoid letting Bob into the house. She let out a sigh of frustration. "They're inside. I was in such a hurry, I forgot to move them to my evening bag."

"Where's your extra key hidden?"

She closed her eyes and rubbed the lump on her head. "I don't know. I don't think I have one."

"Any windows open?" he drilled impatiently.

She shook her head. "Too cold out."

Before she could argue, he swooped her into his arms again and headed back to the truck, mumbling under his breath.

"Put me down, Kevin. I'm not going anywhere with you."

"Are you going to play Casper the Ghost and go right through the door?" He stood by the truck and looked her in the eye. "You have three choices, Emily. I can leave you on the porch, I can call a locksmith, or you can come to my place for the night."

"I don't think so!"

He laughed cynically. "I thought you'd see it my way. Now listen here, lady. You have a lump on your head, a sprained ankle and a very cold porch."

"A sprained ankle? And what did you base your diagnosis on, Dr. MacIntyre?"

He paused, and a twinkle of moonlight caught in his eyes as his gaze met hers. "I've had seventeen of them. And amazingly enough, I limped just like you. As much as I'd love to stand here holding you, it isn't getting us anywhere. Open that truck door for me so you can sit inside, and we can take care of one problem at a time. I'll use the phone in the truck, since I assume you don't have your cell phone in that itty-bitty bag of yours."

Emily looked sheepishly at him and opened the door. Her mouth gaping open. *It's over between us, isn't it? He abandoned me once, he'd do it again.*

He watched her struggling for words. "Must be my charm, huh?" He laughed, but she couldn't. That was exactly what it was. She couldn't think with him holding her, helping her, taking care of her.

He set her down with care and closed the door lightly this time. She watched as he walked past the hood of his hunter-green truck, thinking *she* was the one who took care of people. No one took care of her. Even when they'd been engaged, he'd never taken care of her. *Maybe you never gave him the chance,* said a voice inside her.

Emily realized Kevin was talking, and turned her attention to the arrangements he was making for the locksmith to come to her address. He started the truck and turned on the heater.

"You warm enough?" Kevin switched on the dome light, then lifted his arm to the back of the seat and reached for her hair clip. "May I?"

An unwelcome chill went up her spine and she chastised herself. He only wanted to check her head. "I thought we agreed, you won't play doctor, and I won't play builder."

"Yeah, well, maybe next time, Doc. It's either me, or the hospital staff. Take your choice." Emily hesitantly turned her head so he could look for any swelling. He unfastened the clip and slipped his fingers through her hair.

She pressed her eyes closed, refusing to let herself think of the old days. He carefully touched the perimeter of the goose egg and let out a little whistle. "That's one nasty bump. Let's check your eyes."

She couldn't bear the thought of him looking into her eyes. It was simply too much. "I'm fine."

"Hmph," he said, handing her the clip. "It'll be a while 'til the locksmith can get here. Why don't you recline the seat while I dig an ice pack from my first-aid kit. I'll be right back."

She felt the truck bounce as he slammed the metal box behind the cab closed and climbed back in beside her. He broke the inner sack of the disposable ice bag and mixed the contents, then placed it behind her head.

Suddenly there was an uncomfortable silence between them. Their few attempts at a conversation went dry. A few minutes later, the locksmith pulled into the driveway behind them. After confirming ownership by checking Emily's identification, he opened the front door. Kevin paid the man and came back to the truck for Emily.

Once inside the house, he deposited her on the sofa and closed the front door.

"Thank you for the ride home, Kevin. I don't want to delay you any longer."

Ignoring her, he loosened his tie and turned away, pacing the room. "I know you don't want to believe me, but I'm really not the louse your mother made me out to be. Yet I'm not here tonight to start over, either."

She stared at his broad shoulders, at the curls of blond hair, at the tension in his jaw. Part of her wanted to cry at his admission, and another part wanted to laugh. Not as much had changed about Kevin as she'd originally thought. Cynicism might have overshadowed his sense of humor at times, but he was still as open as could be. "Thank you for clarifying that." She didn't know whether to be hurt or relieved. "However, you don't need to stay. I can take care of myself—been doing it all my life." She didn't mean to sound harsh, but the words had an unavoidable bite to them.

"I just want you to understand, there's no room for dreams of family in my life. We both have other things we have to do now. Life goes on."

"Why don't we just avoid seeing each other altogether?" she snapped. How dare he presume she was even remotely interested in a relationship with him again?

"Come on, Emily. It may be over between us, but we can try at least to be civil, can't we?" He straightened his back, and his eyes narrowed. "Once I'm sure you're okay, I'll be out of here. But until then, sit back, relax, and tell me where I could find your coffeepot. We're going to need something to keep us awake."

"Don't bother, Kevin. I'll be fine."

Kevin glanced around the room, from the checkered sofa to the fresh flowers on the dining room table. Trying to close the door on his curiosity, he looked back to Emily, who was now falling asleep.

"Open your eyes, Emmy."

They popped open.

"What day is it?" he asked.

She looked at him, annoyed. "Friday."

"How old are you?"

She hesitated.

"Come on, Emily. It's not like we have any real secrets, is it?"

"Thirty-two," she admitted reluctantly, as if it would be news to him. He knew she'd be thirty-three in two months. Surely Emily didn't think he'd forgotten her birthday.

"Your sisters' names?"

"Lisa and Katarina. See, I passed the test."

"Your boyfriend's name?"

She laughed. "Nice try."

He smiled. "Never hurts to ask." He looked into her green eyes, noting there was no difference between the pupils. He continued to examine them, while stealing a peek at the woman inside—the woman he had known and loved long ago. There was an impenetrable wall there, and he felt a shock of disappointment zap him back to reality.

"You're free to go home. I know what to watch for—headache, nausea, dilated pupils."

"Time will tell, won't it?" He moved to a chair across the room. "Humor me, prove me wrong."

"It's been a very long day, Kevin, and I'd like to go to bed—er, get some sleep." She turned her body, dropped her feet from the sofa to the floor.

"You know I can't let you do that. Come on, Emmy, pretend eight years ago never happened, just for tonight. I'm not going anywhere." He slipped his loafers off and set them neatly next to the chair. After an uncomfortable silence, Kevin leaned back and crossed one ankle over the opposite knee. "So what's wrong with Laura?"

He saw a sad and pained expression flash in her eyes. "I think that's for them to say." She ran her fingers through her hair, allowing it to veil her face.

"Bryan said you'd explain. You have his blessing."

"She's my patient. You'll have to talk to them."

He'd never before seen her squirm like this.

"I'm going to go change. Feel free to leave." She stood, stumbling as she did so.

He stood up and took hold of her arm, steadying her, but she shook loose. "What's wrong, Emily?"

She hobbled down the hall and slammed the door behind her. Kevin felt his own stomach tighten. He checked his watch, confirming his suspicion that it was too late to call Bryan. Storming after her, he felt the panic rise inside. "Emily. What is wrong with Laura?"

On the other side of the door, he heard her crying. "Go home, Kevin. Just go!"

He turned the knob and stepped inside the room. "You okay?"

Her answer was clear as she blew her nose. Tears streamed from her eyes.

"Come on, Emily, you're scaring me. Is Laura sick?" Kevin took her by the shoulders and turned her toward him.

"She'll be fine."

"Tears and a diagnosis of 'fine' don't go together, Doc. So what's going on?"

Emily pulled away. The delicate straps that formed the heart-shaped cutout on her dress tightened as she hugged her arms to her body. Her long fingers wrapped around the black velvet, and she dropped her chin to her chest, exposing the delicate sprinkling of freckles between her shoulder blades.

He felt his strength waning and stepped behind her, tentatively placing his hands on her shoulders. "I'm sorry, Emily. Of course you can't break your professional confidence. I'm worried, is all. I don't want to see Bryan hurt again."

"It's not going to hurt him, Kevin. It's a joyous occasion."

He heard the slight hitch in her voice when she said "joyous," and realized what she was saying, or, more to the point, what she was feeling. What could he say without making things worse?

He wrapped his arms around her and pulled her close. She needed a friend, and, the way he figured it, so did he. So many times he'd tried to convince himself that he was doing the right thing in avoiding any serious relationship, but holding Emily like this, doubt reared its ugly head again.

He and Emily had dreamed of a large family at one time. Now that was gone. It had to be.

Kevin closed his eyes, wishing he, too, could shut out the pain. Watching his mother's health fail after his father's death, he had promised he'd never let anyone suffer the same way. And when his sister had lost her baby and home to a fire the next year, he knew he could never bear the pain of losing another love, and especially not a child. "Better to have loved and lost, than never to have loved at all" was a total fabrication.

He held Emily in silence, leading her back to the living room. He sure wasn't the person to comfort his ex-fiancée on this one. She didn't want or need to hear *his* prescription for avoiding love.

Where's a joke when I need it?

They sat in silence, Kevin holding Emily, realizing too late that he was brushing the hair off her face and that his lips were near hers. He gave her a chaste kiss, and backed away. "I'm sorry."

She didn't meet his gaze. "Don't be. Even a doctor needs a little TLC occasionally. Thanks. I really shouldn't keep you any longer."

He felt his chest pounding; his mind could only think of escaping unscathed. Or was it already too late?

Chapter Six

Kevin placed the tire jack under the bumper of the sporty teal coupe and pumped the handle. An hour later, he had the tire repaired and put back on the car. Kevin slid into the seat, turned the key and revved the engine. "Not too shabby, Emily," he whispered to himself, then returned to her house and knocked on the door.

He was asking for trouble. That realization had occurred around three in the morning, as he peeked in to make sure Emily was doing okay. Once the knot on her head was nearly gone, he could have gone home. But he didn't. Instead, he sprawled across the sofa and dozed off. Emily was still sleeping when he awoke and took the set of keys laying next to her purse on the table.

Just this once, he promised himself. He would prove that Emily's mother was wrong, that all men were not the same as Em's father.

Kevin would show her that they could put the past behind them without becoming involved. Show her that they could be friends. He'd do her a favor—just because. He'd hand her the keys, ask her for a ride back to get his truck, get on with his life, and let her get on with hers.

It was too late for them. More to the point, it was too late for him. The price of love was too high. Life was simpler without it. Love was for dreamers. And his dreams had faded long ago.

Emily opened the door, her pale face barely visible. "What do you want now?"

He stepped closer and pushed the door slightly with his foot. "Emily, you look awful."

"Aren't you charming this morning? What do you need, Kevin? I thought we agreed last night, our association will be strictly on a professional basis." Her voice had lost its strength—even angry, it sounded as weak as she looked.

"It will be, I promise. After you take me back to the clinic to get my truck."

"What's it doing there?" Her words slurred.

"I took your tire and had it repaired. Could you let me in?" He tried to stay calm. "I like your car," he added, trying to distract her while he eased his foot into the gap in the door. *It has spunk, just like you.*

Before she could answer, Emily collapsed, forcing his foot away and trapping him on the outside.

"Emily!" he yelled. He turned the handle and pushed, moving her just enough to get in, then stepped over her.

She was lying on the floor, a broken lamp next to her. He shoved the pieces aside and unplugged it before kneeling beside her.

"Wake up, Emily. Come on, sweetie, wake up for me." He placed his fingers in the hollow of her neck to check for a pulse. It was beating strong. Brushing her cheek, Kevin felt a draft as she exhaled. It had been almost ten hours since her fall, and so far the only possible sign of a concussion was loss of balance, but that could just as easily be blamed on her sprained ankle.

"You're scaring me, Emmy. Wake up. Please." He mentally scrolled through the first-aid training he'd taken at the community college, then lifted Emily's bare feet above the level of her heart. A minute later she opened her eyes, blinking them wildly as she drew in a deep breath.

"What happened?"

Kevin put her feet on the floor, relieved that she was okay. "You fainted, I guess. Stay here, I'll be right back." He searched through the hall closet for a washcloth and soaked it with cold water, then returned. She remained still while he blotted her pale face with the cool cloth.

When she started to get up, Kevin helped her move to a chair. Her damp hair smelled like apples and tumbled over her sweatshirt. Kevin knelt next to the chair and leaned his elbow on one knee. "I'd feel a lot better if you would have one of your colleagues check you out, Doc."

She studied his face intently, as if she'd forgotten how angry she had been with him just a few minutes ago. Her eyes opened wide, and she leaned forward. "Are my pupils dilated?"

He blinked with surprise, then slowly smiled. "I thought we agreed, I don't practice medicine." Kevin rose to his feet, hoping that from a distance her full lips wouldn't look quite so tempting.

It didn't work.

"Just remember who broke the agreement first." A smile tugged at her mouth as she tipped her head for him to examine her eyes.

Forcing the temptation away, Kevin looked at her pupils, then shaded them from the light and quickly took his hand away. He was relieved to see them make the proper adjustment. "They look fine."

"I'm not nauseated," she mumbled, as if reviewing a medical file. "No headache. Eyes are okay." She shook her head slowly, rubbing her arm. "Probably just need to eat. I missed dinner, and maybe the shower was too hot. I should have cut it short, I guess."

"What does that have to do with it?"

"Dilates the blood vessels and sends the blood rushing from the brain. I heard the doorbell and rushed in here. Your diagnosis was right—I just fainted. It's no big deal."

He wasn't convinced. People didn't just keel over like that. Not without a reason. Must have been her fall.

Emily released the footrest on the recliner and leaned back. She ran her fingers through her hair, trying to make it look as if she was only fluffing it dry. The knot was gone. Her stomach growled. She had to get some breakfast.

"You okay?"

She looked admiringly at Kevin, then nodded. She had treated him horribly from the first time she saw him at the hospital, and yet he continued to be kind to her. "I'm just famished. Why don't I make us something to eat, then I can take you to get your truck."

"Why don't you rest while I make something."

Emily laughed. "I remember your cooking skills. I'll do it."

"Let me help, anyway." A mischievous glint in his eyes tempted her to put her anger aside.

Emily couldn't forget a time when she had really needed his support, and he'd let her down. *Forgive sev-*

enty time seven. You aren't asking much, are you God? Who was to say anything would be different now? He'd come right out and told her he wasn't interested in starting over. Proclaimed that there was no room for dreams of a family. *What happened, Kevin? You loved children.* Then again, he had once loved her, too. And that had changed.

He stretched out his arm, offering a hand to pull her to her feet.

"So, think you could handle the toast?" She took his hand, accepting his help—again. His grip was firm, yet tender and reassuring.

The years of hard work were evident in the calluses and scars covering his hands. Their grasp lingered uncomfortably. She let go and headed for the kitchen, leaving the personal questions behind. She couldn't afford to let herself entertain old dreams. Not with this man.

Kevin made a pot of coffee and searched through the cupboard for dishes, while Emily dug through the freezer for a can of grape juice—his favorite, she realized as she set it on the counter.

She'd gone through enough because of him, and survived despite his dumping her. They'd both moved on. It would be okay. She was happy. She had a job she loved. A home she bought all on her own. What else could she want?

In silence, Emily pulled eggs and homemade wheat bread from the refrigerator. Kevin reached over the door and pulled out a bag of shredded cheese, bringing his face close to hers as she reached for the milk. "Do you mind?" His dimples betrayed him.

The faint remnants of his musky aftershave scrambled her thoughts. *Mind? Do I mind that you've found a way back into my life? That you're right here in my kitchen at eight o'clock on a Saturday morning? That you're* flirting *with me?* She snatched the cheese and tossed it onto the white ceramic-tile counter, next to the eggs. *You bet, I mind!* Emily avoided his gaze, not sure she'd survive one more glance into his baby-blue eyes. How dare he flirt with her!

Emily felt the scars of her broken heart being pulled and tugged by Kevin's familiar voice, his blue eyes, his very being. Her entire soul ached. She'd tucked and stuffed her feelings for him so deep that she thought they'd never resurface. Apparently she was wrong. *Go away, Kevin. You're not supposed to have a place left in my heart!*

She broke the eggs into a bowl and stirred them with a fork, while Kevin placed the silverware on the table and mixed the juice. Her gaze darted to him and back to the stove repeatedly, as if she were trying to convince herself that she wasn't hallucinating. Each glance served to remind her that Kevin was still very real.

When the eggs were done, she placed them in a serving bowl and headed for the table.

"Here, you forgot the cheese." He reached around her and tossed a handful of grated cheddar on top of the eggs, then paused.

Their eyes met, and Emily hoped he didn't sense the jolt of electricity that surged through her and made her shiver.

Kevin's brows furrowed, the sun-drenched skin around his eyes creasing with concern as he pulled away from her. "How are you feeling?"

"I'll be fine once I eat." They each carried an ivy-trimmed dish to the table and sat down. Instinctively, Emily bowed her head, noticing that Kevin had bypassed the grace and gone straight for his fork, then tried to retrace his steps without being noticed.

Emily said nothing, yet silently wondered about the changes she'd seen in only a few visits with the man she'd once loved. Who had he become in the time they'd been apart? *What happened, Kevin?*

Throughout breakfast, he kept her laughing instead of crying, visiting instead of arguing, and eating far more than usual. He watched, a glint of satisfaction in his eyes, as she devoured her meal.

Kevin had been her stability throughout college, watching out for her like an older brother before they started dating. He had always been willing to listen and had never shied away from her family. He had once helped her to take life less seriously, had cheered her up, had encouraged her. He had known how to make her smile.

He still did, she realized.

Emily felt betrayed by her own emotions. She was recalling too vividly the intimate sparkle in his eyes, the gentle way he'd taken care of her, his genuine concern for her happiness.

She looked at her watch. "I'm going to have to get going, Kevin. I have patients to see." It was as good an excuse as any to avoid prolonging this visit.

"I'll clear the dishes, while you finish getting ready." His smile was without malice, almost apologetic. For the love lost? For the years that could never be retrieved?

She longed for the courage to prove him wrong. To show him that his dreams hadn't died, after all. To show him that there was room in their lives for someone else.

Kevin realized he couldn't keep tempting himself, or teasing Emily, either. He'd given her plenty of opportunity to indicate the attraction was still there, and she'd backed away every time.

It was over between them. Just as she had forced her feelings for her father into oblivion, so had she allowed the love the two of them had once shared to fade with the passing years.

For a while, late last night, he had given in to the voice of his ego that said Emily was just being stubborn, that a little wooing would make the pain disappear. Then reality had intercepted and opened up the gaping wounds of the past. No, Emily needed a man who could give her all his attention, a house full of kids and a love that would survive the test of time.

True, there was a part of him that would always love Emily and cherish the time they had had together. But that was the past, and it was best left in the past. Today proved that. It was obvious she wanted nothing to do with him or the love they had once shared.

Later that morning, Kevin tried to ignore the memories of that feeling of togetherness as he walked into the empty trilevel house he loosely called "home." He'd never planned for a life of solitude. Never envisioned a life without love. Never expected life to turn out the way it had.

There was one thing that still mattered. He had his business back, and that would have to be enough.

Chapter Seven

Kevin juggled his work schedule to accommodate the new project. After hiring another crew and evaluating the clinic structure, he met with the electrician, the city's building inspector and a medical design consultant to make final changes on the renovation blueprints.

So far, Kevin had only seen Emily from a distance. Every time he drove into the parking lot and saw her sporty little car, he thought of the night spent taking care of her. He thought of how good it had felt to be with her, to hold her, to imagine the past was just a bad dream. But it wasn't. That night after the reception was the dream. A dream he didn't dare repeat.

He had a job to do, and nothing, and no one would come between him and its completion.

Kevin wiped the dust from his eyes, tired of fighting the spring wind. It was a miserable day to be removing windows, but he didn't have the luxury of changing the schedule. There would be enough unavoidable delays as it was, and there just wasn't that much extra time built into the contract.

As he moved in and out of the building, he could hear Emily laughing with the nurses, talking to patients and rearranging her schedule to help out the other staff. Kevin watched her leave at noon with the pastor who had performed Laura and Bryan's wedding. She returned looking carefree and happy, and Kevin was surprised to find himself wishing it were him bringing a smile to her face.

By midday, though, he could see the signs of stress. Was it her career, or his presence, or a really lousy day? he wondered. The smile she plastered on her face when their paths crossed was as forced as his own. He knew it, and no doubt so did Emily.

Don't get any ideas. She's a doctor now.

Kevin had lost faith in the medical profession when false hope had led his parents down a spiraling path in search of a miracle cure for his father's terminal illness. While his mom and dad had run from one doctor to another, across the continent and back, Kevin had attempted to run the family business. A year and a half later, when the residential construction market hit an all-time low, the business was all but gone, and so was his father.

Looking back, he realized there was no way a twenty-three-year-old son could have done anything differently. It was their money, their business, their decision.

Yet there were days when he felt that all he had achieved was to prolong his father's agony. While doctors had fed his parents' hopes, Kevin did the only thing he could to help—he kept the business operating. Despite Kevin's suggestions to revive the company, his older brother, Alex, convinced the family that it was safest to abandon the business in order to salvage a comfortable cushion for their mother to live on. With three younger siblings to worry about, Kevin swallowed his pride and closed the doors of MacIntyre and Sons, Incorporated.

Now it was just MacIntyre Construction. There would be no "Sons." Of that he was convinced. It had taken two years of back-breaking hours, working for someone else, before he'd been able to bankroll his own company. And finally, everything was falling into place, just as scheduled.

Right before calling it a day, Kevin called one of the new men over to help him nail plywood over the opening left from removing a window. Kevin sent Tom to the top of the scaffolding while he maneuvered the scrap into place. Both picked up their nail guns and began shooting nails into the wood.

Kevin felt a sharp pain in his upper arm and jumped back. The plywood broke loose and knocked him against the scaffolding. "What—!" He pushed the wood away, then turned his head, shocked to find a sixteen-penny nail protruding from his shoulder. "You shot me!"

"I what?" Tom jumped from the scaffolding, the commotion drawing attention from not only the crew, but the clinic business, as well. Kevin heard screams. A few minutes later, a nurse ran outside.

Kevin yanked the nail from his arm and immediately pressed his fingers on the injury. He looked down at the red stain on his flannel shirt. *I hate blood.*

The nurse rushed over to him. "You okay?" As she said it, she pulled his hand away from the injury, then pressed it back again. "Let's go inside where we can clean that and take a better look." Kevin willingly followed, thankful he didn't have to do that himself.

As they walked inside, the nurse kept glancing at him. "You feeling okay?"

"Fine." It was an exaggeration, but in a few minutes it would be true. He hoped.

"You're the boss, right? Kevin, isn't it?" She had a

look of interest that he'd seen way too many times in the years since his broken engagement.

He tried to be polite. "Yeah, and you're…?"

She smiled eagerly. Too eagerly, he thought. *A year ago, I might have been interested, but not now.*

"Lois," she replied, motioning for him to go into the examination room to the right. "You'll need to remove your shirt so I can clean that up." She turned her attention to the cabinet, pulling out a tray with a pile of gauze and some brownish liquid on it. He could almost smell the stench of iodine, and recalled memories of his mother cleaning his numerous cuts when he was a child.

He looked at the cut as he removed the shirt. *This is going to sting like crazy!*

The nurse examined his shoulder, and he looked away. He felt her dab at it with the damp gauze, tug on it, then dab some more. "Hmm. When was your last tetanus shot?"

Kevin looked at the brunette, trying to remain calm. The one thing he hated more than blood was needles. "Not too long ago," he assured her.

"Do you remember approximately what year? Maybe one year ago, five, ten?" She dug through the drawer, seeming unhappy that the item she was looking for hadn't been restocked. She pulled an empty box from the cabinet and threw it away.

He mumbled a reply, not certain exactly which answer would satisfy her enquiring mind.

She laughed, and he realized he hadn't passed the test. "Don't waste your time, Lois. I don't need any shot. Just put a bandage over it, and I'll get out of your way."

"Let me get some supplies, and I'll have you back to work before you know it."

There was no problem, he assured himself when she

left the room. She was getting a new box of bandages, was all. But the longer she took, the more nervous he became. *What's taking so long?*

Tentatively, he lifted the gauze from his shoulder and took a peek. All he needed was something to cover the cut. He stepped away from the table to look for a bandage himself. Not seeing any, he grabbed his shirt and headed for the door.

Dr. Emily intercepted him trying to escape. "Kevin? Where are you going?"

He lifted his eyebrows, almost pleased that she was no longer going out of her way to avoid him.

"Nice to see you, too, Doc, but maybe another time. I'm late to work."

"Not so fast. I understand you have a wound that may need…"

Kevin began to pull his shirt back on. The bleeding had almost stopped. "I'll just get a bandage from my own first-aid kit." There was no way he was going to let her near him with a needle.

She blocked Kevin's exit. "I need to see it, Kevin." Lois filed in behind the doctor with a plastic-covered tray containing several metal tools and bandages.

"Wait just a minute, here," Kevin stammered as he tried to step around the doctor, his hands in front of him as if to stop them both. "Emily… Wait, wait." He took a step backward and ran into the examination table.

"It's okay. It'll just take a minute. Let me look at it, Kevin." She stepped closer.

He moved to the side. "No, Emily."

He bumped into Lois, and jumped even higher.

Emily took hold of his arm. "Just let me look at it," she said calmly, a teasing look of satisfaction in her gaze. "We may not need anything except a tetanus shot." Her voice was authoritative yet soft, her touch strangely comforting, and her gaze—totally *un*businesslike.

If Tom hadn't made such a ruckus over a little mishap, I wouldn't be in this mess, Kevin thought.

Emily turned and reached for a bottle marked Saline Solution and a wad of gauze. "I'm going to irrigate it, make sure we get it good and clean," she explained.

Kevin recalled the tubes, needles and IVs that had failed to save his dad's life, and he began breathing more quickly. When Emily reached for his shoulder he ran out of the room and down the hall. He saw a back door marked Exit and bolted through it.

"Kevin!" Emily followed him through the exit, running right into a construction worker who was trying to complete the job Kevin and Tom had started. Had his employee not caught her, she would have landed in the mud.

Kevin turned in time to see Emily breaking free from the man's embrace.

He jumped onto a pile of plywood, stumbling as he leapt off, intending to hit the ground running. His shirt half on and half off, Kevin made a beeline to his truck. He'd get some ointment and a bandage, and fix his wound himself.

Catcalls followed Emily across the uneven ground, where an audience now gathered. Lois poked her head out the door, patients paused to watch, and even the crew watched with raised eyebrows as Kevin and his ex-fiancée danced circles around each other. Emily caught up to him as he pulled the first-aid kit from the back of the truck.

Kevin looked up, surprised by the firm warning in her green eyes. "This is ridiculous, Kevin. You can't even remember when you had your last tetanus shot!"

He held up his hands to stop her. "Thanks, anyway, Doc, I don't do needles. I'll just put a bandage on it." He winked. "I promise to take very good care of it."

His humor wasn't appreciated. Emily placed her hands on her hips, as if he were a defiant child. "You bull-headed fool. This isn't worthy of such a scene, Kevin. You can't take that kind of a risk." She took another step closer, and he backed away, stumbling over a clump of mud.

"Wanna bet?"

She let out a gasp of exasperation, then looked over her shoulder toward the people laughing and whispering behind her. "You're behaving like a child," she scolded through gritted teeth.

He forced himself not to smile. He loved the way her eyes turned to a deep teal when she was mad. The dusting of freckles that bridged her nose seemed to glow like stars in the night sky. And her hair shimmered in the sunlight like a blazing fire.

"You can't afford to take a chance at getting lockjaw, Kevin. It can kill you."

He tried again and again to convince her that he didn't need any shot, but she remained firm, resorting to threats of making his crew help hold him down.

"You'd love that, wouldn't you? To make a fool out of me."

She smiled. "I don't need to—you're the one running away." She held up her fingers to show an inch. "It's a tiny needle. You'll hardly feel a thing."

"Famous last words." He hesitated, and the doctor made her closing argument.

"You could show a little faith in me, you know. Remember, I'm the doctor, you're the builder."

Kevin allowed his gaze to roam, noticed a frightened

little boy watching. As much as he hated to admit it, he realized Emily was right. "Okay, I'll do it, but be gentle, would you?"

He followed Emily back into the clinic, watching her every step of the way. If things were different... But they weren't. There was no way he could be satisfied with a casual relationship with this woman. He had loved her too much, too deeply to make walking away a second time bearable.

Lois was waiting at the door.

"I'll take care of this, Lois, thanks." Emily stepped past the nurse, then waited in the hall while he went into the room and took his shirt off. Emily moved with confidence, trying to clean the wound gently, as Kevin studied the magazines, the lighting, the wallpaper peeling away from the corner—anything rather than looking at what she was doing.

"This might sting," she explained, holding up the bottle of brown liquid. "This should prevent an infection." She soaked a gauze pad and pressed it firmly over the wound, and he felt the liquid burn its way deep into the tissue of his arm.

As she opened the new box of bandage strips, Emily told him how to care for the wound, explained the indications of infection, and that he could expect a sore arm after receiving the tetanus shot. He suspected most of her spiel was to avoid the conversation turning personal.

A lot had changed about her, he realized. When they had first met, she'd been painfully shy, blushing when he took his T-shirt off to dive into the swimming pool. She'd been quiet and reserved, a sharp contrast to his own personality. He supposed that was what had first attracted him to her. She was a beautiful, intelligent woman with a giving heart. That much was the same. She was gorgeous, smart and still generous to a fault. But she'd also become stronger and more assertive. If possible, that made her even more attractive.

When he looked up, her gaze darted away as if she'd been caught admiring him. *Don't flatter yourself, Kevin. She's a doctor now. Seeing a man's chest is probably an hourly occurrence.* He wanted to laugh at the irony of his sitting here letting his ex-fiancée treat him. *Talk about playing with fire.*

She approached his opposite arm with the syringe, and her gaze strayed to his bare chest, then back to his face. Her cheeks turned a deeper shade of pink, and Kevin fought the satisfaction of realizing he *wasn't* just any other patient.

Despite trying to stop it, his smile turned to a chuckle. "Not much has changed after all, has it?" Before the words were out of his mouth, she stuck the needle into his biceps, and none too gently.

Kevin looked at his arm, felt a cold sweat spread across his chest and face. "Ouch. I thought you said it wouldn't hurt!"

Satisfaction twitched her mouth. "Consider yourself lucky it didn't have to go into the hip."

A laugh rumbled from deep in his chest. "You call that lucky?"

Emily's lips trembled with the need to smile, and she turned her back on him, then broke the needle off into the hazardous waste receptacle. "Have a lovely weekend, Mr. MacIntyre," she said, then walked out of the room.

Kevin was stunned. He hadn't expected her reaction, or his. Why did he continue to tease her? And why did she have to respond with such class? Why couldn't she just have slapped him and walked out? It was almost as if... No, it couldn't be.

He stretched into the sleeves of his shirt and buttoned it, then tucked the shirttail into his jeans before returning to work.

As soon as he stepped outside, Tom approached with an apology, followed by ''Man, who in their right mind would run from a doctor like *her*?'' The comment opened the gates to several bad jokes and offers among the crew to sacrifice themselves for a visit with ''the doctor.''

Kevin had been so focused on Emily, he'd not prepared himself for his crew's razzing. He couldn't react too strongly, or they'd be even harder to quiet. Not to mention that they'd realize the boss had his eyes on the doctor.

''What's your plan, boss? Playing hard to get?''

''Don't even go there, guys,'' Kevin finally said. When that didn't stop the crude jokes, Kevin called the entire crew together and explained that this wasn't a typical construction company. ''A little good humor is one thing, but I don't allow trash on my sites.'' To his relief, the men respected his warning, and cleaned up their conversation.

Even so, Kevin thought he'd never hear the end of it from the crew. He was grateful when his watch hit six o'clock, and he could send the men home for two days. He hoped that when Monday came, the whole thing would be forgotten.

Emily had seen Kevin arrive each morning and had worked hard to avoid him; especially after looking out the window of her office one afternoon to see him hugging a blonde. The two had visited for a few minutes, then climbed into his pickup and left together. Memories of the breakup rushed back, which had actually made it easier for Emily to keep her emotions under control, until his accident yesterday…

When she heard Kevin was hurt, her attention went completely to him. She couldn't have thought of anyone else had her own life depended upon it. *What came over me? I can't believe I ran outside after him!* It went totally against her training, and she was ashamed of her lapse of professionalism. It had never happened to her before, and she'd be sure it didn't happen again.

Why now? she wondered. *Why, when I've survived our split, when I'm through the pressure of school, when I have a career that I love, does the only man who could ruin everything I've worked for have to return?*

How was she supposed to keep herself from falling in love again when he was right in the same building all day, and haunting her dreams all night? She tried to forget the way he had flirted with her in the examination room, held her when she cried over Laura's pregnancy, and comforted her with his tender embrace. She'd resisted him once, but knew she couldn't survive another dose of Kevin's charm. Her immunity just wasn't that strong.

She checked her watch and straightened the flowers she'd bought for the dining room table. Katarina was due to arrive anytime. The moving van had arrived the day before and had unloaded her sister's belongings into the garage, where they would sit until Kat could find a place of her own.

Emily started another load of laundry, then went to the basement to make sure the rooms were ready for her sister to move into. The second phone line for Kat's business had been installed earlier in the week, and the answering machine already had several messages waiting for the owner of Kat's Kreations.

Though it was to be a temporary arrangement, Emily had to admit she was in no hurry for her sister to find another place. She'd moved her own belongings upstairs with welcome anticipation. Having someone else in the house would be a wonderful distraction from her daily routine—wake, walk, work and wonder. She was tired of thinking about the past, the future and the man who wanted no part of either.

The doorbell rang, and Emily ran back up the stairs and through the house. She opened the door and lunged forward to hug Katarina.

She stopped just short of throwing herself at Kevin. She stumbled back. "K-Kevin."

"I'm glad to see you, too," he said, dimples again belying his stoic expression. Humor illuminated his bright blue eyes. "I'm awfully curious to know who that lucky person you *were* expecting is?"

She felt her cheeks flush and wished her hair was loose so it would hide her embarrassment. "Well, it wasn't you."

"That's a safe bet, now, isn't it?"

He glanced inside and lifted one eyebrow. "Am I intruding?"

She knew it was obvious that she was expecting a guest, and even if it was only her sister, she hoped Kevin would take the hint and leave before Katarina arrived and entertained any crazy notions of a reunion between Emily and Kevin.

"Well, if you're asking if I'm busy, the answer is yes. I am expecting someone."

"I need to talk to you."

"You couldn't call?" She licked her lips nervously. "I mean, I'm sure this is strictly business, right?"

He pushed his chin forward. "If I had your number, I

would have called first. Unfortunately, it's unlisted, and you're not the doctor on call today.''

''Oh.'' She glanced toward the street and invited him in, praying Katarina would be late for once in her life. ''Is your arm okay?''

''Fine. Want to see?'' He reached for the hem of his sleeve and pulled it above the wound.

She couldn't help but smile inside, relieved that he'd reached for the sleeve instead of removing the entire shirt, as she had momentarily feared he would. Noting the way his polo shirt hugged his broad shoulders, Emily took a deep breath. ''It's a bit inflamed. Be sure to clean it with hydrogen peroxide and keep a small bandage over it to help keep germs out. You should also try some warm compresses.''

''Nah, needs some air.''

''If that swelling doesn't go down by Monday, you should come in and have someone look at it.''

''Someone? Does that mean you're not going to be my doctor from now on?''

His doctor? She looked him in the eye. ''I can't guarantee I'll be available,'' she answered honestly. There was a long silence. Then she backed into the kitchen and dug through the junk drawer for a piece of paper. She took a pen from the mug next to the phone and wrote down her number. ''I'd prefer you page me, since my hours are so irregular.''

He looked at the note then back at her, and tore the paper up, placing the tiny bits in her hand. ''I don't want to talk to your pager any more than I want to talk to your receptionist, Doc. If you don't want to discuss this like two adults, fine. I'll handle it on my own.'' He turned and walked out the door, greeting her sister, who was on the way in.

"Will I see you again, Kevin?" Katarina asked cheerfully.

"Not likely, but have a nice visit, Kat" was the gruff reply.

Emily stepped outside, the force of his seething reply catching her off guard. Reality hit her like a sledgehammer between the eyes. If she had truly expected any less than directness from Kevin, she had underestimated him.

And if she continued to deny her feelings for him, she underestimated herself.

I still love him. The thought barely crossed her mind before another followed. *Please. No. I can't love him. He left me, just like my daddy.* She simply couldn't survive rejection again.

Katarina sighed. "Things aren't going so well, huh?"

Chapter Eight

⌇

Emily spent her weekend helping Katarina settle into the basement and introducing her sister to her new hometown. Together they perused the classifieds, looking for a suitable building to house Kat's Kreations, the growing mail-order craft business that Katarina had founded right out of college.

Emily assuaged her sister's curiosity with a simple explanation of Kevin's lack of desire for a family. Though it didn't truly explain anything, it quieted Kat's probing into a part of life Emily didn't want to discuss with anyone, especially her Pollyanna sister.

It was becoming more and more difficult to avoid running into Kevin at the clinic, yet she continued to try. She was not ready to deal with her unresolved feelings for the man. As it was, thoughts of him already intruded on her day. With each hit of the hammer, clang of metal and buzz of the saw, Emily wondered exactly what he was handling "on his own."

Monday evening, the outer door down the hall clinked shut, and Emily closed her eyes. *Kevin is finally going home.* She let out a breath and set the journal aside, placing her reading glasses in the drawer.

"Evening, Doc."

She jumped, surprised to see the subject of her thoughts appear before her eyes.

When she didn't respond, he continued, stepping inside her office as he spoke. "I think it's time we get a few things out in the open, don't you?"

Kevin's jeans were white with dust from the plaster walls they'd knocked down that afternoon. Chunks of the same clung to his blond hair. He brushed his lips with the back of his hand as if trying to rid his mouth of the chalky residue.

The image was strong and manly, yet at the same time boyish and irresistible. It was no wonder Dr. Casanova was complaining that the nurses were more interested in the building project than their jobs. Having insider information from the females' perspective, she realized Bob was too proud to admit that his flirtations were now falling upon deaf ears.

"This can't go on, Kevin. I have a job to do, and you can't keep trying to distract me."

He chuckled. "Don't flatter yourself, Doc. If I was *trying* to distract you, you wouldn't stand a chance of resisting."

"Then if you're not trying to distract me, you wouldn't mind keeping your distance." She glared, feeling anger seething behind the smile plastered on her lips. She couldn't help but hear his cheerful greetings to patients echoing through the hall between her appointments. Not to mention the fact that the single female staff members were constantly praising "the boss" of the entire project as if he were the ultimate prize.

She knew better. Kevin MacIntyre was human, just

like her, and everyone else. He'd made his share of mistakes. He had his dark side. His own faults and failures.

Kevin nodded. "And you wouldn't mind parking in the other lot."

"Excuse me?" She popped out of the chair and leaned forward, resting her hands on the cluttered desk.

"You heard me. You can park on the other side of the building. My work is on this side. I have no choice. I can't unload equipment from the other side." His stomach growled. The office had closed over an hour ago, and even Kevin's crew had abandoned the clinic before the sun set.

She watched his callused hand rub his midsection.

"Why don't we continue these negotiations over dinner."

She pushed aside the little voice inside that rattled off the list of questions she was too chicken to actually ask Kevin. Questions that would mean dealing with the past that, until seeing Kevin again, she'd quieted to a dull roar. Now they were blaring again. "There's nothing to negotiate."

He ignored her. "I need to eat. And I'm sure you do, too. You want to ride together?"

"No, I don't." Emily closed the file in front of her and set it in a stack to be returned to the records department, then reached for the next.

She felt his gaze follow her motions, yet he remained silent. From the corner of her eye, she could see him cross one leg over the other and lean against the door frame. *Not trying to distract me, my foot!* His tall lean body was a distraction all by itself, even coated with plaster. She resigned herself from pretending to work any longer and cocked her head as she looked at him.

"Why don't we meet at the café on the corner? Better yet, why don't we walk?"

Emily took her purse from the file drawer and turned back to the desk. "Because I'm going home. There's nothing else we have to say." Emily pushed up from her chair and grabbed her coat. Kevin backed into the hallway ahead of her, waiting as she locked the door behind her. She continued outside and turned toward her car, knowing the battle wasn't over yet.

Kevin took hold of her arm. "Please."

She paused.

He said "Please," she thought.

He didn't bulldoze his way into her office and order her to listen. He had said "Please." The tension in her jaw softened.

She and Kevin had plenty to settle. She couldn't avoid it forever. Maybe it *was* best to talk now, so she could move on with her life. She knew she wouldn't be able to forgive and forget him until they cleared the air.

"Fine. We'll get this over with." He smiled, his subtle way of letting her know he won without saying "I told you so." She glared at him. "Just say it, Kevin. I hate it when you gloat."

He wiped the smile from his face. "What?"

She walked past him, annoyed that he still made her heart beat faster. He hadn't even touched her, yet she felt her palms get clammy, her pulse rate rise and her temper flare. *How dare you come in here and make a mess of my life again, Kevin MacIntyre. How dare you walk out on me!*

Over sandwiches, they ruled out every idea they had to avoid one another. Halfway through apple pie, Emily realized the list was little more than a decoy—and worse, she was as guilty as Kevin for detaining them. She hadn't made one attempt to walk away.

Emily dropped her napkin on the table.

Kevin picked it up and reached for her mouth, wiping some food from her chin. "Neither one of us can afford any distractions from our work." His hand paused at her mouth, and he smiled. Slowly his fingers brushed her cheek, then he backed away. "We agree upon that much, right?"

She froze, momentarily captivated by his tender touch. *Don't back down, Emily. Just pick your battles.* "You asked me to park on the other side of the building. Fine, I'll do it. My office hours are between nine and noon, and one to five, so you'll have to arrange to stay on the other side during those hours."

"That's ridiculous, I can't do that. I'm the boss. I have to oversee the entire project." He looked at his watch and added, "Besides, it's well after seven, and you were still in your office. When do you want me to do my job, Doc?"

She didn't dare admit that she had only been here waiting for him to leave so she wouldn't have to see him. "Oh, yes, that reminds me—would you please ask your crew to refrain from their catcalls when I'm around. I don't appreciate the reminder of your accident."

He stared at her, and she wished the past eight years could be erased. "And, would you please stop flirting in the office."

"Flirting? I haven't flirted with anyone at the clinic." His eyes opened wide, and there was an "I'm innocent" look on his face.

"And what about that blonde you were cuddling with the other day?"

He furrowed his brows. "Blonde?"

"Next to your truck."

"Elizabeth?"

She nodded. "Yes…Elizabeth." It dawned on her that Elizabeth was Kevin's younger sister. "Elizabeth? That was 'little' Elizabeth?"

He nodded. His voice lost its humorous tone. "This is ridiculous, Emily. Surely we can stand each other's company for six months."

"S-Six months?" she stammered. *No, Kevin, I can't do it.* She gathered her purse and slid out of the booth. "Just remember those boundaries, Kevin, and we'll be just fine."

"Emily…" He tried to get the waitress's attention, but finally tossed two bills on the table and ran out the door after Emily. She was at the edge of the parking lot already. He took off running, but by the time he got there, she was in the car and driving out of the driveway.

He stood in the middle of the lane, holding his hand up, forcing her to stop. Then he strolled to her window and motioned for her to roll it down.

"We've settled everything, Kevin. Just promise—no more distractions."

"You want to see a distraction, Emily?" Before she could answer, he leaned his head in the window and kissed her, slowly, just the way she remembered. Then he leaned his elbows on the open window, the look of confidence replaced by astonishment. "No, I definitely don't think we've settled anything, Doc." He took a deep breath. "And I'm no happier about it than you are."

"Move out of my way, Kevin."

"We're adults, Emily. Let's handle it—now. You're accusing me of flirting, of interfering with your life. And up until that kiss, I haven't done one thing to *try* to distract you. I want to finish this discussion. Since your sister's visiting, why don't we go to my house, where we won't be interrupted? Looks like someone's come back to the office for something.''

Emily took a deep breath and looked around, noticing a few cars left in the parking lot. True, the clinic parking lot was no place to be having this conversation. Especially after what had just happened. The last thing she needed was to have one of the other doctors see Kevin kissing her.

''Fine, I'll follow you there.''

A few minutes later, Kevin pulled into the garage and met Emily at the front door. Walking inside felt like walking through a trap door. Her confidence faded, masked by confusion.

She couldn't believe he'd kissed her. With both hands on her hips, she confronted him. ''What exactly was that about, Kevin?''

''Why don't you tell me, Emmy? You're the doctor—you analyze what's going on here.''

Before she said anything, she tried to organize her confused emotions. He was daring her to admit the truth: that she still cared too much for him to leave the past behind them. ''That was not strictly business.''

A look of humor crept into his expression. ''I'm sorry, Doc. I tried. I thought I could make it work. Then your lips asked me to kiss them, and...'' His smile disappeared, and he looked at her tenderly, his gaze melting into hers. ''I don't know what to do about it, Emily. I want to see you again, but the truth is, I can't offer you a future.''

She paced the room like bait in a tiger's den.

How she hated the truth at this moment. Kevin could have lied and at least given her hope for a full recovery. He could have been the louse her mother predicted and abandoned her forever. But he didn't, and he wasn't. He was painfully honest, caring for her when he could just as easily have walked away. He was generous and giving, sensitive and…irresistible.

And how she hated him right now. How she hated his honesty.

Her lips tingled in remembrance of his touch, bringing back a flood of memories of a love that she'd thought would never die. Emily wrapped her fingers around her biceps, squeezing her arms until it hurt. These were questions she'd ignored for too long.

Her thoughts flew back to the day they had met in Laura Beaumont's hospital room, and she tried to keep the memory pure and unsullied. "Then what *do* you want?"

"I want you to forgive me. I want you to stop avoiding me. I want to figure out how to be friends again."

"Friends?" The memory of that kiss was far too new for her to imagine a mere friendship between them. "Friends?" She heard the disbelief in her own voice, and was amazed when Kevin seemed not to have noticed.

Without any reservations, Kevin continued to talk. "You're obviously happy with your career, and I'm busier than ever with mine. It's obvious that neither of us has time for a relationship right now. And the last thing we need is our co-workers figuring out that we were an item at one time."

"An item? Don't you think it was a little more than that?"

He swallowed, and uncertainty crept into his expression. He walked over to the kitchen sink and poured himself a glass of water. "Engaged, then. We definitely don't need anyone to know that. The guys are already getting carried away with the nail gun incident. They don't need any fuel.''

''Of course not,'' she muttered. The counter separated them. ''We wouldn't want *that*. We wouldn't want them to find out you walked out on me when I needed your encouragement, would we?''

He was silent.

She turned her back on him and studied the living room, allowing herself the chance to learn more about the man Kevin had become. He obviously hadn't had Kristen do his decorating. His house was neatly organized, yet lacked a homey feel, and it was apparently the way he wanted to keep it.

She took a deep breath, determined not to let him see her pain. Emily felt it spread through her entire body. How could he kiss her, then tell her he only wanted to be friends? How dare he do this to her again!

Though caution told her not to, she had to ask. ''I want to know what happened. Why you walked away. The truth.''

She watched as Kevin resigned himself to her enquiry, leaning a hip against the counter. ''I had to run the business, I told you that.''

''You also told me it was a family business, that it was your responsibility, that it was our future. Now you have a different company in a totally different town. Since it wasn't just your dreams that were tossed aside, I feel I have a right to know what happened.''

''My dad had cancer, Emily. Thanks to false hope from doctors, we were forced to shut down,'' he said bitterly.

Emily spun around to face him, torn between defending the medical profession, and comforting Kevin. ''I'm so sorry, Kevin.'' He didn't respond. She stepped closer.

''I won't try to defend what anyone told them, but I can tell you it's a very difficult job to give a patient who has less than a thirty-percent chance of survival enough hope to make him want to fight for life. I've seen what God can do when even medicine fails.''

''Yeah, well, even that wasn't enough.'' He paused, then lowered his voice. ''It's too bad our marriage didn't have those odds of survival, isn't it? I guess it was for the best. You have your career now, and I have no time for a commitment.''

She stared at him, puzzled by the sudden irritability in his voice. ''All this time, I thought—''

''What did you think, Emily?'' Kevin looked at her with a sardonic expression that sent her temper soaring. ''That I changed my mind? That I suddenly stopped loving you? What?''

''What was I supposed to believe, Kevin! You led me to believe it was because I wanted to be a doctor. How was I supposed to accept your parents' money when you resented me even wanting my own career.''

''Don't throw that at me! We offered to help. You didn't want to be obligated to anyone. You didn't trust me, or them. And I can't even believe you actually thought I was chauvinistic enough to—'' Kevin set his glass on the counter, then walked to the door and opened it for her. ''You don't know me at all, then, do you?''

All the way home, she thought about Kevin's answer to her allegations.

It was all a blur. So long ago. How had she turned the MacIntyres' offer of help into Kevin being selfish and controlling? It seemed so different now. Suddenly, she was the one who felt selfish and controlling.

Was Kevin's father ill when they made the offer? Could she have helped change the outcome in any way?

Emily went directly to her room, too disturbed to even check in with her sister. From the depths of her closet, she pulled a flat box and stared. It had been years since she'd opened it. Each layer of tape represented a turning point in her recovery. The first, anger. The next, acknowledging the pain. The last, and she had hoped the final step—freedom.

It wasn't. Here it was again—this box of memories that she'd symbolically taped up and buried as deep in her closet as she had buried her feelings in her heart.

Dare she open it?

If she did, would she ever be able to close it again?

She kicked the box under her bed to get it out of sight. She wasn't sure she was ready to open herself up to any more pain. Emily showered, hoping that the routine would ease her tension and wash away the questions lurking in her conscience.

Kevin's kiss filled her memory. His anger broke her heart. She closed her eyes and let the tears wash down the drain, as far away as possible.

I'm not strong enough to resist him, God. And I'm not sure I could recover if he walked away one more time. Protect me, Father. Don't let me love him again if it isn't forever.

Emily dried off and put her pajamas on, then pulled back the heavy quilt and crawled into bed. The memories and random prayers continued. In the drowsy warmth of her bed, she felt at peace. Her anger disappeared. The feelings of helplessness subsided.

Chapter Nine

Emily pulled into the clinic parking lot later than usual, her mind still on the baby she'd delivered that morning. Since the employee entrance was now closed for renovation, she had to go right past Kevin to get to the main lobby.

As much as he visits, I'm surprised he gets any work done at all, she thought as she rushed past. Taking a slight pause from his conversation, Kevin added a casual hello. Still upset about his unexpected visit over the weekend, Emily muttered a greeting on her way past.

She'd found herself asking for more divine intervention since the beginning of the renovation. *Please help me to put the past behind me.*

It had taken years, but she had finally learned to let go of the pain from her father's abandonment. During college she'd come to accept that she couldn't be at peace if she was holding a grudge. It was the same with Kevin. Yet here she was again, struggling with emotions she had thought were long gone.

Inside the clinic, the last thing she'd expected was another delay, but Ricky West ran up to her and started telling her about the preschool's trip to a farm. Emily listened for a minute before hearing Kevin's voice again. "I'll see you in just a little while, Ricky. I have to go to work now."

Kevin's deep voice rounded the corner from the entrance to the lobby long before he did. "Here, let me help you with that."

A sweet voice thanked him, to which he replied eagerly, "Any time." Emily felt her emotions bristle.

Before having to face Kevin, Emily made a quick exit to her office. She tossed her jacket on the back of her chair and locked her purse in the desk drawer, then hurried to the nurses' station to get the file for her first patient. It was going to be a jam-packed morning. The sooner she busied herself with work, the sooner she would forget Kevin.

Three patients into her schedule, she entered the examination room to meet a new mother of six-month-old twins. She stepped inside and introduced herself.

The young mother's sweet voice echoed in her ears all day. It was a woman for whom Kevin had so willingly helped carry two infant seats in from the car. *I didn't think there was a man left who'd do that for a stranger,* she'd said.

Don't bother, Emily. No matter how much you try to turn him into your father, you won't succeed. The voice of guilt wouldn't give her a minute's rest. *Couldn't I have just one day without coming face-to-face with Kevin MacIntyre?*

When she left for lunch, she saw Lois and Kevin visiting outside, and turned away. For the remainder of the week, she forced herself to keep busy with work well past the time when Kevin was sure to have called it a day, which seemed to be later each evening.

Even that wasn't enough to free her from hearing all about him from the nurses. It seemed that his gregarious personality had all of the single women freeing their weekend schedules in hopes Kevin would ask them out. Come Monday, though, all were sorely disappointed. Everyone except Emily.

Despite her outward claim to not want to get involved with Kevin, she silently admitted that she'd be devastated if he asked any one of the nurses out. Inwardly, she knew it was all a last attempt to protect her heart.

In a matter of just a few weeks, progress on the clinic was beginning to show. The foundation for the new wing was poured and new walls were going up. Kevin's crew was working long hard hours, though not nearly as many as the boss. It soon became obvious that Kevin had the total support and respect of his men. In return for their efforts, rumor had it, he was quickly gaining a reputation in the industry as a fair and generous employer.

Emily caught herself looking out the tiny window in her office more than once, entranced with watching him work. It was a distraction she couldn't afford, emotionally or professionally.

"I'm sorry, Dr. Emily is with another patient." The pregnant receptionist straightened her back suddenly, then placed her hand on her stomach.

I've never seen so many pregnant women in my life as in this place! Kevin drummed his fingertips on the gold-and-white-flecked counter. "When will she be available?"

The receptionist looked at the appointment book.

"She's booked for two days. Do you need an appointment?"

He thought a minute. "She said to have my arm checked out if it looked worse, but she didn't mention needing an appointment. Maybe I can catch her before she leaves this afternoon."

"Just a minute, let me see if one of the nurses could do that for you without an appointment."

Before he could stop her, the woman waddled into the back room. She emerged a few minutes later with Lois following her. "Come on back, Kevin. It'll only take a minute to take a look at that."

That plan backfired. Okay, God, maybe next time You could let my timing work out better. How am I supposed to fix things with her if I can't get her to talk to me? Though he knew Emily was a busy woman, he couldn't help but be disappointed. In the past eight years, he'd dated plenty of women, not one of whom had left him with a burning desire to be a better man, the way Emily did. She'd had that effect on him in college, and even more now.

Over the last few weeks, Kevin had spent a fair amount of time in discussion with God about the irony of Emily's and his winding up in the same town. It was more than just a coincidence.

Shortly after Bryan's transfer back to Springville, his friend asked Kevin to join him at the pancake house every Tuesday morning before work for a men's Bible study.

There were issues he hadn't settled in his own mind, let alone with God.

The decision to join the group hadn't come easily. It meant becoming accountable to follow through with the changes he'd made in his personal commitment to God and to himself. Though he'd given up his footloose days, he still wasn't comfortable with the thought of attending church. Bryan didn't pressure him, though he asked Kevin to consider going with him, Laura and the kids, and to come over for Easter dinner afterward.

One on one, he and God were making progress. But he wasn't so sure he was ready to face the congregation.

He continued to struggle with turning his life around, giving up control, and, especially, putting his heart on the chopping block again.

It had been a long battle to recover from, letting Emily move on without him. With each family tragedy, resentment had taken a stronger hold within him. The years of rebellious behavior were over, yet the repercussions lingered as an ugly reminder of his weakness. Funny, he thought. Leaving Emily had sent his life into a tailspin, and finding her had set him straight again. Or, at least, given him the courage to get his life back in order.

Trouble was, it was easier to forgive others' transgressions than it was his own. If he couldn't forgive himself, how could he begin to hope for God's, or Emily's, forgiveness?

She deserved a husband who could share her dreams. One who had dreams of his own.

He and Bryan met for their Friday morning coffee before work. It had been a sleepless night for Kevin, and Bryan seemed to notice immediately.

"What's bothering you?"

Kevin grumbled and took a bite of eggs, chasing it down with a gulp of orange juice. "Nothing much, why?"

Bryan chuckled. "Nothing much, huh? Let's see. That either means work isn't going well, or your love life isn't going well."

Kevin gazed around, hoping no one had heard Bryan's smart remark. "Yeah, well, just shows how little you know."

"You and Emily had a chance to talk yet?" His friend took another drink of coffee.

"Yeah, we talk." *We just don't ever get anywhere with it.*

Bryan wove his fingers together and leaned his elbows on the edge of the table. "About?"

He looked up skeptically, wondering when his friend had taken over Laura's duties as The Great Matchmaker. "Mainly about how stupid it would be to try again."

Bryan lowered his voice. "You didn't tell her, did you? You'd prefer she think you just walked away rather than telling her life dealt you a lousy hand and you made a few mistakes."

"She still has her dreams, Bryan. It's best she keep them, because I can't give them to her anymore."

His best friend was still on his "honeymoon." He'd lost all objectivity. He believed love could conquer all, heal all, forgive all. Little did he know.

"Somehow I can't see Emily wanting or needing anyone to give them to her. But sharing them is another issue altogether, isn't it."

"She deserves better." He and Bryan had been through this countless times in the past few months. Watching Bryan and Laura overcome obstacles had given him hope, until he'd come face to face with Emily.

She wasn't any too thrilled to see him. He'd tested the waters, giving her a chance to knock down the walls between them, or at least leave the door open a crack. In their years apart, Emily had perfected the technique of batting down all passes—including his, and those by his crew. At least she wasn't discriminatory.

"I'm still curious why you think you're beyond forgiveness."

Kevin stared at the Ketchup-covered hash browns on the cast-iron platter. "I made a choice to disobey."

"And you think your mistakes are any different from the rest of ours? Don't we all make those choices, whether consciously or subconsciously? Is the degree of error in His eyes any different?"

Bryan looked at his watch, and Kevin realized it was time to get to the clinic. He placed a bill on the table, and both men stood.

"Open your eyes, friend. He's given you another chance to have everything you could ever want."

Kevin reflected on that for days before finally giving in to the logic. Even if He forgave him, Kevin reasoned, there was no guarantee that Emily could. Her scars went deep, and it would be like moving mountains to convince her that love could see them both through.

Chapter Ten

Kevin was reeling from the realization that Emily had spent the past years believing him a chauvinist. She had no idea how difficult it had been letting her go. How it had killed him knowing he couldn't give the woman he dearly loved her every dream. How far he'd gone to try to bury the pain of *her* silent message—that their love wasn't worth fighting for.

He watched the snow fall, remembering how much Emily loved winter. *I remember my dad making that pathetic snowman, I loved it. We had a snowball fight, and then he took us girls to a restaurant for hot chocolate.* The tears had blurred her vision and soaked his shirt. "Then what happened?" he'd asked. *A week later, Dad left, and never came back. We had so much fun together, and he left.* Kevin had held her and vowed never to hurt her.

Kevin shook his head. *I broke that promise. In her eyes, it was me that abandoned her.* "I'm sorry, Emmy. Honest, I am."

He drove to Emily's house, hoping she wouldn't kick him out.

Katarina answered, "Sorry, Kevin, she's at the hospital. One of her patients had an asthma attack. Care to come in and visit for a few minutes?"

Kevin turned and looked at the snow. He needed some advice, and Emily's younger sister could be just the right person to give it. "Sure. I have a few questions. Maybe you could give me some answers."

Katarina flashed her cheery smile, and Kevin let the encouragement soak in. He stomped his boots outside before walking on the beige carpet. Katarina closed the door behind him and took his coat, while Kevin untied his boots to leave them on the rug by the door.

"Would you like some cookies? Emily was up in the middle of the night baking them. Said something about a peace offering. You know what she's talking about?"

He followed Katarina from the entry to the kitchen to the dining room table. He eyed the flowers on the table and wondered who they were from. Seemed Emily always had fresh flowers. "Maybe."

"Maybe that's why you're here?" the perky blonde added as she poured him a tall glass of milk.

He pulled the chair out for her, then sat down across the oak table and moved the flowers to one side. "Could be, but I'll talk to your sister about that. How's your mom?"

The fine eyebrow tweaked high above Kat's blue eyes. "She's fine. Still works at the department store."

"And Lisa—what's she doing?"

"In her last semester of college, thanks to Emily. Why do you ask?" Katarina dipped the cinnamon-coated cookie in her glass of milk and took a huge bite.

There was no use lying. Kat would see right through it, anyhow. "None of you have married yet, have you?"

The smile faded. "And you think that's because of Mom?"

"I don't mean any disrespect, Kat, but it's quite a co-incidence that three out of three are still single, don't you think?"

Kat was silent.

"She never liked me much, did she?" Kevin took an-other bite of the chewy cookie.

"Mom has never approved of any of our beaus, Kevin. Don't take it personally. You want my opinion? She's incapable of loving any of the male population. She did not, however, pass along that trait to any of her three daughters."

Kevin nodded. "I suppose she had a few choice com-ments when Emily and I called off the wedding."

Katarina laughed. "Whatever happened between you and Em last night certainly stirred things up, didn't it? First, Emily can't sleep, then you show up with a hundred and one questions." She paused. "Let's just say we've learned not to take our problems regarding men to our mother after that night."

"Did Emily—go to her for advice?"

"That was a long time ago, Kevin. It's best just to pick up from where you are today, and move on if you want. Don't try to fix that."

"You can't fix a problem if you don't acknowledge its existence."

Ricky West was back in the hospital after a morning playing with a friend. The combination of ferrets and a sledding trip in a snowstorm's cold air had irritated his asthma.

She rubbed the stethoscope against her tunic to warm it up before pressing it against Ricky's bare back. There was still a loud rattle in the lower lobe of his left lung, yet his oxygen levels were rising, a sign that the nebulizer treatments were going well. His airways had opened back up, and Ricky was finally sleeping.

She turned to Ricky's parents. "I think he's through the worst of it now. It's going to take some time for him to get back to full speed."

"Thank you for coming, Dr. Emily. I hope we haven't ruined your weekend by calling you at home. I'm sure Dr. Walker is a very capable doctor, but he has no patience with Ricky."

Emily felt her heart swell from the compliment, but at the same time was hesitant to let herself care so much. "It's not a problem. That's why I gave you my number. I'll be back this afternoon to check on Ricky, I promise."

On her way home, Emily stopped at the grocery store, then drove to the church to pick up some supplies to prepare for Sunday school the next morning.

When she drove up to her house, she was startled to see Kevin's pickup in the driveway. She left the car in the drive, since Katarina's things were still occupying the garage.

She opened the front door, and was surprised to see Katarina and Kevin sitting at the table, eating cookies and drinking milk.

Kevin jumped to his feet. "Afternoon."

Emily wanted to believe his being here was a good sign, but didn't allow herself to hope for too much. They had been through ups and downs for weeks now. "Hello. I see you found my peace offering."

Kevin's smile took the chill of the spring storm out of

her. "Best snickerdoodles I've had in eight years. I came to apologize for last night."

Emily looked at her sister, who had a grin that spread from ear to ear, then back to Kevin.

"Mostly, I'm sorry we didn't say more eight years ago, Emmy." He stepped closer and looked deep into her eyes. "We owe it to each other to talk it through, don't we?"

"What about demanding careers? And not dreaming anymore? And no commitments—"

"Are you saying you're not interested in going to dinner with me tonight?"

She glanced at Kat.

"Don't be a fool, Emily. We can go out anytime. Go on."

She turned back to Kevin and smiled. "I'm very interested. What time?"

"Now. Thought we could make a day of it, since we're both off. Speaking of which, do you always get called in on your weekends off?"

Shaking her head, she explained the situation with Ricky. "I need to check in on him again this afternoon. It won't take very long. I'm sure he's doing better now."

Humored over something, Kevin wrapped her in his arms. "That wouldn't happen to be the same Ricky that diagnosed you with a broken heart, would it?"

Emily felt her cheeks heat up. Leave it to Kevin to remember that day with the precocious children at the preschool.

"I told you he was a very insightful young man, didn't I?"

He was gloating again. Only this time, she didn't mind. This time, she dared to hope it was merely the beginning of his gentle teasing in her life. There were still a thousand questions she had for him, but she would take them one at a time. For now, she would have to dream enough for both of them, to show him that the schedule of a doctor and the schedule of a contractor could be merged without moving heaven and earth.

She rested her hands on his shoulders, relishing the moment of contentment. "You don't mind my being a doctor?"

"Only when you try to come near me with a needle."

"You don't mind an independent woman?"

He grew uncommonly serious. "I never did. We really don't have to settle everything right now, do we? We have a birthday to celebrate."

Tears stung her eyes. "You remembered? Or did Katarina tell you?" Emily struggled, uncertain she should trust her own emotions. She wanted so badly to believe it would work out between them.

He looked for Katarina, who'd somehow slipped out of the room unnoticed. "I'm crushed. Don't you remember my birthday?"

"Well, of course, but it's rather difficult to forget a July fourth birthday, and the whole *country* celebrates your birthday!" Emily smiled, genuinely happy remembering the past. "What should I wear?"

There was laughter in his eyes, and his gaze softened when he looked her over. "You're fine for our first event."

Emily raised her eyebrows. "First?"

"Put on your coat and gloves and follow me." He led her to the pickup and opened the door. A bulky package with a big blue bow sat in the passenger's seat. "You'll need this."

She removed her leather gloves and unwrapped the box. She pulled out a crumpled top hat, a ratty scarf, a carrot. *A carrot?* She looked back inside and pulled out two pieces of charcoal, and three large buttons. Confused, she turned to thank him. He was standing in the middle of her front yard with a large snowball in his hands.

"Happy birthday, Em. You going to stand there, or come help?"

"A snowman," she whispered. "Kevin!"

"Better watch it, Doc, your tonsils are going to get cold with your mouth hanging open like that." He set the snowball on the ground and started packing more snow around it.

Emily tromped through the foot of freshly fallen snow and started a second snowball. "Do you know how long it's been since I built a snowman?"

"Let me guess." He tipped his head as if doing so helped him calculate each year that had passed. "Spring break, senior year of college, in Breckenridge, at precisely midnight." Kevin smiled. "You take life too seriously, Em. And I'm here to remind you to lighten up."

Emily's blush warmed her clear to her toes. She remembered the rest of that memorable night, and realized they would have a lot more issues to deal with than schedules and careers if this reunion lasted.

But not today. Like he'd said, they didn't need to answer everything all at once.

When they finished the snowman, it was nearly four o'clock, time for Emily to check on Ricky. "Why don't I go to the hospital and meet you back here in—" she looked at her watch "—say, an hour and a half."

"I'll see you then." Kevin stepped back and waved slightly, as if still uncomfortable with the sudden turn of their relationship. "Oh, and dress up. We're going to the theater in Denver."

Emily watched him drive away, then ran inside to

shower and change. *I'll show you that we can work it out, Kevin.* Before leaving, she thanked her sister for understanding.

"If you—" Kat began.

"Don't worry, Kat," Emily said, holding one hand up to calm her little sister. She leaned closer. "I'm not letting him go this time."

When Emily reached the hospital, a nurse pulled her aside. "Dr. Berthoff, Dr. Walker had Maternity call for you. A patient is ready to deliver, and he's with a patient in ER. Seems there's been an onslaught of admissions this afternoon. Ten from your clinic alone. He asked you to handle the delivery."

Emily looked down at her dress and felt her heart sink. "Did you try to reach Dr. Gordon?"

"No one else is in town."

"Another hour, and I wouldn't have been, either. Would you tell Ricky West's parents that I'm checking on a pregnant mother and *will* be there to see Ricky as soon as I can. Then call Kevin MacIntyre and tell him I've had an emergency at the hospital and will have to call him when I'm through here. His number's in the phone book."

The nurse turned and ran down the hall. Emily removed her heels and headed in the opposite direction. She put on scrubs, but since she hadn't even considered an emergency detaining her, had no other shoes to change into. She didn't trust herself on heels, and decided to put shoe covers over her stocking feet, but welcomed the sight of an old pair of tennis shoes offered by one of the nurses. Three hours later, Emily left the new baby in good hands at the nursery, checked in on the mother in recovery, and headed to Ricky's room.

Another hour of her date with Kevin was gone. "What

a start to a reunion! This emergency couldn't have happened a month from now.'' She reached inside her bag for the cellular phone to call Kevin. He wasn't home. Surely, he hadn't gone on over to her house. She called there, only to be greeted by the answering machine.

Her black leather coat slung over one arm, and her bag over the other, Emily exited the elevator and headed for the lobby. Due to the snow, she had chosen to park in the general parking lot tonight. She rounded the corner to the exit, and was surprised to find Kevin seated by the door, visiting across the lobby with the receptionists. ''Evening, Dr. Emily. This charming young man has been waiting for you.''

''Hello, Sally. How are you tonight?'' Emily's questioning gaze met with Kevin's smile.

''Rough night, huh?'' He rose to his feet, his suit wrinkled from an obviously long wait.

''Kevin? How long have you been here? I told you I'd call. You didn't have to meet me.''

He took her coat from her arm and held it out for her. ''I was worried about you driving through this deep snow in that sporty little coupe of yours. Besides, I thought you could use a smile.'' He extended his elbow for her to take as they walked through the snow.

She returned his smile, slipped her arm through his and told the receptionists good-night over her shoulder. A frigid gust of wind blew through the door as it opened. ''I'm sorry about ruining your surprise tonight, Kevin.''

''Doesn't look like Denver was a great plan tonight in any case. Don't you have boots?''

''I wasn't thinking of practicality, obviously. Would you like to come over to my house for some coffee?''

''Maybe after dinner. You haven't eaten, have you?'' She shook her head. ''Where should we meet?''

"I'll drive."

She paused. *Here we go. Not even one date, and we're already disagreeing.* "My car is here, and I'll need my own car in case I'm called back to the hospital."

"You think I won't bring you back?"

She started to argue, but he interrupted her.

"Why don't I follow you to your house. We can leave it there. I'm still a little old-fashioned that way, Em. When I invite a lady to dinner, I pay, I drive and I walk her to the door afterward—even if it is slammed in my face when I get there." Slowly, his lips turned to a smile.

His humor was a refreshing change from that of the men she had dated throughout the years. "Had a few slammed in your face, have you?" She smiled back.

Wind swirled the snow around them, and he pulled her closer. "Enough, let's leave it at that."

"Hmm. I'll have to remember that technique. Is it effective?"

"Guess it depends on what message you want to send. There's only one lady who tried it and stayed a friend. Of course, that was a special circumstance."

Emily felt a twang of jealousy. "And who was that?"

He laughed. "Laura Bates. You should have seen the look on her face when I suggested we go skiing instead of what she expected to hear.

"Laura? You and Laura dated?"

As if he sensed her panic, he rushed into an explanation. "I wouldn't call it a date, exactly. I believe she called it an "outing." He told her about his canceled date, about wanting a chance to see how Laura really felt about Bryan. They'd gone to the theater, then skiing together, and through the course of his best friend and Laura dating, they had become special friends. To Emily, his concern for Laura's health now made a lot more sense.

They reached her car, and he brushed the snow off.

"I'll see you at my house."

"Be careful. There's ice under the snow." Kevin waited to make sure she wasn't stuck in the snow before going to his truck.

She smiled, enjoying being coddled by a gentleman for a change. She had to admit—Kevin knew how to treat a lady. Old-fashioned or not, she wouldn't argue any longer.

A few minutes later, Emily pulled into the driveway, admiring the snowman with his scarf flapping in the wind. Kevin pulled in behind her car and Kat's, then came around to help her get in. "Wouldn't you rather get some boots or even change into something warmer?"

"I'm not taking another chance at getting called in. Bob really owes me, now."

"He takes advantage of you, if you want my opinion," Kevin mumbled. She knew that but certainly didn't want to discuss it tonight, so ignored the comment.

Kevin helped her into the truck and went around to drive. A few minutes later he dropped her off at the door of the restaurant and drove around the building to find a parking place.

When they'd entered and were seated by the stone fireplace, Kevin ordered two cocoas and a platter of shrimp with cocktail sauce.

Emily felt a warm glow flow through her, and it had nothing to do with the fireplace. As much as she wanted to believe it was all going to work out this time, she was still inclined to guard herself. "Kevin, please don't make everything so perfect."

His gaze was soft as a caress. "We're a long way from perfect, Emmy. Just enjoy it for what it is, okay?"

"Which is?" She wasn't sure she wanted an explanation.

"Dinner with an old friend. Don't worry about tomorrow, okay? Let's take it one day at a time."

Easier said than done.

Chapter Eleven

Emily swung her arms in a quick rhythm opposite her feet; two more blocks, and she'd slow her pace. The spring sunshine had a crisp warmth, and invigorated her lungs. She hummed a melody in thanks for the beautiful day, and the fact that she had it off to enjoy.

It was Emily's first day to herself in a month. After the wonderful time she and Kevin had managed to find for each other over the past few weeks, she had hope there could really be a future for the two of them. There were no doubts in her mind that Kevin was still the man of her dreams. The man who would stand beside her, through good times and bad.

It was her mother whom she would have to convince—and Kevin. Though at this moment, she wasn't sure which would be more difficult.

Her mother had never forgiven her father for leaving her with three daughters to raise alone. She lived with bitterness to this day. Emily had grown up believing all men fit the same mold as Dad. Yet Kevin was the first man to show her differently. He would go for visits with

Emily, ignore her mother's cold shoulder and smart remarks, and dry Emily's tears when they left. The day they broke the engagement was the worst day of her life—the day Kevin fulfilled her mother's lowest expectations.

Since then, though, there had been countless other "father figures" in her life who had helped her turn away from the fears and bitterness that had threatened to consume her, as it had her mother. God had given her the gift of freedom to move into other relationships with a sense of self-confidence and hope. Though she had sometimes slipped back, God had always been there to show her another happy couple who would raise her hopes again.

Then there was Kevin. Kevin, who refused to talk about the future, claiming he didn't want to ruin the fun they were having with anything that serious. His hesitation sent up warning flags, yet Emily was convinced that it would take only time for him to realize his dreams, as well as her own, were alive and waiting to be fulfilled.

She realized that changing Kevin's heart and healing his emotional scars weren't within her means. She could only accept Kevin into her life again, and leave the rest to Him.

After her morning walk, Emily dusted the table and placed the flowers in the middle. Once she vacuumed, she would have the day to relax, do some shopping and bake some cookies. The phone rang, and Emily answered eagerly, hoping it was Kevin.

"Emily!" Laura was sobbing. "Gretchen and Jack West were killed in a car accident last night."

Emily's voice caught in her throat. "Oh, no. And Ricky? Was he hurt?" She paced the room.

"No," she squeaked. "He was with us. They went to

Denver for dinner and a play. They were going to be
back around midnight—'' her sobbing grew softer ''—at
three, I started calling their house, their cell phone, everyone I could think of. Finally, I called the state patrol and
explained the situation. At six this morning, they returned
my call with the news.''

Emily thought of the precious little boy, and sank into
the sofa. ''Have you told him?''

''I couldn't. Bryan took the kids to the park to play,
so I could start making phone calls.''

Emily had first met the Wests during Gretchen's pregnancy, then at church. In addition to having them as patients, she had had Ricky in her Sunday school class for
the past two years. As one of her first pregnant patients
after moving to Springville, Gretchen had had a special
place in her heart. It was Ricky who talked Emily into
helping occasionally with preschool. ''Is there anything
I can do? Help find family, or...''

''I already have. I called Gretchen's parents.'' There
was a long pause. ''They can't even make it here for the
funerals. I guess their health isn't good. Emily, could you
go with me to Casper this weekend to take Ricky to see
them? According to them, Jack has no living relatives.''

Emily looked at her calendar. ''Sure, I can fit that in.
When do you want to leave?'' They talked a while
longer, and Emily agreed to join Bryan and Laura for
lunch to tell Ricky about his parents.

As she completed her housecleaning, Emily's thoughts
returned to Ricky. She wondered if he would be living
with his grandparents for a while, or moving on to some
other family member's home. She wrote a note to herself
to make a copy of Ricky's medical records to hand deliver, thus bypassing all the red tape and the risk of their
being lost in the shuffle.

When Kevin called after work that evening, Emily reminded him of the day at the preschool, and told him about the tragedy.

"I'm going to put a playhouse together at the preschool tomorrow. Would it help if I took him for a while?" Kevin offered.

For a man who doesn't want a family, you're awfully generous, Kevin. "Check with Laura. I'm sure she wouldn't mind at all. They're going to keep Ricky with them for the week."

"You want to come along?"

"I work 'til seven this week, so I'd better say no. But thanks for the invitation."

Laura and Ricky met Kevin at the door of the church and escorted him into the preschool, where the teacher was sitting in the middle of a pile of planks and pieces.

"Thank you for coming, Kevin. I'm sorry to bother you, with all the other work you have."

"No problem. Hi, Ricky!" Kevin squatted, resting his rump on his heels, to be close to the boy.

He listened as the little tike explained what had happened to his parents. Kevin gave him a hug, blinking back the unexpected tears in his own eyes. "It's really hard when your parents die, isn't it?"

Ricky nodded. Kevin jangled his tool belt and looked at Ricky. "Mrs. Beaumont called me to help her build something. What are you trying to make again?"

"It's a playhouse, but the instructions are missing. Laura can't figure it out. Neither can Bryan."

Bryan's wife had already explained that her own husband passed the job along to "the expert." Laura hadn't even tried any of the children's fathers, deciding she wanted the job done right the first time, before she left town.

Kevin studied the pieces and began experimenting. "I think Ricky and I can figure this out, don't you, sport?"

Ricky nodded. He ran to the dress-up box and placed a toy hard hat on his head. "Can I hammer some *real* nails?"

"Sounds like a great idea."

"You're looking good, Laura. Feeling okay?" he asked, glancing up. She turned pink, and Kevin laughed, thinking of how much Bryan loved making his wife blush.

"I'm feeling much better now that I'm into the second trimester." Laura sat on the pint-size school chair and reached for another plank to hand him. "I hear Emily wouldn't tell you."

"Who could argue with professional confidence?"

"Nice to know there is some left in the world, isn't it?"

He muttered a response, remembering how little respect he had had for it at the time. He'd been worried about Laura, and couldn't have cared less about ethics, he was ashamed to admit. "When are you due?"

"Late September. Knowing my luck, it'll be October. My kids seem to have my sense of timing—not a minute earlier than necessary. If you two are okay here, I thought I'd run and pick up some groceries while you work."

Kevin looked at Ricky. "Think we can handle it without Laura's help?"

"Yup," Ricky said, puffing his chest out.

Kevin put the frame together, then added the sides, encouraging Ricky to pound the heads of the nails until they were flush with the surface. An hour and a half later, just before dusk, they had completed the new playhouse.

Across the street, three children were playing on a swing set, begging their preoccupied father to push them higher. The hopeful voices beckoned him, sending Kevin back to his own childhood memories—building a tree house, learning to ride a bike, wading in the icy cold stream learning the "art" of fishing.

"You're the only one standing in the way, you know."

He turned toward the feminine voice, and Laura smiled. "What?"

She was carrying a bench across the playground. "I said, you're in the way, could you move, please? We want this inside for the children to sit on. You two did a beautiful job!"

"I helped!" Ricky ran up to Laura.

Kevin jumped to his feet. "You shouldn't be lifting that in your condition. Let me."

He took the bench, realizing when he felt how light it actually was, that he was probably overreacting—to Laura, the children across the way, and to the guilt gnawing at his heart like termites in rotten lumber.

He had no business criticizing that father for ignoring his children, Kevin realized. He wouldn't even consider a family for the very same reason. He had no time. *Had none, or was he just unwilling to* make *time for a family?*

"I can't thank you enough, Kevin. The children are going to love this."

"We enjoyed doing it, didn't we, Ricky? If there's anything else, give me a call."

She helped him pick up his tools, and grinned mischievously. "Don't worry. I have your number."

Kevin thanked Ricky, then watched Laura help him climb into the Suburban.

Emily visited several times to see how Ricky was coping. As expected, he was angry and frightened. She knew from Laura that he was handling it the way any other child his age would. With Laura's past experience helping children cope with losing a parent, Emily knew Ricky was in expert hands.

One evening she decided to entertain the Beaumont children so Laura and Bryan could celebrate their six-month anniversary. Because of Laura's pregnancy, Emily wanted to lighten the emotional load Ricky added. She ordered pizza and gathered a few games for them to play. Kevin joined them eagerly, and Emily pushed aside the temptation to point out to Kevin his natural way with children.

She prayed each night that he would change his mind.

That he would want to make a commitment to her, and to a family.

That God would heal whatever had hurt him so badly.

Kevin pulled out the backgammon board and began setting up. Puzzled, Emily watched from the sofa, taking a break from reading a bedtime story to Ricky and Jacob, as Kevin began explaining the game to T.J. and Chad, the nine- and seven-year-olds.

After a while, T.J. became frustrated and stomped off. Kevin shook his head and followed T.J. up the stairs. A few minutes later they were back, sprawled across the living room floor playing the game again.

"Now, here's your home, and this area here is your yard, Chad." He paused. A few minutes later, she heard him reminding the boys that they always had to have a "buddy" with them or the other player could send them to the "time-out" chair.

Emily gave up trying to read. She listened, entranced by the way Kevin translated the game to the boys' level of understanding. By the end of the game, both boys were rolling the dice and making the moves on their own.

Jacob ran over to Kevin and dove onto his back. The two were especially close since Jacob and Bryan had shared Kevin's house. They rolled around on the floor, and Ricky watched quietly, staying close by Emily's side.

She held him close, wondering what he was thinking, remembering, needing. She was comforted by the fact that he would soon be going to his grandparents', where he would have plenty of time and attention.

As soon as she and Kevin had tucked the five children into bed, Kevin begged off duty to go over some bids that were waiting in his To Do pile.

By the end of the evening, she was exhausted and had an all new respect for Laura's gift of mothering. "I don't know how you keep up with everything, Laura," she said to her friend.

Laura smiled, rubbing her round tummy. "It's one of those roles that you sort of 'grow' into."

Emily rolled her eyes. "Bad, very bad, Laura."

Kevin went with Emily to the memorial service, and together they spent the evening at the Beaumonts'.

"Dr. Emily, when will my mommy and daddy come back?"

Emily felt his pain, knowing what a blow it was to have a parent never return. Except Ricky's didn't have the choice her father had had. That wouldn't make sense to the four-year-old for years. "They can't come back, Ricky. When a person dies, his or her soul goes to live in heaven with God."

Emily looked to Kevin, hoping for some help. He remained silent.

"Why can't it come back here to live with me?"

"Why can't what come back here? Their souls?"

Ricky nodded.

Emily thought. "In a way, I guess they do. You have memories of your mom and dad that you can think about anytime. That way, part of them is always with you."

She asked him about aunts and uncles, to which he just shrugged. It was bad enough that he'd lost his parents, but it was too much to think of him having to move in with a family he didn't even know. Emily shared his confusion with Laura, who became silent. "What's going on, Laura?"

"He has no aunts and uncles. Just Gretchen's parents."

"The ones who are too ill to come here?"

Laura nodded.

Emily felt sick. She couldn't voice her concerns. They were unjust, and she knew it, but she just couldn't stop herself from worrying.

"His grandparents called yesterday and talked with Ricky. The bank called them to let them know there was a will. It's being sent to Casper."

Emily watched Ricky playing with Jacob, thankful that Laura and Bryan had been willing to open their home to Ricky temporarily. Not only was it good for him to be with a loving family, but it was especially comforting that he was familiar with all of them. Laura and his mother had been friends, and she was able to share memories of Ricky's parents with him. Since Laura's children had lost their father, Laura was already well-prepared for Ricky's endless list of questions.

Friday arrived, and Laura and Emily packed up the Beaumonts' Suburban with all of Ricky's belongings. The grandparents had already instructed the church volunteers to donate the majority of Gretchen's and Jack's belongings to the needy, saving only the things the women believed Ricky might be attached to.

Bryan and Kevin were there for support, and Kevin was the one who lifted Ricky into the back seat and buckled him into the car seat. "Take care, Sport."

Emily felt the tears well in her eyes, and was thankful that Ricky couldn't see.

Kevin closed the back door and stepped up to Emily. "You going to be okay?"

"I'll feel a lot better when I know he's in a good home."

Kevin nodded. "He's a tough kid. He'll be okay."

"Tough gets a person through a bad situation—not necessarily in the best mental state, though." Emily spat the correction automatically, then felt bad for criticizing Kevin's attempt to give her courage. "I'm sorry, I know you meant it as a positive attribute."

He smiled sympathetically. "Stay strong for him, okay? When you get home, I'll be here to be strong for you."

She wrapped her arms around his neck and kissed him. "Thank you."

"You're welcome."

The drive was long, and made longer by the barren winter landscape and dreary gray skies. Laura had packed several children's tapes and books to keep Ricky occupied. An hour after they left home, Ricky was sound asleep.

Emily looked back. "I don't know how Social Service workers do this all the time."

Laura chuckled. "Don't you find that comment a little ironic, Emily? You're a doctor. You perform surgery, bring babies into the world of couples who should never have conceived, and tell people they have terminal illnesses. And yet taking a child to his grandparents, you fall apart?''

Emily dabbed the tears from her eyes and added the tissue to the already heaping collection in the trash. ''I can't explain it, either.''

Laura reached a hand over to Emily's and squeezed.

They traded driving responsibilities halfway so Laura could stretch out and rest. Laura had called home four times in the first two hours to remind Bryan of things he needed to do. Emily laughed at that.

''What's so funny?'' Laura argued. ''It's his first weekend as Mr. Mom.''

''You don't think he'll remember to take his own son to the potty? Really, Laura. You're as pathetic as I am.''

Both women smiled, a comfortable silence encompassing them. The mileage sign indicated they were almost there. Dusk was falling into night.

Ricky awoke, rubbing his eyes. ''Look at the big boat.''

Emily and Laura turned toward the bright lights in the distance, unable to tell exactly what they were looking at, yet unable to deny that it did look like a big boat. A gigantic ship, in fact. ''In the middle of Wyoming?''

''Hmm. Remind me to ask George and Harriet about this. I'm sure they can explain what it is.''

''Mommy and Daddy say it's a big boat,'' Ricky reassured them.

''A big boat it is, then.'' Emily smiled at Laura. They took the Center Street exit and turned toward town. Ricky's grandparents' house was settled in the older section, where charming homes had a character all their own. Ricky pointed to a house where a huge ramp had replaced the original stairs. ''Gramma and Papa.''

''Leave it to a child to lead the way.''

"Are you sure this is it?" Emily queried, looking at the paper with the address, then searching the front of the house for numbers.

"I trust Ricky. Right, Sport?"

The toddler had unbuckled his straps and was looking for the handle of Laura's vehicle. Emily didn't argue, but watched in amazement as Ricky jumped down, hitting the ground running before Laura or Emily could stop him.

Whatever reservations Emily had immediately disappeared when she saw Ricky hug his grandparents. By the time they'd unloaded everything, Ricky was dragging his things to the upstairs bedroom.

Through dinner there was a sudden turn of the proverbial tables, when Harriet began drilling Emily about her life and beliefs.

After the meal was over, Harriet instructed George to take Ricky to his room to get ready for bed. Harriet was in a wheelchair, so George didn't argue. Harriet wheeled across the floor with ease, neither asking for nor expecting help.

The weekend went well, easing most of Emily's worries. While age and physical limitations were a slight concern, lack of love certainly was not a problem. Ricky didn't seem to mind that his papa couldn't keep up with him, or that he couldn't sit on his grandma's lap. There were young children living next door, and, according to Harriet, the mother was more than willing to allow Ricky to come over to play.

By seven o'clock Saturday evening, both grandparents looked exhausted. Ricky had missed his nap and fallen asleep on the floor in front of the television.

When Emily lifted the youngster to carry him upstairs, Harriet began to sob. Laura held the woman's hand in silence. Emily paused, then, at a nod from Laura, continued. She dressed Ricky in his pajamas and tucked him into bed.

When she returned to the main level, the silence was ominous. "Emily, sit down, please," George asked. Once she had settled on the edge of a wing-back chair, George continued. "We can't thank you and Laura enough for taking care of our grandson this week, and for bringing him to visit us."

"This isn't a visit, George," Emily reminded softly. "You said he has no other family."

"He doesn't, but—" he cleared his throat "—Harriet and I aren't in any condition to care for a rambunctious little tike. We love him to pieces, but…"

Harriet finished her husband's sentence. "Our health wasn't an issue when they wrote their will, but Gretchen and Jack always spoke highly of you. We know they would want you to be Ricky's guardian."

Emily's mouth dropped open. She looked to Laura for support, and found a tearful smile on her friend's face. "B-But, you and George are his family."

"Oh, they had us as first choice, but knowing our age would one day be an issue, they wanted us to name a second choice in case we couldn't fulfill the obligation. The last time we talked, Gretchen suggested they ask you. I guess they never got around to it."

"Why me? I mean…" How could she tell them Gretchen and Jack weren't nearly close enough friends to have asked this of her?

"Gretchen trusted you above all others with her son, Emily. She praised your way with children, your professionalism, your…"

Emily looked to Laura. "You and Gretchen were closer than we were. This makes no sense."

"I also have four-plus children. I can't say with certainty that that had anything to do with their suggestion, but it would for me. Not to mention Ricky's asthma."

"That's another issue for us, Emily," George continued. "We don't have the knowledge, and I hate to admit it—but for Ricky's safety, I have to—I don't have the capability to keep up with his treatments."

"We would like for him to stay here to visit for a couple of weeks, if you don't mind. Mrs. Smith next door has agreed to help us for that long."

Emily listened numbly as Ricky's grandparents listed every one of her concerns. Their points were valid, but so were her own about becoming a parent. And they wanted Ricky to have a chance for a family with other children, something she couldn't offer him, she argued.

"Your odds are better than ours" was their reply.

Sounds like something Kevin would have said.

"Emily, Ricky has already lost his parents, and most likely we will be next. It's just not fair of us to put him through that again. If he has another young family, they will see him through."

She was a doctor with a sometimes demanding schedule. Kids needed time, had schedules of their own. How could she ever manage to fit more into her days?

Emily's mind reeled long into the night. *A child. Me— a mother. A single mother, just like my mom. What would I do when I had an emergency? I'd have to hire a nanny. I can't see me with a nanny in the house.*

And Kevin. This could send him running forever.

Kevin, or Ricky?

Please, God, don't make me choose between them.

Chapter Twelve

Emily had a difficult time telling Ricky goodbye, and found her own hesitation even more disturbing. The turn of events was overwhelming.

"You knew this before we left, didn't you, Laura."

"I didn't know for sure, but I suspected when they asked if I knew you, and if you could come along."

"You could have warned me it was coming." Emily shifted in her car seat. "I must have sounded like an idiot telling them why I shouldn't be his guardian."

"Knowing earlier wouldn't have diminished the shock, just made matters worse, I would think. You would have waited all weekend for them to bring it up. And what if I had been wrong? What if they had decided to continue to raise Ricky?"

"Guess it really doesn't matter any longer, I know now. What am I going to do?" It wasn't a question directed at Laura, and her friend seemed to understand. Silently, Emily went through the list of arguments at least a hundred more times in the four-hour drive home.

Emily had read the will, the wording of which did

allow her to "find" Ricky a good home if she decided that was "best for all parties."

How can I know what's best, God? You didn't bring him to me as a baby. And why—when Kevin and I are just working things out between us? I love Kevin, Father. I want him in my life. Yet he doesn't want a family. I'm not even sure he wants a wife. How can I even consider bringing a child into the picture?

When she arrived home, a dozen roses were waiting on the table. Scrawled on an adorable teddy bear card was a note from Kevin: I'm just a call away, any time of day. Been thinking of you. Kevin. Katarina had left that morning on a marketing trip, so Emily had the house to herself for a few days.

She pressed her lips to the card and placed it back in the flowers. "Oh, Kevin, not today. I have too much to think about without letting you muddle my emotions more." Emily took her bag upstairs to her room.

In the silence, she tried to imagine the noise Ricky's boisterous personality would bring to the house. She considered how different it would be having someone else to take care of, to fix meals for, to get ready for bed at night. The exhaustion from spending that one evening with the Beaumont children was fresh on her mind. Though she would only have the one, she knew it would be a major adjustment, for both of them.

Emily emptied her bags and started the laundry, then baked a batch of snickerdoodles. She called Pastor Mike and asked him to see her early the next morning.

"Sure," Mike said. "I hoped you would call. Ricky's grandparents made a decision already?"

"You knew, too?" She could imagine Mike's wry smile on the other end of the connection. She and Mike had dated a few times, and had mutually decided their

combined giving careers would be too draining on a relationship to make a marriage work, but the two had remained good friends.

"Yes, but I couldn't say anything. You know that."

"Professional confidence. I know," Emily mumbled.
They were both intense personalities and took life very
seriously. Emily valued him as a sounding board when
she found herself too involved with a situation. "Well,
the cat's out of the bag now, and I need to talk."

For a second night in a row, sleep eluded Emily. She
was anxious to talk to Mike. The phone rang once, and
she ignored it. She couldn't face Kevin yet. Tomorrow
would be soon enough.

At six the next morning, Emily walked into the pancake house and ordered a hazelnut coffee while waiting
for Pastor Mike.

"Morning. Penny for your thoughts."

She looked up, thankful Mike was finally here. "You
may need to start charging for advice soon. This problem
could bring in some big bucks."

Mike laughed. After several minutes of small talk, the
waitress took their order. Mike looked at her with his
deep brown eyes. "So what's the matter, Emily? Why
do you hesitate to follow Gretchen and Jack's wishes?"

Emily picked up the coffee cup and began turning it
around in her hand. The waitress approached and offered
to refill it. "Oh, no, thank you, I don't drink coffee."
She looked at it, puzzled that she *had* already drunk a
cup. She must be more distraught than she'd realized.
Emily set the cup back in the saucer and pushed it toward
the waitress to take to the kitchen, then looked back at
Mike, who was looking sympathetic and waiting patiently for an answer to his question.

"I'm a single doctor, Mike."

"That's not my fault," he said with a grin. "I tried to solve that 'problem.'"

She couldn't decide whether to laugh or cry. The indecision formulated itself as a lump in her throat, and Emily paused for a drink of water.

"Sorry, Emily, I'm teasing. It's just a wonder to me that you haven't found someone to share your life."

She cleared her throat. "That's part of the problem. I have, I think. Remember the man I told you about who wouldn't go with me to Maryland when I was accepted into Johns Hopkins?"

"The one who jilted you?"

The word sounded so much harsher now than it used to. She nodded. "He's back. We started seeing each other again."

He studied her, then added in his casual, jesting way, "Sounds easy enough. What's the problem?"

She shrugged. "Kevin says he doesn't want a family now—that our careers are too demanding. I know there must have been other things that happened after our breakup that hurt him, because he loves children. Kevin wanted a big family."

"And you care enough about him to let that stop you from taking Ricky?"

"I've never stopped loving Kevin."

Mike's expression changed; a smile spread across his face. "Kevin...Bryan Beaumont's best man?"

Emily blushed. "Yes. How did you...?"

Pastor Mike wiped his brow and smiled again. "He isn't the jealous type, is he?"

"Why—?" She followed Mike's gaze...right to Kevin. He was waiting to be seated, and simply tipped his head to her in acknowledgement. When the hostess came to seat him, he motioned toward the other side of the restaurant.

After her long, troubled night of soul-searching, the sight of Kevin made her fear all that much more real. "I can't tell him about Ricky. Not yet."

"You're going to have to sometime."

Emily moved to the edge of the booth. "Maybe Ricky's grandparents will decide they can raise him."

"Maybe, but I wouldn't count on it. They aren't saying they don't *want* him, but that they want what's best for him. And they've determined their daughter and son-in-law made a sound decision in naming you guardian, Emily—"

"Will you excuse me for a minute?"

Without waiting for Mike's answer, Emily walked up to Kevin and motioned toward the chair. "Do you mind?"

"I've only got a minute. I'm expecting Bryan and a couple more friends."

"I'm sorry I didn't call last night. It was a difficult weekend for me, and I needed time alone."

She could see the hurt on Kevin's face, even through his smile. "That's fine. We'll have to talk later—the guys are here."

"Okay." Emily stood up and backed away. "Morning, Bryan."

His response was lost in the confusion of the others moving past to be seated.

When Emily returned to the booth, their meals had arrived, and Mike motioned for her to eat.

She couldn't. Seeing how she'd hurt Kevin made her lose her appetite.

Pastor Mike finished eating a bite, then looked at her. "Emily, if I were in your shoes, I'd have the same questions, I'm sure. No decision is easy, especially when it involves the life of a child. You wouldn't be content with your decision if you didn't question it from all directions. That's who you are. That's probably the reason God led you into medicine. You don't stop with the easy answer.''

She cut her omelette and took a small bite, wondering if that was a compliment, or a concern in *this* case. Should she just accept Ricky without doubts? Was she wrong to find the answer such a struggle? She felt so selfish. What kind of woman would hesitate to take in an orphaned child?

That question alone had been enough to keep her awake all night. She'd tried to convince herself that there were thousands of people who would love to have a little boy like Ricky. That just because she wanted a child didn't mean *now* was the right time. That somehow, she would find just the right couple to take care of and give their love to the adorable boy.

Mike's authoritative voice recaptured her attention. "As you make your decision, I'd like you to think about this story I heard: There was a woman who once asked God why she hadn't been blessed with a child of her own. And God said, 'You were. I did bring you a little boy who had no mother and no father. And I gave you a tender heart for him. He wasn't a baby, true enough, but he needed the care and knowledge and love that only you could give him.'''

Mike paused. "Emily, God's children don't approach Him in the same packaging." He swiped his head, then continued, "Some may be bald, and some may have beautiful red hair, and some may even have a past they would rather forget than deal with. Yet God welcomes each of us. It isn't an easy decision to become a parent, whether it be by adoption, or by birth. Having another person to be responsible for is a great gift, one worthy of much thought and consideration and prayer."

"Thank you, Mike."

"I'm sure you'll come up with the best decision for you and Ricky. And Kevin."

Monday morning had been crazy. Seemed everyone had been waiting through the weekend to call the doctor. She hadn't had a moment to think of anything aside from the stack of files she would still have on her desk at the end of the day.

She had just returned a patient's call and had been put on hold—

"Help! We have a man hurt."

Emily dropped the phone into the cradle and ran toward the construction area. "What happened?"

As she reached Kevin's crewman, he turned and led the way. The two rushed through the tarps and down the ramp as he explained. "We were lifting the window from the truck, and it slipped from my hand. It knocked the boss to the ground. He's out cold."

"The boss?" Emily's heart stopped. "Kevin?"

"Yeah, Kevin."

Emily ran faster, nearly passing the man by. *Hang on, Kevin.* She turned to her nurse, who was trailing behind. "Go get the COR cart."

Kevin was motionless, laying on his back in the dried mud. Several men surrounded him; glass from the shattered window covered the ground. His skin was pale, and there were cuts all over his face.

Ignoring the glass, Emily dropped to the ground and knelt beside him. "Kevin! Can you hear me?" She placed her cheek over his mouth to feel for breathing, automatically pressing her fingers on his neck to check for a pulse.

"He's not breathing. There is a pulse. Call an ambulance!" She wasn't going to take any chances, and there was no way she could chance moving him without a backboard. Emily saw one man holding a bloody rag to Kevin's head, and hoped he hadn't already moved the victim. "Why's he not breathing?" she shouted.

No one answered. Patti returned and dropped to her knees next to Kevin's head, setting the kit beside her. "The ambulance should be on the way." Patti thrust his jaw forward, and Emily checked for an obstructed airway. "Do you want the mask?"

Seeing nothing in his mouth, Emily tried to blow air into his lungs. "Didn't go in. Try the jaw thrust again." Emily stayed in position, ready to move when Patti was ready. "Don't you dare die on me!" she said to Kevin.

Patti continued to hold Kevin's head steady and to pull his jaw farther forward. "You sure you don't want the Ambubag…?"

Ignoring her nurse, Emily blew two deep breaths into Kevin's mouth. "Nothing." She tore the shirt open and straddled his torso. "Oh, no, you don't, buster. You're not getting off this easy!" Weaving her fingers together, she straightened her arms and began abdominal thrusts, then moved back to check for an obstruction of the airway. Emily opened his mouth and looked, swept a red-and-white peppermint candy from his mouth, and resumed the position for rescue breathing.

"Got it! Let's start over."

Patti readjusted his jaw just before Emily's mouth covered his. Holding his nose closed, she gave him two deep breaths, and was relieved to see his chest rise this time. She checked his pulse. The beat was rapid. She checked his breathing, then breathed into his mouth again. "Come on, Kevin, you're not going to give up, are you?"

You wouldn't dare die on me! Don't you dare. She paused, then breathed for him again. *Please, God. Don't let him die. I need him.*

"Breathe, Kevin, three, four..." Emily continued the cycle as the ambulance's warbling siren grew louder, then came to a sudden halt. Kevin coughed—a weak but welcome sound.

Emily felt a surge of relief as voices ordered the crew to move back. A man at Kevin's head offered to take over.

Emily glanced up to the EMT. "He just started breathing again after I dislodged a piece of candy."

"We'll take over, miss."

"I'm a doctor, and I'm *not* leaving the patient. Get the backboard and cervical collars ready. A window fell on him. He could have spinal cord injuries. Possible concussion. He's still unconscious." One medic ran to the truck, while the other quickly wrote the vital information Emily was rattling off on a piece of white athletic tape stuck to his pant leg.

"Sorry, Doctor. How long did you say he went without breathing?"

"Two, maybe three minutes."

"But he's breathing on his own now? That's a relief." While he talked, he took a penlight from his pocket and checked Kevin's pupils. "Good job, Doctor. It looks like you got his airway opened fast enough. The pupils are still reactive. I agree, could still be a concussion. Too early to tell for sure, isn't it."

Knowing that Kevin hadn't been without oxygen long enough to cause permanent damage, Emily felt as if a huge weight had lifted from her.

The paramedic had gone on with his job without waiting for an answer. The EMT placed the oxygen mask over Kevin's nose and mouth. Then they slipped a *C*-collar beneath his neck and fastened it to stabilize his head. As they rolled him to one side, a large laceration was exposed on the back of his blond head. The other paramedic placed a four-by-four gauze bandage over the cut, while they slid the backboard under him.

"Cancel my appointments, Patti. I'm going with them."

Emily worked with the trauma unit until the ambulance reached the hospital. Once the emergency room staff began the exam, Emily emotionally stepped away from her role as a doctor and let the woman in love take over.

She backed into a far corner, out of the way, yet close enough to be assured he was okay. She couldn't leave him. She felt chilled and started shaking. She blinked back tears, watching as nurses prepared him for the myriad of tests to assess the damage.

Please, Father, don't let him leave me again.

Kevin dozed, a fuzzy image of Emily wandering around in his head. He rolled over, felt a tug on his arm, then remembered the IV leash in the back of his hand.

He flopped back and shook his head.

Don't you dare die on me!

Kevin groaned. *Must be the drugs.*

He heard Emily's voice. Felt her touch. "Emmy."

He'd seen a bright light, then immediately felt himself being pulled away from it.

Oh, no, you don't, buster.

Someone was squeezing his arm. "Let me go," he growled.

The feminine voice didn't go with the firm grip. "It's

Darleen, your nurse. I'm just taking your blood pressure.''

He blinked his eyes open, surprised to see a woman standing beside him. The room was dim, machines beeped, and something was pinching his finger.

"You feeling okay?" Darleen asked.

He closed his eyes again.

Don't you dare die on me!

He grumbled, then stretched his neck from side to side. "I must have been dreaming. What happened? I'm okay, aren't I?"

"You're looking better every minute."

"Likewise." He opened his eyes again to see the brunette leaving the room. "Hey, you're not going to leave me all alone, are you?"

Darleen smiled. "You're not alone," she said, and continued out the door.

"You never stop, do you?" There was a welcome familiarity in that voice. He turned, greeted by Emily's smile. "Much as I hesitate to admit it, it's good to see you return to normal, even if you are flirting with someone else. How are you feeling?"

"I only flirt with *my doctor*. You should know that." He blinked sleepily. "What happened?"

She told him about the accident. "It was quite a head injury. I thought I'd lost you again."

"That why my head hurts?"

She nodded.

He lifted his hand awkwardly to his head, found the bandage and began to explore tentatively. "What's that?"

"Calm down, Kevin. You have a nasty gash with a lot of stitches. Don't touch, honey." She took his hand and lowered it to the bed. He wouldn't let it go.

She didn't, either. "You have a severe concussion, but you're going to be okay. We're going to keep you in here for a couple of days to make sure you're okay."

He closed his eyes and struggled to remember the accident, the ambulance, anything relating to the lost time. One memory he was certain of—Emily hadn't called when she returned from Wyoming. He was sure he'd seen her just before his accident, eating with some other man. It was breakfast. It was the last thing he remembered. He winced.

"Do you have any pain?"

Kevin squirmed, sweaty and itchy from the plastic-covered mattress and pillow. "Yeah, there's this one pain."

"Where?"

"I'd better not say, you'd accuse me of flirting."

She scowled at him. "I'm serious."

"You always have been. No reason for that to change now, is there?" He squeezed her hand tighter.

"Well, your memory seems to be good." She took hold of his other hand and spread both arms wide. "Squeeze both of my fingers."

He did as she told him, gazing into her eyes as she studied his coordination. She was beautiful. *Thank You for letting me come back to her, God.*

"Okay, that's good. You can let go now."

He shook his head. "Nope." He pulled her close.

"Nope?" He saw the teasing in her gaze, followed by a sudden look of concern. "Kevin, your doctor could walk in at any time."

"*My* doctor *is* here. Whatever happened to bedside manners, Doc?"

She blushed. "If you don't behave, I'll turn you over to a doctor with *no* bedside manner."

"You mean there are two of you?" He smiled. "Come on, Emmy, one little kiss."

"You're incorrigible." Her eyes drifted closed and her lips touched his. It was a slow, drugging kiss that left him feeling weak. He felt his body relax against the bed as she backed away.

His eyes remained closed, and he was transported to his own dreamy world. "That was you." He furrowed his brow and opened his eyes.

Her look of anticipation offered hope. "When?"

"I don't know for sure. While I was out, maybe? Wait a minute. You were the one to save my life? You were talking to me. It was you...."

Her voice was soft. "I wasn't talking, buster, I was yelling." A tear trickled down her cheek as she hesitantly leaned forward and kissed him once more. "Don't you *dare* do that to me again."

The depth of her emotion confused him. Things were getting serious, and he wasn't sure that was a good idea. Kevin studied her for a minute before coming up with a light response. "Oh, then I suppose you don't want me to mention that you were all over me. Or those loving comments you made. Very unprofessional, if I might say. You might think I didn't hear you, but I did," he teased.

She arched an eyebrow, and stepped close to the bed, her cheeks regaining a subtle glow that softened the worry lines on her face. "I guess you have the wrong person, after all."

Kevin laughed. "Oh, no, it was definitely you. And there was this bald guy." Kevin tried to remember who that was. He gathered by Emily's affections tonight that his first assumption was way off base. Maybe the bald man was his other doctor.

Her green eyes were brilliant and twinkled as if she

had a wonderful secret to tell. Red curls tumbled over her shoulders. "You remember the pastor's visit?"

"The pastor?" He thought, suddenly apprehensive. There was something more he felt he should know about the man. *Why can't I remember anything?* "No."

She was disappointed. He could see it in her eyes. Why did she care that he couldn't remember a visit from the pastor?

"Hmm. Your other doctor will be in shortly to examine you. You know, the one with *no* bedside manner." Emily strolled to the door, then hesitated. "I'd better go check on my own patients before it's too late. I'll be back to see you first thing in the morning."

"Sweet dreams, Doc."

Chapter Thirteen

Emily called the hospital in the middle of the night, hoping to ease her concerns that Kevin's condition hadn't worsened.

Get some rest, she told herself.

It was impossible.

"I'll never tell anyone *that* again!" she said aloud.

Each time she thought of Kevin's accident, she felt guilty for not calling him after returning from Wyoming. Had he been angry with her instead of concentrating on his work? Was she at least partially to blame for what had happened?

After a sleepless night evaluating every aspect of Kevin's injuries and what his recovery would mean to his work, Emily began to worry. How solvent was his company? Had he overextended himself? Would he lose his business if he missed the deadline?

Kevin needed time off, and he wasn't the type to sit back and let others do his work.

She pondered the problem. Kevin and his crew started

around seven. Would his crew be able to continue working without Kevin at the helm?

On her way to the hospital, she took a detour by the
clinic to see if any of the crew had shown up. When she
saw the idle equipment, she immediately called Bryan.
"Does Kevin have anyone who can run the project while
he's out of commission?"

"Not that I know of. He didn't mention it last night
when I visited. A couple of his men showed up as I left.
He must have it under control."

"No one is here. They usually arrive around seven."

"I'm just the silent partner, Em. Sorry. Why don't you
ask Kevin?"

"Because he's already a challenge to keep calm. The
last thing I want to do is make him think about not meeting the deadline. I know the penalty is outrageous, and
Kevin's already cut the budget to the bare necessities on
this, I'm sure. His bid was so much lower than the others—he has to be taking a risk as it is."

Bryan wouldn't confirm Emily's suspicions. Not that
she was surprised: the two men were as loyal as blood
brothers. "He's feeling okay, isn't he? How long are you
talking about?"

"A week or two, but that's if he takes it easy."

"Ouch." Bryan paused, then added, "That's going to
hurt all right. Why don't you see if the crew shows up
later on today. Maybe Kevin put someone in charge."

"I'll keep an eye on it, but in the meantime I have an
idea, and want your opinion. Did you reach any of
Kevin's family last night?"

"His mom picked up Alex at the airport, and they got
in late. They're staying at the Sodbuster Inn. Adam and
the twins couldn't make it. Why?"

"Since Alex and Kevin both worked for his father's

company, don't you think Alex would be willing to help Kevin with the project until Kevin is back one hundred percent?''

There was a long silence at the other end of the line.

''Bryan? What's wrong with the idea? I know Dr. Roberts isn't going to let Kevin go back on the site for a few weeks. He might be able to handle things in the office within a few days, but I'm sure they need a foreman, too. Don't they?''

''You and Kevin haven't talked a whole lot yet, have you?''

Emily felt an emptiness, realizing there was so much that Kevin hadn't shared with her. *What could be so horrible that Kevin wouldn't even ask his own brother for help?* ''I know there must be more than what he's told me about the past few years, but—''

''Maybe it's for the best. It might be the perfect opportunity to let those two make amends. After all, Alex did come.''

Emily stopped him. ''Wait just a minute, Bryan. I need to know what happened.''

''Kevin hoped to rebuild the business after his dad passed away. Alex didn't want anything to do with it, took off to fight forest fires. The family voted to shut down their dad's company.'' He paused. ''I can't imagine Kevin is still upset about it. They've celebrated several holidays together since then, and the house is still standing.''

Bryan offered to arrange a breakfast meeting between Kevin's family and Emily.

''Thanks, I'd appreciate it. It's going to be awkward enough to see them, let alone the fact that I want to ask a favor our first meeting. I need to make my rounds and see Kevin. If it won't work to meet at 8:30, page me.''

Emily said a prayer that the breakfast meeting would go well. After her rounds she went to see Kevin. As she expected, he was flirting again—this time trying to convince the nurse to remove his IV so he could get back to work.

Darleen checked the IV in his hand, and pushed the stand closer to the bed. "No, Mr. MacIntyre, Dr. Roberts wants the IV left in for the rest of the day."

"But it's going to get in the way of my using the saw."

"I think that's the point, Kevin." Emily smiled and stepped into his room. "Thanks, Darleen. I'll handle this charmer." She turned to him. "You should be ashamed of yourself, trying to sweet-talk the nurses into breaking doctor's orders."

His smile was as mischievous as ever, and his eyebrows lifted as he shrugged. "Well, now, I can go right to the source of the problem. You're slowing me down here, Doc."

"Not nearly enough, obviously." She leaned over the side of the bed and gave him a chaste kiss on the cheek. "If you don't behave, I'm going to have to order round-the-clock supervision—"

"Well, now, that just might be worth it."

"—from one of the security officers. How are you feeling?" Emily smiled.

"I need to get out of here. I don't like hospitals."

She smoothed his sheets, wondering how she was ever going to convince him to slow down enough to let his body recover from the accident. "It won't be long 'til you can go home, *if* you cooperate and follow doctor's orders."

"I have a job to do, Emily. You know as well as I do

what a tight schedule we're on. I can't afford to sit in here.''

''I understand, and I want you back at work, too. But more important, I want to make sure you're okay.'' Emily gazed into his blue eyes. *I want you around forever, Kevin.* ''Do you have anyone who can take over for a while?''

He laughed. ''You're looking at him. I have a small operation. Until I cover the expenses for this project, I can't afford to pay a foreman. Everything rides on finishing this project on time. Can't you check me out of here? Ple-ea-se?''

Emily was torn between laughing and crying. ''No, I can't, and even if I were able, I wouldn't. You need rest!''

Kevin pushed the breakfast tray aside, slid his legs over the edge of the bed and looked around the room. ''Where are my clothes?''

''I took them home to wash them. Your wallet and keys are at home. I didn't think they should be left around here. Of course, the shirt's ruined. I'll bring you some clean clothes before you're dismissed.''

He frowned. ''You think that's going to stop me from checking out of here?''

Emily smiled. ''It works on most patients.''

''Smart aleck.'' Kevin let out a weak chuckle and let his head relax against the pillow, then tossed it aside when its plastic cover crinkled. ''As long as you're going to make me stay here, could you please bring me a decent pillow from home?''

''You want me to get things…from your house?'' She didn't mean to hesitate.

''Does that bother you?''

''No, I just didn't want to presume anything, I guess.''

She looked at her watch and realized she didn't have much time before her meeting with Kevin's mom and brother. "I have an appointment in a few minutes. You need to rest, Kevin. We'll talk later."

After a quick goodbye, Emily drove to the Sodbuster Inn. Bryan arrived just as she did. "You ready?"

She had hardly had time to think about the fact that she was going to be seeing her former potential in-laws for the first time since the broken engagement. Her main concern right now was getting Kevin to slow down for a few weeks, which meant finding someone to help during his recovery. "I was before I saw Kevin. He's ready to check himself out and go right to work at the clinic. I know something has to be done, but are you sure I should do this?"

"Bryan!" Alex bound down the stairs and offered his hand. The two men embraced. "Looks like marriage agrees with you."

"Yes, it does. I'm anxious for you to meet the family. We'll plan on you and your mom coming over for dinner tonight."

Alex turned to Emily then, and back to Bryan. "Oh, I thought for a minute that this was your wife, but—" He did a double take, and there was a glimmer of recognition in his expression.

Mrs. MacIntyre's soft voice came from somewhere behind her. "Emily?"

Emily turned toward the woman she'd been too proud to accept help from all those years ago. "Mrs. MacIntyre, I can't tell you how sorry I was to hear about your husband."

"Thank you. What are you doing here?"

Emily had hoped Kevin had at least mentioned they

were both living in the same town, though she doubted he would have mentioned they were dating yet.

Emily looked to Bryan for support, thankful suddenly that he had come along. "I'm a doctor at the clinic Kevin's company is working on."

"Well, that explains a few things, doesn't it?" Alex chuckled. "So, are you here in an official capacity?"

"Not completely." *I'm not going to hide from the truth.* "Kevin and I started seeing each other a few weeks ago, though it's not serious, yet."

"Better have that staff of yours run a few more tests on him, then, Doctor. Until that little brother of mine realizes he needs to *make* it serious, I think he has a few more priorities to get straightened out."

"Alex, stop teasing Emily." Mrs. MacIntyre put her arm around Emily in a welcoming gesture. "I hope everything works out this time. Kevin…well, Kevin wasn't quite the same without you."

Me, neither.

Emily didn't know what to say. Everything in her life had turned upside down in the last week. She had no idea how or where to start straightening it out. Especially now.

While they ate, Emily filled them in on Kevin's condition. The only thing remaining was to ask Alex to do his younger brother a favor. Why did she feel as if she were asking for the world? *They're brothers. Of course he'll help. Won't he?* Since she didn't have brothers, she could only go on her relationship with her sisters. And she knew from experience, they wouldn't hesitate for a minute.

She glanced at Bryan, who winked. When she couldn't speak, Bryan interjected. "Alex, Emily and I have discussed an idea, and we could use your input on the matter. Emily, go ahead."

"As I said, I'm not Kevin's primary-care doctor, but I'm certain Dr. Roberts won't want Kevin working for a few weeks. You know Kevin as well as I do. That won't stop him from trying, unless he has someone capable and trustworthy to do the job in his place—someone who knows the business—who knows the way Kevin works." Her gaze met Alex's. "I'm sure you all know how much this job means to his company. There's no way he can shut down for that long."

Alex took a deep breath and leaned back in his chair. "Who-ee, gal, I thought I was the only firefighter in the family. You sure you're ready to put out *this* blaze?"

Emily's eyes grew larger and she looked at Bryan, pleading for an explanation before she finished. Silently, she prayed, *Am I doing the right thing, God?*

Bryan chuckled. "I'll take the heat if sparks start flying."

With a glance to Kevin's mother, Emily cleared her throat. "I'm not only gambling with my feelings for Kevin, here, but—" Emily stopped. She'd almost blurted out that she had a child to think of, as well. "I'm not sure this is the right thing to do, but I can't let Kevin risk losing his company."

Alex took her hand. "I came to do this job, whether or not anyone asked. I can't think of any better way to show my support."

Emily's mouth fell open. "He already asked you?"

Alex let out a deep laugh. "Don't get happy. What's he going to do, kick me off the site? If Kevin forgives me for the past mistakes in the process, all the better. If not, at least I tried. One thing for sure, I'm not going to let him down this time."

Emily felt tears sting her eyes. "Thank you, Alex."

"You take care of my brother, and I'll take care of his business—'til he's back in shape."

Mrs. MacIntyre's soft voice broke in. "Since we're clearing the air, I'm glad you're here, Emily. I look forward to visiting again later." She looked at Alex. "I want to see Kevin. Are you ready?"

Emily didn't know how to respond. Little by little she was discovering why Kevin was so different from the man she had almost married. "I'll see you all later, I'm sure." She pulled a card from her purse. "Here's my pager number, if you need anything."

They all rose and pushed the chairs in behind them.

"Oh, I took the clothes he was wearing when the accident happened home to wash. I told him I'd bring them back later, but I'd recommend we hold off on that as long as possible. He just may go AWOL if he has any opportunity."

Bryan gave her a hug before heading off to work. "Don't give up on him, Em. You know Kevin's too stubborn to do anything the easy way."

When she visited him that night, Kevin didn't mention Alex's helping out. She decided that it was between the brothers now. Maybe they needed more time. But could the project afford to sit idle while the two made amends?

Dr. Roberts was due anytime. Kevin turned to look at the clock again and shifted in the bed, perspiration gluing his back to the mattress. It had been two days since the accident, and he had to get to work. He was tired of sticking to the bed, eating tasteless mush and being poked and monitored.

Not only that, but being around the hospital so much was obviously bothering his mother, as well. After failing to convince her he'd be okay, and that she could go on home, they finally reached a compromise. She'd keep her hospital visits short. She and Alex would stay at his house. She could stay to take care of him for a few days after he was released from the hospital.

He had to get home before she gave his bachelor pad a whole new look—one with those feminine touches that would remind him of all that was missing in his life.

Alex made regular visits early in the morning and later in the evening. What he was doing with the rest of his time, Kevin wasn't sure. In fact, he wasn't sure why Alex was still here at all. When asked, his brother mumbled something about getting too old to be jumping into flames and looking for a new job.

It was good to see him, without the past acting as a barrier.

The alarm on the IV went off, indicating the fluid was getting low. It was also a not-so-subtle reminder that he had to convince the doctor he was well enough to go home.

Emily's visits were the highlight of his day. Being on the staff, she was the only one not kicked out when visiting hours were over—the only thing that kept him from losing his mind in here. How Emily stayed so cheerful around all this pain was beyond him.

Kevin could still see the fear in her eyes when she told his mother and Alex details about the accident. She ended by telling him over and over again that he'd "better never, ever scare her like that again."

He saw the love in her every action. And it scared the daylights out of him. If anything, the accident had proven to him that no matter how much control he thought he had, in the flash of an eye, it could be taken away.

How can I do this to her? He'd seen what his father's

death had done to his mother. She still couldn't handle being in a hospital. He couldn't do that to Emily.

"Pride goeth before a fall," his father used to tell him. What a time for him to think of his dad—while lying in the hospital.

He thought of him and Alex running the family business in his father's absence—

It hit him like a ton of bricks.

Alex.

That's what he's been doing all day. I've got to get out of here, get back to work before Alex shuts down my company, too.

Kevin sat up in bed and swung his bare legs over the side, trying to figure out how he was going to get to the construction site.

Alex probably has my truck, too.

"Morning, Kevin. How are you feeling?"

Dr. Roberts had rotten timing.

"Well enough to get out of here."

The doctor laughed. "Let's take one more look and see what your file says before you check yourself out of here." He looked at the chart and set it aside. "No more headaches, dizziness…"

"None," Kevin snapped.

The list of questions went on and on, adding to Kevin's irritation. "Dr. Roberts, I really need to get back to work."

He thought of his mother. Emily. Alex.

None of them had given him a clue as to what was happening in the outside world. "I have people to see. I don't have time to sit around here doing nothing."

"Now, now, Mr. MacIntyre. Let me review a few things with you."

Before Kevin knew it, he'd been sidelined for a indeterminate length of time.

In the back of his mind he heard the doctor mention seeing him in three to four days for a checkup without saying exactly how long he would have to stay away from work.

No lifting, no physical exertion, nothing.

The old codger winked. "I'd hate to have to pull the clinic contract in order to make sure you take care of yourself. Don't worry, your brother has everything running smoothly."

Kevin snapped inside, but somehow managed to remain calm on the outside. "My brother may have come to help, but I still run the project. With all due respect, I can't afford to stay off clinic property for another day."

Dr. Roberts chuckled. "Fine, but I'd better not see you lifting even a hammer, Kevin. First it's a hammer, then the saw, then a plate-glass window. Don't push your luck. I'm serious."

Kevin laughed. Weren't all doctors always serious? *Must be an occupational hazard.*

Kevin couldn't believe that Alex filling in hadn't crossed his mind earlier. Kevin hoped he didn't look half as foolish as he felt. His brother wasn't just looking for any job; Alex was taking *Kevin's* job.

"When can I go home, Dr. Roberts?"

"I'll sign the release—shouldn't take too long. Why don't you get dressed and call a ride to get you out of here."

Kevin held out his hand. "Thanks, Doc. See you in a few days."

The doctor gripped Kevin's hand firmly and smiled. "Someone upstairs gave you a second chance. Don't take that for granted."

Nodding, he waited for the physician to finish signing the papers.

Kevin knew better than to look for his clothes—all he would find were empty closets. He'd searched for a way out yesterday, hoping Emily had put them away while he wasn't looking.

Now, not only did he need to call home for a ride, but he had to wait for his clothes to arrive, as well. When he called the house, no one was home.

He called Emily. In the background he heard pounding and sawing. "Emily, my brother is doing my job, isn't he?"

The silence lengthened, and he heard Emily close her door to the noises that were as comforting to him as a worn-out sweatshirt. "This is no time to let your stubborn pride stand in the way, Kevin."

"I want a straight answer, Emily."

"I don't know where he is right now, but yes, Kevin, Alex is making sure things continue to run smoothly with your project."

"You couldn't have told me two days ago?" he said, and failed to keep the anger from his voice.

Emily's words were tart with professionalism. "Two days ago, you were so out of it you wouldn't have understood what I was saying if I *had* told you. I thought you'd appreciate your brother's help. He's making sure the work is getting done."

"You just had to take over, didn't you?" The minute he said the words, he was sorry.

"It won't happen again."

"I'm sorry, Emily—" She'd already hung up.

Kevin closed his eyes. *Great way to make amends, Kevin.* He wove his fingers together behind his neck and lay back on the bed. *I think it's time we have a talk, God.*

* * *

An hour later his brother walked into the hospital room, carrying a change of clothes and the keys to Kevin's truck. "I understand you're not terribly happy with me."

Alex always did know how to make an entrance.

"If you wanted a job, you could have asked."

Alex nodded slightly, not looking at all remorseful or worried. "A lot less headache this way. When that old codger gives you your life back, I'll be tossed aside like a dirty shirt, and you know it."

Kevin didn't know how to deny it. Though he had forgiven his family for the decision they'd made years ago, he wasn't sure it was good business to bring "family" into the picture again. "It isn't that I—"

Alex dropped into the chair across from the table and crossed one ankle over his opposite knee. "I want to help, to tell you I'm sorry. To let you know how proud I am of you and what you're doing. You're not too proud to accept that, are you?"

He struggled with his stubborn pride, afraid of making matters with his brother worse. It wasn't that he didn't want Alex here. Admittedly, he wasn't up to speed yet, and he would have been scrambling to run the job from afar. But he was in no position to offer his brother what a foreman should earn—even temporarily.

Kevin took a deep breath and repeated the verse silently: "A friend loves at all times, and a brother is born for adversity."

"Thanks. I'll admit, I'm not at all happy with having to sit the bench on this, but if there's anyone I trust to do it right, it's you. About the pay—"

"Don't worry about it." A look of trepidation crossed Alex's face.

Kevin knew the spring thunderstorms made this the

busiest season for smokejumpers, and Alex's presence here was costing him plenty. "I plan to worry about it. And I plan to pay you."

"You don't need to, okay?"

He looked suspiciously at his brother. "You dropped your job, flew down here on the spur of the moment—which couldn't have been cheap—and you don't want to be paid? What's going on, Alex?"

Kevin heard dainty footsteps enter the room.

"I paid him already, and before you start yelling, I asked him not to say anything," Emily's soft voice explained. "I wanted to help."

He turned toward her. It was bad enough that he was incapacitated physically and facing his ex-fiancée who'd already saved his life once, but to have her taking care of his business obligations was totally out of the question, and he didn't hesitate to tell her so.

She looked at his hospital gown and back at his face. "So, let me get this straight. It would have been okay for your parents to pay for me to go to medical school, yet I can't help you out?"

"This isn't at all the same situation, Doc. We aren't—" He stopped short of saying they weren't committed to one another the way they had been then. "I pay my own employees."

She looked as if he'd just punched her, and an unwelcome tension stretched between them.

"I see." Emily's eyes revealed her mounting anger. "Consider it an investment, Kevin. The sooner you finish the job, the sooner we can both move on with our lives."

Emily whirled around and walked out of the room.

Kevin tripped over the hospital tray and headed after her, the tails of his gown flapping as he ran down the hall. She ran into the elevator, and the door closed before he could stop her.

Kevin hit the button and pounded his fist against the stainless-steel door.

"Ah, Kevin?"

"What?" he growled. What could his brother have to say *now?*

Alex stepped behind him, tugged the back of Kevin's gown together and whispered, "You're putting on quite a show, little brother."

Kevin turned and waved to the wide-eyed audience, furious that his brother and the hospital staff had seen him chasing after a woman—especially Dr. Emily Berthoff. "I can't wait to get out of here," he muttered.

Chapter Fourteen

Emily leaned against the wall of the elevator and closed her eyes. *You are so stubborn, Kevin!* She ran her fingers through her hair, pulling the bulk of it into a clip.

She had been fool enough to think there was a chance she could actually become whole again. That Kevin would wake up, anxious to tell her directly what he'd told Pastor Mike while in his stupor from painkillers—that he loved her.

Mike had come to visit as soon as he heard about Kevin's accident, both to pray for Kevin and to offer Emily support. They had both stayed with Kevin for most of the day. Emily was grateful that Mike had a wonderful sense of humor and already knew how Emily felt about Kevin, or it could have been quite an eye-opener when Kevin warned the pastor not to get any ideas about her. The warning had been followed by an emotionally garbled, "I love her."

It had been two days since Kevin's babbles had given her hope, only to have him dash them again in his alert, clear-minded stubbornness.

I've waited eight years to find this kind of love again, God. Why can't Kevin give us another chance?

Her pager beeped, and she pressed the button to silence it, seeing the code from the maternity ward. *Mrs. Apple's labor pains must be getting closer.* Emily took a deep breath and pushed the elevator button to return to the third floor.

A few hours later, Emily finally made it home with a bag of French fries and a burger. Katarina was home from her business trip and met her at the door.

"I thought you had the evening off."

"I filled in for Bob."

Katarina scolded her with a tip of her head. "That's the third time in the month that I've been here! Doesn't the man realize you have a life?"

"I do?" Emily said sarcastically. She moved into the living room and dropped onto the sofa. The picture of a rainbow that Ricky had drawn for her sent her back to the weekend—before Kevin's accident. Had it only been four days since she'd learned of Gretchen and Jack's request?

"What is bothering you? You haven't looked this sick since you caught the flu from Stanley What's-his-name right before Homecoming."

"Nothing's wrong with me," she said, then filled her mouth with an oversize bite of hamburger.

Katarina made a show of checking Emily's forehead for a fever. "Something *must* be wrong if you stopped at a fast-food place for dinner."

Emily forced a smile. "I'll be okay. How was your trip? I want to hear all about it." There was nothing Katarina could do to alleviate her concerns. Only Kevin could do that. And it didn't appear he was inclined to do so anytime soon. "Did you get any contracts?"

"Oh, no, no, no. Don't you change the subject." Katarina dropped into the seat next to her, pulled Emily's shoes from her feet and began massaging. "Come on, sis, spill it."

Emily collapsed against the back of the sofa and let herself relax as her sister worked the aches from her feet. *Maybe it would help just having someone to share my worries with.* "You wouldn't believe the week I've had."

She told Katarina about the turn her weekend with Ricky's grandparents had taken, and about Kevin's accident.

"You're serious. I mean, Kevin almost died?"

She tipped her head to the side in disbelief. "I'm a doctor, Kat. I don't joke about things like that."

"But he's fine now? He's thrilled to have another chance to make you blissfully happy? To be the father of your children, and Ricky?"

Emily rolled her eyes. "Where do you store all that optimism?" Her sister kneaded a knot from Emily's left arch, and Emily jerked the foot away, only to have it snatched back. "No, Kat, in fact, he's furious with me for trying to help. I can't believe I ever let myself hope it could all work out."

"Give him time."

"I don't have that luxury. Ricky doesn't, either." Emily felt the weight of the world on her shoulders. "After today, I just keep thinking how wrong I am to even consider adopting him. What would I do if I had to respond to an emergency?"

"Child care. A nanny. For now, I can certainly help watch him. There are a lot of single parents, Emily. It's not like when Mom was trying to raise us."

"Look at my hours," Emily argued. "It's ten o'clock,

and I'm just eating dinner. I couldn't do that to a little boy.''

Katarina's eyebrows arched in an I-told-you-so expression. "You'd get used to cutting the day shorter. You wouldn't take others' calls quite so readily. You would have time for yourself, which, quite honestly, would be good for you. And becoming a mother would be a wonderful excuse that no one would argue with.''

Emily looked at her sister longingly. She wished she had even one-fourth the enthusiasm her sister did. "Mother should have named you Pollyanna. How do you even make decisions? You can't possibly look at both sides of a problem.''

"Usually the negative is already in front of me. That leaves me to focus on the positive. Which is what I want you to do. Think of three reasons why you *should* adopt Ricky. You obviously feel something more for him than for your typical patient, or you'd already have said no.''

Emily thought of the adorable little boy. That was the easy part. But a child's adorableness was no reason to adopt. She needed a better motive.

He needed love.

He is so lovable. Yes, she could easily love Ricky. *I could love a dog, too, but I don't have one.*

"Ricky will have a lot of emotions to deal with.''

Kat tickled the bottom of Emily's toes, and Emily felt her body relax.

"Turning that one around to fulfill the requirements, Doctor, you would need to add 'And who better to help him than me?' After all, you do have the training.''

Emily frowned. "I'm not a psychiatrist.''

"Never stopped you from giving advice before. Now, think of a positive reason.''

Pulling her pampered feet from her sister's lap, Emily sat up. "Don't you have something else to do?"

Katarina rubbed her hands along her blue jeans and crossed them in front of her. "Nothing. Get busy thinking. Come on, think positive."

After trying to sort out her feelings, Emily finally came up with one she really wasn't sure should qualify. "I want a family?"

Katarina smiled. "Good."

"But I have such a demanding career, horrible hours. And what would I ever do about being on call?"

Her sister's animated groan almost made Emily laugh. "Oh, no, and I thought you were actually going to come up with one."

Katarina looked at Emily as if she were some forlorn old maid whose days were numbered. "Your career is your life because you let it be. You knew you wanted a family when you decided to become a doctor. You knew there would come a time when you would eagerly make time for a husband and children."

"Which is another point. I'm single."

Katarina sighed. "Having two parents doesn't guarantee happiness *or* a good family life. You have so much to offer a child, Emily. Besides, what happens if you never meet Mr. Right?"

How could Katarina even think such a thing? In the back of her mind, Emily thought of Kevin. She recalled the way he had looked in a suit, romping on the floor with Jacob and Laura's children.

He denied wanting children, even though he was wonderful with them and at one time wanted a houseful. She and Kevin were just now beginning to work things out, and adding a child would throw a definite wrench into the works. She hoped that one day Kevin would change his mind and realize what he was missing. *Surely he'll change his mind.*

"I could lose Kevin if I choose to adopt Ricky."

"That's not at all positive, Emily! You're thinking of this all wrong. I hate to break my own rule, but I will, for Ricky's sake." Her voice lowered. "If Kevin leaves because you have a child, it was never meant to be in the first place, and Ricky would save you another huge mistake. You wouldn't truly be happy, even with Kevin, if you sacrificed a family for marriage."

The gaze in her sister's eyes was sympathetic, silently sharing the misery of the truth.

"I think you missed your calling, Kat. I think you should be the psychiatrist."

Her sister pushed herself to her feet and shrugged. "Not me! That's way too serious. By the way, Kevin called while you were at the hospital. He asked you to return the call when you got home."

Emily tried to tame the glimmer of hope before it consumed her again. She watched her sister head toward the stairs. "Oh, Kat. Don't mention Ricky to anyone, please. I need some time to make a decision."

"As long as you need me, Em, I'm here. Remember that."

Emily smiled. She knew she could count on her sister.

"I can do all things through Christ who strengthens me." I believe You, God, but I can't do it alone. Help me make the best decision for Ricky.

She called Kevin, prepared for the worst yet hoping for the best. Emily took a deep breath. She hadn't meant to interfere with his business. She'd wanted to help. To show him that he was important to her. They had both been through so much recently, it was no wonder tempers were flaring.

Kevin answered immediately. "Emily, I'm so sorry I yelled at you. I'm not handling any of this well. It hit me so unexpectedly. I appreciate your help, and—I'll pay you back, if you want to consider it…"

She couldn't answer.

"Are you there?"

"Uh-huh. I don't consider it a loan, so we don't need to bring it up again. I gave it because I wanted to, and I would really like it if you'd simply learn to accept help graciously."

The deep timbre of Kevin's voice faded to a low whisper. "Thank you."

Emotion caught in her throat. Relief wasn't far behind. She took a drink of water and tried to compose herself.

"I didn't mean to make you cry." He paused. "You're supposed to save those for when I'm there to dry them, don't you know?"

Emily laughed at his unexpected advice. "I didn't know you were so fond of tears. Been breaking a lot of hearts, have you?"

"Only one that matters."

She couldn't speak. Her heart beat faster. The tears started again. It had been so long since she'd let herself care for anyone. Emily decided God had other plans for her life, after all. "I'd better go, Kevin. I'm sorry."

"It's okay, Emmy. I hate to admit it, but I am tired. Looks like I'm going to have some free time tomorrow, if you can get away for lunch or something."

"I have the day off. Why don't you let me fix you and your mother lunch."

"That sounds great. We'll see you then. Sweet dreams, Doc."

"You, too." Emily went to bed, hope blanketing her in warmth. Her thoughts drifted to Ricky, and she wondered how he was doing. She was ashamed to realize she hadn't called him once since Kevin's accident. She jotted a note, reminding herself to call him first thing in the morning on the pad next to her phone.

Emily pulled her Bible from the shelf and opened her study guide for the first time in a week. It seemed a lifetime ago. She read the lesson from the day of Kevin's accident, and paused. "'I will not leave you as orphans; I will come to you,'" she read in a whisper, then read it again.

Emily called Ricky first thing the next morning and visited. He sounded happy and seemed to be enjoying his "visit," as he called it. She was relieved. When his grandparents got on, she explained why she hadn't called sooner. His grandparents sent him next door then, and bragged about about how well Ricky was adjusting to his parents' death.

"We can thank Laura for that. She's had a lot of experience answering little ones' questions about death." Emily sipped her orange juice and jotted down a few more things to pick up at the grocery store.

George suggested Emily plan for Ricky to come spend a couple of weeks with her. They were enjoying their grandson, but were wearing out already. Emily looked at her calendar, and promised to come pick him up in a week and a half.

"Have you made any decision yet, Emily?"

She sighed. "No. I adore Ricky, but I'm just not sure I am the best person for the job. I look at this week and wonder how a child would have fit into that."

"I'm sure it's very difficult for you, and we don't want to pressure you. Really we don't—" George's voice broke. "If you don't think you can take him, we really need to start looking for the right family. He's been through so many changes already. I want him to get settled soon. Harriet's not doing well.''

Emily rubbed her forehead. "I understand." After asking about Harriet's health, she added, "I'll be in touch soon, George." Emily hung up and immediately thought of the verse in her study last night.

As soon as she composed herself again, Emily went to the store and picked up steak and vegetables to make fajitas. After slicing the meat, she put it in the bowl with the marinade, then cut up the peppers, onion and tomatoes and set them in the refrigerator, her mind still on the conversation with George.

She tossed a salad, annoyed by the steady drip of water from the faucet. While setting the table, Emily turned on the stereo, hoping the music would drown out the noise. The rhythms were out of synchronization, and it only made matters worse. "How long has this faucet been dripping, Kat?"

"A few days, I guess. I meant to call a plumber before my trip, but didn't get around to it."

"Probably needs a washer tightened or something. It'll take forever for a repairman to get here. That's going to drive me insane with company here." Emily went to the drawer, pulled out the pliers and tried to tighten a nut that went around the base of the faucet. The drip got worse. "Oh, come on. Don't do this now."

"I have a meeting with a Realtor. I'll see you later."

Emily offered her halfhearted best wishes to Kat on finding a studio that had room for a few employees and storage for her stock. The door closed behind her sister as Emily pried the cover off the handle and started turning the screwdriver. *Maybe if I readjust the handle, it'll make it through lunch, anyway.*

"Morning, beautiful. I saw Katarina outside, and she told me to come on in." Kevin closed the door and walked across the living room. "What are you doing?"

Emily turned, relieved to see Kevin. "Hi. Where's your mother?"

"She thought we should have some time alone after..." He stepped closer. "You're not taking that off, are you?"

"I'm just going to see if the washer needs to be replaced."

"You did shut off the main water valve, didn't..."

Emily lifted the screw out and jiggled the handle, and the water exploded like a fountain all over the kitchen. "Help!" She tried to put the handle back on, which only made matters worse.

"Move. Hold a bowl or pan over that so it will at least force it back into the sink." Kevin dropped to the ground, pushing her aside. He reached under the sink, tossing bottles of cleaner out of his way. He let out a grunt, then yelled, "Wrench!"

She grabbed the pliers and handed them to him. He popped his head out of the cabinet and gave her a look of disgust.

She shrugged her shoulders. "It's all I have."

Groaning, he banged on the handle and began twisting. "Give me some oil. Maybe that'll loosen this rust."

Emily looked at the pan, knowing that the minute she let go of it, water would spray everywhere again. At least his idea kept it somewhat contained. "It's in the cabinet across the kitchen, to the right of the stove. Can you get it? If I move, the water's going to spray everywhere again."

Emily looked at the pictures on her refrigerator that were ruined, the Victorian lace curtains that were dripping water, and the puddles inching their way toward the carpet.

He scooted across the floor and returned with the towel and oil. A few minutes later, the water finally slowed to a stop. Kevin slid out of the cabinet again and slumped against the refrigerator. "You forgot one itty-bitty detail, Doc."

"Sorry."

Kevin laughed. He looked at her and smiled. "What was that agreement we made? I won't practice medicine, you don't do any building? Let's add plumbing to that list."

Soaked, Emily knelt next to him and lifted one eyebrow. "Don't suppose I could beg for mercy and ask you for a favor?"

He pulled her into his soggy embrace. "Gee, I don't know. You haven't saved my life, or my business, or...anything." His words faded into a whisper as he gave her a kiss that made her very happy she was already sitting down.

Chapter Fifteen

The next morning, Kevin discussed the clinic plans with Alex, answering his questions about the next phase of the project. Kevin struggled over leaving his "baby" in someone else's hands, though he knew Alex was more than capable of handling everything. Throughout the first week, he made excuses to stop in daily. Kevin soon realized everything was under control and that he might as well get other work done.

Knowing the project was back on track made it easier for him to follow doctors' orders—both Emily's and Dr. Roberts's. The last thing he wanted was *more* medical attention.

With any luck at all, Monday morning the doctor would give him the all-clear to return to work next week.

Taking advantage of Alex's help, Kevin prepared bids for future projects and caught up on paperwork. After looking at the stack of potential contracts, Kevin ran a few figures through the computer, and smiled. He was beginning to see real benefits to having his brother around.

Despite his initial anger, the two were working well together, and Kevin was beginning to wonder if there was room to add *Brothers* to the name MacIntyre Construction, after all. If Alex was serious about giving up fire-fighting, he and his brother had something to discuss.

Kevin stopped by the clinic to check on the progress the crew had made under Alex's sole direction. He had to admit, the results were impressive. Still, though they were back on schedule without him and he'd been relieved to get ahead on the office work, Kevin was itching to get his hands dirty again.

Kevin walked inside, greeting the staff along the way. As he got closer to Emily's office, he overheard Bob Walker trying to sweet-talk her again.

"I had a small mix-up for this weekend, Em. I didn't realize it was my turn to be on call already, and I made other plans. Could you fill in for me?" the man begged.

Emily didn't respond. Kevin peeked around the corner, trying to decide whether to walk on in or wait in the hall. A smile remained plastered painfully to her bright face. She was going to give in, again.

Oh, no, you don't, Doc. If you're too generous to say no, then I'll take care of it for you.

Kevin stepped into the room, startling both Emily and the other doctor. "Hi, sweetheart, sorry I'm late. I just picked up our train tickets for this weekend. It's all planned. Hot springs, here we come."

"Kevin!" Her green eyes widened in amazement when he wrapped his arm around her and kissed her on the cheek, then turned to the arrogant Dr. Walker and smiled.

The man's face went blank as he stammered, "I—I didn't think you'd be busy. Sorry. You and the builder are…?"

"Very close," Kevin confirmed, hugging Emily.

"Oh, Kevin and me? Yes, we go way back." She looked up at him with "I can't believe you did this" twinkling in her eyes.

Bob backed slowly away. "I didn't realize. Well, if you'll excuse me. Ah, have a nice weekend."

"Same to you, Bob," Kevin said, loosening his hold on Emily.

She was still gazing up at him, but said to Dr. Walker, "Sorry I can't cover for you again, Bob."

"I'll figure something out." The man backed out of the office, his stare boring through Kevin as he turned around.

"I'm sure you will." How she managed to sound sweet was beyond Kevin's comprehension.

Kevin watched to make sure Bob was out of earshot, then closed the door. He studied her sanctuary lined with medical books and journals. There was nothing in here that revealed the Emily he had once loved, just the doctor she had become. Her many honors lined the walls of her study. *Summa cum laude,* Johns Hopkins School of Medicine. Fellowship, American Academy of Obstetrics... Kevin turned away from the reminders of what had come between them and what it had already cost them.

"Why didn't you just tell the jerk 'no'?"

"I was going to, before you interrupted with that *outrageous* claim of yours. And where in the world did you come up with 'sweetheart'? Good grief, Kevin. Do you realize the implications?" she asked with quiet emphasis.

His blue eyes narrowed speculatively. "I would have thought that removing yourself as my physician would already have opened up the 'implication' file."

"The only one who knows—make that *knew,* was Dr.

Roberts. But that's obviously not the case now. Everyone will know by Monday morning.''

"I'm tired of watching you work yourself into the ground. Don't you ever take time to relax?''

Emily tilted her head to the side and placed one hand on her hip. "Aren't you one to talk? If you weren't working all the time, you wouldn't know how many hours I put in, now would you?''

He didn't bother pointing out that he'd just taken time "off," since, just as soon as he was able, he'd be making her statement true again. "So we both work too much, which is all the more reason we need to get out of town.''

"I hope you enjoy yourself,'' Emily said absently as she stepped behind the desk to the chair and opened a patient file.

Kevin saw the phone book standing on her desk and looked up a number, while Emily returned to her work. He reached for the receiver and dialed a number. "Yes, I'd like to see if you can reserve two tickets for the train ride to Glenwood tonight.'' He smiled. "Great, I'll be right over to pay. My name is Kevin MacIntyre.''

Emily popped back to her feet. "You wouldn't dare.''

Kevin looked at the phone and handed it to her. "I just did. We're going to relax if it kills us. I might as well take a few days to get away while Alex is still around, right? Can you be ready at five?''

Emily thought of Ricky. He'd be arriving next weekend, and she had to get a room ready for his visit. Even though it was officially just a visit, she was thinking of it as—sort of a trial run—and she wanted everything to be just right. "I can't go.''

He leaned over and kissed her cheek, whispering in her ear, "The break will be good for both of us. We haven't had much time together. I think it's time we do, don't you?''

Emily felt her heart skip a beat. "Oh, Kevin. I don't know." She felt the blood rush to her cheeks. He sounded so—serious.

She thought of Ricky, and becoming a mother, and the fact that this might be her last chance to get away, as well. Though Katarina claimed she'd be willing to continue living with her in order to make the transition smooth, Emily was still hesitant. *If I adopt Ricky, I'm going to have to rethink everything I do.*

His gaze bore into her in silent expectation. Before she knew it, Kevin was standing next to her and lifting her chin to him. When he spoke, his voice was tender. "Come on, Emily. With our careers, you never know how long it might be before we have the chance to get away again."

Suddenly the distance between them faded, and Emily could think of only one reason to stay home—fear.

A lot had changed since they had been engaged. "Older and wiser" was more than just a quaint phrase to her—it was what had given her the courage to accept God's forgiveness and rededicate herself to Him. *You have to talk to Kevin before it's too late.*

Two hours later, Kevin drove up to the house and knocked on the door. He loaded her bag into the truck for the short drive to Union Station in Denver to catch the train.

Once the truck door closed and they pulled away from the curb, Kevin took her hand. "I want to give it another try, Emmy."

For the past two hours she'd practiced how to tell him there was someone else in her life that was now her first priority. She took a deep breath, yet her courage faltered.

Give me the words to tell him, Father. Would he understand why it had to be different between them this time?

"What makes you think anything has changed, Kevin? If anything, we're even more set in our own lives now."

"Hasn't this past month been enough to show you that we can juggle schedules with the rest of this crazy world? Before my accident, I didn't think I could let Alex help with the business, either, and that's working fine." Kevin told her in detail about the disagreement between Alex and him that had led to closing down his father's business. Until Alex had come here, the two men had simply ignored the issue, finding that the only way to get along.

"I realize now that life is too short to harbor anger and bitterness, Emily." He paused, then added with quiet emphasis, "I don't have time for it."

Hope took another step up the ladder to her dreams.

If he could allow himself to change in that respect, maybe he could eventually change his mind about a future for the two of them, and a family to fulfill all of their dreams.

"I've spent my time off in my office, preparing bids, and filling out contracts. God's been good to me. I'm going to have to hire help to keep up with everything if I want a life at all."

He went on excitedly about his hopes of asking his brother to stay on permanently, and eventually expanding to two totally separate divisions.

Emily was thrilled to see Kevin's excitement over the changes Alex's presence had made. They pulled off the interstate and turned into the Friday evening rush-hour traffic. Kevin unplugged his car phone and stashed it in the glove box. "Do you want something to eat before we get to the station?"

She shook her head. "I'm fine, but feel free to get

something if you want." The opportunity to get into a new discussion had passed, she realized.

Traffic moved like molasses on a winter day, and Kevin pulled into the first burger joint they saw. "We may as well eat something while we sit in the traffic. I know you're not fond of junk food, but they do make a great bowl of chili."

She smiled. "That sounds good. Here, let me." Emily pulled a bill from her purse.

"I thought we covered this already." He quirked his eyebrow.

"So did I," she said, gently reminding him of the conversation they had had the previous week about the joy of giving, and learning to receive graciously. "I didn't argue when you made the reservations for both of us, did I? Well, not too hard, anyway."

He placed the order and accepted the twenty. "Thank you for dinner." She didn't fail to notice the note of resignation in his voice.

"You're welcome. And thank you for making me take time to relax." Emily tried to keep her own tone playful.

Finally the traffic thinned, and they were able to find a parking spot at Union Station. After checking their luggage, they boarded the train. Emily sat next to Kevin, feeling snug and comfortable. Conversing quickly became awkward over the noise of other passengers. The rhythm of the train ride was strangely relaxing. Emily fell asleep with her head resting on Kevin's shoulder and didn't wake until they pulled into the station at Glenwood.

The shuttle driver met them inside the small station to take them to the hotel. Emily and Kevin found their bags and climbed into the van. Immediately offended by one of the young men whose breath smelled like the inside of a beer barrel, Emily leaned closer to Kevin.

Kevin wrapped his arm protectively around her shoulder. "We should be there soon."

A few minutes later the driver pulled up in front of the historic Rockfront Inn. Kevin grabbed their luggage from the back and escorted Emily to the registration desk. "Why don't you pick up a few brochures, see if you can find something fun for us to do tomorrow. I'm taking care of this," Kevin whispered.

She started to speak, then saw the look of reproach in his gaze. Reluctantly, Emily glanced at the advertisements, picked up a few that looked interesting and waited for Kevin to return.

"We're on the second floor. The pool is closed for tonight, but opens at ten in the morning." With Kevin leading, they climbed the wide stairs and turned left.

Emily paused momentarily to admire an antique chest in the hallway. Kevin set their bags in front of a door and inserted the key.

I have to say something, she thought.

"Here you go." Kevin opened the door and motioned her inside.

Her feet were like lead. She dragged herself into the room and looked around. Her stomach churned with anxiety. Though she was relieved that he'd reserved a two-room suite, she still had to make a few things clear. The door closed at the other end of the room, and Emily panicked.

"Kevin, we can't share a room," she blurted out, rushing on before she lost her courage. "There's someone more important in my life now—"

Emily spun around. The room was empty.

"Kevin?" She searched the bedroom, the bathroom, the closet. No one.

She ran to the door and opened it. Across the hall, the door opened and Kevin stepped out.

"How's your room?" He gave her an irresistibly devastating grin, and she knew she'd been set up.

"You...are so ornery!" The tension broke, and Emily began laughing.

The smile in his eyes contained a sensuous flame. He lifted her room key and quirked a brow questioningly. "May I? I'd like to explain, in private."

Emily took the key defiantly and crossed her arms in front of her. "I don't know," she teased. "I'm not very happy that you made me agonize over this for the last six hours."

"Forgive me?" His brilliant blue eyes sparked with excitement. "I wanted to see how much you trusted me."

"Now you're testing me?"

"Us." Kevin took her by the shoulders and pulled her close, his gaze as soft as a caress. "Testing us," he whispered. He paused as if asking for permission before his mouth covered hers.

A few moments lost in the velvety warmth of his kiss, and all the emotions of their past returned. The warmth of his embrace was so male, so comforting. Emily wanted the moment to last forever. Kevin leaned against the wall, holding her firmly against him as the kiss ended.

Emily opened her eyes, drinking in the sight of him. A small one-inch scar from the accident was all that was left to remind her that she'd almost lost him. Tentatively, she reached up and touched the tender skin on Kevin's chin.

Kevin jumped slightly, releasing his hold on her, both

emotionally and physically. "It's late. Why don't we talk tomorrow." His voice was low and ragged.

Emily felt her own control wavering, and appreciated Kevin's wise decision. "Call when you wake up." She kissed him again, then backed out of his embrace, turned and opened her door.

Chapter Sixteen

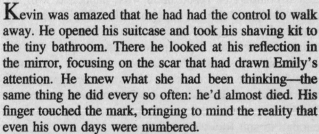

Kevin was amazed that he had had the control to walk away. He opened his suitcase and took his shaving kit to the tiny bathroom. There he looked at his reflection in the mirror, focusing on the scar that had drawn Emily's attention. He knew what she had been thinking—the same thing he did every so often: he'd almost died. His finger touched the mark, bringing to mind the reality that even his own days were numbered.

After that kiss, he had thought he was protecting her, but as he lay in bed trying to sleep, he realized it was himself that he was guarding. He was afraid of losing her. Once had been torture, but to think of going through that again was more than he could comprehend.

The next morning, Kevin awoke and showered. It was still too early to take the chance of waking her, and he made a pot of the complimentary coffee included with the room. He turned on the television and occupied the time mourning the degeneration of Saturday morning cartoons.

When he called Emily's room, there was no answer.

He left a message. A few minutes later she returned the call, saying she'd gone for her morning walk.

"Why didn't you call? I've been waiting to call because I thought it was too early. I'd have gone with you."

"I hoped you were getting some rest, I guess. I try to walk every morning. It's my chance to start the morning on the right foot." They decided to walk down the street for breakfast, then tour some of the historical sites in town. While they ate, Emily told Kevin little bits about her visit with Ricky's grandparents. She was tempted to tell him that she was named to be Ricky's guardian, but still she hesitated.

She'd convinced herself that it was her decision solely, that it couldn't be based upon what happened with her relationship with Kevin, or anyone else. While she would love to have someone else she could talk to about the situation, her sister's persuasion made it clear that the more opinions she sought, the more muddied the waters would become. She couldn't take any more pressure. It was something she had to trust God to help her answer in His own time. She only hoped that happened soon enough to suit Ricky's grandparents.

After shopping the morning away, they visited Doc Holliday's grave, had lunch, then stopped in to see the vapor caves before returning to the hotel.

Throughout the day, there had been an undercurrent of tension that became stronger as they approached the hotel. "Why don't we meet down at the pool," she suggested.

"You sure? We have a lot to talk about, Emily."

"After that kiss last night, I have a feeling it would be better if we avoid being alone. Hopefully we can find a quiet corner of the pool to have our visit."

His blue eyes brimmed with passion and understanding. Awkwardly, Kevin nodded, and they both escaped into the retreat of their own rooms.

Twenty minutes later, Kevin knocked on Emily's door, and the two of them walked to the pool together.

Keeping her voice low, she said, "I want to thank you for not presuming we'd continue from where we left off eight years ago, Kevin." She wasn't sure if that was a promising sign or not, but she knew it was right.

"I couldn't do that to you. I'm sure it was as difficult on you as it was me when we broke up last time. I want to be sure before we make that decision."

Emily took his hand and looked into his eyes. "With your charm, you make your restraint as flattering as a full seduction."

"I'm not trying to be charming, Emmy. I mean it. I care too much about you to hurt you again."

His smile showed the agony he, too, was feeling.

They reached the lobby and separated long enough to enter the pool area through the segregated locker rooms. After the required shower, they met on the other side and stepped into the two-block-long hot springs pool.

Emily had pulled her hair into a bun atop her head. She dipped into the water, clear up to her chin. It felt like a soothing massage on her tired legs.

"Now this ought to work off some of that work-related tension!" Emily looked at Kevin. "Wanna race?"

He smiled. "To that shady corner. Looks quiet there."

Emily looked to the corner he was referring to, squinting. "You've got to be kidding me! That's like a marathon."

"Are you forfeiting? Too tough for you?" The laughter in his eyes was a refreshing sight.

Emily turned and started swimming, knowing she would need every advantage available. She felt Kevin's hand around her ankle, and he tugged her backward while he took the lead.

Halfway to the goal, she reached over and reciprocated. It was obvious he wasn't half as interested in winning as having a relaxing swim. He could have beaten her with both hands tied behind his back.

Finally they both reached the end and grabbed hold of the edge. "I forgot how much more tiring it is to swim in warm water," he groaned.

"Yeah, that's my problem." Between the altitude, the heat, and her own foolishness for actually trying to win, Emily was light-headed. "I need to get out for a few minutes." She climbed out, staggered to the chairs, and collapsed into the curves of the chaise longue.

Kevin grabbed two towels from the towel stand and sat down next to her. "Next time you decide to swoon, let me know ahead of time, would you?" He laughed. "You okay?"

She rolled her eyes and tossed her head back. "I've never had this reaction to hot water before you came back into my life."

Kevin snapped the towel open and covered her. "It's still a bit chilly."

"Speak for yourself."

"I'm going to go get us something to drink. I'll be right back."

Emily watched him walk away, acutely aware of his athletic physique. His shoulders were already more tanned than her own arms, and summer hadn't even started. When he returned, she studied his face, imagining Ricky all grown up and looking just like the man in front of her.

"Do you want orange juice or grape? I had to tell them you nearly fainted to get them to let me bring the bottles out here, so you'd better make a good show of drinking one of them.''

She chose the orange juice. Kevin sat down and guzzled his grape juice in silence.

"What are you thinking about?" she asked.

"I'm not the same man you walked away from eight years ago—and much as I hate to say it, I'm probably not the man you need now.''

If she didn't know him so well, she would have found him almost convincing.

"I have a business that takes a lot of time, and that isn't bound to improve if I expand the company.''

"I don't believe that, or we wouldn't be here now. I don't think you do, either." Emily dragged in a deep breath of the thin mountain air.

She shaded her eyes from the late-day sunshine. "I'm not the same woman you loved, either, Kevin. There's someone else in my life whose love is more important to me than anything. It was His love that carried me through the years without you.''

Kevin sat up, straddling the chaise longue. He looked at her, pain filling his gaze. "That's just it, Emily. You had that one love, and I spent eight years running from Him. Until I saw how Laura's love changed Bryan, my conquests were about as far from what God wanted of me as they could have been.''

Emily reached over and placed her cool hand against his cheek. "We all have things in our past we want to forget, Kevin. I'm not condemning you. I just want you to know that my relationship with God is even more important to me now than it was before. I loved you, and it was beautiful. But it was nothing compared to what it could be once God is part of both of us.''

"He is, Emily. But it still isn't easy to change everything all at once.'' Kevin heard voices behind them and turned to see a family set down their towels. The kids ran and jumped into the water. ''We're here, together. What more do you want?''

Emily couldn't believe what she was hearing. It was like riding a roller coaster. ''Why did you ever make your way back into my life? You could have used *any* project to launch your commercial career, so don't give me that line again.''

He closed his eyes and shook his head. Maybe she was right. Maybe deep inside, he had once hoped they could try again. Unfortunately, he had enough honor left in him to know that he couldn't take a chance on hurting her. There were plenty of ways he could have handled things when his life fell apart, but he'd run away from God and even shunned his own morals. Admitting as much to the only woman he'd truly loved would only hurt her more. He couldn't lie to Emily, and he couldn't tell her the truth. He had to walk away now, before it was too late.

Kevin stood up and gathered his towel.

''Don't even think of leaving here without giving me an answer, Kevin James MacIntyre.'' She felt her voice crack, felt herself losing control. She couldn't do this. She couldn't let him walk away again. Something had hurt him. She had to know what had changed the man she loved. The only man she would ever love.

''I didn't come to Springville for you, Emily!'' He raked his hands through his hair and took hold from the roots. ''Or to prove anything to you. And especially not to hurt you. Yet that's all I've done. You deserve better.'' He hesitated before meeting her gaze.

''What's that supposed to mean?'' Emily rose from the chair and stepped closer, lowering her voice. ''You brought me here, Kevin.'' She wondered if he understood the reference to the resort where he had planned to surprise her on their honeymoon. "Why?"

"For some R and R. I'm tired of that jerk taking advantage of your generosity!"

"You could have done that *any* place. It didn't have to be here."

A faintly uncomfortable look of understanding flashed in his eyes. "I didn't realize you knew," he quietly admitted.

"The hotel called the day after our—when we never showed up. You weren't at home, so they tracked me down, somehow."

Kevin dropped into the cushioned sofa. "It was a lousy idea, coming here. You have dreams I can't share anymore."

Dare she hope he would change his mind? Could she convince him that there was hope for a future together? It felt so right telling Dr. Casanova that she and Kevin had plans. It felt right accepting his invitation. It felt right being here with him.

Despite her inner turmoil, she had known all along that she still loved Kevin. But was their love strong enough to heal the pain that had cost him his dreams?

"I had hopes that your bringing me here was a positive sign." She moved next to him and brushed his smooth cheek. Kevin pushed her hand away.

"I'm not going to have this discussion out here."

"Fine, Kevin. Go on up. I'll call when I'm dressed."

Kevin went on ahead, and Emily waited. She took her time, wanting some space to think without the temptation of Kevin's nearness.

Emily showered, anxious to rinse the drying minerals off her skin and out of her hair. When she was dressed, she went to Kevin's room, surprised to see that it was tiny, with only a bed and chair.

"Do you mind if we go downstairs for dinner first?"

"Yes, Kevin, I do mind." Emily turned, opened her door again, and walked in and sat down on the sofa, struggling with the sudden uncertainty that had been wakened between them.

She recalled his proclamation of love while he'd been taking the strong painkillers, and longed to hear those words again, ungarbled and clear-minded this time.

Emily placed her arm on the back of the sofa.

Kevin squirmed away, forcing a smile. "Don't do this, Emmy. I...want you in my life. I don't want to, but I do."

"I know. I feel the same way." She moved away. The harder she tried to deny the truth, the more it persisted. She couldn't hold her feelings inside any longer. "I love you, Kevin."

Their eyes met, and Kevin's smile disappeared. "This was a mistake." He jumped up, his long gait carrying him quickly to the door. "Do us both a favor. Lock the door behind me."

Emily hugged her legs to her chest and rested her head on her knees. *God, I can't do this alone. I can't stop loving him. I can't change him, but I can't let him give up, either.* She let the silent tears fall, and listened to the door bang on the other side of the hall.

Several minutes later, she stood and crossed the empty hotel room, locking the door on her way to the kitchenette. As she opened the tiny refrigerator, she heard a quiet knock on the door. Emily set the apple on the counter and tentatively walked to the entrance to put her eye to the peephole.

It was black. Someone was holding a hand over the glass.

She paused. "Take your hand off the peephole." She waited a second, then looked again. It was Kevin, his head drooping as if he'd lost his best friend.

"I have one more thing to say, Emily. Please give me just a minute."

She opened the door, praying that it would be the last barrier between them.

He stood, hands braced against the doorjambs. "I can't predict the outcome, Emily. I've spent eight years learning to block out all the emotions you've brought back to life in a matter of weeks."

"I hope you don't expect me to apologize for that."

He wrapped her in his arms and held her. "Part of me wants to thank you, and the other is just too plain scared to do anything. It's not fair to move on to the next level until we've made that promise. I won't put us through that again. You have my word."

Emily's body relaxed against him. "Whether you like it or not, Kevin, you are my dream come true."

"I'm not worthy of your love, but I'm selfish enough to take it." Wrapping one arm tightly around her, he gave her a kiss that she wouldn't soon forget. Then he turned, walked across the hall to his own room and locked his door.

Two hours later, there was a knock on the door, followed by "Room service."

Suspicious, Emily looked out the peephole again. On the table was a bouquet of wildflowers and two dinner trays.

"I'm afraid you have the wrong room."

"Is this Dr. Emily Berthoff's suite?"

She placed a hand on her hip. "Yes, but I didn't order anything. Possibly it belongs across the hall."

Kevin's voice interrupted. "I'll take care of this."

She opened the door a crack, and saw Kevin tip the man. Kevin placed his hands on the table and looked up at her. "Would you like some dinner?"

She opened the door. "You told me to lock the door. I trusted you meant it."

He looked like a broken man. "You bring out the best and the worst in me, Emily."

She smiled. "Not much has changed, after all, then, has it?"

"I don't know if you're willing to take another chance…"

For a long moment she stared back at him, waiting for him to finish the suggestion. He didn't. "I am."

Kevin stepped around the table, then brought two chairs over; he held one out for her to be seated.

She looked at the elegant table, then at their jeans and sweatshirts. "I feel underdressed."

A mischievous grin was the immediate response. "Don't go there, Emmy. The dining room downstairs is formal. That's why I ordered it for the room."

She smiled back. "And the flowers…I don't think those come complimentary with a meal, do they?" As she spoke, she leaned forward to smell them. "They're gorgeous."

"They pale in comparison to you."

Emily sipped her water. "Kevin…"

"I wanted this trip to be special, Emily. And I guess deep inside, I did choose it because it seemed like an appropriate place to pick up from where we left off, so to speak." He hesitated. "Not completely, mind you."

Her heart raced. "Right, we've talked about that." Emily felt the color rise to her cheeks.

"Emily." Kevin took her hand, and paused.

The suspense was making her dizzy all over again. Tears welled in the corners of her eyes.

Kevin jumped to his feet, ran to the bathroom and returned with a handful of tissues to dry her tears. Kneeling beside her chair, he dabbed at her cheeks. "Emmy, I haven't even said anything yet."

She blinked. "Then say something!"

He smiled. "After all these years, you're still the one I want to share my life with. You're the only one I'll ever want."

She watched the play of emotions on his face and felt his hand gently brush her tears away again.

"Will you marry me?"

Emily gasped. "Yes, yes, yes." She wrapped her arms around him, her hands shaking, her breathing much too quick. "Ooh," she squealed. In one forward motion, she was in his arms, and the two crashed to the floor. She drank in the sweetness of his kiss.

Suddenly Kevin pulled away. "Dinner's getting cold," he said as he unwrapped her arms from his neck. "We'd better back off while we can."

She smiled, understanding too well the dangerous emotions sparking between them. They sat back in their chairs, and Kevin took her hand and bowed his head.

The full impact of his proposal hit when she opened her tray and found an engagement ring.

But her vision was filled with a mental image of sweet Ricky. She looked again at the ring, then up at Kevin. Though she thought of Ricky, something cautioned her not to ask.

"Emily? What's wrong?"

His ability to understand her silent messages unnerved her. She chose her words carefully. "Kevin, I want nothing more than to spend the rest of my life with you."

"But...?"

Tears blurred her vision. "I can't be content with half a dream. I want it all—marriage, children and my career."

He sighed heavily, and a new anguish seared her heart. He asked, "Can't we knock down one wall at a time?"

Chapter Seventeen

Emily had put on a brave face with Kevin, determined to give him time to think about what she'd told him. Though she hadn't made a final decision about adopting Ricky, she knew Katarina was right: Emily could never settle for less.

Kevin was given permission by his doctor to resume working. As indecisive as a child in a candy store, he didn't know what he wanted to do first. Emily traded her on-call schedule with Dr. Roberts, which would give her two weeks off while Ricky was visiting.

Between their two schedules, the only meal they managed together was Friday. Emily picked up burgers for herself, Kevin and Alex, and came along when they drove to Denver to trade a door of the wrong size that had been mistakenly delivered. When they returned, Kevin and Alex were determined to install it before forecasted thunderstorms made another mess of a deadline.

The next morning, Emily and Katarina went to Wyoming to bring Ricky for his visit. Emily was astonished by the joy that consumed her when she wrapped her arms around him and felt the strength of his embrace.

They spent the afternoon with his grandparents, then stuffed as many of Ricky's belongings in the trunk as would fit.

It was late when they pulled into Emily's driveway and unloaded. Ricky had taken a nap as they drove and wasn't ready for bed until after ten. He ran into "his" room, and up and down the stairs, despite reminders not to run in the house.

When she and Kevin finally had a chance to talk in private, it was nearly midnight. Kevin suggested they take Ricky for lunch at the local pizza parlor the next day after they went to church.

Emily tried to hide her surprise, and agreed immediately, trying to leave His work in His hands. She woke several times in the night, sure she'd heard Ricky, only to find the little boy sound asleep.

The sermon that day was based upon a verse from the New Testament in which Paul prayed for sinners to turn away from darkness in order to receive the freedom of forgiveness and enable them to see the riches God promises for their future.

As they were leaving the sanctuary, Ricky ran to greet his friends, and Emily and Kevin made their way to the doorway where Pastor Mike was waiting. Emily reached out her hand to shake his, and was surprised when Kevin lifted her left hand to show Mike the engagement ring. Still unsure whether Kevin had made a decision about having a family, she had been hesitant to make any announcements.

Kevin's voice was deep and matter-of-fact. "We need to set up a time to visit, Mike."

Mike smiled, a knowing look of confidence on his

face. "Call me this afternoon, and we'll set up an appointment." He looked at Emily and winked. "I see Ricky's here."

She hoped Kevin missed the question in Mike's remark.

"He's here for a visit. His grandparents need a break."

The pastor's smile gave her courage to hope. "I see."

When Laura and Bryan rushed up to her, she realized everyone already knew about her tentative engagement.

After Sunday school, Kevin took them home to change; then they went for lunch. Ricky was a chatterbox. It took nearly an hour for them to get him to eat. Before leaving, they let Ricky play games and ride the kiddie rides until well past his quiet time.

Once they were home again, Emily read a story to Ricky and left him to rest. "Katarina will be here with you. Kevin and I need to run some errands."

"Okay. Bye." The look of trust in his eyes was something Emily would never take for granted. His blond hair was the same color as Kevin's, and she could almost imagine he was their natural son.

Emily descended the stairs, mentally preparing herself for a difficult conversation. Katarina and Kevin were joking around together, and Emily had to interrupt. "Kat, could you keep an eye on Ricky? We need to get out for a while."

Kevin's smile softened her nervousness momentarily. As soon as they were alone in his truck, however, it started again.

"This is a pleasant surprise. I thought you'd want to stay home with Ricky this afternoon." He paused, then leaned back and started the engine. "Where are we going?"

"I don't care." She smiled, though panic was building inside her. "We need to talk."

"About what now?" He turned off Main Street, across town, and headed up the hill to his house. The clouds rolled in, making the skies dark and dreary.

"Your telling Pastor Mike that we need to set up an appointment, for one thing."

Kevin ran his hand over his chin. "Isn't that the usual step after getting engaged?"

The pickup lumbered up the curb and to a stop in his driveway as drizzle clouded the windows. Kevin shifted into Park and looked at her impatiently. He motioned toward the house. "Do you want to go inside?"

The more distance there was between them, the easier it would be to ask all the questions she'd avoided asking, and the ones he'd carefully avoided bringing to her attention, as well. She shook her head. "This is fine."

"I need to know everything, Kevin. Why you wouldn't come to Maryland with me, why you never married, why you don't want children. Why you haven't told me once that you love me."

"What brought this on?" he mumbled.

"We broke through to the next level of commitment last weekend, but there's one issue you seem to have forgotten. I want a family, and love, and you. I've waited a long, long time, Kevin. I need to know exactly what it is that's standing in our way."

Kevin was a complex, sensitive man, and she could feel the pain his recollection of the past eight years revealed. Holding nothing back, he shared the roller coaster of family joys and sorrows all over again—his father's death, his sister having and losing her child, having to close the doors of his father's business. She respected him all the more for his honesty.

Emily was filled with guilt. All these years, she'd thought Kevin had selfishly walked away. She'd thought he'd abandoned her. She couldn't have been more wrong. Yet still, she felt betrayed. He hadn't trusted her, hadn't let her share his pain. And that confirmed he hadn't been ready for sharing good times and bad.

"You didn't even tell me your dad was sick before the engagement, Kevin!"

He looked at her, tears hiding in the corners of his eyes. "Mom and Dad asked me to wait until after we returned from our honeymoon. They didn't want anything to ruin the wedding for us."

Emily swallowed, grimacing as tears fell. "I wouldn't have left you to handle that alone."

"Why do you think I didn't tell you? I couldn't promise you a degree. I couldn't give you what Johns Hopkins could. I couldn't take your dreams away. And even now, after seeing what losing baby Lexie did to Kirk and Elizabeth, I just don't know if I can take the chance of losing a child." He reached out and took hold of her hand, pulling her across the seat.

She let out a deep sob and raised her fists, pounding softly against Kevin's solid chest as he pulled her into his embrace. "How dare you, Kevin?" She wept, not only for her own loss, but for what it had cost Kevin, as well. "How dare you?"

"Yeah, yeah." Kevin tenderly brushed the hair from her face. "I'm sorry, Em. I didn't want to take all your dreams away."

"You did cost me my dreams, you fool! All these years, we could have been together. We could have been sharing the good *and* bad, Kevin. Isn't that what you told me? Marriage is a fifty-fifty agreement?" Emily wondered if there was any hope for them to live happily ever after. If anything, they were even more independent than they had been then. "I still want those dreams, Kevin," she whispered.

Her face was tucked against Kevin's neck, and she felt him swallow. A deep sigh was followed by a ragged heave. "I wish I could give them back, Emmy. Truly I do. I thought maybe being together would be enough."

"You can, Kevin. You changed your mind about marriage...."

Emily felt him shake his head. "I don't think so."

She pulled away and looked him in the eye. "Why?"

"I thought it would be enough to have each other. I hoped I could at least be the man of your dreams in one respect. But a child is so helpless.... You deserve better."

She laughed bitterly, searching frantically for a tissue to dry her tears. "How could I ask for better than a man who selflessly put my dreams ahead of his own? Who respected his parents' needs over his own desires? Who will take time for a hurting little boy! Who is so afraid of hurting me again that he's choosing *not* to love?" Tears blinded her and choked her voice. "Tell me you don't love me anymore, Kevin."

He backed away. Emily turned his jaw, forcing him to look at her. Silently she pleaded with him. As each moment of silence passed, her hope faded a little more.

"Say it—'I don't love you, Emily... I can't ever love you, Emily.' *Say it.* Once and for all, set me free, if that's what you want!"

"You're a doctor," he whispered. "Surely you know how to fix a broken heart."

Emily was filled with inadequacy. There was a long, brittle silence between them. "God gave me a lot of knowledge, Kevin, but this wasn't in any textbook I ever read." She hugged him close. "I can give you my love.

I can tell you that whatever it is you think I can't deal with, *we* can. I can tell you that if you want it badly enough, God is waiting to take your pain away."

Kevin's eyes misted, like the drizzling rain outside. Emily knew she had reached the true crux of his battle. *Please, God, give me the words to comfort him. I need him. Ricky needs him. And he needs You so badly.*

"It's just not that easy, Emmy."

Emily reached her arm behind him, the confines of the truck making it awkward to hold him. "Let's go outside."

They walked to the ivy-covered gazebo in the backyard and sat down on the porch swing. Emily watched the rain fall as she coaxed Kevin to dig deeper. Finally, he admitted that he had lashed out in anger at God for allowing the doctors to give his father false hope, and for taking a tiny baby away, tearing apart his sister's marriage. "I turned to the only comfort I could without risking losing my heart again. So you see, Em, even though I'd like to be the man you fell in love with, I can't go back."

Emily had to admit to feeling a twinge of jealousy after Kevin's admission, yet quickly forced the negative emotion away. He wasn't giving himself credit for turning away from the temptations that had led him so far from Christ.

"Look at those leaves, Kevin. Every day wind and dirt gather on them, just like humans who can't stop sinning. Yet just as easily as that rain washes the dirt away, Christ died on the cross to free us from sin. You're no different from anyone else, in that respect. It's human nature."

"There are always going to be reminders, Emily."

"Only if you let there be. If God doesn't keep tally of our sins, who are *we* to keep a list? If you've handed them to God, they're gone. I don't care what happened before we met again—just so's it's only me now.''

''I couldn't bear to hurt you again, Emily.''

''I can't bear another day without you in it. You were my first and only love, Kevin. I want to marry you, to have your children, to be there on good days and bad ones.''

''Which is exactly why you deserve better than what I can give you now. Our careers barely leave time for ourselves. We've already seen that. How can we fit each other, let alone a family, into this craziness?'' Kevin stood, pushing the swing into frantic motion.

Emily stopped the swing and followed him to the arched opening in the gazebo, where she smelled the sweet hint of lilacs already in bloom. She took hold of his arm and leaned her head on his shoulder. It was time to tell him about Ricky. About her decision to become the little boy's mother.

She couldn't allow Kevin to commit to her without understanding that she absolutely refused to give up her complete set of dreams. If he wanted her, he had to accept her—and Ricky. She felt the tears sting her eyes. It wasn't the way she had expected to become a mother, but He had given her a child nonetheless, and she wouldn't walk away from Ricky any more than she would walk away from Kevin.

Kevin turned to face Emily and buried his face in her hair. His hands moved gently to embrace her.

She had to tell him, before…

Her misgivings increased by the second. What if he said no? Could she survive his walking away again? ''Kevin—''

''You're right, Emmy. I've never stopped loving you. I always will.'' His words were a bridge that she hoped would continue to build as he allowed God to heal his pain.

She looked into his eyes and drowned in the truth. He loved her. Always had. Always would? She blinked, feeling light-headed.

Emily forced her gaze to lock with his. "Wait. Please. Don't say anything more."

Kevin laughed. "Now that's just like a woman to change her mind. I thought this is what you wanted. You and me forever, just the way it should have been eight years ago."

Emily tore herself from his embrace. "Listen to me. I'm going to be a mother."

A sudden icy contempt flashed in his eyes.

"A what?"

"I'm going to have a child. A son, actually."

"All this talk of a future, of love, of acceptance, and lies and repentance, and you somehow managed to forget to mention you're pregnant?"

She reached for him, and he backed away. "It's not what you think."

Emily was going to be a mother?

Kevin felt his chest tighten. *A baby.* He dragged in a deep breath, choking on the heavy scent of spring. Flowers and rain, and love. He looked for an escape from this cage.

"How—" His voice caught. He didn't really want to know any more. Didn't want to have to walk away. Didn't want to see the pain in Emily's green eyes when he broke her heart again. His voice caught, as he tried to recall the information she'd told him. His eyes roamed over her slender figure.

She placed a hand on her stomach and shook her head. "It's Ricky."

"Whoa, Em. You said his parents died—" he paused to think "—and that he was only visiting."

Emily nodded, her red hair bouncing with the slight movement. "His grandparents can't care for him full-time. They didn't want him in limbo any longer. I tried to put it off, but inside I knew they were right. It was time to decide—either I adopt him, or find him another family who could give him a permanent home." She paused. "When I got there to pick him up, I knew."

"And why didn't you tell me sooner?"

"Because my love for Ricky will matter in his life. It isn't something I can turn away from any more than if I'd carried him in my own womb. I can't explain it, Kevin. I just know that God brought Ricky to me for a reason." She spoke with bitterness. "I guess I kept hoping you would tell me you were ready to make all of *our* dreams come true. You, me, happily ever after, kids, dogs—all of those things that turn a house into a home. I want it all, Kevin. For once in my life, I thought there was a chance to—" Emily's voice broke, and he felt a knot in his own throat, as well. "If you remember, you were the one who wanted a house full of children."

He couldn't look at her. "I was young and idealistic."

There was a long painful silence, and Emily turned, tipping her head up as if to question God Himself. "I guess we both were, then, because I believed in those dreams. And I'm tired of waiting for someone else to make them come true." Her voice was edged with confidence and determination. "I guess the only other question I have for you is, Will the man of my dreams be able to make the rest of my dreams come true?"

Chapter Eighteen

Kevin struggled to understand how Emily could have made such a decision alone. Yes, he wanted them to be together—but kids? They'd overcome one hurdle; surely they would eventually have come to some sort of agreement about children, too.

He rubbed his temples. *What a lousy day!* He didn't want to accept that the doctors were right about having to take it slow in returning to work. Kevin dropped onto the sofa and spread the full length, propping his head on that all-too-familiar pillow.

Alex came into the room. "You feeling okay?"

"Growing up is the pits, Alex. I thought I could stay twenty-two forever, just live it over and over. You know?"

His brother sat down in the recliner. "I'm sorry, Kev. I thought we did the right thing at the time. Maybe not."

"I'm not talking about Dad's business, Alex. I'm happier running my own company than I ever was having to worry about whether Dad would have done it the same way, or whether a job would bring in enough to pay the employees and leave enough money for Mom, too. I should've told you that long ago. It hurt at the time, but we did the right thing.''

"If that's not it, what is it?''

Kevin chuckled. "Life, love, the pursuit of those pesky dreams.''

"I saw Emily walking off. She okay?'' He paused. "Doesn't she realize it's raining?''

"She insisted on walking home.'' Kevin leaned his head back, wishing this headache would subside. "She just became a mother.''

"She what?''

"She's going to adopt Ricky—the little boy whose parents died. They named her as guardian, and she just decided today to adopt him.''

Alex let out a whistle. "That woman has spunk.''

Kevin couldn't argue with that. In her quiet conservative way, she had overcome a lifetime of obstacles. He, on the other hand, had life pretty easy in comparison, had taken it for granted, and was doing a lousy job rebuilding it after the few catastrophes he'd experienced.

"You know, Kevin, I think you need to get away and spend some time talking to God. Get your priorities straight before you lose Emily again.''

"That's like the pot calling the kettle black. You never married. Why?''

"Never found a lady who could commit to a man who jumped into forest fires for a living.''

Kevin nodded. "Then why do you keep doing it?''

"Hey there, bro, this is your analysis, not mine.''

"Not yet, anyway.'' Kevin closed his eyes, hoping his brother would take the hint and leave him alone.

"Why are you afraid to be a father, Kevin?''

Alex never was one to take a hint.

Kevin took a deep breath and exhaled. "After seeing all of us suffer after Dad died, then Elizabeth and Kirk's marriage fall apart when baby Lexie died, it seemed a whole lot easier to avoid the issue all the way around."

Kevin heard a soft agreement from across the room and looked up at his brother.

Nodding, Alex added, "Same reason I spent eight years jumping into fires. We're all going to die, and I suspect it isn't nearly as frightening to go as it is to be left behind. But, Kevin, losing Emily a second time would be twice as rough as it was the first time. You know that, don't you?"

He nodded, remembering the day he and Ricky had built the playhouse, and the evening they'd watched the Beaumont kids, and all those months Jacob and Bryan had lived with him. He loved kids, he couldn't deny it. But becoming a father was such a huge commitment. And his business alone was enough to keep him busy at this point in time. How would he ever make time for being a husband *and* father?

"And what's standing in your way?"

Kevin thought. Was it really his past that he couldn't deal with, or was that merely an excuse? Was it Emily's dreams, or Ricky? "You know, when I was twenty, being a dad and a husband and keeping a job didn't seem like it would be any problem. But now...I can't even handle my job."

"You can't beat yourself up over that. You need some time, then you'll be right back on top of things."

That wasn't what he'd meant. Since his accident, he had felt unsettled. Edgy. Out of control. Everything he'd worked for was in jeopardy. He couldn't even accept Emily's love and forgiveness. He'd been offered a priceless gift; unworthy as he was, Emily had offered it to him. Her love. Acceptance. Support.

"You know, Kevin, a friend out in the field told me one day that it wasn't as important to know who you are, as *whose* you are. Once you have that straight, all the rest falls into place."

"I can tell you from experience, that's a whole lot easier than it sounds."

"We're all lost sheep, Kevin. Not one of us is worthy of His grace." Alex shook his head and took a drink of his soda. "I know what you've been going through these last few years. I've had my share of arguments with God, too. But here's a reason you didn't die. Take some time off. Get some rest. Open your eyes, before it's too late."

Alex went upstairs to the den. Kevin heard his brother thumbing through papers on his desk.

A week later, Kevin called Alex at the clinic and told him he was taking a few days off. "You're right, I'm no good to anyone like this."

"It's not all that bad, bro. Looking at what-all you've accomplished with your business in a mere six years, it's obvious you haven't had a life outside the company. You need someone to share your load here, permanently. We would make a great team," Alex said.

Kevin shook his head. "I know we would. I've been meaning to discuss that with you. First things first, and sorry, but my business isn't it. I need you to hold things together."

"Not a problem. I'm here for you." They reviewed the building schedule. Alex had come in and taken over the supervisory position on the site with poise, gaining the respect of the entire crew by asking what he didn't already know about the job. For the first time in six years,

Kevin felt at ease taking a week off. "Alex, I am thinking seriously about your suggestion. I can't thank you enough for helping me out. By the way, the crew's paychecks are on my desk in the den. Yours is there, too."

"Thanks. You take whatever time you need. We're going to finish this project on time."

Kevin left him the phone number at Laura and Bryan's cabin. The couple had decided to add on to the bungalow to accommodate their growing family. He couldn't blame them. It was a great place to get away from the pressures of the city.

He hoped that a few days up there would put his problems back in perspective. He'd do a little work, fish for a while, have a talk or two with God; get his priorities straight.

Just what the doctor ordered. He laughed at his own bad joke. It had been a week since Emily had dropped the latest bomb on his life.

Kids. She wanted not only one, but several. She didn't just want love, she wanted the complete dream, as she'd reminded him in a phone conversation the previous day. She wanted him despite his past. Wanted to share his life, his burdens, his business, fifty-fifty. Kids, dogs and all the upgrades, as she put it.

He pulled into the dirt driveway and opened the gate, then closed it behind him before continuing to the back side of the cabin. He unloaded his duffel bag, the fishing pole, then the groceries: a sack of man-size frozen dinners, a few assorted snacks, plus two gallons of milk. He filled the refrigerator and plugged it in.

The June sun was high in the sky, warming the cabin through the big plate-glass window. Despite its warmth, Kevin brought in an armful of kindling, dropped it in the copper boiler and went back outside. He dug through the shed out back 'til he found the sledgehammer and splitting wedge. He and Bryan usually tried to save the split wood in the wood box for the dead of winter when it was too cold and blustery. Which left out today. Spring had made an early arrival in the Rockies.

What little snow had fallen the past winter had melted, and the ice was gone from the river below. He tossed a few logs away from the sod-covered garage. He propped a log on the old tree stump, tapped the wedge into the wood and swung the sledge. The broken pieces fell to the ground.

It felt good to exert some energy. The ache in his muscles sure beat the ache in his heart. He repeated the motions several times, then carried the wood inside and built a fire as the sun set.

Kevin had spent the past week thinking about little besides Emily and Ricky. He popped a frozen dinner into the microwave and moved the chair so he could watch the sunset. He went to bed early, thankful for the full bin of firewood that had exhausted him so he could sleep.

First thing the next morning, Kevin strung his fly pole and headed to the river. A couple of hours later, he headed back, his stringer loaded with half a dozen twelve-inch rainbow trout. He cleaned the fish, then planned to get busy drafting the layout of the cabin so he could give Laura and Bryan his suggestions for remodeling.

He and Bryan had agreed that a new fence around the cabin, in order to keep the kids away from the river, was the first project they would tackle. The next question was whether they wanted to add on a traditional frame structure, or hire a log-home contractor to try to match the original cabin. Kevin had agreed to start with his suggestions, then let them consider the other as an option.

He walked through the gap in the pole-fence and onto the Beaumont property, just in time to hear car doors slam at the front of the cabin. Female voices carried through the trees.

"Who in the world could be here?"

Kevin climbed the steps to the veranda and propped his pole against the corner joint of the logs, then walked in the back door of the cabin.

Ricky's bright blue eyes greeted him. "Kevin!"

Emily followed, her arms overloaded with luggage. "Kevin?"

Next were Emily's sisters and her mother.

Kevin staggered back, feeling as if he'd just been ambushed. "Hi. I didn't realize you were coming."

Emily looked at him, and the room grew silent except for the sound of Ricky's feet running on the bare oak floors.

"Let me get some of that for you." He reached for the luggage, and accidentally slung the stringer of trout at one of the bags. "Oh, sorry."

Lisa and Katarina jumped back, screeching. Ricky ran back down from the bedroom to see what had happened. Kevin took the fish to the kitchen sink and rinsed his hands, then returned.

"Are you going to take me fishing, Kevin?"

Kevin looked at Ricky, then Emily, waiting for her to answer. When she didn't, he said, "I don't know, sport. I didn't know anyone was coming up here this week, so I should probably get out of your hair."

Ricky scratched his head. "He's not in our hair, is he, Emily?"

"I'm sure Kevin doesn't want to stay here with a cabin full of women," Emily's mother snipped.

Emily grinned, pursing her lips to keep from laughing

aloud at the irony of her mother's remark. She could think of no more comfortable place for Kevin than a room full of women, unless one of those women was her mother. She looked to Kevin for understanding, sending a silent apology.

"Someone forgot to mention you were scheduled to use the cabin for this week. I came up to see what they're going to need to do to make room for the whole family. I'll have my things packed up in just a few minutes." Kevin turned toward the kitchen.

Katarina looped her hand through Kevin's, stopping him. She addressed her sister. "What a perfect time to celebrate the engagement, isn't it, Lisa? You have to stay, Kevin."

The youngest of the sisters gazed at her mother, then at Emily. "Of course it is. Congratulations, Kevin. Ricky, why don't we go outside and get your things from the van."

It was Kevin's turn to look to Emily for an explanation.

Emily's mother, Naomi, turned her back. "I won't believe it until I see it. He left you once, Emily. There's nothing to stop him from doing it again."

"Mother, I love Kevin more than ever. I'm not asking for your approval. If you want to let your bitterness ruin your life, that's up to you. I'd rather forgive than live in the chains of unhappiness."

"You can't be serious, Emily. You're telling me that you've forgiven even your father? How can you forgive a father abandoning his wife and children?"

Emily swallowed hard. "Oh, Mom." Emily wrapped her arms around her mother. "I don't ever deny the pain. I just don't let it control me any longer. I've handed it to God." Her mother started to complain about her husband again, and Emily interrupted. "I don't want or need to hear it anymore. I've put that behind me. There's no reason to rehash something I have no control over."

Naomi looked at Kevin, then back to Emily. "Don't expect me to help with another wedding."

"I didn't plan on it, but if you'd like to come, you'd be welcome." Naomi stomped out the door, and Emily's shoulders drooped.

Kevin wrapped his arms around her and kissed her forehead. "I don't want to ruin your mother's visit, Emily."

"If you want to stay, stay, Kevin. Your leaving won't improve her attitude."

"What do you want?" He took her left hand in his, touching the ring he'd given her. Dare he believe there was a chance it would remain on her finger forever this time?

"I want you here. You know that. Question is, do you want to stay?"

Chapter Nineteen

Emily was grateful that Kevin agreed to stay. Her sisters offered their continued support for her and Kevin, each taking a turn talking to Naomi. Emily doubted there was any hope of her mother changing her attitude after all these years. Though Emily longed for her mother to be happy for her just once in her life, she no longer depended upon it.

She and Ricky "helped" Kevin take measurements of the cabin for Kevin's drafting, while Katarina and Lisa took Naomi to Estes Park to shop. When they were finished, Kevin fixed a pitcher of lemonade and poured three glasses. He and Emily sat on the veranda, while Ricky gathered pinecones.

"I'm sorry I put you on the spot this morning, Kevin."

He took a long drink, then rested the glass on his knee. "I noticed a load of bricks falling, but for the life of me, I couldn't figure a way to dodge it." He turned to her and his whole face spread into a smile.

She took his hand, grateful he could laugh about it already.

Kevin tipped the chair back and stretched. "I must admit, under the circumstances I'm surprised you're still wearing the ring. I half expected it to come off immediately when I couldn't commit, and definitely thought you'd take it off when your mother arrived."

Guessing that meant he hadn't come to any decision yet, Emily said simply, "It gives me hope."

Kevin leaned over the side of the chair and pressed his lips against hers, and Emily fought the temptation to assume everything was going to turn out the way she wanted it to. She was too old to presume that. Despite her fears, though, she wouldn't give up hope. *God is still in the miracle business.*

"Mommy? I mean Emily..." The soft words were accompanied by a gentle tap on her knee.

Emily jumped and looked around. She looked back to Kevin, tears instantly forming. "Yes, Ricky?" Even though it was a mistake, it tugged on her emotions and gave her hope that one day he would accept her as his mother.

She rested her hand on his shoulder. "What, Ricky?"

"Can we go see the water?"

"Sure. We can take a walk to the river. Ask Kevin if he wants to come with us. Maybe he'd even show us how he caught all those trout for supper." She smiled at Kevin, daring him to turn the charming little boy down.

Kevin waited casually, pretending he hadn't heard a word Emily had said. *Please, help Kevin to see how much he would love being a daddy, God. And help me to give him the time he needs to decide.* She looked up, thrilled to see Kevin put Ricky on his shoulders and grab the fishing pole.

They spent the afternoon fishing and hiking along the banks, gathering sticks and pinecones. The flowers were just beginning to bloom, and Ricky wanted to pick all of them.

"If you leave them for a few more days, they'll be much prettier," Emily suggested. "Then we can pick two or three, but not all of them." He scrunched up his face at the advice, but settled instead for making a pouch from his T-shirt to hold the collectibles he found along the path. When they returned to the cabin, Emily helped him make a centerpiece from the twigs and clusters of cones and various other "treasures."

While Kevin prepared the fish, Emily put a bowl of broccoli in the microwave and buttered a loaf of French bread. Her mother and sisters returned while dinner was cooking. After they all ate, Emily bathed Ricky and put him to bed upstairs on a folding cot.

Kevin was increasingly disappointed that he hadn't spent much time alone. There was nowhere to escape, and he was impatient to get started on the cabin. He knew Bryan was, too. Kevin couldn't imagine what four kids sounded like within these walls. Ricky seemed to echo off them all by himself.

Emily brought some needlework with her, and filled any spare time with that. Naomi had her knitting, Katarina brought books, and Lisa had her paints and easel. Her project for this week was a portrait of Emily and her new son. Kevin loved watching her work, especially when the subject was so interesting.

Once they were satisfied that Ricky was asleep, Emily suggested a moonlight walk. They both welcomed the break from the stress inside.

"Mom seems to be adjusting to everything. She's thrilled to have a grandchild, finally," she said as they strolled.

Kevin laughed. "How did she expect to get grandkids

when she did her best to chase any husband-prospects away?''

Emily didn't say anything, but snuggled closer. Even he was chilled by the cool evening air. ''I guess I'm a fine one to talk, aren't I? It's not that I don't like kids, Emily. It's not even that I don't want them. You know I always wanted us to have a house full of little ones.''

''I remember,'' she said softly. ''I'm not trying to pressure you, Kevin. I just need you to know where I'm at. If you decide you can't commit to me and Ricky...I'll manage, and so will you.''

He leaned his head against hers. ''I feel like some ogre. We were younger then. Young and naive. Taking a chance at hurting you again is bad enough, but to think of involving kids...like Ricky. He's already lost his mother and father. What if I had died after that accident?''

''You didn't die, Kevin. It was a freak accident. If you hadn't choked on that candy, we wouldn't have made nearly the issue over it.''

He shrugged. ''It's not just that. We weren't absorbed in careers eight years ago. I don't know how I can back off now that business is booming, Emmy.''

She knew what he was feeling and understood his doubts. There were no easy answers. ''Kevin, don't worry. I'm not going anywhere. You don't have to give me an answer today.''

Kevin stopped walking and pulled her into his embrace. ''I think Alex was right.''

''About what?'' Emily asked, wrapping her arms around him.

''I need my head examined for having even one doubt, don't I?''

* * *

Kevin pulled a sleeping bag and pillow from the closet and moved out to the veranda to sleep. The stars were bright and the mountain air was crisp. Even when he snuggled to the bottom of the bag, his shoulders stuck out.

He went back inside to grab a sweatshirt from his bag and was surprised to hear the sisters still giggling as if they were having a slumber party. He slipped back outside unnoticed, wondering how Ricky could sleep through the noise. The little tike was his last thought upon falling asleep, and his first upon waking up.

Ricky greeted him early the next morning, completely dressed, well before anyone was awake inside. Kevin left a note on the table and took Ricky fishing. They made a short pole from a willow branch and fishing line, and sat on a grassy spot along the bank, next to a quiet spot in the river.

The little boy's cough started with an occasional ticklish sound. Kevin didn't think much of it, but after a while it became more constant. "You catching a cold, Ricky?"

"No, just a cough. I have medicine to take. Dr. Em—Emily gives it to me."

"Let's head back and see what Emily has planned for breakfast, shall we?"

Ricky eagerly pulled in his empty line and ran up the hill to the cabin, with Kevin puffing and panting close behind.

Kevin got Ricky a glass of juice and told Emily about the cough. After listening to Ricky's chest, she gave him his asthma medicine. By midmorning, Ricky was feeling better, his cough was much quieter, and he went from one activity to another at lightning speed. Kevin worked outside until lunch, trying not to intrude on the women's time together.

Before long, Ricky made his way outside, too. "Kevin, will you play football with me?"

Kevin reached his hands out, expecting a little toss. Ricky wound up and slammed him in the chest with the sponge ball. "Nice throw." He stepped farther back and returned the ball. They continued playing until Emily called them for lunch.

The tension among all of them eased as the week went on, so much so that Naomi eventually offered to watch Ricky so Kevin and Emily could get away for an afternoon.

Emily didn't hesitate for a moment. On the way out the door, she grabbed the pole in one hand and took his hand in the other. "I want to fish. Will you teach me?"

"We've been fishing all week. Why haven't you asked earlier?"

She shrugged. "I was busy keeping an eye on Ricky. Since he's napping now and Naomi's baby-sitting, I can relax and enjoy it."

They hiked farther downstream to an area with fewer trees to get caught on, then set down the tackle box. Kevin tied a fly and showed her how to "strip" the line. Then, standing behind her, he held her arm, showing her the rhythm of casting the line back and forth, letting out more line with each cast.

Emily began to get the idea, so Kevin let her go on her own. He whispered suggestions as if it were some sort of secret. She turned her head to talk to him, and the line went wild. She cast forward, and her arm jerked to a sudden end.

"Oh, no, I'm caught on something."

Kevin felt a tug on his shirt and laughed. "Looks like

a big one." He twisted around to try to grab the hook from his back, then saw the line arc from him to the willows at their right, then over to Emily. Kevin walked over, hoping to untangle it without losing the fly. Emily turned. Kevin ducked under the pole, and the line snapped loose. The hook tugged his shirt again, and Kevin swung his arms, trying to avoid the line getting tangled around him.

"Emily! Kevin!" Lisa called. "Ke-e-e-vin! E-em-m-m-ily!

Kevin turned just as Emily did, and the two wound up fighting each other's efforts. "Lisa, we're down here."

"Hurry up here. Something's wrong with Ricky!"

Emily started up the hill, and was quickly jerked backwards. "Kevin!"

"I'm trying to reach my knife, just a minute. The hook is caught in my shirt." Emily turned to look, and whacked Kevin in the head with the pole. "Stop tugging, Emily, you're making it worse. And drop the pole, would you?" Once he was able to get his hand into his pocket, he cut the line, and they both bolted up the hill.

Emily ran into the cabin, directly toward the horrible wheezing sound. "Get his medicine."

Katarina handed it to Emily, adding, "We just gave him two puffs a few minutes ago."

"Let's get him to the hospital. Call ahead for us."

Kevin carried Ricky outside, then tried to hand him to Emily, but the little boy tightened his grip around Kevin's neck while continuing to gasp for air. "I guess you're driving, Em. I'll sit in back with him."

He turned to the preschooler. "Watch, Ricky. I'm going to buckle my seat belt right here next to you. But I need you to sit in your seat, so we're both safe. Okay?"

Before Kevin detached the boy's arms from around his neck, he buckled his seat belt across his lap and showed Ricky. "It's your turn now."

Kevin couldn't believe the drastic change in Ricky's condition in such a short time. It was a struggle for him to breathe.

"See if you can get him to take another puff from the inhaler. I don't think he's breathing deeply enough to help much, but we're going to have to keep trying. As soon as we get him to the hospital, they'll set up the nebulizer treatment."

Kevin shook the medicine, then held the mask over Ricky's nose and mouth. "Come on, sport, I need you to take a really deep breath." Kevin gently coaxed him to keep inhaling. He brushed the damp hair from Ricky's brow and wiped the perspiration with his shirtsleeve. Just as Ricky tried to inhale, he went into another coughing spasm. By the time they reached the hospital twenty minutes later, the wheezing had deteriorated to a high-pitched whistle, and Ricky seemed too weak to care who was holding him.

Emily pulled into the emergency room parking lot. "I'm going to go order the medicine and get him admitted, while you bring him in."

"You're so good at giving orders," he teased, giving her a wink of encouragement.

She put the car in Park and ran inside.

"Ricky, we're going into the hospital to get you help."

"Daddy?"

Kevin stopped dead in his tracks. "It's me, Kevin."

"My new daddy," the boy said slowly. He smiled and put his head on Kevin's shoulder. "Emmy, my new mommy." Just saying those few words seemed to exhaust him.

Kevin felt love seep through him. He was unconditionally loved by a little boy who had lost everyone dear to him, everyone except his new mommy. A little boy who had every reason to be angry, yet trusted God, trusted Emily, trusted him. Just because. There were no strings, no conditions, just love.

It was enough. Just love... *Okay, God, I get the message, loud and clear. If I could ask a favor, it's that You let me have a chance to be Ricky's daddy.*

Kevin closed the car and was inside before he realized it. When Ricky saw the doors to the emergency room, his body grew tense, and Kevin held him closer than ever.

"I know how you feel, Ricky. I don't like this place, either, but they're going to help you. Just take it easy. I'll stay right here with you."

I'm not about to let you go. All the way down the corridor Kevin found himself breathing more deeply, as if doing so would benefit Ricky.

He suddenly realized that Ricky would be alone if it weren't for Emily. Of course, somebody would see that his essential needs were met, but it wouldn't be the same.

He recognized the love in Emily's gaze when she looked at Ricky; it was the same tender gaze she gave Kevin.

Suddenly it was no longer a matter of Ricky needing Kevin, but of Kevin needing Ricky—the little boy who had the wisdom to teach Kevin all about what was important in life.

Love.

Not money. Not jobs. Not business commitments.

Just *love.*

Emily met him at the door and led Kevin to the nurse who was waiting with the treatment, then paused. "I need to finish filling out the forms."

"You go ahead, Em. I'll take care of Ricky." He sat down and turned Ricky in his lap so the nebulizer pipe could blow directly on Ricky's face. With each gasp for air, Ricky's laboring lessened slightly.

"We'll need to take his vitals and listen to his lungs, Mr. Berthoff, if you could please undress your son."

Kevin laughed to himself, suddenly flattered to be mistaken not only for a married man, but for a father. He must be doing okay at the job if he'd already convinced one nurse. The moment of humor was a welcome reprieve. "Come on, Ricky. Let's show the nurse your muscles."

She took over holding the pipe, while Kevin undressed Ricky. Kevin tugged on the sleeves of the boy's gold-and-black CU Buffs football sweatshirt and gently worked it over his blond head. The toddler squirmed in Kevin's lap, snuggling closer as if cold. Kevin indulged in the chance to wrap his arms around the boy to keep him warm.

After the treatment, the nurse put an oxygen mask over Ricky's mouth and nose. A doctor arrived and wrapped his hand around the metal disk of the stethoscope to warm it for a minute, then placed it against Ricky's back.

It was as if Kevin were back in the hospital himself, watching as the doctor listened to the little boy's lungs and heart. Kevin looked up, surprised to see Emily standing calmly in the doorway with her gaze fixed on him.

In that moment, he realized that God had given him another chance to have the love and happiness he had pushed so far away. He had allowed Emily's love to heal him. Kevin winked, and gave her a slow, secret smile, which he knew she understood.

They were a family.

Emily stepped closer and knelt next to the chair. "How's he doing?"

"Better. Aren't you, sport."

Ricky nodded.

"Thank you for coming along, Kevin."

"That's part of being a dad, isn't it?" He smiled.

Emily's mouth gaped open. As soon as they were alone, she looked at him with hope in her eyes. "Are you serious?"

"Of course I'm serious. I'd never joke about becoming a father."

The nurse returned a while later. "Mr. Berthoff, Dr. Berthoff, this is a prescription for Ricky's medicine…"

Emily looked at Kevin and started to correct the nurse, but Kevin shook his head and winked. *What in the world are you up to, Kevin MacIntyre?*

"If you'll just sign here, you can take your son home. The doctor is comfortable with you monitoring his treatments." The nurse gave Emily more instructions and handed her a form to sign, while Kevin dressed Ricky.

On the way out the door, Emily looked up at the two blond men in her life. "'Mr. Berthoff'?" she repeated incredulously. "Isn't that carrying your point a bit far?"

He chuckled. "I thought it was kind of cute, myself. And I will say, I definitely liked being mistaken for your husband." He paused. "Ricky, what do you think of adopting a mommy and a daddy?"

"Yeah! Can I have a brother and a sister, too?"

Kevin laughed. "We'll have to wait and see what God has planned on that one." He looked at Emily. "I know it's been like beating your head against a wall, Emily, but this little guy here finally drove the point home. What do you think of becoming Mrs.-Dr.-Emily-Berthoff-MacIntyre? Or whatever you want to be called."

"I think...it's about time." Emily smiled and leaned forward to give Ricky, then Kevin, a kiss.

"Are you twitterpated *now,* Dr. Em—Mom?" Ricky asked, his voice raspy.

"Yes, Ricky, I am." She looked at Kevin again. "Always was," she murmured.

"Don't I know it! We'd better get back to the cabin. Your mom and sisters are going to wonder what happened to us."

Chapter Twenty

First thing Monday morning, Emily arranged to take a few weeks of family leave. She and Kevin took Ricky to see a specialist so they could learn more about controlling his asthma. As far as they could tell, his attack in the mountains had been caused by the high levels of pollen and dust. Now he was improving.

Emily was scheduled to sign the adoption papers that Wednesday, but postponed it so she and Kevin both could do so after the wedding ceremony.

With all the changes Ricky had already been through, she and Kevin had decided it would be easier on everyone if there wasn't a long engagement. That way, when Emily went back to work, their family would already have settled into their own routine, however chaotic.

She called George and Harriet and put Ricky on the phone. "I'm going to get a new mommy *and* a new daddy. Dr. Emmy is getting married to Kevin this Saturday." Emily laughed at how quickly Ricky was picking up new expressions from Kevin, such as calling her

Emmy. The two were inseparable, just as a father and son should be, she thought.

Though this was the busiest time of the year for weddings, Pastor Mike had worked to fit them into the church schedule. She and Kevin agreed to have the ceremony in the courtyard, and have the reception at a nearby restaurant.

Her sisters and mother were troopers, pulling everything together for the small ceremony. Emily took the box out of her closet and tried her wedding dress on for the first time in eight years. Once she had it cleaned, it would be perfect.

Kevin came in after work and looked around at the piles of fabric and ribbon. "I thought this was going to be a simple ceremony—me in jeans, you in…oh, never mind, that's later. Sorry, got the ceremonies mixed up." He winked, pleased to see her cheeks turn a brilliant shade of pink. He lifted the corner of material and took a peek. "Have you seen Ricky under all this stuff recently?"

"He's playing at Laura's. They're going to bring him home after supper. By the way, what are you fixing?"

"Fixing? For dinner? Me? How about my specialty, pizza?"

Emily laughed. "Good idea. Mom doesn't like mushrooms, but anything else goes."

He looked at Naomi and smiled. "We have one thing in common, anyway."

Emily's mother smiled back. "It looks like I owe you an apology, Kevin. I should have put my own selfishness aside and let my daughters find happiness years ago."

Kevin wrapped an arm around her. "I'm in no position to criticize. I am glad you're putting the past behind you, for your own sake, as well as Emily's. And I want to thank you for giving me such a precious gift.''

Naomi looked at Emily, confused. ''You haven't opened my gift yet, have you?''

Emily shook her head, and Kevin chuckled mischievously. ''I'm talking about Emmy. Your daughter is an incredible woman. Thank you. I promise to take good care of her and to be faithful 'til the day I die.''

''I have no doubts you will, Kevin.''

The doorbell rang, but Ricky didn't wait for an answer. He ran inside, dragging the Beaumont family with him. ''See, Chad, I get a new daddy, too. Kevin's going to be *my* dad.''

''So what, I get *two* babies!''

''I can have two, too,'' Ricky argued.

Laura and Bryan trailed in behind the rest of the gang. ''Guess our news is history, huh?''

Emily looked at Laura, her eyes open wide. ''Twins? I was wondering…''

The couple laughed. ''The ultrasound you suggested was scheduled for this morning. No wonder I'm getting so big.''

Kevin patted his friend's shoulder in congratulation. ''Six kids? Wow.''

Saturday morning was warm and sunny, a perfect day for a wedding. The organist played, and Kevin and Bryan tossed the football across the tiny church parlor as they waited for Pastor Mike to come for them. Finally the oak door opened, and Mike gave Kevin a wide smile. ''That bride of yours is beautiful, you know.''

''About that visit we had in the hospital, Mike…''

''It's okay, Emily had already told me about your relationship.''

Kevin put a hand on Mike's shoulder. "I was going to remind you that I meant every word of it. I love her, and I'm not going to let her go this time."

Mike laughed. "And I'm going to hold you to it! I think she's ready, what about you?"

"Ready. This is the best day of my life." Kevin turned from Mike to Bryan. "Now don't forget to give me the ring, would you?"

"Turnabout's fair play," Bryan said as he followed Mike and Kevin to the church courtyard.

"Why's that?" Kevin murmured from the corner of his mouth.

"You set Laura and me up." Bryan turned to look at him. "But I don't think either of us could have taken Laura's matchmaking much longer!"

"Remind me to thank her." Kevin smiled and heard Bryan's soft chuckle.

The organist played more loudly, then eased in to the processional, and Emily appeared at the end of the grassy aisle.

Kevin had never seen her more beautiful. The ivory dress flowed over her curves, simple yet elegant, perfectly Emily. Kevin's smile grew wider and his heart beat faster. *Thank you, Father. I don't know what took me so long to get here, but I'm sure glad You didn't give up on me.*

Naomi walked Emily down the aisle and offered her daughter's hand to Kevin. They shared a special smile, and Naomi gave him a hug.

Kevin looked into the eyes of his bride. His heart skipped a beat. The sprinkling of freckles across her nose was as charming as on the day they had first met. Flowers circled the bun on top of her head and delicate strands of her beautiful red hair framed her face.

Kevin took her hand in his. It was small and delicate, warm and reassuring. Today he was marrying his best friend, the bride of his youth, the only woman he'd ever truly loved.

"In Ecclesiastes, King Solomon tells us that two are better than one, for if one falls down, his friend can help him up...." Pastor Mike's voice faded, and Kevin realized the truth of His words.

"... Though one can be overpowered, two can defend themselves. A cord of three strands is not quickly broken. Emily and Kevin, your relationship has proven the strength of the bonds of love and forgiveness can survive the tests of time."

Emily's eyes sparkled with tears, and Kevin lifted his hand to dry them. *I love you,* he mouthed silently, as they turned to face the altar.

I love you, she mouthed in return, a look of admiration filling her gaze. Standing hand-in-hand, they bowed their heads.

Kevin heard Ricky's voice among the congregation, and knew that His timing was perfect, and that the rough eight years he and Emily had survived hadn't been wasted. He was finally ready to be a husband and a father.

"Do you, Kevin James, take Emily Ann..."

Kevin said his vows, which were echoed by Emily's softer, gentler voice, then placed the ring on Emily's finger. Surprised to find her trembling, he winked. She smiled confidently and slid the gold band on his finger.

Pastor Mike smiled. "I now pronounce you man and wife. What God has joined together, may no man put asunder." He turned to Kevin. "You may kiss the bride."

As Kevin and Emily sealed their vow with a kiss, the wedding march began.

From the corner of her eye, Emily could see Ricky squirming in his seat next to her mother. Kevin's family had all made it just in time for the ceremony.

She looked at Kevin, overwhelmed by the reflection of her love in her husband's blue eyes. She'd waited a lifetime for this day—to marry the man of her dreams. Never, though, had she imagined a day so perfect. She was not only marrying her only love and officially becoming Ricky's mother, but, most wonderful of all, she had her own mother's blessing.

"I now present Kevin and Emily MacIntyre—" Ricky ran up the aisle and into Kevin's waiting arms "—and their soon-to-be son, Ricky."

"That's my *new* mommy and daddy, Mike. They're twitterpated."

"That's my boy!" Kevin's laughter was joined by a chorus of background accompaniment.

Following the ceremony, the adoption papers were signed. Then Kevin lifted Ricky into the crook of one arm, embraced Emily with his other, and the three became a family.

When they left the church, she could see Bryan and Alex had taken it upon themselves to make certain that Kevin's truck was appropriately adorned for the festivities. Brushing the crepe paper and pop cans aside, Kevin lifted Emily and Ricky into the cab for the ride to the reception.

Her sisters and mother had left early that morning to complete the decorating. The reception area was stunning. On each ivory table were small clusters of wildflowers. And Laura had insisted on making the cake—

three oval tiers of ivory with fresh wildflowers between cakes.

Among the guests were Kevin's employees and Emily's co-workers. The receiving line was one long "I told you so" followed by "playing hard-to-get, my foot!" and many hugs of joy.

"These last few weeks on the clinic are going to be interesting, aren't they?" Kevin said as he followed Emily to find his brother and twin sisters, who had arrived just before the ceremony.

Emily turned her head and smiled mischievously. "If you had just let me give you that tetanus shot without making such a scene, they wouldn't be having nearly so much fun with this."

He wrapped his arms around his wife's waist and smiled. "Then again, neither would I."

He savored the sound of Emily's deep laugh and the vanilla scent of her perfume. His willpower was wearing thin.

Kevin and Emily visited with relatives for a while before cutting the cake. Ricky and his friends were there immediately, ready for the first bite, having already eaten half a plate of the homemade butter mints.

Emily gracefully cut a bite of cake and lifted it to Kevin's mouth.

"Can we leave now?" he whispered.

"Not until you give me a bite."

"Oh, yeah, I forgot. I'd hate for you to get light-headed—yet."

Going against tradition, they served the cake themselves, enjoying another chance to visit with each of their guests.

Then they changed from their wedding clothes and rushed out the door, but the truck was gone.

"Uncle Alex moved it. I got to ride with him," Ricky exclaimed. Birdseed pelted them as they hugged Ricky goodbye.

Emily was torn over leaving him already. "Aunt Katarina will take good care of you. We'll be home in two days."

"I know," he said confidently. "Uncle Alex says he'll take me for pizza."

Emily prepared to toss the bouquet, and smiled at Kevin. "You go find a car, while I find our next bride."

Emily turned her back to the gathering of women. Just as she let the bouquet go, Kevin's clean truck pulled to a stop in front of them.

The bouquet flew high into the tree and caught in the branches. Kevin jumped up and grabbed the limb to loosen it, and it bounced off another branch and into Alex's hands.

"Oh, no, you don't." Alex batted it away, directly to Katarina.

"You two had better give in now," Kevin exclaimed as he helped Emily into her seat.

An hour later, they arrived at the hotel, and Kevin carried Emily over the threshold. "We finally made it, Doc."

"Kevin, don't you dare refer to me as your 'doctor' again, because the minute you touch me, I don't think or feel a bit doctorly. I only want to be Mrs. MacIntyre, a woman in love."

"Excuse me." Kevin stopped. "But to me, you'll always be the heart specialist. Not only did you save my life, but you fixed my broken heart, too."

"I don't know—you're the one who gave mine a jump start, remember?"

He laughed. "That kid…"

"I miss him already." She looked into his eyes. "Think he misses us?"

"With the brood at Laura and Bryan's, and his Aunt Kat and Uncle Alex to entertain him? He's probably going to be lonely once we get him home. Maybe we ought to get busy filling that house of yours—ours. After all, we were supposed to be the first ones down the aisle. We've got some catching up to do."

"We are *not* competing with the Beaumonts, Kevin."

"Maybe not, but we can sure give it a try!"

Emily blushed.

* * * * *

Dear Reader,

It's been nearly seven years since I first "met" the characters in this book. They became my friends over the course of *There Comes a Season,* my May 1998 release. I can't remember what made me choose their professions, as I'd never personally know either per se, yet two years ago, into my child-care home walked a very special couple. A builder and a doctor, and their son. The Lord truly provides for all of our needs. A month later, the idea for *Second Time Around* sold, and I began writing Kevin and Emily's story, along with my own "in-house" research team.

I've come to learn that where a door is closed, God often opens a window. I hope you enjoyed reading about the opportunities and second chances facing Kevin and Emily, and how they respond to God's open windows.

As always, I love to hear from my readers. You can write to me c/o Steeple Hill Books, 233 Broadway, Ste. 1001, New York, NY 10279.

Carol Steward

REQUEST YOUR FREE BOOKS!

2 FREE INSPIRATIONAL NOVELS PLUS 2 FREE MYSTERY GIFTS

Love Inspired.

YES! Please send me 2 FREE Love Inspired® novels and my 2 FREE mystery gifts. After receiving them, if I don't wish to receive any more books, I can return the shipping statement marked "cancel." If I don't cancel, I will receive 4 brand-new novels every month and be billed just $3.99 per book in the U.S., or $4.74 per book in Canada, plus 25¢ shipping and handling per book and applicable taxes, if any*. That's a savings of at least 20% off the cover price! I understand that accepting the 2 free books and gifts places me under no obligation to buy anything. I can always return a shipment and cancel at any time. Even if I never buy another book from Steeple Hill, the two free books and gifts are mine to keep forever.

113 IDN EF26   313 IDN EF27

Name	(PLEASE PRINT)
Address	Apt.
City	State/Prov.	Zip/Postal Code

Signature (if under 18, a parent or guardian must sign)

Order online at www.LoveInspiredBooks.com

Or mail to Steeple Hill Reader Service™:

IN U.S.A.
P.O. Box 1867
Buffalo, NY
14240-1867

IN CANADA
P.O. Box 609
Fort Erie, Ontario
L2A 5X3

Not valid to current Love Inspired subscribers.

Want to try two free books from another series?
Call 1-800-873-8635 or visit www.morefreebooks.com

* Terms and prices subject to change without notice. NY residents add applicable sales tax. Canadian residents will be charged applicable provincial taxes and GST. This offer is limited to one order per household. All orders subject to approval. Credit or debit balances in a customer's account(s) may be offset by any other outstanding balance owed by or to the customer. Please allow 4 to 6 weeks for delivery.

LIREG06

Love Inspired.
CLASSICS

TITLES AVAILABLE NEXT MONTH

Don't miss these stories in January

SECOND CHANCES
AND
LOVE ONE ANOTHER
by **Valerie Hansen**

Love blossoms during an Arkansas summer
for two Southern couples.

NEVER ALONE
AND
NEW MAN IN TOWN
by **Lyn Cote**

Children help two women find the men
they've been waiting for.